# Also by

**Also by A.L. Hatcher**

<u>The Tess Dane Thrillers:</u>

*The Blood Eagle*

*River of Lies*

*Hill of Bones*

<u>Other titles:</u>

*Little Jar of Teeth: Dark Stories to Keep You Up at Night*

## Praise for The Blood Eagle

"From the first chapter, I was absolutely hooked. Fast paced, engaging, twisty, and downright horrifying (in all the best possible ways)."— Alex, Amazon review

"... the crime scenes were very realistic.... I might or might not have looked behind me often last night after reading some of the murder scenes!" —Kiara Yaeger, author of *Annoy Me More* and *Back Home at Shawnee Creek*

## Praise for River of Lies

"...if you're searching for a book that will consume you, captivate you, and leave you breathless with anticipation, look no further than *River of Lies*." —Robin G-V, Amazon review

"Put your seat belt on and hang on for this one! I can't recommend this book enough!!"—Heather, Goodreads

"Tess is back and with a vengeance, proving she's one tough cookie... and a smart one at that, when she picks up a missing person case that has several twists and turns. Fun read!"—J.C. Fuller, author of *Black Bear Alibi* and *The Push*

## Praise for Little Jar of Teeth

"...Great choice for a campfire read— provided you are willing to risk being wrenched from sleep by the screams

# Hill of Bones

A Tess Dane Thriller

## A. L. Hatcher

A L Hatcher Author

For My Little Bug, I love you

# Prologue

*July 21, 1996, 4:02 AM*

The body at his feet stared up at him with sunken, unseeing eyes. As a shiver coursed down his spine, the man bent over the body and quickly shut the lids. It didn't improve the situation, but at least the sightless orbs wouldn't creep him out so much. He had too much to do to chicken out now. After all, he was the reason the corpse lay at his feet.

He grabbed the handle of the old shovel, the wood smoothed from use, and began digging again. The sound of the metal blade scraping through the earth was nearly drowned out by the sound of the frogs and insects that ruled the hot, summer night in rural Ohio.

A twig snapped from somewhere in the darkness behind the man, causing him to jump and whirl around, nearly twisting his ankle as he went. He knew this particular spot was sacred and protected. *Probably haunted.*

That's why he'd chosen it.

Once he left this place, he'd never think of the dead man at his feet again. The bastard didn't deserve another thought, another second of his time. He'd made sure of that. And now, as he finished digging a shallow grave, camouflaged amongst the others, sweat beaded up on his brow. He paused to cast a wary glance over his shoulder again, distractedly wiping a dirt-smudged hand over his face. The lantern near his feet let out a persistent, low hiss as it sent shadows dancing across the landscape, causing the eerie sensation of being watched.

And maybe he *was* being watched. Maybe the dead man at his feet wasn't the only creature watching his every move from the shadows, biding their time to reveal themselves and attack him for what he'd done.

With a quickening pulse, the man gave up on digging and cast the shovel to the side. Bending to grasp the corpse's cool ankles, the man pulled and grunted until he had the body lying in an awkward fetal position in the bottom of the grave. The man paused, sweat-drenched from exertion and woozy enough that he leaned out to hold onto a nearby tree for support. After catching his breath once again, he took one last look at the dead man in the hole.

"See you in Hell, you son of a bitch," he sneered, a look of hatred etched into his dirt-smeared face. Bending quickly to retrieve his shovel, the man hastily refilled the grave with dirt, making sure he'd covered his sins, certain no one would ever find them.

Until they did.

# Chapter One

---

*(Twenty-eight years later, present day)*
*Friday, August 17th, 11:48 a.m.*

Another flash of lightning stabbed down towards the earth, and in the distance, thunder grumbled. It had been raining for five days straight, and Kevin O'Leary was over it. He stood in the open doorway of his old farmhouse, looking across his once beautiful yard, and was disgusted by the muddy mess it had become.

He'd heard on the radio that the old Crawley Bridge had to be cordoned off on account of the rising water levels from all the flash floods in the area. It had been a dry, hot summer with little rain, so much so that the O'Learys had been looking for other forms of income. If the crops failed, then they would have nothing. It had been a dry year the previous summer, and the yields weren't that high. Another bad harvest could be their undoing.

This summer had threatened to be the same until last week when the sky turned black and the rains finally came, causing flooding in the tri-state area. Still frustrated at the weather, Kevin was now worried about the flooded fields. *Maybe I just need a new livelihood*, he thought to himself as he pulled on his rubber boots and headed out to check on the chickens. It was almost noon, and he still hadn't checked on them for the day due to the storm. The rain finally seemed to be letting up, though marginally, and now was as good a time as any to check the livestock.

He plodded across the farmyard through muck and mud to the chicken coop. Opening the door, he stuck his head in and found his feathered ladies all perched together looking sodden and miserable. The hens eyed him as he deftly filled their feeder and then sprinkled some scratch grains for them in a flat metal pie pan. He'd usually cast the grains on the ground and let the chickens busy themselves for a while, but the rains had proved to be an obstacle, covering everything in a thick layer of mud.

"Sorry, girls. Don't know when this mess is supposed to clear up," Kevin said as he puttered around the coop. "One station says today, another says tomorrow." The chickens just stared at him with their beady eyes.

Suddenly, there was a loud cracking sound, followed by another rumble of thunder, but this time, Kevin could smell something burning. *Shit.* Lighting had struck something. Tossing the lid back on the chicken feed, he swiftly made his way back outside to take a look. It wasn't the barn. Not the house. Confused, Kevin slogged through the yard, looking around for the source of the smell of burning wood. He was halfway around the large old barn when he saw it.

A tree, down near the fence line, had been struck by lightning and had hungry flames dancing in its branches in direct defiance of the rain. The crown of the tree was split in two, crushing part of the fence separating the pasture from the woods. The creek that had once meandered along the fence line near the forest was now overflowing its banks. *What a mess.*

Kevin glared up at the sky with a look of disdain etched across his face. He'd have to repair the fence and cut up the tree once the deluge was over. Work was never in short supply on a farm. With a grumble, Kevin O'Leary slugged toward the barn door to finish his chores and wait out the storm.

*Saturday, August 18th, 6:42 a.m.*

By the next morning, the storm had finally passed. The sun filled the azure sky, and except for the puddles, mud, and occasional fallen tree branch, the storm had left nothing behind.

Kevin O'Leary downed some coffee as the sun crept over the horizon and then pulled on his work boots, hoping to make quick work of the burnt-out tree. After feeding the cows and chickens, he headed down across the pasture, chainsaw in hand.

The fenceline was a splintered, charred mess, much to Kevin's dismay. The trunk of the old oak still smoldered from deep inside, where the lightning had struck. There was no saving it. Setting about cutting off the charred and broken branches, Kevin began working up a sweat despite the early morning coolness. Slipping off his jacket, he stepped over to a remaining fence post to hang it up when his eye caught sight of something in the woods beyond the creek.

The O'Leary farm sat on over 1,500 acres of fertile farmland and virgin forests that had provided years of adventure to Kevin and his siblings growing up. The old two-story farmhouse had once been in pristine condition, and everyone in Swain County, Ohio, knew of the O'Leary farm. Whether it was because of the roadside farmers market that the house had once boasted, or the Native American burial mounds tucked into the woods, or simply because of the farm's dark history, O'Leary Farm had made a name for itself over the years. Kevin was the third generation of O'Leary's to live there and work the land.

As Kevin stood there now, looking deeper into the woods from the fenceline of the cow pasture, his mind wandered. What was that in the woods? He could see the burial mound from the tree line, just as he always could, but today, something looked different. *Better not be damned wannabe historians again, sneaking around looking for ancient artifacts*. He'd had to chase off the last batch of them, and it was beginning to get ridiculous.

His mother had taught Kevin and his siblings all about the Mound Builders and how to respect the dead buried in the hill. He'd always given it a wide berth, more worried about ghosts or something grabbing his ankles as he passed by. As he'd gotten older, though, Kevin just ignored the mound and left the dead alone. Was it creepy to have dead people buried on his property? No more than a cemetery near a church. The dead were dead, and they didn't cause problems, so Kevin was okay just letting them rest.

With resolve, he decided to look closer at the burial mound. It looked different today, and he couldn't determine why from where he stood. Leaving his jacket on the fence, he quickly hopped over the railing and walked to the swollen creek separating him from the woods and the burial mound beyond.

Forced to walk upstream to find an easier place to cross, Kevin finally made it with a flying jump. Landing with a loud splat, his rubber boots made sucking sounds along the creek bank as he made his way through the mud. Advancing into the woods, he noticed a large felled tree that had been uprooted in the storm. Once butted up against the burial mound, the large oak had an impressive root ball that had been torn from the ground when it fell. The large chunk of missing soil at the tree's base caused the burial mound's silhouette to look different.

Kevin was relieved to find it was only a tree and not looters. He walked through the woods toward the mound, which appeared to be no more than a leaf-littered hill in the woods. As he approached and got a closer look, he realized why it looked so strange.

The tree's root ball had not only torn away a huge mass of dirt away from the base of the hill, but water from above had run large rivulets down the sides of the hill, causing even more dirt to be displaced. The rainwater had settled in the hollow recently vacated by the tree roots, forming a large, muddy puddle.

He came to a sloppy halt near the edge of the puddle, absently gauging how deep it might be, when he noticed something sticking out of the clay mud. Was it a stick? No, it was too white. Interested, Kevin leaned over the mud-filled hollow, reaching for the pale object.

Spreading his fingers wide, he tried to grasp the object and failed. It was too far away, just out of reach. He stepped into the puddle to assess the depth, the muddy water coming halfway up his rubber boot.

"In for a penny, in for a pound," he muttered to himself as he decided to just step into the water with both feet. Much closer to the mysterious object that had caught his eye, Kevin reached for it once again, only for it to fall below the surface of the water. Rolling his eyes in frustration, Kevin began running his hands blindly through the rusty-colored water. At first, he felt nothing, but then his hand bumped something. He wrapped his large hand around the object and pulled it up from the water for inspection.

It was then that he understood what he had found, for in his hand lay a human jawbone. His initial reaction was to cast it away out of revulsion, but something had caught his eye. This wasn't part of an ancient Native American skull buried there generations ago. This was from a much newer skull, as evidenced by the modern-day dental work visible on the molars. This body wasn't meant to be there. Had there been an accident? Or was it murder?

# Chapter Two



"Uno!" Nine-year-old Natalie Haywood squealed as she slapped down a green card. She grinned triumphantly, and Denny Haywood sighed, a grin creeping across his face.

"Better draw until you get a green one, Daddy!" Natalie laughed, watching as her father began picking up cards in search of a green one. After selecting four from the pile and still not finding the correct color, he groaned, and Tess and Natalie began giggling.

"Maybe you shouldn't have challenged your daughter to a game of Uno after all. She told you she was good," Tess smirked from behind her glass of orange juice.

The trio sat around Tess's dining room table, having finished eating a late Saturday breakfast. The storms from the recent days had kept them busy with their respective jobs, so when Tess suggested a breakfast get-together, Denny and Natalie eagerly agreed. They showed up early that morning with fresh bagels, orange juice, and strawberries.

Though they'd only just finished breakfast, things had quickly devolved into a cutthroat game of Uno— Natalie being the instigator and apparent victor and Denny her unsuspecting victim.

Suddenly, Denny grinned and stopped gathering cards. "Aha!" he exclaimed, turning towards Natalie. "I'm changing it to red." He laid a "Draw Four" card down with a slap. Now it was Tess's play, and Natalie leaned in to see what she would do, an ornery smirk on her little face.

Tess made a show of carefully studying her cards before selecting one and laid down a red card with the number '3' on it. She turned, watching Natalie just as the young girl laid down her last card and announced herself as the winner.

"*What*?" Denny gasped, eyeing the girl's winning card. "How did you...?"

"I knew you'd change the color as soon as you could, and your favorite color is red. I knew the odds were in my favor," Natalie said smugly. An ornery grin spread across her face, and her eyes danced with mischief.

"The odds were in your.....where did you even learn that?" Denny asked, laughing. Tess and Natalie laughed along with him when Natalie made an exaggerated shoulder shrug.

"You two never cease to amuse me," Tess commented as she stood, stretching before she began clearing the breakfast mess. Denny stood to help as Natalie gathered up the Uno cards and shoved them back into their box.

Otter, Tess's black Labrador Retriever, began sniffing around under the kitchen table, looking for fallen scrambled eggs or bagel crumbs. Tess tried to act like she didn't notice Natalie slip a small piece of bacon under the table for the dog to eat.

"Do you have any plans for the rest of your day?" Denny asked Tess as he scraped their plates clean into the trash.

"Just hanging out with you two," Tess replied as she filled the dishwasher. With a glance over her shoulder to see where Natalie was, she looked at Denny and lowered her voice. "Any word on the job transfer?"

Just a few weeks ago, after wrapping up a case in Cleveland, Denny had been informed that he'd be transferring to the BCI (Bureau of Criminal Investigation) office near Cleveland instead of his current location in London, Ohio. Had Denny not been a widower raising a young daughter all alone, he may have been interested, but his support system was in Swain County.

So was Tess.

They'd known each other for a few years now, long before his wife, Cassie, had died from Lymphoma. Then, Tess had been in the police academy where Denny had taken on some adjunct instructor duties while also working full-time as a detective with the county. He'd been so impressed with her abilities and drive for law enforcement that when she'd applied to work for Swain County Sheriff's Department, he'd specifically requested to be her training partner for her rookie year. Once Tess had proven herself capable of working effectively on her own, Denny had eventually moved on, taking a job with BCI. They'd stayed in touch, though, sending each other pictures of Natalie or Otter, random texts, and occasional Christmas cards.

It was only recently, after Denny was wounded in the line of duty, that they each finally admitted to themselves, and each other, that there was something between them. Since then, they'd tried to spend every moment they could with each other, and yet a dark cloud seemed to hover over their heads. The Cleveland job.

Denny had gone to the "mandatory" interview only to find out once he got there that it wasn't mandatory at all. He'd been nominated for the promotion, and it was up to him to accept.

"So I told you that they gave me the week to think about it, right?" Denny asked, putting the butter and jelly back into the fridge. Tess nodded.

"I told them thanks for the interview, I'd think about it—even though you and I both know I'm staying here—and then I called Shaw." Denny made a face when he said his supervisor's name. "I told him I went for the interview, and he asked when I'd start. I informed him that I hadn't accepted the position and didn't intend to. That's when he got pissed."

"Why? What's it to him?" Tess wrinkled her nose in confusion, a dirty coffee cup in her hand. She shook her head in disbelief and placed the mug in the top rack of the dishwasher.

"Well, that's what I was wondering. Why would Shaw care if I took a job in Cleveland or not? And that's when Claybourne heard something of interest." Denny grinned, glad his coworker-turned-friend had passed on the information.

"Ohhh, you got some hot goss?" Tess smirked, wiggling her eyebrows. Denny rolled his eyes.

"Relax, it's not hot. But it *is* gossip that's been confirmed."

"Well...?" Tess pleaded impatiently, abandoning the dishwasher to give Denny her full attention.

"Come to find out, Shaw applied for a promotion in Cleveland. The catch? They'll take him, but only if I come too, hence why he told me the transfer was mandatory. If I don't go, he doesn't get the position and there goes his dreams of cruising a bass boat on Erie in his free time."

"He lied to you to get a promotion!?" Tess exclaimed, her voice shrill, her eyes angry. "Mother fu–"

"Daddy, can I go outside with Otter?" Natalie asked, coming into the kitchen holding a ratty old tennis ball, the neon yellow fuzz sticking out in all directions like Albert Einstein's hair. The dog was about to lose his mind over it, following alongside the young girl, tail rocking back and forth like a metronome.

"Sure thing, baby. Just make sure the gates are closed." Denny smiled, helping her with the sliding glass door. Leaving it slightly open so they could hear the child and dog playing, he turned back to Tess.

"So, what happens now? If you don't take the job and Shaw is stuck here, won't he make your life miserable?" Tess huffed, not even trying to hide the ire in her voice.

"He could, but I'm still not taking the job. You're here, my family is here. I'm not uprooting my daughter if I don't need to. She's doing great in school, despite everything she's been through the past few years with losing her mother. I'm not going to tear her away from the rest of her family or you just to appease the higher-ups."

"If it's any consolation, I'm glad you aren't going, and I'm relieved you found out the truth before doing something regrettable." Tess dried her damp hands on a towel and stepped into Denny's open arms. He returned her embrace, resting his chin on her head.

"Can't you report him for lying like that?" Tess murmured against his chest. At first she thought he wouldn't respond to her question and contented herself by listening to the strong rhythm of his heart. He gently ran his hands up and down her lower spine, relaxing her with each stroke.

"I thought about it, but really, I'm not sure it would do anything," he finally answered. "I'm pretty sure Coban, the agent in charge of interviewing me, figured out what had happened around the same time I did. He called and left a message asking me to call him back to discuss the promotion. When I did, he didn't hide that he was put off by the fact that Shaw had been less than honest in his efforts to move up the ladder."

"Yikes. Now I wonder if IA will get involved. I'm gonna need popcorn for this," Tess grinned mischievously. Denny snorted lightly, pulling away to look down at her face.

"You're ornery." A grin spread across his handsome face. "But yeah, popcorn will be needed. Ask for extra butter." That earned him a laugh from Tess.

Just then, her cell phone rang. Glancing at the caller ID, she cast Denny a defeated look. She let out a sigh and hit the green button.

"Detective Dane," she said as a greeting, turning to watch Natalie and Otter rolling around in the grass in the backyard.

"Hey, Dane," Sheriff Malone's voice came across the phone. He sounded tired and mildly irritated. "We have a situation down at the O'Leary farm. Kevin just called the station, carrying on about a bone he found in the burial pit."

Tess nodded along to his explanation, wondering if this was a new case to solve or just a false alarm. Everyone in the area knew about the old mound in the woods on the O'Leary farm.

"It's not a pit, Malone. It's a Hopewell Burial Mound. It's full of remains," Tess corrected him. "What does this have to do with me? Shouldn't you call a historian or something? An anthropologist?"

"Well, I thought that, but he says there is a bridge."

"A bridge?" Tess asked, confused. "Like the Crawley Bridge? He found the bone there?"

"No. No, you misunderstood." Malone chuckled, "O'Leary said the bone he found looks like a jawbone that's had some dental work done."

"Oh! Like a dental bridge!" Tess exclaimed, finally understanding. "I gotcha. Okay, well, sure, I can head out there and check it out. If it's legit, we'll have to get somebody from OSU to help us. Bones, especially ancient ones, are out of my wheelhouse."

"Sure, Dane. It's probably nothing, just some animal bone, but we need to check it out."

"Okay. I'll head out after I change," Tess said as she caught Denny's questioning gaze. She said goodbye to Malone and laid her phone on the counter with a sigh.

"Gotta go?" was all he asked. When Tess's shoulders slumped, he went over to her and pulled her into a hug. "It's okay, honey, we can let ourselves out."

"I wanted you guys to stay for a while. I can't believe I'm getting called in on the one Saturday that I made plans with you," she said, with a huff. She looked down at her jean shorts and red tank top. "I gotta change. Don't leave yet." She leaned in to press a kiss to his lips as he continued to hold her for a few more seconds. She pulled back enough to gaze up into his face. His deep blue eyes stared back at her, and he began to grin. With a returning smile, she turned from his embrace and raced down the hallway to her room, stripping off her shorts and tank top. She changed quickly into some dark pants and a white button down shirt, her typical detective 'uniform', pulling her long, dark brown hair back into a ponytail.

Denny was still in the kitchen when Tess reappeared. Shoving the rest of the breakfast dishes into the dishwasher, he looked up as Tess walked in.

"Oh, you didn't have to do that!" Tess gave him a grateful look as she reached for her wallet, phone, and keys. Sticking her head out of the sliding glass door, she called for Otter.

The black Labrador bounded over, panting around the tennis ball he held between his teeth. She bent down to rub his head, planting a kiss on the dog's forehead.

"Sorry, I have to go, boy," she said regretfully, looking into his soft brown eyes. He just wagged in response.

"You gotta go?" Natalie sighed, eyeing Tess's change of clothes, firearm, and badge. "Can't the bad guys just commit crimes Monday through Friday, nine to five, for once?" She swooned dramatically onto a red lounge chair on the patio. "Just go," she fanned Tess away with her small hand, "Leave me to my sorrows."

"Oh, good grief, Nat," Tess laughed, stepping down onto the patio, "I'm just checking on something. Hopefully, I'll be back soon, silly goose." She tousled the young girl's hair before bending to kiss the top of her head. She was rewarded with a grin.

Tess found Denny standing in the doorway to the house, watching them, a bemused expression on his face. The sight of him standing there watching her was enough to give her butterflies in her stomach like a teenager. She gazed up into his eyes as his arms came around her waist, "Thank you for cleaning up the kitchen. I've got to look at some old bones at the O'Leary farm. Hopefully, I'll be back soon. You guys can stay as long as you want. Just lock up if you leave. Otter should be fine with his doggie door." She gave Denny a quick kiss, but as she pulled away, he gently grabbed her for one more, taking his time. When he eventually pulled away, Tess immediately felt his absence. He smiled down at her, as though feeling her frustration at being torn apart so soon, and gently pushed some loose hairs behind her ears.

"Hurry home. We can hang out for a little bit in case it's nothing. Mind if we take Otter to the dog park?"

"Oh, he'd love that! Sure!" Tess smiled as she pulled from Denny's embrace and headed toward the front door. "I'll keep you posted. Have fun, take pictures, Nat." And then, with a wave, she was gone.

# Chapter Three



As Tess drove down the winding rural roads leading toward the old farm, she let her mind wander. If she were lucky, she'd be able to wrap up this call out quickly and get back home to Denny and Natalie. *Maybe they'd stay for dinner and or even ice cream? Otter would love that!* She smiled at the thought.

A few moments later, Tess slowed to turn onto Quaker Hollow Road, following her GPS to the O'Leary farm. Unsure of what she'd find once she got there, she made a mental checklist of her supplies. She had her duty belt with her, even though it was part of her deputy uniform. It was one thing that she'd felt weird parting with since becoming a detective a few months ago. Although she had a department-issued firearm with her at all times while at crime scenes, she also had her father's old service weapon safely tucked into her ankle holster. She'd only recently gotten it back from Internal Affairs after they had done a thorough investigation into the untimely shooting death of Sheriff Burrows, Malone's predecessor.

Following her GPS, Tess slowed the SUV to turn down a long, winding driveway marked by an old wooden mailbox. The mailbox, once painted white with green trim, now sat chipped and faded, listing to the side precariously. The name 'O'Leary' was barely legible, having been battered by the elements for many years.

Her vehicle bounced over the ruts in the long gravel driveway leading up to the house, the puddles splashing up over the tirewells. Coming to a halt in front of the once-grand old farmhouse, Tess looked around for any signs of life. According to the 911 dispatcher, it had been Kevin O'Leary who'd called in about finding the human remains.

Not seeing anyone at first, Tess cautiously turned the ignition off and gathered her phone and some latex exam gloves and exited the vehicle. Her shoes, once nice and clean, were instantly covered in mud and made squelching sounds as she slammed the car door and made her way to the trunk.

Suddenly, the front door of the farmhouse opened, and a man in his early fifties approached, shadowed from the midday sun by the covering of the porch.

"Hiya, Officer," he called down to Tess as she fiddled with the trunk latch and began pulling out her rubber boots. Out of sight of the man on the porch, she impulsively felt her hip for the firearm holstered there. She knew it was there, but her father, who'd also been a detective, had reinforced the idea of always being prepared at an early age.

"Hello, I'm Detective Tess Dane with the Swain County Sheriff's Department," Tess announced, squinting up at the man on the porch. "Are you Kevin O'Leary?" Keeping her eyes on the man, she cautiously changed into her rubber boots.

"Yep," he said, stepping forward into the sunshine. "It's a good thing you brought those." He pointed to the rubber boots. "It's a mess out there, and we gotta walk a ways."

"So you found the bones this morning?" Tess asked, giving the trunk a good slam and then sloshing her way toward the porch where the man stood.

"Yep," he answered again, his hands shoved in the pocket of his denim overalls. A sleeveless tee shirt, possibly white at one point, was layered underneath. An old John Deere hat sat atop the man's head, small wisps of graying brown hair sticking out around the edges. Kevin, tall and lanky, seemed to be a man of few words, and Tess groaned inwardly. This was going to take a while if he insisted on exclusively answering her questions with one-word answers.

"Can you show me where you found them?" she asked, trying to move the conversation forward. She was rewarded with a grunt and head nod before Kevin O'Leary turned and started walking around the house towards the pastures beyond. Tess quickly locked her vehicle and shoved the key fob into her pocket before racing to catch up with his long-legged stride.

They walked in silence for a few moments, the sounds of mud sloshing underfoot and the occasional braying of cows in the distance the only things interrupting them.

"So....Mr. O'Leary, how did you come to find the bones?" Tess finally asked, more to break the silence, but she'd take any information she could get. The farmer remained quiet for a few strides before he finally offered a reply.

"Well, I was down at the fenceline cutting up a tree when I noticed something different in the woods. Went to check it out." he shrugged. "Once I was in the woods, I noticed another tree had fallen near the burial mound. Took a chunk of ground with it. The bone was there."

"Okay.....so you found a bone near a known burial mound?" Tess asked, trying to decide if this was even her jurisdiction or if some state historian or tribal entity should be dealing with this. She'd never found herself in such a situation and made a mental note to find out the proper protocol.

"Yep," O'Leary said, pausing to open a gate leading into the pasture. Tess eyed the black and white Holsteins wearily as she followed O'Leary. "The bone wasn't ancient like you think. This one was newer."

"How do you know that?" Tess asked as O'Leary latched the gate and took up the lead again.

"Well, unless the ancient Moundbuilders used modern dental techniques, then I'd say it's newer. I found a jawbone, complete with a bridge and some fillings." He gave her a look that told her he wasn't stupid and didn't appreciate her treating him like he was.

"Sounds fair," Tess said dismissively, trying to keep up with the man's long strides. Tess was tall, standing at 5 feet 10 inches, but O'Leary seemed to walk quickly, causing Tess to play catch up.

"Was it only a mandible? Or were there more bones?" she asked, sidestepping a sodden cow patty camouflaged in the tall grasses. A hoard of angry flies swarmed in discontent at being disturbed.

"Just the jawbone that I found," O'Leary said as they approached the remains of a burnt-out tree. "Once I saw it was human, I dropped it where I found it and went to call you guys. I ain't never seen nothing like it."

They stopped at the fence line; the wooden planks cracked and split in several areas from where the tree had fallen on them. The scent of campfire mixed with freshly cut wood still lingered in the air. Tess noticed a chainsaw resting on the ground near some freshly cut branches.

"I was cutting this tree when I looked into the woods and saw that the mound looked different," O'Leary said, pointing across the fence into the woods beyond. Tess could just make out the shape of a hill just inside the woodline.

"You're gonna have to hop the fence. No gate on this side." O'Leary informed her as he climbed on the fence and swung his leg over. Tess grasped the railing and began climbing over, her large rubber boots making it awkward. She landed on the other side with a gentle squelching sound and resumed following the farmer.

"I had to walk down here a ways because of the creek being so high," O'Leary commented as he slowed to a stop and carefully worked his way across the swiftly moving creek. "It was a lot worse just an hour or so ago. Water's already going down."

Tess thought about jumping across but, figuring she'd fall flat on her rear end, gave up and sloshed through the shallowest area she could find. Barely missing a rock to stand on and wobbling off balance for a second or two, she wondered if she was going to end up soaked and muddy just to look at a cow jaw instead of getting back home to Denny before noon. Thankfully, she finally righted herself and made it to the other side of the creek.

Feet once again on firm ground, Tess looked up to find Kevin O'Leary watching her with a slightly amused look on his face. She chose to ignore it, feeling her cheeks flush in embarrassment.

They slowly made their way into the woods, the forest floor littered with briars and honeysuckle. The undergrowth finally gave way, and the trail became easier. In the distance, Tess could see the burial mound.

Approximately thirty feet long and roughly twelve feet high, the hill had a flat top and was surrounded by trees on all sides. The hill itself was littered with fallen leaves and short vegetation. At one end, Tess could see that a rather large tree had fallen over, most likely in the recent storm, taking a huge chunk of earth with it.

"Over there," O'Leary pointed toward the fallen tree. "The bone was sticking up out of the water where the tree had been."

The two came to a halt in front of the base of the fallen tree, an old oak with a thick trunk. The root ball alone was well over their heads.

"That's a pretty old-looking tree. I'm amazed it hasn't fallen over before now," Tess commented as she squatted next to the muddy puddle. "Here?" she pointed.

"Yep. I dropped it when I saw what it was. You'll have to feel around."

Groaning inwardly, Tess slowly reached into the puddle barehanded. The mud squelched loosely between her fingers, promising to be too deep for her short exam gloves. Keeping an eye on O'Leary, she gently leaned forward over the water and began to feel around, wincing as the water seeped in at the glove's edge.

The water was very cold, the mud thick and lumpy. It took all of Tess's willpower not to pull her hand back out in revulsion, especially knowing what the murky depths held.

Her hand bumped something hard and she grabbed at it, pulling it above the surface. To her dismay, it was just a water-logged stick. Throwing it over her shoulder, she reached into the water once more.

Kevin O'Leary began walking around the area, hands in his pockets, looking for what Tess didn't know. More bones, perhaps? Evidence of foul play?

"Sir, I'd like it if you could not touch anything if you find something out of the ordinary. Chances are the bones you found have been here for some time, but this could be determined to be a crime scene, and I'd like to not have it mucked up any more than it already has been."

"Surely, all the footprints are gone after this long, right?" Kevin shrugged. Tess nodded, her hand still moving below the murky surface of the deep puddle. The water was almost up to her elbows when suddenly she felt something hard, smooth, and U-shaped. *This is it*, she thought to herself as she pulled the human mandible from its watery grave.

"That's it," Kevin commented from where he stood a few yards away, watching.

Tess tried not to think about the fact that she was holding the skeletal remains of someone's jaw in her bare hands. She looked at it from various angles, noting the dental bridge that Kevin had mentioned, as well as two metal fillings in the molars of the left side. She had to concur with Kevin O'Leary. The mandible did not appear to be ancient Native American bones, buried there with respect and honor. It appeared, unfortunately, that someone had been buried there more recently, hidden in the mound to conceal their whereabouts.

# Chapter Four

*Saturday, August 18th, 2:35 pm*

"Hey, Dane," Mike Seawell, Swain County's lead crime scene investigator, greeted Tess as he and his assistant approached the burial mound.

Looking up from where she'd been logging her findings in her notebook, Tess nodded in his direction. Closing her notes and shoving them into her back pocket, she walked toward the CSI as he stopped and set down some of his supplies, his assistant following his lead.

"I heard you found human bones?" Seawell commented, glancing over at the mound.

"Yep." Tess held up a cardboard evidence box holding the mandible. "One human mandible. Now you get to help me find the rest of them."

"Do we have the ME headed out?" he asked, sliding his wire-rimmed glasses up his narrow, sweaty nose, only for them to immediately slide back down.

"Yeah, Dr. Summers is en route. She was in Columbus when I called her." Tess looked at her watch. "That was almost two hours ago, though. She may be a while."

Seawell took the box from Tess's outstretched hands and opened it. Scrutinizing the contents with a shrug, he closed the box and handed it back to her.

"Alright, well, I'll have Stacey start taking photographs while I start taking measurements. Then we'll have to start draining that puddle." Seawell bent down and began digging around in his tacklebox of investigation tools. Eventually he came up holding a measuring tape. Meanwhile, Stacey, his assistant, began taking area photographs from various angles.

"So who found the bone?" Seawell asked as he began logging measurements of the distance between the burial mound and the uprooted tree. They would eventually measure the length between each bone and a specific reference point on the mound. Measuring the puddle itself was useless as its depth and circumference varied by the hour, depending on the rainfall in the area.

"The homeowner, Kevin O'Leary," Tess answered, casting a glance back toward the house and barn, where O'Leary said he'd be if she needed him. "Apparently, he was out cutting down a tree that crushed his fence during the storm. Saw this mess through the trees and came to investigate." She waved her arm in the direction of the uprooted tree.

"That was one helluva storm," Seawell commented as he wrote more notes to himself in his log book. Tess murmured in agreement and then left him to do his work.

Slowly skirting the area, mindful of tree roots and soggy underbrush, Tess made her way around the entirety of the burial mound. The only thing she knew about such mounds was what she'd learned in grade school.

If she remembered correctly, the Adena and Hopewell tribes that had once called central Ohio home had been Moundbuilders. They'd received that name due to the flat-topped hills or mounds that they'd built for spiritual reasons like honoring their dead. Since the mounds and surrounding lands were considered sacred, they were protected by law, but that didn't stop people from defacing them. Some mounds were found on private property, such as this, while others, like The Great Serpent Mounds, had been turned into historical sites with museums for learning the histories of the Native Americans that had built them.

When Tess was on the other side of the mound from where Seawell and Stacey were busy at work, she was suddenly overcome with a strange feeling. It was almost as though she were being watched. Trying not to be obvious, she continued to act casual and glance around her, to see if she could find the source of her unease, but she didn't see anyone. She didn't hear anyone either. And then she realized...

She couldn't seem to hear anything at all. It was as though she'd been dropped into a vacuum, and all outside noise had simply vanished. Feeling her heartbeat quicken, Tess began to turn around, looking at her surroundings, feeling disoriented. What was happening? Where were Stacey and Seawell? Why couldn't she hear anything?

Taking a stumbling step forward, towards the leaf littered mound in front of her, Tess began to panic. Eyes were on her, but from where, she didn't know. She could just feel them. Was she somehow cursed now for disturbing a sacred mound? No, surely not. That would be crazy. *She* was going crazy. That was it; Tess herself was going crazy.

Suddenly, the shrill ring of her cell phone filled the air around her, causing Tess to jump. Slapping at her pockets, trying to find her phone, she took in huge gulps of air. Feeling the hard rectangle in her pocket, she pulled the phone out and tapped the green button.

"Hello?" she said shakily as she held the phone to her head, suddenly aware of the birds chirping in the trees overhead.

"Hey, Tess..." Denny's deep voice filled her ear, "What's wrong? You sound upset."

"I.... I'm fine," she said, shaking her head to rid herself of the uneasy feeling. Slowly, her heart rate decreased to a normal level and her breathing came easier.

"You don't sound fine." Concern filled Denny's voice. "Did something happen?"

"No," Tess sighed, leaves from the previous autumn slick underfoot as she made her way around the mound. "I just... I don't know. I got this weird feeling, like I was being watched, and then suddenly I felt like I couldn't breathe or hear anything." She let out a pitiful laugh. "I know I sound crazy."

"You don't sound crazy. It sounds like you might have had a panic attack or something. Do you feel better now? Do you want me to come get you?"

"No. No, I'll be fine," she said, trying to smile at his concern. "I'm already feeling better. It was just so weird." She still felt a little off but didn't want to worry him any further.

"Well... okay, if you say so." He didn't sound like he fully believed her but let her do her thing. "I was calling to ask where Otter's leash and travel bowl is. You know, that collapsible one you bought him a few weeks ago? Natalie and I wanted to take him to the park." In the background, Tess could hear Otter barking and Natalie giggling.

"The bowl is in the dishwasher and.... crap... His nice leash is in my car I think. You'll have to grab his backup one. It's hanging in the laundry room on the hook by the door." Tess could hear shuffling from the other end of the phone.

"Found it!" Denny exclaimed. "You sure you don't need anything?"

Tess smiled, "Yeah, I'll be fine. I already feel back to normal." She'd rounded the far end of the mound and could again see Seawell and Stacey in the distance. Movement from the direction of the farmhouse caught her eye, and she turned to see Kevin O'Leary leading a tired-looking Dr. Abby Summers through the woods toward the crime scene.

"Okay, well just call me if you need anything." Denny was saying in her ear.

Distractedly, Tess thanked him again and disconnected the call. Walking back to the crime scene, she waved at Dr. Summers when the medical examiner saw her approaching.

"Hey, Detective Dane," Dr. Summers greeted Tess with a warm smile. Her dark hair was pulled up in a messy bun on top of her head, and she looked exhausted.

"How have you been?" Tess asked, watching the woman carefully.

"Well, I have two sick kiddos at home, and my husband is out of town for work for two weeks—thank God my mother lives with us! And I just finished a fourteen-hour shift on my feet, and I'm exhausted." She cast a tired smile at Tess.

"That's a lot!" Tess empathized. "Well, hopefully, this doesn't take forever, so you can go get some rest."

"How are *you* doing? You look a little pale," Summers commented, leaning closer to look in Tess's face.

"I just had a panic attack or something. Just a strange feeling, really," Tess mumbled, not wanting to make a big deal about it. "I'm fine now."

Dr. Summers didn't look convinced but didn't press either. "So what do we have so far?" she asked, changing the subject and turning to look over toward the mud where Seawell and Stacey were hard at work draining the water from the puddle.

"Human mandible, modern dental work, not part of the prehistoric Burial Mound." Tess rattled off as she watched one CSI fill a bucket and then carefully dump it through a large strainer held by the other CSI. The water level had already gone down substantially, and Tess wondered what else they would find buried in the mud.

As she and Dr. Summers approached the uprooted tree, Tess took note of Kevin O'Leary standing near the edge of the clearing, watching. Had it been his eyes that Tess had felt watching her? No, surely not. She'd just seen him walking from the direction of the farmhouse, which was on the opposite side of the mound that she'd been on.

Tess sighed. She didn't know what had happened, and she felt fine now, so with an inward shrug, she squatted down next to the now-drained mud puddle. She could already see a few more white things sticking up from the thick, brown sludge. Bones.

Dr. Summers must have seen them, too, because she was soon down on her knees next to Tess. Seawell and Stacey set their strainer to the side as they too looked at the bones.

Abby Summers pulled a pair of black nitrile exam gloves out of her pocket and pulled them on while Seawell took photos of the empty hole in front of them. Except it wasn't empty. It held the remains of some poor soul that had been left there to rot.

*There goes the rest of my weekend,* Tess muttered inwardly as she got down on her knees next to the makeshift grave and prepared to help Dr. Summers however she could.

# Chapter Five

*Saturday, August 18th, 5:39 pm*

"Here's another rib," Dr. Summers announced grimly, holding up a long, thin bone covered in thick mud. So far, that made one hundred fifty-six bones they'd collected from the mud.

The group had partitioned the area off in a grid pattern for easy cataloging of what bones were found where. The thin neon pink string used to make the grid crossed the burial site where the skeleton had been found, the knotted ends fluttering in the breeze.

Even though the day had started cool and overcast from the storms, the sun had decided to come out and had begun drying everything. The air was humid, and sweat trailed down Tess's spine as the group worked in the mud. She could hear a gnat buzzing around her head and absently swatted at it as annoyance at the insects grew. She moved around slowly, appraising the scene, her county-issued black rubber boots making squelching sounds as she slipped through the mud. Despite the rain from the previous few days, the woods seemed vibrant and alive, and the scent of the freshly churned mud mixed with that of the newly fallen tree, creating a pungent bouquet of growth and decay.

It must have been almost dinner time, if Tess believed her rumbling stomach. She wiped at her sweaty forehead with the back of her arm and left a dirt streak on her skin.

Suddenly, Tess heard voices coming up behind her. She turned to look over her shoulder and saw a group of five adults briskly making their way through the woods, carrying video equipment and microphones.

"Oh, hell no," she muttered as she quickly stood and went to intercept the group of media personnel barreling towards her crime scene.

"Stop!" she commanded, holding up her hand to halt them. "Do not come any further. This is a crime scene, and by the jurisdiction of the Swain County Sheriff's Department, this area is off limits."

Four of the adults–two men carrying cameras and two women with perfect "ready for television" makeup on—skidded to a halt. The fifth person, a woman, continued walking toward Tess and the crime scene. Why hadn't they cordoned off the scene? And how did the media already hear about this? Just a few hours ago, they were unsure if it even *was* a crime scene. Tess inwardly berated herself for not keeping a closer watch on the perimeter.

"I said stop!" Tess ordered as the woman continued towards her, an angry look etched into her tanned face. Tess matched her look, glaring at the approaching woman. "I will arrest you for trespassing and tampering with a crime scene."

"*You're* the one trespassing," the woman snapped back, finally coming to a halt a few feet in front of Tess. The rest of the intruders stood in a huddle, setting up their cameras.

"I am Detective Tess Dane of the Swain County Sheriff's Department, and this is a crime scene. Please back up and remove yourself, or I will have you arrested." Turning to glance over her shoulder, Tess motioned for the two patrol deputies milling around the area, documenting the scene and photographing as they went. They saw her beckon to them and quickly headed in her direction, their footfalls making sucking noises in the thick muddy landscape.

"This isn't a crime scene," the woman in front of Tess seethed, her dark eyes boring into Tess. "These are the ancient burial grounds of my people, and you are the one trespassing here. *You* are the one that needs to leave."

"I understand this is a burial ground, ma'am, but I am confident that this is also the site of a crime. Now, if you will allow me to explain, out of the earshot of the media, we can work through this...misunderstanding." Tess ground out through clenched teeth. "Please stand over there while I get rid of these goons." She pointed toward the edge of the clearing. The woman sighed dramatically, her black hair swirling around her shoulders.

"Go on, guys, while I talk to this... detective," she sneered at Tess before casting a glance over her shoulder at the other four people in her entourage. She turned back toward Tess but still addressed them. "Just wait for me in the car. They will be leaving soon and then we can too." Her dark eyes, black as coal, bore into Tess's blue ones, each woman not willing to give an inch.

Tess could hear the media leaving... for now. She knew they'd be back and made a mental note to get some more officers to patrol the crime scene until they cleared it.

"So, I've given you my name. Now give me yours," Tess commanded, her eyes never moving from the woman in front of her. Irritation coursed through her at having people trampling through her crime scene. In the distance, she could hear Summers and Seawell continue to work in hushed tones.

"I don't owe you shit," the woman snapped. Tess glared at her through slitted eyes. Taking in the woman's tanned skin, black hair, and tribal necklace, Tess was sure she had something to do with the Mound more than the crime scene itself. But regardless, Tess couldn't have her running around the scene at will.

"Look, ma'am, we are out here working on a crime scene. That's it. We aren't digging up the mound, we aren't messing with your ancestors," Tess sighed. "We are trying to be as respectful as possible, but we need to collect all of the evidence and bones to find out who is buried near the mound and who is trying to get away with murder."

The two women stared at each other for a moment, and when it was apparent that neither would be cowed by the other, the newcomer finally shrugged.

"Remi," the woman said with a sigh. "Remi Nightsong," she added when Tess gave her a confused look.

"Nice to meet you, Remi Nightsong," Tess replied, trying to keep the irritation from her voice.

"How do you know it's a murder and not the ancestral bones of my people?"

"I don't know that it's *not* your people," Tess stated. "All I know for sure is that they are not ancient bones. There is evidence that points to a more modern death. It's my preliminary belief that someone used the mound as a way to dispose of a body. A murder, from the looks of it."

Remi seemed to mull the information around for a moment, her face finally relaxing. When she wasn't scowling and angry, she was very beautiful. "Will you be leaving soon? Leaving this place alone?"

"Yes, Remi. As soon as we can, we will release it back to Mr. O'Leary, the property owner."

This caused another angry look to pass over Remi's face once again. "This land belongs to the Mound Builders. I don't care what the deed says. The O'Leary's have always respected it, though. Hopefully, you will, too."

"I will do my best," Tess declared solemnly. "I understand that this is a sensitive subject and a sacred place for your people. I also understand that it appears that someone has tried to hide a hideous crime. If that was your loved one, wouldn't you want to know what happened to them?"

Remi looked up at Tess and then nodded, the long beaded earrings on her lobes dancing gently. She sighed, "Look, I'm sorry for being such a bitch. We've just been dealing with a bunch of people being disrespectful to the various mounds in the area. Just last month, some kids were riding their bikes along the ridge of the one in Newark. People have even dug into the more hidden mounds, like this one, just looking for artifacts and relics to make a quick buck or exploit the dead. It's disgusting."

Tess shook her head in dismay. The audacity of some people was appalling. "Well, if it makes you feel any better,

I plan on having an officer guard the area until we release the scene. Hopefully, that will deter any looky-loos from creeping around here."

"Thanks, Detective," Remi nodded. She paused for a moment, her dark eyes scanning the burial mound and the forensic team busy at work. "Any idea who it is?"

"No, not yet," Tess replied, joining Remi in watching Dr. Summers gently examine a bone she'd just pulled from the mud. "All I know is they are human. We'll get an anthropologist to look at them and give us more information."

"Sounds good," Remi sighed. "I'll let my dad know what's going on. He wasn't too happy to hear about you all digging around in here. That's why my friends and I headed over here. To get the dirt firsthand."

"Who's your dad?" Tess asked, interested. "And you're friends with the media? I thought they were just pesky news anchors and ambulance chasers. You know the type."

Remi snorted softly and grinned, "I am a member of the Wyandotte Nation and the head of the Native Women's Media Group at my college. We have a podcast, among other things, that shines a light on Native issues, like the alarming numbers at which native women are murdered or go missing. We travel the state mostly, but we've even gone out West to interview people for videos. So many crimes and indignities to Native people go unreported or unresolved." Remi explained. "I am my father's daughter. He's Gordon Nightsong."

"*The* Gordon Nightsong?" Tess asked, surprised and mildly impressed. She'd heard of the man but didn't know much about his personal life. What she did know of him was what she'd gleaned from newspapers or online news outlets. Once the manager of one of the most successful casinos in the country, Gordon Nightsong had changed courses and become somewhat of a self-help guru. Tess had seen his books at various stores and even caught the tail end of an interview or two on early morning talk shows.

"Yep," Remi shrugged, "That's the one and only."

"Interesting," Tess commented, suddenly wondering why someone like Gordon Nightsong, who had a ton of money from his casino days and now had a successful guru career, would get upset over a skeleton found near a burial mound. Just because it disrupted Native people? Or because he somehow had deeper ties to this site?

Always the detective, Tess decided to ask just that. "So why was your dad so upset about us being out here? How did he even hear about it? Isn't he living in a mansion out west somewhere?"

Remi smirked. "I wish!" When Tess gave her a quizzical look, Remi added, "He lives locally in a log cabin on a few acres. He has a couple of chickens and some old hound dogs. Seems to be happy living the stress-free life baking things and listening to the police scanner."

Remi's cell phone chimed, distracting her for a moment. Tess watched as the woman, a few years younger than herself, read through a text message and made a face.

"Look, I have to go," Remi said, sliding her phone back into her jeans pocket. "You'll let us know when you've cleared the area?"

"Sure," Tess agreed. She handed Remi one of her business cards. "Call me if you hear any chatter that may prove useful."

"Will do, Detective." Remi gave a friendly smile and nodded to the crime scene techs. Turning around in the muddy terrain, she retreated in the direction where her friends had gone.

# Chapter Six



Tess sat at her desk, sipping coffee as she inspected the photographs of the skull and mandible found at the O'Leary farm over the weekend, pondering the dental bridge and if it would help them identify their John Doe.

After finishing up at the crime scene, Dr. Summers had packed the skeletal remains up to take to the Swain County Crime Lab for further analysis, saying she'd be in touch within the next few days. All she had been able to tell Tess definitively at the scene was that the victim was most likely male but that she'd know more once she examined it. Summers had also mentioned calling her friend and colleague, Dr. Jenn Brezdika, a forensic anthropologist at The Ohio State University in Columbus. Tess was hopeful that Dr. Brezdika would agree to help them with the remains and finally get justice for the victim.

Curious about the dental work, Tess did a quick internet search and found that there were three major suppliers of dental implants in the country, depending on the needs and geographical location of the patient. Perhaps if she called local dentists, she'd be able to determine the owner of the implant or, at minimum, the manufacturer.

Crawley, though still considered a small town, was the county seat of Swain County. Camden Town sat adjacent to Crawley, and between the two communities, there were only two dental offices. Tess crossed her fingers that at least one of the offices could and would answer some of her questions.

According to the internet, however, Shively Family Dental had only been open for five years, and Tess was doubtful that if the skeleton was a local, Dr. Shively would have been their dentist.

She clicked on the "Our Staff" tab on the website, and within seconds, Tess found herself staring into the smiling face of Dr. Amelia Shively, DDS, who appeared to be in her early to mid-thirties at most. There seemed to be little hope that Dr. Shively would have been the victim's dentist. The age of the doctor didn't match up with the possible age of the victim. But, until forensics came back with more information, there was no way of telling how long the skeleton had been buried in the mound.

The other dentist in town was the one Tess had gone to as a child, Camden Dental and Orthodontics. Old Dr. Beeson had retired long ago, but perhaps his son, who had taken over the practice, could shed some light on Tess's current case.

Tess picked up her phone and called Camden Dental. After a few rings, a bored-sounding woman answered the phone.

"Camden Dental, this is Marcia. How may I help you?" came a monotone voice.

"Hi. This is Detective Tess Dane with the Swain County Sheriff's Department. I was wondering if you have a moment to answer a few questions for me."

"You'll have to talk to the doc, Detective. That's out of my pay grade," Marcia stated in her dry, nasally tone. Tess could practically hear her roll her eyes. "He's busy doing a root canal at the moment. Can he call you back?"

"That is fine. I look forward to speaking with him." Tess smiled her way through her frustration with the woman's attitude. She quickly terminated the call after supplying a good callback number and leaned back in her chair, thrumming her fingertips on the desk in front of her.

The only information she had was that skeletal remains were found next to a Hopewell burial ground. Until she spoke with Drs. Summers and Brezdika, she wouldn't have anything else to go on about the victim. But what about the mound? Other than being a sacred place to the indigenous peoples of the area, was there something else in particular about that mound that drove the killer or killers to use it to conceal their crimes?

Leaning into the desk again, Tess quickly ran an internet search for burial mounds in central Ohio. Instantly, results flooded in about Mound Builders Park in Newark, The Great Serpent Mound in Adams County, and more. They seemed to be scattered throughout the state from Marietta and Cedarville, to Worthington and Zaleski or even further.

Most, but not all, seemed to be registered as state historical sites and reserves. One had been turned into a golf course but, luckily, had been permanently closed. Tess felt anger rising in her at the thought of someone being so callous as to build anything–much less a golf course–atop a highly spiritual and sacred place. Tess thought about how well those same kind of people would like it if someone plopped a vacation resort on their family's final resting place. *Bet they wouldn't like it one bit.*

Grinding her molars together in frustration, she ran a quick search for specifically Swain County. Two known burial mounds popped up, both of which were situated on private property: one on O'Leary land and one on the southeastern corner of the county belonging to a man named Derek Boone. Tess made a note of the man's name and the location of the mound for future reference before pooling her efforts into the O'Leary Mound.

A basic search revealed that the O'Leary mound was registered as a historical site but was closed to visitors. There were some references to a farmers market back a few decades ago and some people had posted chatter in local forums about paying to see the mound, while others admitted to having "recovered" artifacts. A few people even claimed to have snuck onto the O'Leary's land in search of an opening into the mound.

According to another website, the mounds were built by various indigenous tribes and were eventually termed collectively as the "Mound Builders." The earthen structures themselves were made up of subterranean chambers, most containing artifacts such as pottery, weapons, pipes, and pelts. Other mounds were used for the burial of tribal members.

"Too bad someone thought they could use a mound for something nefarious," Tess muttered to herself as she clicked through a few more websites. Eventually, she pushed back from her desk with a sigh. Was she even on the right track? Did the Mound Builders have anything to do with the John Doe Kevin O'Leary had found?

Rubbing her temple as a headache threatened her day, Tess stood and headed toward the breakroom to refill her coffee.

The small staff room was empty of people at the moment, much to Tess's relief. She quickly approached the coffee carafe in anticipation only to realize too late that the pot was nearly empty, the contents cold.

"Damnit, how hard is it to rinse out the carafe and make a new pot?" she huffed as she did just that. As she watched the last of the previous shift's coffee swirl down the drain, she heard someone enter the room behind her.

"Oh hey, Dane!" greeted Deputy Miles, a broad smile cracking his round face in two. "How's it going? You find out anything about them bones?" He held a chipped green 'Just Add Coffee' travel thermos in one hand and something wrapped in a napkin in the other.

"Hey, Miles," she smiled at her colleague. "You with Scafferty today?" Glancing around for his partner, she didn't see him, but she knew he was somewhere close by. The two officers seemed to be attached at the hip.

"Yeah, he's just slacking," Miles whispered with a laugh as he watched Tess refill the coffee filter and set it to brew.

"I heard that!" Scafferty rebuked, walking into the room, mug in hand. "Oh, good. You're making a fresh pot."

"Yeah, apparently it's too hard for anyone else to do around here so...." Tess rolled her eyes at the two men. Miles and Scafferty shrugged and grinned.

"Thank you, Tess," Scafferty smiled with exaggerated sweetness and then snorted out a laugh when Tess punched him in the arm playfully.

Suddenly, Deputy Evans stalked into the room, ignoring the trio of officers waiting patiently for the coffee to brew. They watched as he grabbed a mug from the cupboard and poured the first cup from the carafe, even as it continued to drip and sizzle on the burner.

"About time someone made some fresh coffee," he muttered as he slipped past them again and exited the room.

"The audacity...." Tess seethed. Some people were so rude and self absorbed. On one hand she tried to understand their point of view but then they did something like steal the first cup of coffee that they were too lazy to brew themselves before it was even done! She took a few deep breaths to calm herself.

"Sorry, Dane. Men are pigs," Miles shrugged sheepishly. "Scafferty and I were thankful you made a fresh pot though, aren't we?" he jutted out an elbow into his partner's paunch. Scafferty wheezed out an agreement.

"As we were saying..." Scafferty tried steering the conversation back to more neutral topics. "Have you found out anything new about the bones found at the O'Leary farm?"

"Not so much the bones themselves, but I do have a call in with a local dentist to ask a few questions about the dental bridge. I've also been researching the Mound Builders."

"The Indians who built the mounds?" Scafferty asked thoughtfully.

"Yes," Tess answered slowly, "except we don't call them Indians. They aren't from India. They are Native or Indigenous people."

"Noted," he nodded sheepishly. Tess pulled the full pot of coffee off of the burner and motioned for the men to set their mugs on the counter. Filling each, including her own, she replaced the pot before adding French vanilla creamer to hers.

"Do you still think the bones are newer and not part of the original mound?" Miles asked, sipping his brew before uncovering the item he'd been holding in his hand. It looked like some sort of homemade breakfast pastry.

"Your mom baking again?" she asked. When he nodded, she grinned and continued, "Yes, to answer your question, I do think the bones are modern. The dental work leads me to believe that. Until I hear otherwise from the anthropologist, that is."

"When do you see them?"

"Hopefully Dr. Summers calls today or tomorrow with more information. Otherwise, I'm waiting on the dentist to call me back. I can't really do an effective missing persons search until I have some search parameters to enter into the database."

"Detective Dane?" Bertie's voice crackled over the intercom, "You in there?"

"Yes, Bertie. What's up?" Tess called across the room to the receptionist's disembodied voice.

"There's some dentist on line two for you."

"Awesome. I'll get it in my office. Thanks, Bertie."

"Copy," Bertie replied before the intercom staticked.

"See you two later," Tess smiled, holding her mug up in a feign salute to her friends. They reciprocated the gesture as she quickly made her way back to her office.

Picking up the receiver, she greeted the caller. "This is Detective Dane."

"Hi, Detective. This is Dr. Lowel Beeson over at Camden Dental. My receptionist told me you'd called with some questions...?"

"Oh, hi Dr. Beeson, thank you for returning my call. Yes, I had a few questions about a case I'm working on, and I was hoping I could have a few moments of your time."

"Sure, Detective. I've got about thirty minutes before I have another root canal coming in."

"Ugh, that doesn't sound fun," Tess commiserated. A snort sounded over the line.

"Nah, it's not. And the patients don't seem to care for it either!" The dentist barked out a laugh at his lame joke.

Tess shook her head and let out a laugh of her own. "Nice one, Doc."

"Hey, I gotta amuse myself somehow, right? Anyway, what were your questions?"

"Well, I've been working a case involving some old bones–"

"That skeleton out on the O'Leary place? Son of a..." Beeson interrupted in a rush. Tess pulled a face of frustration he couldn't see over the phone. Small town gossip mills could be the worst sometimes.

"I'm not saying one way or another. Either way, you understand that I'd appreciate your discretion, considering this is an open investigation, right?"

"Of course, Detective. I hear ya," Beeson answered. "Is what they are saying true, though? Is it a murdered person? Someone said the woman was shot two times clean through her head."

*Oh, good Lord, how misinformation spreads faster than the truth.* Tess shook her head.

"No, that isn't true, and I would advise that you help shut down the gossip mill before this gets out of hand," she instructed, an edge to her voice. "Now, my question is this: How far back does your office keep records, specifically those pertaining to dental implants like bridges?"

"Well, in Ohio, we technically only have to keep them for ten years. Pops liked to keep everything, and I mean *everything*, but when the basement flooded back in 2011, most of his boxes got destroyed. Fine by me, to be honest. I'd been harping on him to either digitize them or throw them out, but he wouldn't. When he retired, they sat down there, forgotten. Well, until the flood, that is. After that, I pulled out all the files that were destroyed and threw them away. Most of them were well over twelve years old! If the patients wanted their records when Pops retired, they would have come by and picked them up by then."

"And did any of his patients become your patients?"

"Oh, sure, most did," Dr. Beeson answered. "Of course, when I took over the office, I updated a bunch of things, including digitizing records."

"So, all of the older records that are still in the basement are just... not current patients? And they aren't in your new database?" Tess asked, the task at hand seeming insurmountable. She was mentally picturing a large basement with row after row of bankers' boxes shoved full of disorganized medical charts. How would she ever weed through them all to find the owner of the dental bridge currently affixed to the mandible lying in the county morgue? And that was *if* the skeleton was even a local! Then another thought hit her: what if her victim's records were one of those that were destroyed in the flood?

She may never be able to determine who the victim was based on dental records.

"Yeah," Beeson replied. "I know technically I don't need to keep them anymore, but they mean something to Dad. I figure they aren't costing me anything, sitting in the basement collecting dust. I've just left them where Dad put them." He let out a long sigh. "It's not worth the arguing about it, you know? You're welcome to come over and dig through the boxes. They seem to be somewhat in alphabetical order so if you know the name of the person you're looking for...?"

"No, not yet. I'm waiting to get more information from the ME and forensic anthropologist. They'll take radiographs of the skull for us to compare with possible patients." Tess answered, trying to sound hopeful. "I do know that the victim had a bridge on their mandible. Would that be traceable in any way?"

"Well, I guess it depends on a few factors. Most of the older ones don't have markings of any kind. I mean, the bridge itself is supposed to appear as natural as possible, right? Well, some companies have started putting their own form of ID numbers on the underside of the bridge. It's not a fail-safe, and not every single one does it, but all is not lost, Detective." He paused to take a breath. "There are... I think three major manufacturers of dental implants. Some regions of the county get their implants from whichever manufacturer is geographically closest to them. So, say, if once you get radiographs of the mandible, we can hopefully ID your victim by determining which region of the country their implant came from. That is, if they are even from the United States."

Tess sighed, her mind absorbing this new information. "So, hopefully, this person is a local where we can find their actual dental records. Searching a potential third of the country, if not more, sounds insurmountable at the moment."

"I'm hoping for your sake, and the victim's, that the anthropologist will be able to give you more information to lead to an official ID," Beeson empathized.

"Thanks, Doc. I may contact you again soon to come poke around in the basement," Tess said grimly.

"Sure, anything I can do to help, just say the word," the dentist offered before he disconnected the call.

With a sigh, Tess rubbed a palm down her face, thinking about the rest of her day. She was waiting to hear back from Dr. Summers and still had to finalize her report from the day before.

She glanced at the clock. If she hurried, she might be able to head over to Tolliver Care Home and visit with her dad before his usual afternoon nap. She'd missed seeing him over the weekend because she'd been tied up at the farm on Saturday and then had spent all of Sunday with Denny and Natalie to make up for her hasty departure. She felt bad skipping out on her dad, but when she'd called to check on him, his nurse, Angela, had told her that her father had been sleeping all day. After that, Tess had decided to make a day of heading into Columbus with Denny and Natalie to visit Franklin Park Conservatory and grab lunch at Katzinger's Deli on 3rd Street. She'd even conned Denny into stopping at The Book Loft in German Village, where she bought the latest title from her favorite dark romance author.

He'd quirked his eyebrow when he'd read the title and grinned. "Really? Are you trying to tell me something?" his eyes sparkled with mischief.

"Don't judge me," she whispered before snatching the book from his hands and heading down the labyrinth of book-filled rooms that was The Book Loft.

"Yeah, Daddy..." Natalie inserted, as though she knew what the adults were talking about. "Don't judge her."

Tess snorted a laugh as she threw a grin over her shoulder at Denny. She could hear him laughing all the way down the hall.

Since he'd bought her the book, she'd already managed to read half of it. She looked forward to finishing it after work if the rest of her Monday went as planned.

Mondays rarely went as planned though.

# Chapter Seven



"So what do we have?" Tess asked Dr. Abby Summers, the medical examiner, as she approached the doctor's desk while carrying two cups of coffee. Standing at the end of a stainless steel examination table across the room, Dr. Summers was just finishing rearranging the bones that were found at the O'Leary farm.

Abby looked up with a smile. "Hey, Dane. Thanks for coming down so early. Jenn will be here any moment." She paused, eyeing the disposable coffee cups in Tess's hands. "Is that what I think it is?"

"Venti caramel macchiato?" Tess grinned, holding it out to Abby. The doctor let out a happy squeal, held up a finger to wait for a moment, and went to wash her hands.

"So who's Jenn?" Tess asked, sipping her French vanilla coffee.

"Dr. Jenn Brezdika, a forensic anthropologist from OSU.... and my bestie from college." Abby grinned as she came to join Tess at the desk. Abby let out a contented sigh as she swallowed a mouthful of her coffee and nodded at Tess. "Perfection. Thank you!"

Just then, there was a knock at the morgue door, jarring Tess and Abby from their caffeine-laden bliss. Tess looked up to see a dark-haired woman peeking around the doorframe at them.

"Knock knock!" The woman's bright smile and singsong voice instantly put Tess at ease.

"C'mon in, Jenn! How have you been?" Abby greeted her friend with a hug. "This is Detective Tess Dane with the Swain County Sheriff's Department. She's the one who is officially working this case."

"Nice to meet you, Detective Dane." Dr. Brezdika extended her hand.

"You, too. And you can call me Tess if you'd like," she smiled as she shook the anthropologist's hand.

"Oh, good! Because I was just about to ask you to call me Jenn!" Brezdika beamed, her smile lighting up her round face. "All that Dr. So-and-So stuff seems so... impersonal."

"See, Tess? This is why Jenn and I got along so well in college. She's a unicorn." Abby took another swig of her drink before setting the cup on her desk. "I remember being so introverted back in college. Didn't have many friends, but then during freshman year anatomy lab, in walks this girl who wasn't shy at all." She paused to look fondly over at her friend. "She introduced herself as Jenn, said she got geeked out by bones, and sat down next to me. That whole semester, she followed me around, talking incessantly and inviting me out to do things and meet new people. I honestly think that's why I finally came out of my shell and became more extroverted."

"Oh, Abby, you always had that person inside of you," Jenn scolded playfully. "She just needed help busting out from under your xiphoid process." Jenn cackled at her joke. "Get it? Xiphoid process? Your breast bone?" She turned to Tess and made a gurgling sound and a hand gesture like something was bursting out of her chest.

"Wow....I could only imagine you two drunk at a party," Tess said, sorting, which only made Jenn laugh harder.

Abby just rolled her eyes and grinned. She was used to her friends' antics and seemed unphased.

"Okay, though.... Time to get serious," Jenn declared, absently smoothing some stray hairs. "Who *is* the handsome devil on the table?" she nodded towards the skeletal remains arranged precisely on a blue fabric sheet laid over the stainless steel table.

"This," indicated Tess as she stepped back toward the remains, "is the skeletal remains that were found on the O'Leary land. You probably heard about it on the news. We're waiting to contact a dentist in the area to confirm some dental work that appears to have been done on the molars. Hopefully, there is some kind of serial number on the dental bridge. I wanted you to have a look at the skeleton first, take pictures. This is your and Abby's party now. I wouldn't even know what photos the dentist would need."

"Alrighty! Sounds like you've been working hard on this case already," Jenn commended as she came close to the table to examine the bones. "Let's see what these bones can tell us today."

Tess watched as Jenn Brezdika carefully studied the skeletal remains, lifting various bones and turning them this way and that before replacing them on the table. She made notes to herself, took measurements, and logged everything inside of a pink, leather-bound journal she'd brought with her. While she quietly worked, slowly making her circuit around the table and back again, Tess and Abby congregated near the ME's desk to finish their coffee and discuss their theories.

After some time, Jenn finally looked up from her journal and beckoned Tess and Abby over.

"Well, I've got some good news and some bad news. Which one do you want first?"

"The bad?" Tess wrinkled her nose in dismay. She'd honestly rather not hear the bad news at all.

"Your victim was stabbed approximately eight times, and that's just the stabs that went deep enough to cause damage to the bones. There could have been more wounds to the soft tissue but we'll never know at this point. Whoever did this was very angry indeed. The frustrating part is the markings on the bones are so degraded that it will be difficult to differentiate the exact type of blade used."

"Meaning what exactly?"

"Meaning it doesn't look like a serrated knife was used, but if you need individual characteristics to determine the *exact* blade used in the killing then…. I'm sorry. The bones have been out there for too long. They've been nibbled on by insects and animals, exposed to the elements to some degree even though they were buried under the tree."

"And the good news?" Tess asked with a sigh. She felt her frustration increase as she became aware of the job ahead of her.

"Well," Jenn smiled mischievously. "Not only do we have the dental implant to use for identification, but we also have this that could prove valuable." She pointed to a small, bony bump on the left femur. "This is a bony callus from where this bone healed after a break. It healed in such a way that it is slightly shorter than the other femur." She held up both femurs for analysis. "See? This just means that, at some point, our vic had a broken leg that healed shorter than the other. He most likely walked with a slight limp."

"And what about race, gender, age..." Tess asked hopefully.

"This is a Caucasian male somewhere in his late thirties to mid-forties," Jenn announced confidently.

"So, to be clear, it's not a Native American skeleton?" Tess reiterated, knowing that Remi Nightsong would be very interested in hearing the news.

"Most definitely not, but why do you ask?"

"The skeleton was found buried up against a Hopewell Mound, and I just want to triple-check that we aren't overlooking anything important."

"Oh, well, these are not the bones of indigenous people as you'd find inside of an Adena or Hopewell burial mound." Jenn picked up the skull and turned it so that Tess could see inside the oral cavity. "See how his incisors are kind of blade-like? Smooth across the back?"

When Tess and Abby nodded, Jenn continued. "Well, with Native Americans, and even people from eastern Asia, the backs of their incisors are more scoop or shovel-like. It's almost like they are slightly bowed in the back. But that's only one way to determine race. The nasal aperture size aids in racial indentification, as well as this little boney knob here." She pointed to a piece of bone extending off of the base of the skull behind the mandible. "This little guy is called the Mastoid process. It actually varies in size and shape among the different races. Then there is the zygomatic arch or the cheekbones and orbital

...." She paused, looking at Tess and Abby. Glancing down at the skeleton, she grinned.

"Sorry. I'm a total nerd when it comes to bones. They just fascinate me. I could talk about them all day if you let me!"

Tess and Abby laughed along with Jenn as she gently replaced the skull and stepped back from the table in an exaggerated, dramatic way, a smile spread over her face.

"It's all good," Tess consoled. "It was very educational and interesting. It also helps give us a direction of inquiry. I'm sure at this point we won't find the murder weapon, but hopefully, we can find enough evidence to track down his killer."

# Chapter Eight

*Friday, August 24th, 9:05 AM*

A few days later, when Tess opened her work email, she was delighted to find a message from Dr. Brezdika. Opening it, Tess smiled as she read the short personal message:

*Hey Tess,*

*Hope you're doing great. Attached are radiographs, photos, and final report for that handsome devil you had at Abby's the other day. Upon further examination, I didn't see any identifying marks on the dental hardware.*

*Quick question for you… Why did the skeleton drop out of medical school? He didn't have the stomach for it! Ha! ha! I crack myself up! Let me know if you need anything else!*

*Best,*

*Jenn Brezdika*

Tess grinned and shook her head at the ridiculous joke as she clicked on the attachment. Within seconds, she was viewing the dental radiographs of the victim found in the mound.

In addition to the obvious bridge, there were three cavities that had been filled. As she wasn't a dentist she couldn't tell if there were any unfilled cavities or other anomalies but she was hoping the good dentist Dr. Beeson could help her with that.

Reading through the rest of the report didn't reveal anything new that they hadn't already discussed. Glancing at the clock, she determined she had a few hours before her next appointment. Maybe she could fit in a quick visit to Camden Family Dental.

****

Twenty minutes later, Tess smiled at Dr. Beeson as he came out into the lobby of his practice to greet her.

"Ah, Detective Dane! I'm so glad you called when you did! I'd just had a cancellation. This works out perfectly," the dentist beamed, his smile bright enough for Hollywood. Wearing green scrubs and a white lab coat, he looked professional despite what his older patients might have to say about his full-sleeve tattoos and ponytail. Everyone in Crawley and Camden Town knew Doc Beeson was part of the local biker club that rolled through town on the weekends.

"Thanks for letting me come dig through your basement. There aren't any spiders down there, are there?" Tess asked, making a face as she followed Beeson down the hallway toward his office. He barked out a laugh and shook his head.

"Nah, we have it sprayed down there just to be safe." He paused long enough to gesture for her to enter his office ahead of him. "So you brought some x-rays?" he asked as he slipped behind his desk and took a seat.

"Yes, and photos. Here." Reaching into her pocket, she pulled out a zip drive containing all of the information on the Burial Mound John Doe.

"Thanks." Beeson stuck it into his computer and began hitting buttons and clicking things that Tess couldn't see from where she stood. He seemed to notice her finally still standing and pointed toward the chair opposite his desk. "Oh, sorry! Sit, sit... Ahh, here we go..."

Tess took a seat and situated herself so that she could easily see the computer screen. Illuminated in all its pixelated glory was the mandible of Burial Mound John Doe. The radiograph showed the two fillings in the lower arcade and the dental bridge. The third filling was in an upper premolar.

"Can you tell what kind of bridge that is?" Tess asked hopefully, crossing her fingers in her lap like an excited schoolgirl about to be asked out to prom.

"Well, I have some news for you... This isn't a bridge. It's dental implants." Dr. Beeson commented, clicking through another radiograph.

"Isn't that the same thing?" Tess wrinkled her nose. A sinking feeling began filling her stomach. Just when she thought they were onto something, were they hitting a dead end?

"Eh... yes and no," Beeson answered, turning to take in her confused expression. "Dental bridges have been used for decades, centuries even. Over time, they've gotten better and better, to the point that we can use computers to survey the surface of the person's mouth and then make the bridge fit almost exactly. However, dental bridges are built onto the root structures of broken teeth. They smooth them out some, add some adhesive and attach the bridge. This doesn't help in the long term. You can still get bacteria in there, the root can continue to rot away, leading to bone loss of the mandible. Is it better than just having a rotten or broken tooth? Yes. Are there better options available? Also, yes." He smiled at Tess before continuing. "In the 1960s, they came up with the dental implant. The dentist removes the entire root of the tooth, not just smoothing it out to add adhesive to. Once they drill out the entire root, they implant a metal insert that mimics the tooth root. Once that's secured, a false tooth crown is added, and BAM! Now you have a tooth that is impervious to bacteria and rot. Ideally, getting dental implants is the way to go."

"Okay, but then why does anyone even bother with bridges anymore?" Tess asked, still confused how this information would help her case at all.

"Well, a bridge doesn't involve surgery for one, and two, it's less expensive."

"Okay... So I give up. How is this going to help me other than making sure I brush my teeth and floss so I don't have to get either of these options?"

"Well, because I said dental implants came out in the 1960s but only became widely popular in the 1990s. Also, my dad was the first dentist in Swain County to offer the service. Chances are, your victims' records are downstairs unless they were wiped out in the flood." Beeson grinned.

"Well, why are you still sitting there?" Tess stood in a rush, "Show me!"

Besson let out a laugh as he led her out of the office and back down the hallway toward a closed door at the end. Opening it revealed a darkened stairwell and a musty odor. Luckily for Tess, nothing seemed to skitter away.

The dentist reached out and flipped the light on, illuminating the worn, wooden stairs. "Follow me if you wish to live," he whispered with a poorly done accent of some sort, and Tess snorted. They descended the stairs, the boards creaking under their weight. At the bottom, Tess was instantly overwhelmed.

There were at least two dozen bankers boxes stuffed with patient files lined up on some old metal shelving. Along the cinder block walls, she could see the old water-marks from where the flood waters had risen so many years ago; up to her knees by the looks of it. It was amazing that the recent rains hadn't flooded the building a second time!

"Here you go," Beeson gestured. "I know it looks like a lot, but at least you have search parameters now, right?" When she nodded, he continued. "Feel free to take the files out of the boxes. You can use that table over there," he pointed to a long six-foot folding table set up against the back wall. A few promotional displays sat on top of it, and the dentist immediately cleared them away. "If you find something you think might be a possible match, just bring it up with you. I'll help you check it."

"Sounds good." Tess nodded as Beeson headed back toward the stairs.

"I have an appointment starting in a few minutes, but I'll have my hygienist check on you shortly."

"Thanks, Doc," Tess called as he climbed the stairs and disappeared. With a sigh, she turned around and pulled the first box off the shelf and took it to the table. Quickly separating the files into two groups– male patients vs female patients– she set the female patient files back in the box. Dr. Brezdika's report stated that the descendant was between thirty-five and forty-five years old when he died.

Taking this into account, Tess flipped through the male patient's folders and pulled out any where the patient was significantly younger or older than the age range suggested by the anthropologist.

After pulling out the wrong ages, she was left with eight charts. She decided to whittle them down by race. Knowing the Burial Mound John Doe was caucasian, she pulled out any charts left where the man was not. Now, she was left with five charts.

"Five charts and twenty-three more boxes to go..." she sighed. Feeling overwhelmed, exhausted, and yet also excited for the search at hand, she pressed on. Carefully, one by one, she opened each of the five charts and looked at the records. It was time-consuming and mentally draining, but she had to find something, anything, to ID the victim.

After looking at the old x-rays and records, none of the patients from box one fit the victim profile.She moved on to box two and then three. She was lost in her work and when she was halfway through box number eight, her stomach began to growl. Glancing at her phone she was surprised to see it was already half past two in the afternoon. No wonder she was hungry!

She looked over at her small stack of 'hopefuls' which included four files that she didn't feel too confident about. Then she turned and looked at all the boxes that still hadn't been checked. This is going to take forever, she moaned inwardly as she stood to stretch her back.

Grabbing the four 'hopefuls', she decided to head upstairs and grab something to eat. She found Dr. Beeson washing his hands after finishing up with a swollen-faced woman rubbing her jaw as she walked slowly to check out.

"Ah, Detective! Did you find anything good?" he asked brightly, eyeing the folders in her hand.

"I've made it through almost half the boxes and have only found four that might be matches. Everyone else is either the wrong age, wrong gender, or wrong dental work," Tess shrugged.

"Well, here, let's see what you have real quick. Were you going to get lunch, or are you done for the day?"

"Food for sure. I'm planning on coming back today if that's okay. I need to find out who this guy is."

"Not a problem. We are here until six, so stay as long as you'd like," Dr. Beeson offered as he flipped on the lightbox in his office to view the old x-rays. "Okay, let's see who you have..." he flipped through the small stack and frowned. "Well, I know for a fact that this guy is still alive. He was my next door neighbor until about two years ago when he moved to Thailand." He waved around a file labeled 'Conners, Stuart'. "But just so you believe me and can tell the courts you did everything..." he grinned at Tess as he slipped the x-ray under the holder to view it. Even Tess could tell they weren't a match. The front teeth were obviously different, Stuart's being slightly overlapped compared to a small gap noticeable on John Doe's.

Tess sighed and nodded. Doc was right. He shrugged and flipped through the other three charts. Sticking the x-rays up on the lightbox one at a time, they were each slowly scrutinized and then discredited.

"I'm sorry, Detective. I don't think you've found a match yet, but that doesn't mean it's not down there," Dr. Beeson comforted. "Go get some lunch, try to relax. I think I can sneak down and help you around 4:30, okay? We'll find out who this guy is."

Tess, too disheartened and hungry to argue, nodded and mumbled her thanks as she slipped out the door and headed for her county vehicle.

Within moments, she found herself tucked into a corner booth at Ida's Diner, a greasy spoon at the edge of town. Her back to the wall, she quietly perused the laminated menu even though she'd been there multiple times growing up.

The diner itself was still busy from the lunch crowd, the steady hum of chit chatting and laughter mixing with the clank of dishes and silverware.

"Order up!" called a voice from the recesses of the kitchen and Tess watched as a young woman with dark hair and wearing a pink waitress uniform slipped behind the counter to grab the plates.

It was then that Tess recognized Remi Nightsong. The waitress must have recognized her as well as evidenced from the flash of a smile she threw Tess's way as she passed by, her arms laden with a tray of plated food. Tess returned the smile and then continued to study the menu.

"You decide on what you want, Detective?" Remi asked, pulling Tess out of her musings. She glanced up to find the waitress standing at her table, tapping out a rhythm with her pencil on her order pad.

"Hi, Miss Nightsong," Tess greeted brightly. This caused Remi to snort.

"Sorry, I don't mean to be rude, Detective, but please, just call me Remi. That Miss Nightsong stuff is..." Remi wrinkled her nose in displeasure and then laughed.

"Noted... Remi," smiled Tess. "And yes, I did find something that sounds good." She pointed to a lunch special involving a bowl of soup and half a sandwich. "I'd like to have a turkey Club and a bowl of French onion soup, please. Oh, and you can call me Tess."

"Sure thing," Remi replied, jotting down the order. "Anything to drink?"

"Do you have lemonade?"

"Fresh squeezed, every morning." Remi held her arm up and flexed her bicep. Rolling her eyes, she leaned in and whispered, "That's what we're supposed to say, anyhow. Reality? It comes concentrated and we dilute it down with good ol' Crawley tap water. You sure you want it?"

Tess snorted a laugh at the humor in Remi's dark eyes. "Well, with that eloquent description, I think I'll just get a bottle of Goldpeak."

"Can't go wrong with sweet tea." Remi nodded and disappeared toward the kitchen.

While Tess waited for her lunch, she checked her phone for texts or emails. She had an email from Angela, her father's nurse, who had been sending daily status updates. Today, Tommy Dane was doing okay, considering he'd been dealing with some respiratory issues recently. Angela claimed his spirits seemed bright for the most part and he was having some times of lucidity. Tess smiled and quickly responded, planning on trying to visit later that evening if possible.

"So, is it true? Did y'all find a murdered woman hacked to bits out on the O'Leary land?" a male voice next to her said, startling Tess. Turning to the voice, she eyed the man before responding.

He was older, possibly in his early sixties, wearing a safety yellow tee shirt that was straining to cover his prominent gut. His stained denim work parts were in need of a wash as the entire lower part from the knees down were covered in drying mud. Work boots encased his feet while dropping chunks of dirt and mud every time he moved.

The man watched her through dark, beady eyes enshadowed by bushy gray eyebrows. He chewed on the end of a toothpick while waiting for her to answer.

"I'm not at liberty to discuss an open investigation," Tess informed him, looking him directly in the eye, daring him to pry further. He eyed her for a few seconds, pink tongue jutting out occasionally as he mouthed the toothpick.

"Is that so?" he grunted, leaning back in his seat, seeming to size her up.

"It is. Always has been, always will be," Tess informed him, giving him a pointed look, indicating she was done discussing the matter. She turned back to her table and opened her phone to scroll absently. Out of the corner of her eye, she could see the man still eyeing her.

Thankfully, Remi arrived just then, carrying a black plastic tray laden with Tess's lunch. It smelled amazing, and Tess's stomach grumbled in response.

"Dang, I'm glad I came when I did, Detective! Your stomach sounds like it's about to start eating your backbone," laughed Remi, her dark eyes sparkling with humor. "Oh, and here's your tea." She set Tess's lunch on the table before pulling a bottle of cold sweet tea from her apron pocket.

"Thanks, Remi." Tess accepted the tea and immediately opened the lid to take a drink.

"Is that guy bothering you?" Remi leaned closer to whisper. She rolled her eyes in the direction of the man with the toothpick.

"Meh…I've had worse," Tess mumbled back, reaching for a napkin and acting as though they weren't discussing the man sitting mere feet away. "He didn't like that I didn't want to discuss an open investigation."

"I saw him trying to talk to you," Remi explained. "We've had some complaints about him pestering people. Just thought I'd ask, make sure I didn't have to get my Louisville Slugger."

Tess raised an eyebrow, "Please tell me you aren't admitting to have attacked or have threatened to attack people with a baseball bat?"

"I plead the fifth." Remi grinned before turning on her heel and heading to serve someone at another table.

# Chapter Nine

---

*Monday, August 27th, 5:40 PM*

After returning to the dental office and working through the rest of the boxes, along with Dr. Beeson's intermittent help, Tess had found nothing helpful. They'd found an additional three charts that could be considered 'hopefuls' but, in reality, when compared with the dental radiographs provided by Dr. Brezdika, were not a match. Burial Mound John Doe was not in the basement files, at least not currently. Frustration ate at Tess, churning her stomach with anxiety.

She'd already fielded two calls from the sheriff and one from the mayor. Luckily, Bertie was blocking most of the calls from the local media and nosey neighbors looking for a story.

"Who are you?" Tess whispered, staring at the photograph of the skull staring back at her from an open file on her desk. "Were you a local? Were your dental records wiped out in the flood?" She tapped her fingers against the wooden desk.

Her phone chimed, pulling her attention away from the dead man. It was an alert, letting her know that the doggie daycare closed in twenty minutes, and she had to go get

Otter. She grinned. It was an indulgence, but one she was willing to pay to get him some socialization a couple days a week. Besides, it wasn't like she was getting anywhere today. She was mentally exhausted and needed some time to relax and think. John Doe had been out there for years; what one more night of waiting to be ID'd? The DNA tests wouldn't be back for a few weeks so that she could run them through the state and national database.

Grabbing her phone, keys, and the file, Tess headed to the parking lot, pausing long enough to tell Sheriff Malone and Bertie she was leaving to grab Otter. With a promise to Bertie to kiss Otter for her, Tess stepped out into the balmy summer evening and headed toward her vehicle, an older model red Jeep Wrangler.

As she unlocked the door, she suddenly felt the strange feeling that she'd had at the mound, as though someone was watching her. She glanced around over her shoulders but saw no one. A look in the backseat told her it was empty.

The tiny hairs on the back of her neck raised as the uneasy feeling persisted. Who or what was watching her and why? Where were they? The cop in her told her something wasn't right... But what was it? She'd always listened to her gut, and so far, it had kept her safe. Hopefully, it would continue to do so.

Trying to appear calm, she quickly got into her Jeep and locked the door. In the distance, a dog barked. The parking lot was deserted except for a few on-duty officers' vehicles and the sheriff's SUV.

After turning the ignition, Tess hurriedly buckled her seatbelt and backed out of her spot, staying alert as she went. Across the street, movement caught her eye.

An older man with snowy white hair and a blue ball cap jogged down the sidewalk in the evening dusk. From the opposite direction, a young family with a toddler were taking an evening stroll. They waved at the older man when they passed on the sidewalk.

No one seemed to be concerned with Tess. So why did she have such a feeling of unease?

Steeling her spine, yet still staying alert, Tess put the Jeep in drive and went to pick up Otter.

# Chapter Ten



Early the next morning, the eerie feelings of the previous evening long gone but not forgotten, Tess found herself mulling over cold cases throughout Swain and adjoining counties. She felt much better, both mentally and physically, after a night of snuggles with Otter, Facetiming with Denny and Natalie, and some good sleep. She'd felt so well that morning that she'd even stopped to get herself a new coffee maker for her office so that she wouldn't have to be bothered by going to the breakroom to clean up after someone else just to brew a cup. She was a woman on a mission this morning!

Smiling at her new red Keurig as she sipped a mouthful of her steaming brew, Tess thought about how to go about the missing persons search in the database now that she had some more information.

According to Dr. Brezdika, the bones had probably been buried in the mound for at least ten years or more. The skeleton was male, around 6 foot 3 inches in life, and between thirty-five and forty-five years of age at death. The various stab marks found on the ribs led to the fact that the death had been a violent one.

As she sat at her desk, scrolling through various search parameters, trying to narrow down the number of cold cases to a workable few, her mind began to wander. What if this crime was never even reported? What if the man found in the burial mound wasn't even local as she'd previously feared and had been missing from some distant city or state before interagency computer networking was even a thing?

Tess sighed at the thought, hoping that wasn't the case. So far, she'd whittled the caseload down from twenty-two cold cases in the past forty years in the surrounding five counties, including Swain.

Now, after changing the search parameters to male subjects, the number fell to twelve. She quickly got rid of any cold cases that were newer than eight years.

Now she was looking at seven missing men or teens in Swain or the surrounding counties within the past forty years.

She studied the list but paid special attention to the top four cases listed. They were all men who had gone missing or were found dead within the past thirty years. Based on her own Google searches and what the dentist, Dr. Lowel Beeson, had told her, dental implants like those found in the skull were only widely used within the past 30 years or so, meaning the victim would most likely fall into that category. Consulting her notes, she remembered that Beeson had said that type of implants came out in the 1960s but only became popular in the 90s. She sighed. That could mean adding thirty years onto the search parameters.

Deciding to stick with her gut, she went with the thirty-year parameter search first, since that would be the most likely. If nothing turned up, she'd add the additional decades.

She took another sip of coffee while the computer program hummed, searching for cases. Within moments, the results popped up on her screen.

The first missing person, Austin Cramer, was 21 years old at the time he went missing. He also had a metal plate on his right humerus. Not their guy.

Tess deleted Cramer from the list and continued to the next: Isaiah Winkler, age 34, African American .... Tess sighed. Their skeleton was from a caucasian male. She took Winkler off the list with a frustrated huff.

She'd whittled down two more possible cases, but would she find the right one?

Clicking on the third one, she tapped her foot while it loaded. Finally, a picture appeared of a man with close-cropped red hair and ice-blue eyes. Under the photo were the words, "Missing: Garrett O'Leary, age 44, male."

*"O'Leary?"* Tess mumbled excitedly to herself as she mulled over the information. "Why hadn't Kevin said they had a missing family member somewhere?"

Intrigued, she clicked on the report to read through the events leading up to and including the investigation:

*Garrett O'Leary, 44, of Quaker Hollow Road, Swain County, was reported missing on July 20th, 1996. Kevin O'Leary, Garrett's son, reported him missing when he failed to come home after a night out with friends. Marissa and Brandon, Garrett's other children, also report that they hadn't seen their father since the afternoon of Saturday, July 20th, around 3:00 p.m. when they went to play at a friend's house. Tina O'Leary, Garrett's wife, claimed to have been bedridden with a migraine and hadn't seen her husband since approximately 7:45 p.m. on July 20th.*

*Upon investigation, it was determined that Garrett O'Leary's last known whereabouts were at The Booby Trap, a strip club just south of route 72 where he was seen drinking and socializing with his brother, Kane O'Leary, and close friends, Fred Krinsel and Kenny Novak. The bartender, Sid Miliron, claims he saw Garrett O'Leary leave alone and in good health at around 1:15 a.m. on July 21, 1996. Miliron also stated that O'Leary did not appear intoxicated or impaired in any way and saw him drive away in his blue F250 pickup truck.*

*Although all parties noted to be at the bar and conversing with O'Leary that night were interviewed, nothing new or pertinent was revealed {SEE ATTACHED WITNESS STATEMENTS}. This case will remain open until O'Leary is found.*

*Signed: Deputy Glenn Burrows*
*Date: July 22, 1996*

Tess's stomach churned at the sight of Sheriff Burrow's name. Even in death, he could elicit such a response from her. But even back then, when he was just a deputy, he had worked the same case that Tess was working on now.

She went ahead and checked the final cold cases to be thorough, but she was sure that the skeleton in Dr. Summer's morgue was that of Garrett O'Leary. It was just too much of a coincidence to be otherwise. DNA results would confirm identity without a doubt, but they would take weeks, if not months, to get back, and she'd only just sent them out.

After jotting some notes to herself, she grabbed her jacket and keys and headed for her county-issued vehicle. She had some questions for the O'Leary family.

# Chapter Eleven

*Tuesday, August 28th, 11:03 AM*

The wooden planks of the old farmhouse porch sounded hollow under Tess's feet as she stepped up to the front door which hung open, the home's interior darkened and in full view.

"Hello, Detective," came a male voice from somewhere close by, causing Tess to jump, her hand raised midway to knock. Whirling around, she found herself staring at Kevin O'Leary, sitting on the green porch swing that was nestled in the shadows of the purple clematis that grew up an old trellis at the end of the porch.

"Oh, hello, Mr. O'Leary. Just the man I came to see," Tess smiled, stepping away from the open doorway.

"Did you find something out? About them bones in the hill?" A stream of tobacco spit barely made it over the porch railing.

"Well, that is what I'd like to discuss with you, sir," Tess began, stopping to stand in front of the porch swing but out of the line of spittle fire. O'Leary nodded for her to take a seat in a white wicker chair opposite him.

"I've been working with Dr. Summers, the medical examiner used by Swain County, as well as an anthropologist from OSU who has done an exam on the bones found in the burial mound on your property. I've been going through old cold cases from around here and surrounding counties. Mr. O'Leary... why didn't you tell me your father was reported missing nearly thirty years ago?" Tess watched the older man carefully, wondering why he hadn't brought up the possibility in the beginning that the bones could have been those of his father.

"Can't honestly say, Detective," the farmer sighed, pausing to scratch his balding pate. "He's been gone for so long that I almost don't even remember him. I mean, I was what .... sixteen... when he disappeared. He's been gone for longer than he was here."

"And you haven't heard from him in all that time?" Tess furrowed her brows. "Have any idea where he may be?"

"You think it's him in that hill?" Kevin O'Leary's voice suddenly filled with a mix of panic and horror. "I picked up the jawbone! You sayin' I picked up my dad's jaw bone?" He leaned forward abruptly, causing the porch swing to jump on the chains and groan in protest. Running a work-hardened hand over his face, O'Leary let out a groan.

"Mr. O'Leary, please remain calm," Tess soothed, leaning towards the man in an attempt to console him. "I'm not saying that the skeleton is your father–yet–but I just need to look into any possibilities at this time. It could be anyone at this point. I just happened to stumble upon your father's missing person report and, well.... The timing works. I don't want to give you false hope, nor do I want to ruin your day. I'm just being honest and open with you. Can you understand that?"

The farmer nodded, his eyes fixed on the painted wooden planks beneath his feet. He swallowed audibly as he ran a calloused hand over his stubbled chin again.

"Can you tell me about your dad? About that night?"

"Hell, Detective.... That was nearly thirty years ago now," O'Leary paused, seeming to gather his thoughts. The porch swing groaned slightly as he shifted his weight. "I remember being here with Marissa and Brandon, back before Brandon died."

"Your siblings, correct? I read that Brandon died in an auto accident the year after your dad disappeared?" Tess asked, consulting the notes she'd jotted to herself.

"Yep. Brandon was the baby. It was me, then Marissa, then Brandon. All two years apart. I was only sixteen when Dad left. The three of us were home that night, a Saturday if I remember correctly. We were just hanging out, like teens do, after we finished our chores."

"You weren't hanging out with friends? Night out on the town?" Tess asked, curious as to why three teenagers were just hanging out at home on a Saturday night.

Kevin snorted and slumped his shoulders. "Well, Marissa was super shy and never went anywhere. She'd rather just stay home with her books. Brandon, well..... He was.... Different. Didn't have many friends. Kept to himself, too. I think nowadays they'd say he was on the spectrum? I don't know for sure. Mom and Dad didn't really believe in goin' to the doctor much."

Tess nodded in understanding. She'd heard stories like that before, parents unwilling or unable to take their children to get proper medical attention whether due to cost, availability, or in some instances, the parents' belief system. In a situation such as Brandon O'Leary's, it saddened Tess to hear that the boy had possibly missed out on proper care due to parental ignorance.

"Is that why you were here that night? To look after Brandon?"

A blush crept up Kevin's weathered face and neck. "Nah. I was just grounded. Dad caught me out in the barn with Cindy Whitestead. It didn't go over too well if you get me." He shot a grin at Tess that told her he still wasn't repentant.

Tess returned his bemused grin and shook her head playfully. "Oh, the joys of being young." She was rewarded with a quiet snicker from Kevin.

"Well, after Dad came charging through the barn that night, carrying on like he'd never done such a thing, Cindy ran for it. She grabbed her shirt and just took off through the cornfield out yonder. 'Course I shoulda ran after her. She was the one for me, but I didn't know it at the time. Apparently, Cindy didn't know it either, but because she was the preacher's daughter and obedient to a fault, she avoided me. Ended up marrying someone else. Six months after the barn incident, I ended up meeting someone new, too.... Gina. I married Gina, had my son, and then got divorced ten years later. Found out she was cheating."

"So, whatever happened to Cindy? Is she still around here?" Tess asked, totally vested in the story even though it most likely had nothing to do with Garrett O'Leary's disappearance.

Kevin grinned up at her like a cat who'd caught a canary. "Her husband turned out to be a piece of shit. Smacked her around a lot. Luckily for her, he died of cancer three years ago. Cindy moved back to town shortly after that and looked me up. We've been seeing each other on the down-low ever since."

"Why in secret?" Tess was so intrigued that she didn't realize she was leaning forward in her seat until the wicker creaked.

"To add mystery and some spice, of course!" Kevin erupted in laughter, "My son doesn't know. He thinks I'm too old to have a girlfriend. I'm forty-six; I ain't dead. It just started as a funny joke, us having to be sneaky, like we were when we were teens, and now we just do it because.... Well, it's fun. And not too much is fun when you're my age."

"Fair enough," Tess grinned. "So, you were grounded for doing the dance with Cindy out in the barn. Your siblings were off doing their thing in their rooms. Where was your mom?" She tried pulling the conversation back in line. If she didn't, they'd be there all night.

"Mom was working on some sewing project, if I remember correctly. She ended up getting one of her migraines and went to bed early that night. None of us kids were too concerned because that was normal for her."

"Did your dad go out frequently on the weekends?"

"Not every weekend. Maybe once, twice a month? He always went to the same bar, hung out with the same crowd, and got the same boring drink."

"And how do you know that?" Tess asked, watching Kevin carefully.

"Uncle Kane and Kenny Novak, Dad's best friend always used to pick on him about it." Kevin laughed, but it sounded forced. "Said he was as boring as plain mashed potatoes."

"And what bar did they like to go to?" Tess asked, flipping through her notes to find the bar's name listed in the missing person's report.

"The Falcon's Nest, that old dive bar on Route 72 outside of Crawley."

"Kevin, the police report says your Dad was last seen at a strip club called The Booby Trap, near Camden Town," Tess explained, referring to her notes. "Does that sound familiar at all?"

"A strip club?" Kevin's eyes were large and round when he met Tess's gaze. "Why would my dad be there? That has to be a mistake."

"A lot of men go to strip clubs, Mr. O'Leary. I'm not saying it's right or wrong, but it's not completely out of the realm of possibility. Can you think of a reason why he'd go there this particular night instead of The Falcon's Nest?"

"No, ma'am," Kevin's shoulders hung, disappointment radiating off of him. Disappointment in his father perhaps, although Tess couldn't be sure.

"Do you know where Kenny Novak and Fred Krinsel are these days?" Tess referred to her notes again, trying to get some new angle or lead on this case.

"Dad's old friends? You think they had something to do with all of this?" Kevin stopped moving the swing and stared at Tess with a look of horror on his face.

"Never said that," Tess calmed him. "They were just listed as some of the last people to see him before he vanished. Them, your Uncle Kane, and Sid Miliron, the bartender."

"Ahh, well, let's see..." Kevin rubbed his stubbled chin deep in thought. "I haven't spoken to Krinsel in years, other than a friendly wave when I see him in town. As for Kenny Novak, I think I've only seen him maybe twice, three times since Dad left. I was a teenager then, and I never really paid attention to Dad's friends, you know? I mean, Kenny was nice and all when I was growing up. Brought us candy when he thought my mom wasn't looking, but I wasn't close to him, no."

"How about the other two?"

"Uncle Kane and Sid Miliron?" Keven asked, sounding confused. "Uncle Kane is... Uncle Kane," He shrugged as though Tess's question was weird. "He lives in some assisted living community outside of Columbus on account of being confined to a wheelchair. I can get you the address and his cell phone number if you'd like. I've never heard of Sid. Who's he again?"

"The bartender at The Booby Trap," Tess consulted her notes before looking at Kevin expectantly.

He shook his head, "Sorry, Detective, I have no idea who that is."

"That's okay, Mr. O'Leary. Maybe it'll come to you and trigger a memory, who knows," Tess said before changing the subject. "One other thing... You wouldn't happen to have any of your dad's old medical or dental records here, would you? To help ID the skeleton while we wait for the DNA results?"

"Maybe; there's some old boxes in the attic that might have something helpful," Kevin sighed and his shoulders slumped as though the weight of the world had suddenly been laid upon him.

"Would you mind also providing a DNA sample for comparison? If it's a match..."

"Sure, Detective, whatever I gotta do," the farmer's deep voice cracked with emotion. He sniffed and leaned back in the porch swing, wiping his nose with the back of his hand, avoiding Tess's gaze.

She gave him a moment to compose himself and went to grab a buccal swab kit from her vehicle. When she stepped back onto the porch, she found Kevin standing near the front door, a lost look on his face.

She felt horrible for him. He'd lost his father years ago, and now, nearly three decades later, she'd ripped that scab off and watched him bleed. If Burial Mound John Doe was indeed Garrett O'Leary, then Kevin was only going to lose his father all over again after having just found him. And for what?

# Chapter Twelve

*Wednesday, August 29th, 9:05 AM*

After obtaining a DNA sample from Kevin O'Leary and overnighting it to the lab the night before, Tess had decided to go home to grab some dinner and spend time with Otter. On her way home, though, she'd stopped by Tolliver Care Home to visit her dad.

Tommy Dane had been alert but seemed sedated due to the medications he was on for his upper respiratory issues he'd been fighting. Angela, the charge nurse, had assured Tess that Tommy seemed to be holding steady with his breathing issues at the moment, but that he wasn't out of the woods yet.

Tess was worried, as she had been for years now. Her father had early onset dementia. That was a fact that she couldn't change. There was no treatment, and inevitably, it was a death sentence. The question was, when? For the most part, Tommy seemed to do well, considering his memory lapses. Sometimes, when Tess would visit, he would seem indifferent to her, not excited or scared that she was there. Other times, he would get disoriented and begin yelling or throwing things; those were the visits that always managed to bring Tess to tears. Seeing her father like that, a stranger trapped in a familiar body, was one of the hardest things she'd ever had to endure.

She was still thinking of her father and aching for the Detective Dane she'd grown up with, all shrewd analysis and rough bear hugs, when she walked into the lobby of the Swain County Sheriff's Department early the next morning. Since seeing her dad the previous night, she felt renewed in the prospects of making progress in the Burial Mound John Doe case.

With a nod at Bertie, the ever-faithful receptionist turned dispatcher, currently tucked away behind her wall of Plexi-glass, the phone receiver cradled on her thin shoulder, Tess made her way toward her office.

It was then that she heard someone calling her name from the lobby. How had she missed them? Turning on her heel, Tess strode back down the short hallway to find Kevin O'Leary standing in the lobby.

"Ah, Mr. O'Leary! Good morning. I'm sorry I missed you," Tess apologized as she approached the farmer. He shrugged her off, standing there in his worn denim overalls and yellow tee-shirt. His usual John Deere hat donned his head, its green bill frayed and stained from use.

"It's nothin', Detective. I was looking at the bulletin board in the corner," the farmer said, jabbing a thumb over his shoulder to indicate a community notice board covered in flyers and alerts from concerned citizens.

"Well, if you'd like to discuss something in my office...?" Tess gestured toward the hall. He nodded and followed her.

"Coffee? Tea?" she offered as they entered her small office. "I just got a new coffee maker." She pointed to the shiny red Keurig taking up residence on the shelf under her window.

"Sure is pretty," Kevin commented with a smile. "My mom always liked red." He stood in the doorway, his thin frame taking up the space. "But I'll pass on coffee, Detective, if it's okay. I haven't felt like myself since your visit last night. I figure the coffee won't help my stomach none."

"That's fair," Tess nodded, her voice full of empathy for the man in front of her. She turned then and began preparing herself a cup to brew. "And for what it's worth, I'm sorry about last night. About..."

"It is what it is, Detective. It isn't your fault, you were just doing your job." He paused, a sigh escaping him as a look of sorrow crept across his sun-kissed face.

"You can have a seat if you'd like," Tess said, gesturing toward the worn leather office chair opposite her desk. He nodded and took a seat, pausing to pull a bent manilla envelope from the back pocket of his overalls.

"I... I went through the boxes like you asked. The ones in the attic," he began, idling playing with the wrinkled edge of the dog-eared parcel. "I..." He paused again, seeming to be at war with himself.

Tess waited patiently for him to continue, sure that he had something important on his mind to share with her. Why else would he have driven all the way to town to speak with her? Her curiosity for the envelope had her heart rate elevated, and she wanted to snatch it away from him, tear it open and read the contents. Was it a confession letter? Was it a piece of evidence that would crack the case wide open?

Instead, Tess remained externally calm, going about adding creamer to her mug before sliding into her desk chair to wait for O'Leary to speak again.

A moment passed. Then another. Finally, he sighed and held out the envelope for her.

"Here. I found this, like you asked for. This just makes it... so real, you know? Part of me wants it *not* to be my dad. I've always had the hope that maybe someday, he'd come home. And I know that eventually, the DNA results will confirm your theory one way or another, but this may make it quicker, and I guess I'm just not ready for the truth. Maybe I never will be."

Tess reached out and took the manila envelope from him, both excited and apprehensive. Once she saw what was inside, there was no going back, and for that, she was sorry for Kevin O'Leary. If the contents did indeed identify the Burial Mound John Doe as Garrett O'Leary, it was a step forward for her and the investigation but a tragedy for the O'Leary family.

Unwinding the red cotton string twisted around the closure, Tess opened the envelope and peered inside. With a frown, she carefully pulled out the stack of papers and laid them before her on her desk.

They appeared to be old medical records for Garrett O'Leary. Her heart rate quickened again. This could be the evidence she needed.

"I don't know why Mom and Dad kept them, or why I even kept them, but there were packets like this for both of my parents. There's medical and dental stuff in there. X-rays of his teeth, too. Isn't that what you needed to ID him?" Kevin asked, watching Tess anxiously as she flipped through the records.

"Yes, the radiographs will help us make a match," she paused her search to look up at him. His eyes were watery, a turbulent sea of emotion churning within. "I'll contact Dr. Beeson immediately to compare these with those taken of the remains found near the mound. We should have an answer very soon."

Kevin nodded, his emotions barely contained. To cover them, he stood abruptly, rubbing his work-hardened hands down the front of his thighs.

"Whelp... I guess I'll be headed back to the homeplace. You'll call me?"

"Of course," Tess nodded, "And Mr. O'Leary, I know this isn't easy, but thank you. This is truly very helpful."

Kevin just nodded, the bill of his ball cap obscuring his face momentarily.

"Oh, and I almost forgot," he paused to dig around in the front pocket of his overalls before pulling out a folded piece of paper torn from a notebook. On it was a hastily written phone number. "This number keeps calling me."

"Oh? And what do they say?" Tess asked, taking the paper from him.

"That's the weird part. Nothing. They just breathe all creepy like," he made a face. "It's happened twice in the past week or so and again last night. Always in the evening, always from this number. They never make a sound, just breathing. I don't know if it means anything or not, but with all this going on with..." his voice trailed off.

"I'll look into this; hopefully, it's just kids prank calling you," Tess told him. "It's probably nothing, but it shouldn't be happening."

The older man just nodded, mumbling his thanks and avoiding eye contact, as he quickly strode out of her office and back down the hall.

# Chapter Thirteen

*Wednesday, August 29th, 11:15 AM*

"It's a match, Detective," Dr. Beeson announced confidently. "There's no doubt in my mind that those remains belong to Garrett O'Leary." He lightly tapped the radiograph currently illuminated on the light box in his office. Holding up his laptop to compare the more modern digitized radiographs from the Burial Mound, John Doe, even Tess could see the similarities.

The fillings of the cavities, the dental hardware, and even the slight gap in between the front incisors all matched. Garrett O'Leary had been murdered nearly thirty years ago and left to rot next to a Hopewell Mound, just yards from his family home. But how? Why? And most importantly, by whom?

"Thank you, Dr. Beeson," Tess sighed, her mind reeling with all the questions she needed to find answers to. "You've been a huge help. Now I just have to go and officially tell the family."

That was the part of her job she liked the least. Telling a family that their loved one wasn't coming home. That they'd befallen a painful and hideous end. It was never easy and every time, Tess felt as though she lost a little part of herself. She tried to compartmentalize her job, thinking about it objectively, separating the humanity of it all from the depravity of the crimes, but it was still hard.

Even when she'd been investigating the Torture Killer, she'd managed to find some empathy for the man committing the despicable acts. She'd been disgusted by the crimes and devastated by his cruelty, but she'd managed some empathy. Did that make her a horrible person? To empathize with a killer who would perform a Blood Eagle on another human being? Sometimes, Tess thought she was horrible for thinking certain things about the Torture Killer. On one hand, she could understand how he'd justified his slayings to some degree. On the other hand, she recognized the descent into horrific acts after the criminal justice system failed again and again. Regardless of what happened to someone in their lifetime, Tess knew that murder was wrong, and the cop in her wouldn't allow it. The way Tess saw it, no one was above the law, and the law must prevail. Without it, people are no better than animals: feral and barbaric.

With a resigned sigh, Tess gathered her things and headed back to her office to call Kevin. She wanted to speak with the family and let them know what she knew so far, which wasn't much.

After dropping into Sheriff Malone's office on the way to her own to inform him that she'd ID'd the body, she quickly called the O'Leary farm.

"I was worried you'd call, Detective," Kevin answered, his voice hoarse. *He must have caller ID*, Tess thought.

"I'm sorry, Mr. O'Leary…" her voice trailed off. "But I know you understand why I'm calling…I wish I didn't have to do this."

"I know, me too," he sniffed. Tess suddenly felt bad for not driving out to the farm to tell him in person. Typically, she would have, but since he'd already been expecting the news and had asked her to call, she had. "I'd like to tell your family in person if I could, let them know what's going on with the investigation, and answer any questions that I can. Could you–"

"I'll call 'em, Detective." Kevin's voice sounded gruff with emotion. "Just let me know when you want us to come in."

"How about I come to the farm? Would that be easier? How about tomorrow afternoon? Are most people local?" Tess asked, writing a note to herself to check into family members of the O'Leary family.

"Most are within an hour or two, yeah. Tomorrow should work. If they don't come, that's on them," Kevin said.

"Thank you, Mr. O'Leary," Tess replied before disconnecting the call.

# Chapter Fourteen

---



"C'mon in, Detective," Kevin O'Leary greeted her wearily as he held open the screen door of the old farmhouse. "Everybody else is already here."

Tess nodded in acknowledgement as she slipped past the man and entered the cool interior of the home. A murmur of voices could be heard coming from the living room to the left of the entryway. Straight ahead of her, a wooden staircase, its treads worn but clean, ascended to the second floor. To the right of the entryway appeared to be a dining room, the space dark and quiet.

"Through here," Kevin motioned for Tess to follow and quickly strode across the hardwood floors, his footfalls echoing in the hall. Following close behind, Tess continued to take in her surroundings.

Although the wallpaper was old and faded, and the paint in need of touching up, the farmhouse was tidy inside. From the antique baseboards and trim to the wide planked wood floor throughout and even the slightly rippled hand-made glass panes in the windows, the O'Leary family home was beautiful, and Tess could only imagine how much more amazing it would have been during its heyday.

"This is Detective Tess Dane, from the sheriff's department," Kevin announced as he and Tess came to a halt in the living room doorway. Multiple pairs of eyes suddenly stopped to look at the detective.

"Hi, I'm Detective Dane. I wanted to thank everyone for coming out here today, so that we could get to know each other, ask questions, try to get some answers," Tess began, stepping into the room and looking at each person in turn. They'd all been through a lot recently and she'd hoped to alleviate any undo stress by answering their questions at the house versus down at the station.

"Hey, Detective, thanks for coming," a woman in her mid-forties greeted, attempting to stand from where she'd been sitting on an old sofa near the fireplace. She struggled with her arm braces as she tried to pull her thin form up but was stopped by the man next to her.

"It's okay, ma'am," Tess answered, taking a step forward to assist the woman to stand completely as the man seemed to want to pull her back down on the couch.

"Jamie, for the love of God, let me stand up," the woman lightly hollered at the man, gently shoving his hands away. "I'm not dead yet. Besides, I need to stretch."

"Sorry, Lori, I just worry you'll fall," the man sighed glumly as he watched her slowly shuffle towards Tess.

"Have a seat, Detective, if you'd like." Lori gestured to an empty armchair as she used her arm braces to slowly make a circuit around the living room. "I'm Lori O'Leary, and that worrywart is my husband, James." She cast a loving grin toward the man on the couch, and he shrugged.

"It's true. I'm a worrier," he admitted sheepishly.

"We all are when it comes to Mom," a blond man in his mid-twenties commented from where he sat in the window seat, holding a book on his lap. He looked up at Tess, "I'm Luke O'Leary. James and Lori's son. My sister, Courtney, will be here soon. She had to pick up Grandpa."

"And how do you fit into this family dynamic?" Tess asked, turning to Kevin as he sat down next to a younger version of himself.

"This is my son, Breck," Kevin introduced the man next to him, even though it seemed obvious as the family resemblance was uncanny. Breck, Tess noted, barely looked up at her, seemingly too engrossed in his phone to pay her any mind. Tess decided to let his lack of good manners slide for now.

"Jamie... James... is my cousin," Kevin continued. "He's my Uncle Kane's son. Kane is who Courtney is picking up now."

"Your father and Kane were brothers, correct?" Tess confirmed. Kevin nodded. Tess took a seat in the chair nearest to him and made a few notes, her paper soon a mess of names and scribbled arrows on her makeshift family tree.

As Tess was about to ask another question, the front door opened and in walked a tall blonde woman in her early twenties, pulling a wheelchair backwards through the door frame.

"Grandpa Kane is here!" the woman announced as she deftly turned the wheelchair around to push the old man into the living room. His tanned, weathered face lit up when he saw his family all around him.

"Hey, Grandpa!" Luke exclaimed, closing his book and heading over to greet the man in the wheelchair.

Tess watched the exchange, noticing how Kane O'Leary resembled a thinner version of Santa Claus: snowy white hair, rosy cheeks, and twinkling blue eyes. His smile was contagious, though and when his eyes fell on Tess, he startled.

"And who is this?" he asked, reaching a hand out towards her. "You guys said we were having a family get-together, but I don't know this pretty lady." He wiggled his white bushy eyebrows at Tess and then laughed when Courtney playfully swatted him.

"Grandpa, I think that's the detective that's come to talk about everything that's been going on around here," Courtney informed him. "Stop trying to flirt. What will Beth think?"

"Who's Beth?" Kevin asked, bending to hug his uncle.

"Oh... just my lady friend that lives down the hall." Kane grinned over at Tess and winked, soliciting a laugh.

"Grandpa lives at that new senior home, Glade Springs," Courtney explained to Tess as she set the brakes on her grandfather's wheelchair. "It's more like an assisted living type of place. He has his own apartment and can take care of himself for the most part, but there are nurses there to come check on him from time to time. He likes to make friends with all of the women." She snorted and shook her head in dismay.

"What? I may be seventy-five, but I'm not dead yet!" Kane chastised with a grin.

Tess suppressed a smile as she tried to get control of the situation so that she could get on with her evening. She cleared her throat and stood. As everyone took the hint and quickly found a seat, Tess began.

"If we could get started, I'd like to introduce myself officially. I am Detective Tess Dane with the Swain County Sheriff's Department. I am here to discuss the official findings of the skeletal remains that were found on this property a few days ago. As you all know, they have been analyzed, and dental records have confirmed that they belong to Garrett Michael O'Leary, who has been missing since July 20th, 1996. As Dr. Abby Summers stated in her final report, it appears that the cause of death is sharp force trauma, and the manner of death has been ruled a homicide. This was no accident."

"Sharp force trauma? What does that even mean?" Lori asked, her eyes large and worried.

"He was stabbed, ma'am," Tess answered gently as she watched the reactions on the faces of those present. Some of the family members in the room were too young to have even met Garrett, but those old enough to remember him looked anguished.

Kevin, having already discussed the matter with Tess, just hung his head in silence. Kane closed his eyes, his lips trembling as tears began to course down his wrinkled face. James, the dead man's nephew, sat in stark, shocked quiet until he broke, a sob escaping his chest.

"Oh, Uncle Garrett..." James's voice cracked.

At hearing his son's cries, Kane's quiet sobs mixed with the sniffles of the family around him. This was the part of the job Tess hated the most: the shattering of a family, watching it splinter into a million pieces, never to be the same again.

Kevin stood abruptly and stalked out onto the porch, the front screen door slapping the frame behind him. Tess could hear the quiet grinding sound of the porch swing swaying on its chains as Kevin sat on the other side of the wall from her, lost in his torment. His father wasn't just missing. He'd been murdered. Stabbed repeatedly. The sheer brutality of the slaying was not lost on Tess, and she felt sorry for the family, especially Kevin.

"Detective," came a voice, wet with emotion. Tess looked over to see Lori, James' wife, calling for her from across the living room. The woman's hand was gripped around the handle of her arm braces, her wrists wobbly as she struggled to make it over toward Tess.

"Here, I'll come to you," Tess offered, giving the family a moment to absorb the news of the murder while she went to see what Lori needed.

"Lori, just come sit down," James said, standing and acting as though he meant to drag her back to her seat. "Don't tire yourself out. You know it's not good for you."

"Jamie, for the love of....! I have MS, but I'm not dead!" Lori harped at her husband as though it wasn't their first go-round on the topic.

Tess motioned for James to sit back down and approached Lori, quietly escorting her to a quiet corner of the large living room. They stopped in front of an old piano, its top covered in framed photographs of happier times.

"You sure it's Uncle Garrett?" Lori asked, leaning toward Tess and watching her closely.

"I'm afraid so. All signs are pointing that way. Of course, the official DNA results won't be in for a few weeks, but we are pretty confident at this point. The DNA is just a confirmation."

The older woman hung her head, seeming to collect her thoughts. Tess pulled out the bench to the antique upright piano they stood in front of and guided Lori to sit. Lori slumped down onto the bench before extracting her arms from her braces. Setting them next to her, she let out a sigh.

"I never got to meet Uncle Garrett; he was gone before I met Jamie. But Jamie... Now he remembers him. Used to tell me stories all the time about how Garrett would take him fishing when he was a kid, taught him how to change the oil in his truck," Lori sighed, a sad smile on her face. "Jamie said he always felt that Garrett went out of his way to do special things for him, to make him feel loved. Garrett was there for him his whole growin' up years. When Kevin called us and said they may have finally found Uncle Garrett, Jamie didn't take it well." She leaned closer to Tess and lowered her voice to a whisper. "If you ask me, Garrett was a better dad to Jamie than Kane ever was."

Tess nodded at the woman's words, feeling empathetic for the little boy that James had once been. Losing someone in such a violent way was hard, especially someone who'd once been such an important part of your life.

Kevin strode back into the house then, his work boots clumping loudly on the wooden floor of the old farmhouse. The family sat in small groups, talking quietly among themselves. Over the quiet murmur of voices and the occasional sniffle, Tess heard someone say her name.

Glancing up, she found herself staring into Kevin O'Leary's red, sorrowful eyes. He motioned with his head from across the room that he needed to speak with her.

"What do you mean by that?" Tess asked Lori, trying to wrap up the conversation while holding up a finger to acknowledge Kevin.

"Because Garrett was always there for him, his whole life. Kane wasn't. He didn't hurt him or anything; he was just... absent." Lori sighed. "Go on now, see what Kevin wants. I'm just rambling, anyhow. What do I know? Nothin'. I've never even met Garrett, I just married into this family." Lori shrugged, casting Tess a broken smile.

Tess nodded and thanked her for speaking with her, making mental notes to herself as she headed out to the entryway where Kevin stood waiting at the base of the staircase leading to the second floor.

"Hey, Kevin..." Tess said as she approached, noting the haunted look in his eyes. The tall farmer stood leaning up against the newel post, a sorrowful expression on his weathered face. He was only in his late forties, but years of toiling in the sun had aged him.

"Hey..." he greeted. "Is there anything that I can do to help? Anyone I can get to talk with you? I just need to know what happened to my dad." His voice was thick with emotion.

"I am here to answer any questions that may arise, and at some point, whether today or tomorrow, I'd like to speak with all the family members that were around during the time of the disappearance. People like Breck, Courtney, and Luke weren't even born yet, but the others—Kane, Jamie...your sister, Marissa. Where is she, anyway?"

"She's a nurse in Toledo. She couldn't call out on short notice to be here, so I'm supposed to talk to her tonight about everything." Kevin sucked in a breath, "You think one of them did this?" He slid a glance into the living room at his family. Tess watched as his weary gaze traveled over each one in turn, his face a blend of hurt and despair.

"We don't know that, Kevin. It's much too early for me to say one way or another, but I'll be honest," Tess said, lowering her voice so she wouldn't be overheard. "Statistics show that most murders are done at the hand of someone close to the victim."

Kevin nodded, his shoulders slumped. "I'll come down later and give my official interview. I just want justice for Dad. Whatever I need to do."

# Chapter Fifteen

*Friday, August 31st, 1:30 PM*

Kenny Novak's house was just off of Main Street in Crawley, right behind the CVS pharmacy. Tess called ahead to verify he'd be home and willing to speak with her. At first, she thought he wasn't going to answer, but after four or five rings, his deep, gravelly voice came across the line. When she'd explained who she was and why she needed to speak with him, he'd agreed to meet with her.

Tess parked her county-issued SUV at the CVS due to lack of street parking in front of Novak's before walking briskly across the cracked parking lot to the yard beyond. The verdant lawn, lush from the recent rain, was in need of mowing, but the squishing sound of her footsteps told Tess the ground was still much too water-logged to mow. The entire county was hit hard by the recent storms, and some areas were still under water.

She climbed the steps to the freshly painted white front porch, making sure to wipe her wet shoes off on the rug before knocking on the front door. A wind chime made a tinkling sound from somewhere on the porch, and a fat orange cat lay rolled up, sleeping on a black rocking chair near the door, painting a quaint, country aesthetic.

"Hey, kitty," Tess greeted it but the cat merely opened its eyes a slit to look at her and then resumed its nap. Not surprised by the feline's disdain for her, she shrugged and knocked again.

This time, the door opened, and a tall, slender older man wearing an OSU Buckeyes tee shirt and jeans greeted her. He looked to be in his early 70s, yet fit, his skin kissed by the sun. *Must be a golfer*, Tess mused, an assumption confirmed by a golf bag leaning against the inside entryway wall, the titanium heads sticking out in different directions.

"Ahh, Detective Dane," he greeted, a wide smile splitting his face. "Do come in." He stepped to the side to allow her entrance, and as she stepped through the door, he cast a withering look at the cat on the porch.

"Oh, Poundcake... There you are, you fat schlub." He scooped up the cat, who let out a quiet growl at being disturbed. "It's time for your medicine. I just know how you love it!" Kenny caught Tess's gaze over the cat's ginger head and rolled his eyes. "This boy and I have been through it, let me tell you. Here, why don't you have a seat in the living room while I give him his pill? It should only take a moment." He gestured toward the living room while he carried the wiggling cat on through to the kitchen.

Tess grinned at the man's retreating form and made her way into the living room. Taking the moment to look around and get a feel for who Kenny Novak was, she slowly made a circuit of the cozy room.

The wooden floor, though old, was well cared for, as were the bookshelves that lined three of the walls. The fourth wall, which faced the street, was dominated by a large picture window. An antique glass table sat directly in front of the window and held an array of various houseplants and photographs.

Bending to look at the photos, Tess noticed one of a much younger Kenny Novak and a blond woman sitting on the edge of an old dock, smiling at the camera. In another photo, Tess saw Kenny standing in between two other men, one of whom she was pretty confident was Garrett O'Leary. The trio of men appeared to be standing on the banks of a river, somewhere with snow-capped mountains in the background.

"That was our annual guy's trip. We went to Alaska that year." Novak broke the silence as he entered the living room. The orange cat was nowhere to be seen.

"Is that Garrett O'Leary?" Tess asked, pointing to the red-headed man to Kenny's left in the picture. She stood up, waiting for his response.

"Yes," he murmured, his face saddened for a moment. "And that's Fred." He pointed to the third man in the photo. "Fred was always the jokester."

"Fred Krinsel?" Tess confirmed with her notes. That had been one of the men last reported to have been seen with Garrett O'Leary the night he went missing.

"The one and only," Novak sighed fondly. "We had some of the best times. The year we went to Alaska... 1984, if I remember correctly... Fred signed us up for some kind of backcountry hiking adventure deal in Talkeetna."

"Sounds like fun, but by the look on your face, I'm guessing it wasn't.....?"

"No, Ma'am," Novak shook his head and smiled. "See, Fred told Garrett and me that it was an all-inclusive backcountry hiking expedition. They provide everything:

a guide, food, supplies, you name it; we just needed to show up. So we did..."

"And...?"

"It wasn't until the helicopter dropped us off at the 'trailhead' that Garrett and I realized what it was that Fred had signed us up for." Novak paused dramatically, staring Tess in the eye. "A backcountry *survival* expedition! We were dropped off with just the clothes on our backs and three items: a compass, a knife, and a water bottle. Oh, and a GPS thingy that we could push a button on to get extracted if we gave up. All we had to do was make it back to civilization."

"That sounds miserable and challenging all at once," Tess commented, her interest piqued. She loved to backpack but had never tried doing it in survival mode.

"We were pissed at Fred. He thought it was funny, though, and said we were just being wimps. I just wanted to get home. Garrett, too. Garrett's kids were young at that point, and I had a wife at home. We fought about it for a while but then decided we best look for shelter and food. Before we knew it, we were doing it—surviving. Catching our food, picking berries, walking a ton. It took us like four days to find our way out, but we made it back to Talkeetna." Novak grinned as he spoke of the memories.

"Do you see Fred anymore?"

"Haven't seen him in years now," Novak sighed. "We went on guy trips every year, or at least as close to every year as money would allow back then. Once Garrett disappeared, we kinda... fizzled out. It's hard being the Three Musketeers when one of you isn't there, you know?" He walked over to a black leather loveseat and sat down abruptly. Staring across the living room to the photo of the Alaska trip, he said nothing for a few seconds. "We used to do everything together. We all met in grade school, in Mrs. Fornsby's class. Got into mischief in middle school, chased girls in high school. And then one day... Garrett was gone." A look of deep sorrow crossed his face as he gazed at his feet.

"Did you have any thoughts or theories about where he'd gone?" Tess asked, slipping into a matching sling-back chair, the black leather creaking in protest. "Was it like him to just... disappear for a few days, especially with having a young family?" Novak looked up at Tess, seeming to mull over her words for a moment before answering.

"Nah, not really. He woulda told Fred or me. Shoot, he'd probably try to talk us into going with him." He stared out the front window as a car drove past the house. "I thought it was suspicious from the beginning. He wouldn't have left without telling us, he wouldn't have left his family. I tried telling the police that, but no one would listen. They just assumed he'd had a lady friend on the side and had skipped town."

"And did he? Have a lady friend, I mean?"

"Shoot, no. He couldn't handle the one he had, much less get another one." Novak let out a barking laugh.

"Was Mrs. O'Leary hard to get along with?" Tess chose her words carefully. Perhaps there was some level of truth to the rumors. Maybe there was another woman involved, and Mrs. O'Leary had found out and stabbed her husband to death in a furious rage. Tess jotted down a note to herself at a possible, though unlikely, motive.

"Nah, not really. She was pleasant enough," Novak shrugged. "She liked her house a certain way, her kids to act a certain way, and if it wasn't like that, well... You better look out. She'd give you a verbal thrashing to end all thrashings." He grinned then. "I remember once, I made the mistake of walking into the farmhouse with Garrett and Fred with my boots still on. I'd tracked mud in on her clean floors, and boy, did I hear all about it! To this day, if I visit out there, I make sure my shoes are left on the porch. And that woman had been dead for over twenty years!"

Tess gave him a small grin, amused by his ornery reaction to the late Mrs. O'Leary. Kevin never mentioned that his mother had ruled the family with a firm hand and a quick tongue. She'd have to ask about that.

"So, Mr. Novak, on the night that Garrett O'Leary went missing, the police report says that you guys were out drinking and hanging out. Tell me about that," Tess asked, turning the questioning back to the night of July 20, 1996. "Where did you go?"

"We went to some new strip club out on 72. It used to have a different name, but I can't remember. Something goofy... The Booby Trap? I think it's called Sid's Place now." When Tess nodded, he continued. "It was Fred, Garrett, me, and Kane O'Leary, Garrett's older brother."

"Did he hang out with you guys frequently?"

"Oh, sure, when he was around," Novak nodded. "He travelled a lot for the Army, so as we got older, he was sent to various places. He would go on the guys' trips if he was in town, but for a while, he was stationed overseas, so we didn't see him."

"So why did you all go to The Booby Trap that night instead of the Falcon's Nest like usual?" Tess asked, watching Novak carefully.

Kenny shrugged, "Because it was the new big thing, I guess. Besides, Fred wouldn't shut up about it so I think

Garrett finally agreed to go just to appease him. Me? I didn't care where we went just as long as there was music and good beer on tap."

"Okay, so he was in town the night you all went to the strip club. How did everybody seem that night?"

"Everybody seemed fine. Kane was a little quiet, but he'd just come home recently from a long stint overseas. Fred and Garrett were like they always were. That was around the time I was thinking about putting a bid on this house, actually. Kane talked about buying some property for himself at one point, so he knew more about the process than I did. Garrett, of course, lived at the farm and had no idea how to go about doing any of it. Fred was too busy chasing women, so he wasn't helpful." The old man rolled his eyes, grinning over at Tess.

"So Kane was helping you with making the offer for the house. What else did you all discuss?"

"Everyday stuff, I guess. Ma'am, it's been nearly thirty years now. I don't remember much from that night, just that none of us drank more than usual, and everyone seemed relaxed."

"Do you remember if anyone else came up to the table, said anything, or interacted with you all in any way?"

"Not that I remember, no."

"And when you all left, did anyone leave with Garrett?"

"Might sound crazy that I remember, but when he went missing, I must've said the same thing a hundred times, so I'll likely never forget. He drove off on his own, headed toward the farmhouse."

# Chapter Sixteen



*Saturday, September 1st, 12:15 PM*

"It's so great to see you, Tess!" beamed Stephanie Anderson, Denny's younger sister. "When was the last time? Gavin's fifth birthday party?" She nodded toward her gangly nine-year-old son, who was currently showing Natalie how to play Mario Kart.

"Oh my! Has it been that long?" Tess gasped as she slipped into the other woman's open arms for a hug. Had it taken a family barbecue to finally get them all back together? Tess truly enjoyed Steph's company, and as she thought back to recent months, she realized just how busy her job had kept her. As she released Steph from their embrace, Tess inwardly vowed to make more of an effort to stay in touch with Steph and get to know her more.

"Yeah, it has. Denny's been keeping you all to himself!" Steph playfully chastised her brother.

"What? Do you blame me?" Denny asked with a shrug. Steph rolled her eyes and playfully swatted at him.

"How about you go man the grill while I catch up with your girlfriend?" Steph suggested as she shoved a platter of raw hamburger patties, bratwursts, and hotdogs into Denny's hands. With an eye roll at his sister and a kiss on the cheek to Tess, Denny accepted the platter and disappeared out the patio door and into the fray of children playing in the yard.

"So.... What's new with you? Tell me everything!" Steph gestured for Tess to take a seat at the kitchen island as she puttered around the kitchen. "I don't get out much, so I want to live vicariously through you." The woman grinned, her eyes, the same deep blue color as her brother's, sparkling with mischief.

"Well, let's see..." Tess grinned, leaning into the counter on her elbows. "You know that little puppy I brought over last time I saw you? I named him Otter, and this is him now." She scrolled through her phone and found a photo of her best friend, tail wagging, and a tennis ball in his mouth. Stephanie squealed when Tess turned the phone around.

"Oh man! He's a cutie. You shoulda brought him," she said. "Lenny would have loved him."

"Lenny?"

"The cute little mutt out back with the kiddos. They snookered me into getting a dog about a year ago. I'd been telling them no for a while because I knew it would be yet another chore for me to deal with. But really, the kids have been surprisingly helpful. Brielle walks him nearly every afternoon and Gavin scoops the poop without complaining. Super weird, right?" Steph shrugged, causing Tess to laugh.

"Hey, if he likes to scoop dog poop, I have a whole yard he can come clean up. I'll pay," Tess offered. "I'm serious. Send him with Denny sometime."

"So, is it true then?" Steph asked over her shoulder as she started rummaging through the refrigerator for ingredients to make pasta salad.

"Is what true?" Tess asked, wrinkling her nose in confusion.

"That Denny's over at your house all the time, and you guys have slumber parties?" Stephanie grinned wickedly, and Tess felt her face heat and her ears redden.

"Relax, Tess. I'm totally okay with it," Steph smiled. "In fact, when Natalie told me, I had to try to remain calm. You have *no* idea how long I've been waiting for this moment!"

Tess coughed out a surprised laugh. *Stephanie had been waiting for Denny and her to get together.* The idea made Tess both relieved and happy at the same time.

"Really?" she smiled. "Well, that makes me happy. *He* makes me happy." Tess's cheeks warmed in a deep blush at the admission.

"Oh, no," Steph laughed. "I've seen that look before. You better watch it, or I'll be calling you 'sister' before too long." She walked around the island holding a block of cheese and a knife. "I'll quit messing with you, but I am excited for you two. Denny deserves to be happy after everything he's been through and I think he's found that with you. I haven't seen him this smitten since.... Forever. Now here, you cube the cheese. I'll get started on the veggies." She grinned and set the cheese on a cutting board in front of Tess.

The two women worked in silence for a moment, each busy in their task. Tess was quietly happy to have the cheese to cube as she didn't want to get anything on her sundress. She so rarely got to wear such things, it was a special treat.

The dress was a beautiful floral print in a periwinkle purple color with spaghetti straps. Although it was supposed to hit just above the knee, Tess was tall enough that it landed almost mid-thigh. She'd almost decided not to wear it until she saw Denny's expression when he stopped to pick her up. She'd even taken the time to curl the ends of her long dark hair and apply some simple makeup and lip gloss. She felt pretty, which was something that didn't happen often on account of her uniform of  dress pants and a button-down shirt—a casualty of the job.

"Can I have a piece?" came a whisper from somewhere behind Tess. She turned, trying to find the source, and noticed a small boy crouching on her side of the kitchen island.

Confused for a moment, she held a cube of cheddar up questioningly, and he nodded vigorously. She grinned and quietly passed it to him. When she looked back up, she caught Steph watching her, an amused expression on her face.

"Seems you have a mouse problem." Tess shrugged as the boy slunk away so his mother wouldn't see him.

"More like a cheese-eating rat problem. A rat named Grady." Steph shook her head as she went back to preparing various side dishes. "That kid would survive on cheese if we let him. I don't know what else to pack for his school lunches besides cheese sticks and apples. It's all I can get him to eat!"

Just then, the patio door slid open, and Brielle, Stephanie's eldest child, strode in, followed by a gray mixed breed dog hot on her heels.

"Hey, Tess," Brielle greeted her with a shy smile. She turned to her mother. "Uncle Denny said the meat will be done in about five minutes."

"Perfect timing," commented Steph. "Here, can you take this stuff out to the table?" She piled Brielle's open arms high with paper plates, condiments, and a small basket holding napkins and silverware.

Tess filled her arms with the bowl of pasta salad and some delicious looking bean dip and followed the blond haired teenager outside.

The backyard was freshly landscaped and decorative paving stones dominated the patio area. A newly painted pergola sat next to a small man-made garden pond nestled in the corner of the fenced-in yard. Thin, gauzy white material had been draped over the pergola to aid in enclosing the seating area beneath. In the slight shadows of the awnings, Tess could see white lawn furniture punctuated with bright turquoise cushions set circularly to aid in conversation.

Across the large corner lot was a swing set complete with a lookout tower and zip line. Tess would have loved that as a kid!

"You know you want to try that," Denny called to her from where he was plating the perfectly grilled burgers. He grinned at her when she realized he'd caught her eyeing the zip line.

"Have you?" she asked, turning to make her way to him.

"I'm not admitting anything," he shrugged. "After lunch, it's on."

"It's for kids, it's not going to hold me."

"Paul souped it up. Trust me," Denny laughed. Just then, Paul, Denny's brother-in-law, came out of the house.

"Hey guys! Sorry I'm late. I got called into the office. On a Saturday! Can you believe it? Anyway, great to have you! Tess, you look happy. It's been a while since we've seen you. How have you been?" Paul gushed, a huge smile splitting his face. Tess couldn't help but smile. She'd forgotten how much Paul liked to chat.

"Hi, Paul," she greeted him with a smile. "It's been a few years. Gavin's fifth birthday!"

"No!" Paul exclaimed as he opened the cooler and extracted a beer. He offered it to Tess, but she declined, so he passed it to Denny before grabbing another one for himself. "Are you working on any cool cases? Denny said you're a detective now! How cool is that!" He paused long enough to take a swig of his beer.

"Just a few smaller cases. The biggest one at the moment is a cold case," Tess offered. She was used to people asking about her work but wouldn't talk about current cases. "Oh, man.... You got the skeleton that was found by the Hopewell mound?" Paul asked, his eyes round with wonder. "I saw that on the news. That's crazy. It makes you wonder... How many other dead people are randomly buried where they shouldn't be? Like, when I dug up this yard to do the landscaping, I'm not gonna lie. I was kind of wondering if I'd find something creepy like that. Interesting things like that don't happen to me, though." He laughed before taking another swallow of his beer.

Tess didn't know if she'd classify finding skeletal remains buried in the backyard as 'interesting, ' but she smiled nonetheless.

Denny strode over to the picnic table adjacent to the pergola and set down a steaming platter of freshly grilled meats. It was like a siren call for the kids; once they saw that the hotdogs were ready they came running over to the table en masse.

"Did y'all wash your hands?" Paul hollered over the din of young voices as he headed toward the chaos. Tess took that distraction to go find Steph. She didn't want to discuss work all day, especially the O'Leary case.

Today was for relaxation. A time to unwind with friends and family, eat good food, and maybe even play some games. Although Tess tried to stay present in the moment and enjoy her day off, there was a weight on her shoulders. The oppressive need to solve the case hung over her like a dark cloud, even as she tried to ignore it. Regardless of what she was doing, the detective in Tess was always working, analyzing data and looking for clues that would lead to the truth. Even when she was at a barbecue.

# Chapter Seventeen



*Monday, September 3rd, 12:32 PM*

Fred Krinsel's single-wide trailer sat nestled at the top of a washed-out driveway. Tall grass and old tires surrounded Tess on both sides as she slowly drove up the rutted gravel to meet with him. He'd agreed to speak with her about Garrett but would only do it at his house.

Given the detritus around the yard, it appeared that Mr. Krinsel hadn't done any home improvement in quite some time. Tess counted at least four abandoned vehicles, their windows busted out, their bodies covered in rust and moss. And that was just what she could easily see as she pulled up to the place.

Several cats scattered into the weeds and decrepit looking shed that listed precariously to the side. A few fifty-gallon drums were stacked behind the house. Tess got out of her vehicle and stood looking around for a moment, her eyes stopping on the old barrels. Her mind wandered as to the contents of the barrels but she quickly decided she didn't really want to know.

A faded orange kayak leaned up against the side of the old shed, and two old riding lawn mowers were parked next to it. By the look of the parts and pieces from the engines scattered around and the state of the overgrown lawn, it was evident that the mowers hadn't worked in quite some time.

Minding where she stepped, Tess made her way through the unkempt yard before quickly climbing the rickety front porch steps to stand before the paint-chipped door. She wondered if she should have dragged Deputies Miles or Scafferty along with her. The house was the last one on a single-lane country road near the edge of Swain County. Surrounded by woods on three sides, Tess could just barely make out the neighbor's house through the trees.

Absently placing her hand on her firearm strapped to her hip, she raised a hand to knock on the grimy front door. Inside, she could hear movement as she patiently waited for Fred Krinsel to open the door.

With a rattle, the door flew open to reveal an older man with a balding head and a paunch that hung over his belt. His bushy beard was long and grey, masking the lower half of his weathered face.

"You the detective?" he asked, squinting up at Tess through a large rent in the screen. He looked her up and down, pausing on her chest a moment longer than necessary before sliding back up to her face.

"Yes, I'm Detective Dane with the Swain County Sheriff's Department. We spoke earlier. You're Fred Krinsel?"

"Sure am, Detective," he smiled as he shoved open the storm door so she could enter. "C'mon in, c'mon in." He turned and shuffled deeper into the shadows of the house.

Tess took a deep breath before following the man into the trailer and was instantly assaulted by stale air, heavy with body odor, cat urine, and old cigarettes. Schooling her face against the smell, she looked around, taking in her surroundings.

The interior of the Krinsel home wasn't any better than the outside. Stacks of old newspapers sat around a ratty old armchair in the corner of the living room. The brown thread-bare shag carpet under their feet did little to help make the house homey. Walls, once papered in light blue and white stripes, had long ago yellowed with age and decades of cigarette smoke curling through the air.

"Here, have a seat," Fred offered as he grabbed at a pair of old jeans that had been thrown over the end of the sagging couch. Seemingly as an afterthought, he reached out and grabbed a handful of empty beer bottles resting on the coffee table before heading to the kitchen to discard them. Not wanting to sit on the couch, Tess decided to sit on the edge of it to be polite. The musty smell that wafted up when she sat down did little to appease her senses.

An overflowing ashtray sat on the coffee table where the beer bottles had been. Grimacing inwardly, Tess glanced to see if Fred Krinsel was in view before gently pushing the stinking cigarette graveyard away from her.

"So, you wanted to talk about Garrett, huh?" Fred smiled at her as he came back into the living room. Gratefully, he decided to sit in his old armchair, which was opposite Tess. She'd almost worried that he'd come to sit on the couch next to her.

"Yes, that's correct," Tess began as Fred wiggled his large belly into a comfortable position. Once he was finally nestled into his chair, he sat back and watched Tess intently.

"I'd like to know about your relationship with him. You know, where you met, what you all used to do together, what happened the last time you saw him...." She let the last part hang in the stagnant air between them as she continued to watch his facial expressions for any sign of distress.

Fred Krinsel leaned his head back against the stained fabric headrest of his chair, seeming to be deep in thought. After a moment of awkward silence, he rolled his head back up to look at Tess.

"I met ol' Garrett back in school, maybe fourth, fifth grade. I don't remember what year, just that the teacher had really big ti–" he paused, suddenly looking sheepish. "Er, she was well endowed, if you know what I mean, and me and the others would make jokes about them."

"How delightful." Tess's deadpan comment landed perfectly, causing Krinsel to begin tripping over himself to explain.

"Well, I mean, she was a nice teacher and all, but it was hard to concentrate with.... those things.... in our faces," Krinsel insisted. "Anyway, we made jokes. That's how we met." When Tess didn't commend him for his actions, a scowl darkened his face. "What? You're the one that asked."

"I asked how you met, not when you became a pig, Mr. Krinsel," Tess cringed inwardly the moment the words escaped her lips. She knew she needed to calm her feminine rage and play into his misogyny if she were to get anywhere with him.

"Well, aren't we hoity-toity..." Krinsel sniped under his breath.

"So you met Garrett O'Leary in grade school, along with Kenny Novak, correct?" Tess asked, deciding to ignore his snide comment and try to get the conversation back on track. At first, she didn't think he was going to answer her, much less look at her again, but he eventually turned to study her.

"Yes."

"And did the three of you remain friends?" Tess inquired, knowing full well about the annual 'guy trips.'

"Yeah, all through school and even through college," Krinsel answered, absently scratching his rotund abdomen. "Garrett and I didn't go to college, but Kenny did. Business or something like that."

"And what did you and Garrett do while Kenny was away at school?" Tess asked, not expecting to learn anything new or useful but hoping nonetheless that perhaps something may come to light that she hadn't learned already.

"Garrett was busy working the farm with his dad since his brother skipped out on them. I got a job down at the quarry."

"Garrett's brother... You mean Kane?"

"Yeah."

"I heard he joined the Army. You said he 'skipped out'... which was it?" Tess asked, making a mental note to look into Kane's possible military background.

"His parents *said* he joined the Army. I think he just left. He didn't want to work the farm, that I know for a fact."

"And how do you know that?" Tess asked, writing some notes to herself on a small notebook she'd brought with her.

"He told me. More than once, too," Krinsel shrugged. "Kane and I were kinda close, even though he was a couple years older than the rest of us. He always hated working that farm. Said it was too much work for so little reward. He often talked about going off on his own, seeing the world. Wouldn't surprise me none if he said he was joining the Army just to escape Swain County."

"Tell me about the guy trips you went on together," Tess said, deciding to steer the conversation elsewhere.

"We went to a few places... California, Alaska, Mexico... We tried to go somewhere each year just to hang out and forget about adulting," Krinsel sighed, seemingly deep in thought. "Eventually, with Kane gone off somewhere and Garrett starting a family, we just started to drift apart. And then, Garrett just... disappeared completely. At first, I thought he was just blowing off steam or something. That he'd come back in a better mood, pick up where he'd left off, you know?"

"Come back in a better mood?" Tess noted. "Had he seemed off to you in the days leading up to his disappearance?"

"Yes and no," Krinsel sighed, his forehead wrinkled in thought. "You see, Garrett always seemed laid back. Happy. Even when his old lady was going off about one thing or another. But then both his parents died, and Garrett had the burden of the entire farm on his shoulders."

"How did he seem to handle that?"

"At first, he seemed overwhelmed. He had his three kids–Kevin, Brandon, and Marissa. They were just youngsters at the time, but eventually, they all seemed to get in a groove, you know? Working the farm, making things move like a well-oiled machine. And then Kane came back into town." He paused then, staring off into space as though conjuring up an old memory.

After a moment of silence, Tess pressed on. "And how did Garrett handle having Kane back? Was there any friction between the brothers that you saw?"

"Shoot! Between those two?" Krinsel scoffed, "They were thick as thieves. If there was anything amiss between the two, I never saw it. All I do know is that when Kane came back, things changed around here. Changed on the farm."

"Changed how?" Tess asked, leaning forward in her seat. Had Kane had something to do with the murder of his brother? She shook her head slightly in disbelief at the possibility.

"Kane came back from wherever the hell he'd been, and it seemed to upset the balance at the farm. Garrett was stressed more. He cancelled more times than he showed up to things. I didn't think much about it, to be honest. Like, sometimes we'd all try to get together for a poker game or head down to the bar to play pool and drink. When Kane was in town, he would come hang out more often than not. But Garrett? He seemed tired and overworked. Wouldn't show up."

"Any idea why?"

"Not that I know of. Just figured he was busy and didn't want to hang out."

"Well, if it was the family farm, why didn't Kane settle down and help out some while he was in town? You know, take some of the burden off of his brother?"

Krinsel let out a puff of air that wasn't quite a laugh. "I said they got along well. I didn't say Kane was a hard worker." When Tess pulled a face, Krinsel grinned.

"It might have been the family farm, but there was little to no chance of Kane ever working that soil. Working on vehicles? Sure. Chasing women? Guaranteed. But farm work? He'd rather cut off his own nose."

Tess mulled over this new information. She'd met Kane O'Leary once and the man reminded her more of Santa Claus than some lazy womanizer. He was confined to a wheelchair and lived in a senior assistance home even though he was only in his mid-seventies. The Kane that Tess had met was a far cry from the Kane that Fred Krinsel was describing.

"So, if there wasn't any friction between the brothers or Garrett's wife, was there anyone else that might have had a beef with him?" Tess asked, consulting her notes.

"Not that I can think of, really. Garrett was a nice guy. A real straight shooter. It's such a pity that happening to him," Krinsel sighed heavily, casting a woeful look down at his belly.

"What can you tell me about the night he disappeared?"

"Pretty much just what I told the coppers back then. There was a new strip club, The Booby Trap, that we wanted to check out. The 'we' being me and Kenny Novak. Anyway, we called Kane and Garrett and asked if they wanted to meet us there to check it out. It took some work, but we finally got Garrett to agree to come down and meet up with us."

"Did Kane come too?" Tess asked, listening intently.

"Yeah, he came down, too, but they arrived separately. Garrett arrived first, and I don't know how Kane got there.

I just remember because Garrett seemed super agitated and had already been drinking by the time he got to the club."

"Any idea why?"

"No. He wouldn't say. He pretty much sulked the whole night, even when Kenny bought him a lap dance. I just figured he'd had a fight with the missus and let it go," Krinsel shrugged before pulling a crushed package of cigarettes out of the breast pocket of his tee-shirt.

"And how did Kane act that night? Was he agitated, too?"

"Kane was perpetually moody back then," Krinsel breathed out a laugh. "He was always bitching about something so it's hard to say." He pulled a lighter out of his pocket and gave it a few flicks before producing a flame. Lighting a cigarette, he inhaled a deep breath and then exhaled slowly, savoring the nicotine.

"Okay... so was he worse than normal?" Tess asked, trying not to cough from the sudden plume of smoke swirling around her head.

"That night?" He took another long drag on his cigarette. "Maybe a little. Angry and quiet. Sullen? Ain't that a word?"

Tess nodded as Krinsel let out another lungful of smoke, which ended in a hacking cough. After the coughing fit subsided, Krisel leaned to the side, withdrew a stained bandana from the back pocket of his jeans, and blew his nose loudly. Tess lowered her gaze to her notes to give him some privacy.

"I remember Kane got there later than Garrett. Much later, almost near eleven or so. Kenny and I had gotten to the strip club around... 9:00 if I remember correctly. Garrett didn't show up for another forty-five minutes or so. He'd been down at the Falcon's Nest with Kane. When we called him to join us, he said they'd come over, but it took him a while. It took Kane even longer."

"Do you have any idea why?"

"Nope," Krinsel shrugged, "You'd have to ask Kane that."

# Chapter Eighteen

*Tuesday, September 4th, 10:00 AM*

Kane O'Leary's senior living apartment was located on the outskirts of Columbus. A newer building, Glade Spring Senior Living boasted an exercise facility and a game room filled with small tables and stacks of puzzles and board games for tenants to use.

From where Tess stood at the reception desk waiting for Kane O'Leary, she could see two elderly women playing cards through the large glass window in the wall to the game room. To her right was another glass wall that showcased the exercise room. Tess watched as a wiry-looking older man began aggressively pressing buttons on a treadmill. As the treadmill began accelerating, so did the man's wobbly legs.

She turned to the woman at the front desk to voice her concern for his safety, but the woman held up a dismissive hand.

"I know what you're about to say, Detective. That is Stefan. He may look like he has one foot in the grave, but trust me... He does this every single morning without incident. He'll be swimming laps," she paused to glance at her watch, "in about thirty minutes."

Tess raised her eyebrow in skepticism and was rewarded with a light laugh from the receptionist.

"I was afraid to look away too, when I first started here," the receptionist leaned forward and whispered, "but really, a lot of our tenants are very capable of looking after themselves." She winked at someone conspiratorially as they passed behind Tess.

Tess turned in time to see another man with poorly dyed black hair and a spray tan sashay past the front desk, pausing only to wink at the receptionist. This caused the young woman behind the desk to giggle and smooth out her hair subconsciously.

Tess turned her back to the man with the spray tan and overly white teeth and began wondering what kind of Twilight Zone she'd entered when she suddenly heard someone calling her name.

She turned then to find Kane O'Leary steering a motorized wheelchair toward her. He lifted a frail hand in a wave as she began walking toward him.

"Hi, Mr. O'Leary," Tess greeted, extending her hand in a formal greeting even though she hated handshakes. Kane's grip was weak, his skin soft.

"Ah, Detective Dane," Kane beamed, his blue eyes sparkling. "What a great surprise! When Shayna at the front desk said you were here to speak to me, I raced right down. Vroom! Vroom!" He laughed lightly at his joke.

Tess smiled and shook her head at his silliness. "I'm glad you were available to speak with me today, Mr. O'Leary. Is there somewhere private we can talk?" She looked around again, taking in the large centralized atrium that was used for visiting and relaxing.

The high, domed ceiling was completely made of glass, as were the walls. Large potted plants and palm trees filled the area, providing privacy for tenants and allowing quiet conversations. In the center of the large open space was a shiny black baby grand piano and a small group of chairs. In the farthest corner, a large flat screen TV hung from the wall, its volume low. A few people were currently sitting on couches surrounding the common TV area, watching one of the multitude of baking shows that always seemed to be airing.

Through the glass walls, Tess could see pathways and gardens in full bloom. A small pond sat within view of the Common Room, allowing tenants and visitors alike to watch the ducks swim around.

Tess was suddenly overcome with a feeling of sadness at the thought that her father would have loved a place like this. But instead, he'd needed more of the one-on-one care that Tolliver Care Home provided. This place was for individuals who were mostly capable of taking care of themselves but still needed some assistance.

"Sure, Detective. Come this way," Kane said, turning his wheelchair around easily with just the push of a joystick. He took off down a side hallway with more speed than Tess was anticipating. She took long strides to keep up with him as they went down one corridor and then another.

He stopped abruptly and turned into a darkened room. Casting a look over his shoulder at Tess fast approaching, he announced, "I win!"

Tess snorted a laugh and shook her head, which, in turn, made Kane smile.

"Hit the lights, will you?" he asked as Tess arrived at the doorway behind him. She reached out, blindly feeling for the light switch. After several seconds that stretched out into eternity, she found the switch and flipped it to illuminate a small room containing two couches, a large wooden table surrounded by matching chairs, and a boring piece of artwork on the walls.

"Is this where you conduct all your secret business?" Tess asked playfully as Kane rotated his wheelchair around.

"Shhhh!" Kane whispered, holding an arthritic finger to his lips. Tess rolled her eyes and grinned as she found a seat at the table.

"Okay, so now it's time to be serious," she cautioned, looking through her file and notes quickly. From her pocket, she pulled out her digital recording device.

Kane watched her curiously, his face suddenly concerned. When Tess was ready, she looked up and found Kane still watching her intently.

"So, as I told you over the phone, I am here to speak with you about your brother. Since you are all the way here in Columbus, and getting you to come down to the station in Crawley may be..." she glanced at the wheelchair, "difficult, I've decided to record our session instead. Is that alright?"

"I already made a statement about that night, Detective, but sure. If it helps find who did this to Garrett, then do what you gotta do." His voice cracked, causing him to look away from her to compose himself.

"Yes, I have your original statement, at least the paper report. The audio file seems to have... been misplaced." Tess sighed. "I've been going through the old case files for your brother. Trying to determine what's already been done and what still needs to be done. What witnesses I should interview again. That kind of thing."

"Well, if they talked to the cops back then, what makes you think they'll have anything new to say now? I don't even know if I remember what I wore that night, much less who said what or where they were."

"Well," Tess looked at Kane thoughtfully. "Whenever we reopen a cold case like this, we review the case. Sometimes, it's helpful to re-interview witnesses because occasionally they will remember something that seemed insignificant at the time but could break the case now. Or perhaps they were afraid to tell the truth back then, but now, thirty years later, their abuser is dead, or their allegiances have changed. Does that make sense?"

"Yeah, I guess so," Kane shrugged. "If you think it'll help, then let's do this."

"Okay," Tess nodded, picking up the recorder. She pressed record and rattled off the date, their names, and the purpose of the interview.

"When was the last time you saw your brother, Garrett?" Tess asked, lightly tapping her pen on her notes subconsciously.

"That night at the bar," Kane sighed, looking down at his lap.

"And which bar was that?" Tess asked, wanting to confirm the different stories she'd been told.

"Some strip club. I got there late and didn't really feel like partying, if you know what I mean."

"Do you mean The Booby Trap?" Tess asked, cringing inwardly at the ridiculous name. Kane nodded.

"Why were you late?"

"I had something to take care of first, so I just met the boys over there," Kane answered, looking Tess directly in the eye and daring her to dig further. She knew the look and decided to come back to it.

"By 'the boys, ' I'm assuming you mean Kenny Novak and Fred Krinsel?"

"Yeah, and Garrett."

"How did everyone seem that night? Especially Garrett?" Tess asked, consulting her notes.

"Fred and Kenny seemed like their normal selves. Garrett seemed angry about something but I don't know what."

"You didn't think to ask?" Tess asked, raising a well-manicured eyebrow. "Your own brother seemed upset about something, and you didn't ask him about it?"

"I didn't say I didn't ask him. I said I didn't know," Kane snipped. "He wouldn't tell me. I assume it had something to do with his wife."

"You mean... Tina?" Tess asked, consulting her notes. Kane nodded.

"Yep, that's the one. Tina the Tornado," Kane frowned. "She was always bitching about something, complaining about this or that. It was nauseating. She caused destruction wherever she went. I always hoped they'd split up. It woulda made everyone a helluva lot happier."

"Is she why you left and didn't come back for so long? Avoided the farm?" Tess asked cautiously, watching for any facial tells. Kane gave her nothing.

"I left that farm because it was a never-ending load of work. And for what? Nothing. I wanted to be free to travel, do what I wanted, and learn what I wanted. I couldn't do that if I had stayed. I would still be working in those fields.

Well... except for this stupid thing." He tapped the arm of his wheelchair for emphasis.

"Is that why you joined the Army? To get away?" Tess asked, baiting him to gauge his reaction. She'd heard two different versions of his military service. She'd follow up officially, of course, but for now, she wanted to get it straight from the horse's mouth.

Kane laughed, but it held no humor.

"Did I ask something amusing?" Tess asked, raising her eyebrow again.

"I never joined the damn military. My parents came up with that bullshit to make themselves look better. 'Oh, look! Shamus and Lenore have a son serving his country!'" Kane sneered at the memory. "In truth, my parents—Mom especially—couldn't stand the idea that I didn't want to stay home and work the farm. She thought it was disgraceful that I wanted to live my own life. Live by my own rules."

# Chapter Nineteen



"Thank you for calling me, Angela," Tess said as she rushed past the waiting room at Tolliver Care Home to where her father's nurse stood waiting for her.

"I'm sorry I couldn't call you earlier. We've only just got him stable.... But Tess, I must warn you. He doesn't look good. This pneumonia has been very rough on him." Angela gave Tess a sympathetic smile as the two women headed toward the hallway that led to Tommy Dane's room.

Tess steeled herself for what she was about to see as they walked the freshly waxed hallway. The typical antiseptic smell mixed with the ammonia scent of urine engulfed them, and Tess tried not to think about what a dismal place a care home could be.

As far as nursing homes went, Tolliver was highly rated and had always provided excellent care for her father. Early on, when Tess had been forced to bring her father there, she'd made friends with the charge nurse, Angela. She was unsure how old the nurse was, but Angela's caring attitude and support for her meant a lot and helped fill the empty void left by Tess's absent mother.

"He's resting now," Angela stated softly as they paused in front of Tommy Dane's closed door. She quietly turned the handle, and the two women entered the room.

The curtains were pulled closed, and a small bedside table cast a slight glow around the darkened room. On the bed lay her father, his pale face calm and thin. Tess gulped back tears at the sight of him. That wasn't her father. Of course, the *body* was his, but the mind, the part that made him...him...was no longer there.

"He'd been improving some with the medications, but the pneumonia is persistent. Now, he's barely able to eat and has trouble swallowing. I believe Dr. Hanover will be contacting you later today about possible treatment options," Angela informed Tess as she carefully adjusted Tommy's blanket around his shoulders.

"Treatment options?" Tess wrinkled her nose in confusion. "The dementia is here to stay, and the pneumonia is being treated with antibiotics, right?"

Angela nodded, then paused, seemingly unsure if she should say anything more. She glanced toward the half-closed door, as if to bolster herself before looking Tess straight in the eye and whispering, "I'm talking about... feeding tubes, possible respirators versus potential palliative care.... But it's not my place to say so you didn't hear it from me." Her empathetic gaze met Tess's for a moment before she looked away.

Tess's eyes rounded in understanding, her lips held firm in a grim line. Tears threatened the backs of her eyelids.

"Shit..." She quickly wiped at her eyes, trying to regain her composure, but inside, she was lost. How would she survive if anything happened to her dad? She knew she would persist, but how would life look if he were gone? If he wasn't just a short drive away? If she couldn't call him on his good days just to hear his voice? He'd always been a source of wisdom, guidance, and strength for Tess and the thought of going through the rest of her life without him there by her side left her feeling shattered.

"How is his overall demeanor?" Tess asked cautiously. The last time she'd seen him lucid, when she told him about Chief Burrows and how Detective Malone was now the interim sheriff, Tommy Dane had become extremely agitated and confused. It was then that Tess vowed to herself that she wouldn't discuss police work with her father anymore. The thought saddened her, of course, as police work had been her father's lifeblood. Tess came from a long line of law enforcement officers.

She remembered times as a small girl when her father would be sitting around talking with her uncles and grandfather, discussing crazy stories from their years on the force. Even now, Tess had family in law enforcement. Her cousin, Ian, was an FBI agent out in Denver, and another cousin served as an Alaska State Trooper.

"He's been sleeping a lot the past couple of days. The doctors were talking about possibly sedating him to keep him calm due to the pneumonia because when he gets agitated, he starts coughing and gagging. It makes his breathing worse, and in his current condition..." Angela offered, her dark eyes soft and her voice low and smooth. "He was awake earlier when I called you. He's just so weak now... I've been trying to get him to eat some softer foods, but he seems to be struggling. That's why Dr. Hanover wants to speak with you."

Tess walked over to stand next to her father's bed, watching his weak chest rise and fall, his breath sounding raspy. Reaching down, she took his hand and was surprised at how cold it felt. Almost as though he were already dead.

"I'll leave you to visit, sweetheart," Angela whispered as she patted Tess's shoulder reassuringly before turning to leave the room. Tess watched her go for a moment and then turned back to her father.

"Hey Dad, it's me, Tess," she greeted softly as she pulled a chair over to sit on. Her father remained asleep, yet she felt compelled to continue. "I don't know if you can hear me or not, but.... I just wanted to tell you that I love you." Her voice broke, an overwhelming feeling of loss hanging over her. She knew her time was limited, and she wasn't ready. It made her so angry when she thought of how it was so unfair for Tommy Dane to suffer the way he had with his early-onset Dementia.

There had been subtle changes at first, all those years ago. Tess had been around fifteen, and her mom, Kathy, was still in the picture. As far as Tess knew, life was great; she was in high school track, had a small but loyal group of friends, was saving up money from her first after-school job at McDonalds to buy a Jeep, and she spent every waking minute not at school or work with her dad down at the Swain County Sheriff's Department. He'd been a detective, and she'd been his self-ordained partner, trying to solve cases before he did.

Of course, Tommy Dane and his fellow coworkers wouldn't let Tess just have free-range with actual case files and evidence, but there was a time or two when Tommy "accidentally" left a file for Tess to find so she felt included.

It was one of those times of "accidentally" leaving a case for Tess to find when Tommy Dane really messed up. It was one of the first times Tess could remember noticing that something wasn't right with her dad.

The case in question was a murder case. Due to the graphic content, Tommy wouldn't let Tess see it. That is, until he forgot and left the crime scene photos lying out for her to find.

The victim was one of Tess' classmates.

When Tess saw the photos, she let out a cry and ran from the room. It was then that Tommy and his partner realized what had happened. When Sheriff Burrows had questioned Tommy about leaving sensitive case files out where civilians, especially children, could find them, Tommy couldn't remember doing it.

At home, little changes happened. Tommy would forget to turn off the stove, or he'd put on two different pairs of shoes and call it good. He'd forget the keys in the ignition or wake up in the middle of the night and wander outside.

Then he started forgetting words, facts, dates, and eventually faces. The episodes eventually began happening more frequently and were longer in duration. It was during that time that Kathy, his wife, decided it was too much for her to deal with.

Tess remembered the day her mother left like it was yesterday. Kathy hadn't said goodbye, hadn't even hugged her only child farewell. She'd just ripped a page out of Tess's school notebook, scrawled out, "I can't do this anymore," in pencil, laid the note on the kitchen table, and left. She didn't even bother locking the door behind her.

"Oh, Dad..." Tess heaved a sob as she sat with him now, thinking about all the things they'd weathered together.

"Please don't leave me. I'm not ready for this. I don't think I'll ever be ready for this..." Sobs wracked her body as she leaned over in her seat, laying her forehead on his thigh, his cool hand still held in her grip. Tears fell in rivulets, soaking the blanket covering his legs.

Her heart felt as though it were shattering into a million pieces. She struggled to breathe as the sobs erupted from her.

Suddenly, she felt a soft pressure on the crown of her head. She looked up and found her father looking at her, his eyes tired, his face pale. He gently patted her on the head.

"It's okay, Bug..." he wheezed, his voice weak. "You'll be just... fine." He sucked in another labored breath. "I love you, too... Always have, always will."

# Chapter Twenty

*Tuesday, September 11th, 2:00 PM*

They laid Tommy Dane to rest four days later. The entirety of the Swain County Sheriff's Department, the Crawley Police Department, and many other law enforcement officers from BCI and surrounding areas all attended to support Tess and pay their respects to one of their own.

Tommy Dane had been a great detective and a dedicated officer, as was evident by the sheer number of people who stood soberly at his grave.

Tess stood next to the open pit, Denny by her side, as the minister gave some final words about Tommy and the joys of the Heavenly Afterlife. Tess felt anything but joy. Her heart was shattered. She was broken. The one person who knew her best, loved her the most, and supported her in all she did now lay in the cherrywood coffin at her feet.

Of course, she knew it was just the shell of her father. The real Tommy Dane– the loving father, the caring officer, the beloved friend– had been slowly disappearing for the past few years. But his death hurt nonetheless. The finality of it stung, and Tess wasn't prepared for the flood of emotions that threatened to unravel her.

As the sermon wound down, the group of mourners stood silently as an officer stepped forward and, trumpet to his lips, began playing Taps.

When the Twenty-one Gun Salute began firing off, Tess turned into Denny's embrace. He held her as tears wracked her body. She'd thought she'd cried all her tears, but apparently, she was wrong.

The rest of the funeral was a blur. Vague silhouettes of fellow officers and their spouses coming to her with words of condolences and saddened looks cast her way as the crowd began to disperse... None of it managed to come into focus. Tess stayed within arm's reach of Denny. It was all she could do to smile politely and nod at, hopefully, the correct intervals. But truly, Tess just wanted to be alone. She wanted her father back, alive and well. She wanted things to be the way they had been before he'd gotten sick.

But those days were gone forever– a blip on the timeline of her life. Wishing she could press rewind and re-experience the good times with her father, or at least pause them in an effort to enjoy the moments to their fullest, Tess took one last shuddering breath as she finally lifted her head to take in the grave.

She and Denny stood alone next to what remained of her father as the late summer sun beat down on them. Taking a careful step forward, the ground lumpy under the outdoor rugs that had been laid around the grave, Tess bent down to say her final goodbyes.

Tess felt her heart break even further as she uttered her final words. Her head throbbed from crying, her eyes red and swollen. When her sobs finally quieted and she felt spent, she stood back up, numb, her eyes never leaving the cherry coffin.

"I'm here, sweetheart," Denny murmured from close behind her as she felt his hand gently come to rest on her hip. "Whatever you need, just tell me."

"I need my dad, but I don't suppose you can help me with that," Tess whispered, looking up at Denny's drawn face and giving him a wilted smile. "But I'll settle for some more tissues, a hug, and maybe some lunch."

"It's about time you ate something. I was getting worried but didn't want to pester you about it. You've been dealing with a lot," Denny said. The relief was clear in his tone and his gentle but persistent affection. "Come here." He pulled her into an intimate embrace, encircling her thin frame with his muscular arms. She leaned into his strength, a sigh escaping her. She'd been trying to stay strong for the past few days, and it was growing heavy on her, both emotionally and mentally. With a sniffle and a sigh, Tess let herself slowly relax in Denny's arms.

After a moment, he nuzzled her hair with his chin. "You ready to go?"

She nodded. He gently took her hand and led her gently through the cemetery to his Tahoe.

# Chapter Twenty-One

*Thursday, September 13th, 10:00 AM*

The next couple of days were a haze of emotion and exhaustion. Tess felt like she'd been in a daze since her father's funeral. She just wanted to be alone and found herself avoiding calls, even from her Aunt Sharon in Anchorage. She'd been given time off for bereavement but found that the sudden idle time lent itself to a wandering mind. Thinking about happier times with her dad. Of him coming home in the evening after a long day on the job, looking handsome in his dark uniform. He'd scoop Tess up like she weighed nothing, and her little girl giggles would fill the room.

She remembered the moment, at six years old, when she'd decided to be a cop, just like him. She'd been sitting on the wooden porch swing, its surface covered in a thick layer of peeling white paint that Tess liked to pick at. Tommy Dane had just gotten home and was walking slowly up the front walk, head down, deep in thought.

"Daddy!" Tess squealed, running toward her father, jarring him from his thoughts. When he looked up and saw her running at him, long braids bouncing, a large smile crossed his once solemn face.

"Hey, Bug!" he exclaimed, stooping low to pick her up. Then, it was game on. She told him all about her day: what she did at school, how she got to eat some of her friend Liberty's animal crackers at lunch because they decided to share, and how Josh Moeke farted in class and everyone started laughing.

The whole time Tess prattled on about her day, Tommy simply led her over to the swing, and they sat, watching the sun set low in the western sky. At some point in the conversation, Tess tugged at Tommy's badge, and he took it off to let her hold it as he always did.

She sat on the swing, feeling the weight of the brass police badge in her small child-size hands. Gently tracing the letters on it with her fingers, Tess glanced up at her dad and smiled.

"Daddy?"

"Yes, Bug?"

"I want to be like you. I want to be a police officer and catch the bad guys."

"You'd be a tough cop, Tess. With your personality and your desire for justice, you'd catch all the bad guys." Tommy smiled down at her.

An exciting thought occurred to her, and she suddenly sat up straighter. "Maybe we can even be partners! You could be the driver, and I could turn on the lights and sirens!" Tess exclaimed.

Tommy grabbed her then, swinging her up into his arms. "Those bad guys wouldn't have a chance against us!"

he smiled in agreement as he carried her into the house for dinner.

***

Suddenly, the doorbell chimed, jarring Tess from her memories. Otter began barking and running to the front door. Tess stopped folding clothes in the laundry room long enough to stick her head out into the hallway and look towards the front door. She wasn't expecting anyone. Confused, she laid the half-folded towel down and went to answer the door.

Peering through the beveled glass next to the door, Tess recognized her visitor and instantly smiled.

"Aunt Sharon!" she squealed, opening the door and throwing her arms around the older woman. Sharon laughed in delight at seeing Tess again and returned the embrace.

"Hi, Otter!" she said, reaching out to pat the prancing dog's ebony head. The Labrador gave a happy yip and nudged her hand happily. "Nice to see he hasn't forgotten me!"

"Aunt Sharon, you're hard to forget." Tess smiled, ushering her only close relative into the house. "Why didn't you tell me you were coming? I would have asked for extra time off work. It's been over a year since I've seen you!"

"Oh, baby girl, I wanted to be here for you. When you told me about your dad's passing, I knew you'd be needing somebody." Sharon sighed, glancing up at Tess, her eyes misty.

"Oh, Sharon! That means so much to me! It's such a long flight from Anchorage." Tess swiped at her eyes. "Where are your bags?"

"Out on the porch," Sharon grinned. As Tess moved to retrieve them, Sharon grabbed her arm gently.

"I need to talk to you about something. Soon," her aunt cast a glance towards the front door somewhat cryptically.

"O-kay," Tess said, drawing the word out. Confusion and concern clouded her face. "I'll grab your bag. Go ahead and take the guest room."

As her aunt made her way down the hall, Otter at her side, Tess shrugged to herself and headed out to the front porch to grab her aunt's suitcase and tote bag. The day, once sunny, suddenly seemed to darken as another mass of charcoal colored clouds moved in overhead. *More rain? Ugh!* Tess cast a withering glance at the darkening sky.

The wind began to pick up, blowing leaves and an empty discarded soft drink cup down the road, when a white car pulled up to the curb outside Tess's house. Holding the suitcase in one hand, the tote bag in the other, Tess watched curiously as the back door opened and a woman climbed out.

Tess's blood ran cold.

"Contessa! Darling!" the woman called shrilly over the sound of the wind. Tess's cringe wasn't just at the use of her full name. Her day, and possibly her life, were about to become a shitshow.

"Mom."

# Chapter Twenty-Two

*Thursday, September 13th, 12:34 PM*

"What are you doing here?" Tess demanded, not budging from where she stood on the porch step, her aunt's luggage hanging useless at her sides.

"Is that any way to greet someone, dear?" Kathy Dane-Humphries chided.

"I wouldn't know. My mom never taught me," Tess's voice dripped with ice. "She dipped out when I was a kid, so..." With a sarcastic shrug, Tess turned and walked back towards the front door, tuning her mother out.

"Contessa, you know it wasn't like that!" Kathy started as she turned to pull an over-sized purple suitcase out of the back seat of the white car and pay the driver. With a nod and a wave, the driver peeled away from the curb.

"Stop calling me that. You know I hate it," Tess fumed. "And why do you have a suitcase?" There was no way in Hell that she was letting her mother stay in her house.

"But it's your name. After your grandmother Lucy. Contessa Lucille," Kathy grunted as she tugged her suitcase through Tess's lawn instead of up the driveway like a sane person.

"Yes, I know. Doesn't mean I like it any more now than I did when I was a kid." Tess glared at her mother through slitted eyes, setting down Sharon's suitcase to open the door. "You still didn't answer my question. What's with the suitcase?"

"Why do *you* have a suitcase?" Kathy asked obnoxiously, still dodging the question.

"Because *I* have a house guest. And it's not you," Tess growled as she entered her home and slammed the front door in her mother's face, effectively halting the woman's response.

Sharon came out of the guest room just then, a look of guilt on her face. The doorbell rang. Then it rang again and again. Tess knew Kathy wouldn't leave without a fight, and anger coursed through her at the sudden chaos her life had become.

"Somebody better tell me what the hell is going on right now!" Tess seethed. "Is *that* what you needed to discuss with me?" She stabbed her finger at the front door. Sharon lowered her head in shame.

"I tried to stop her, Tess, but you know my sister. Persistent to a fault." As if on cue, Kathy began loudly knocking on the door. Otter was going crazy. He emitted a low growl as he stood in front of Sharon and Tess, staring at the front door.

"Dear God," Tess sighed, shaking her head frustratedly. As she stalked over to the door, she felt Sharon come up behind her.

"I tried to keep her away, but she wouldn't have it. You know she only wants trouble. The moment she found out Tommy was dead, she said she was coming here. I tried to intercept her to protect you. I'm sorry, Tess."

Steeling herself, Tess whipped open the door, catching Kathy with her hand raised mid-knock. After a second or two of staring like a deer in the headlights, Kathy dropped her hand and smoothed her shirt as though she hadn't just been acting erratic.

Looking past Tess's shoulder, her eyes narrowed to slits when she saw Sharon standing there.

"What are *you* doing here?" she barked at her sister. Otter let out another deep growl, his hackles up, ears back. Kathy's gaze left her sibling's face and slid to the dog at her feet.

"Please get that animal away from me. It seems dangerous." Kathy balked, suddenly nervous.

"I will not. This is his home," Tess stated, unwilling to back down or shut her dog away. "His name is Otter. He's four. But you'd know that if you ever bothered to call me back."

"Please, Tess, I just want to talk to you. Can I come in?" Kathy sighed, casting a glance at her sister in the process.

"You aren't going to leave until I let you talk, are you?" Tess asked, folding her arms across her chest. She knew she'd harbored bad feelings for her mother after all these years, but never knew just how deep they ran until she was face to face with the woman again.

Over the years, since Kathy had left Tess to fend for herself and care for her ailing father on her own, Tess had built a wall of resentment toward her mother. She'd tried multiple times to contact her, but Kathy would always ignore her efforts.

After a while, Tess just gave up.

During that time, however, Aunt Sharon had been there for Tess as much as she could be. They'd talk every few weeks to catch up, email back and forth, and visit when they could.

A sigh of disdain escaped Tess's lips as she stepped to the side and let her mother into the house against her better judgment.

With an air of victory, Kathy brushed past her daughter, dragging her suitcase behind her.

"Just because I let you in for now doesn't mean you'll be staying, so don't get comfortable," Tess warned, trying to put boundaries in place to protect her from the vulnerability of having her mother in her home. At this point, Kathy was a stranger. She'd been absent from Tess's life for nearly the same number of years she'd been present. Tess both hated her mother and craved her attention, because no matter how terrible she'd been to Tess through the years, she was still her mom. Tess was feeling torn between wanting to toss Kathy out on the street or pulling her into a close embrace. The child in Tess wanted to remember the good times with her mother despite the woman having hurt her so willingly.

"I've already taken the spare room," Sharon commented quietly, watching the exchange from the corner of the living room, Otter now by her side.

Kathy cast a sharp glare at her sister and then wheeled her suitcase to a halt near the hallway. She straightened her shirt again and smoothed her hair before looking at Tess.

"Might as well have a seat, ladies," Tess offered, gesturing towards the tan leather couch and an oversized chair that dominated the living area. "Would you all like something to drink?"

"I'll take some water, please," Kathy requested, sliding onto the couch while keeping an eye on Otter. The

Labrador seemed just as leery of her as she was of him but he'd quit growling and had resorted to avoidance and sniffing the air.

"You got any of that sweet tea?" Sharon asked with a grin. Tess nodded.

"Of course." She headed into the kitchen to get her guests' drinks before heading back into the living room to tackle a conversation nearly ten years in the making.

# Chapter Twenty-Three



It didn't take long for Tess to figure out that her mother was only feeding her half-truths. If her years in law enforcement had taught her anything, it was how to tell when someone wasn't being completely honest, and her mother had all the tells.

The three women sat around the living room, Tess making sure to keep the greatest gap she could from her mother. She watched silently from her place in the oversized chair, Otter spread across her lap, as Kathy relayed a watered-down version of her past ten years.

According to Kathy, she'd left her husband, Tommy, and young daughter because she needed to find herself. She'd felt as though she were drowning in a sea of anxiety and turmoil and couldn't bear to see Tommy slowly forget her. Claiming guilt had eventually kicked in, Kathy stated it just made it harder to admit her transgressions and come back home. By that time, she'd heard that Tess had graduated from the police academy with flying colors, and it seemed as though she didn't need her. It was simply easier to stay away.

At some point along the way, Kathy had met her second husband, and then eventually her third. Both of those marriages ended for "various reasons," and when asked which ones, Kathy became flustered.

It was with that revelation that Tess's mounting suspicion of her mother's shady motives went from undercurrents to screaming alarm. Sure, she could understand feeling overwhelmed at seeing her spouse slowly fade away and feeling the need to take a breather. She could understand staying gone so long that it would be awkward to come home, but she didn't even try to reach out or contact Tess in any way.

But *choosing* to stay away? Choosing to remarry, not once, but twice, when you have a family at home that needs you? Unacceptable. Just thinking about it caused Tess's anger to surge.

"So why come back now?" she asked her mother, swallowing her anger before it got the better of her. "Why wait until Dad's dead before you come crawling back?"

Kathy cast her daughter a reproachful look. "You don't have to be so hurtful, Tess, really. I heard that Tommy had passed, and I just wanted to make sure you were okay. Taken care of and all. Help you take care of all the estate stuff. It can be pretty stressful. Overwhelming even. I know because I had to deal with estate stuff when Reggie passed." Reggie was husband number two if Tess remembered correctly. Keeping her true emotions under a professional mask, Tess mulled over her mother's words for a moment.

"So, you're here for money," Tess accused, not hiding the angry bite in her tone. Sharon sat next to Kathy, her head hung in dismay as she listened to the exchange.

"Now Tess, dear—," Kathy began, a patronizing edge in her voice.

"Don't 'Tess dear' me. You left Dad and I high and dry, and now, after he's dead and buried, you're groveling back looking for handouts," Tess growled. "Unbelievable." She shook her head in disbelief and looked away.

"That's not true, I..."

"I'm not selling the house, Mom, and you aren't in the will. Dad left everything to me, which isn't much, given the cost of his care."

"That's good, Tess. I'd hate for you to lose your home," Kathy replied cryptically as she took a sip of her water. She swallowed audibly before turning her face to gaze out the front window at the rain coming down.

It looked gray and dismal out there, just like Tess's mood.

"What the hell does that mean? 'Lose your home'? I've been making the mortgage payments just fine and the deed is in both mine and Dad's name," Tess pointed out, eying her mother suspiciously. If Kathy thought she was going to come here and wreak havoc on Tess's lif,e she had another thing coming.

The news of the deed having been changed into Tess's name seemed to catch Kathy off guard as she sat up straighter. Had Tess not been paying such close attention, she would have missed the quick intake of breath that accompanied the motion altogether. *So, Mom thought she'd swoop in and take my house? Fuck that.*

"I hadn't realized that your father changed the deed and everything." A nervous laugh escaped Kathy's lips. "And here I was so worried that you'd be stuck with a house in my name that you couldn't sell..." She dramatically fluttered her hand through the air as though she were talking about something inane as afternoon tea.

Sharon remained seated at the opposite end of the couch, listening but saying nothing. Tess could tell she was uncomfortable but was glad she was there as a potential mediator nonetheless.

"Don't bullshit me, Mom. When you walked out, filed for divorce.... Things changed around here. I had to grow up quickly and learn all about this kind of stuff. Dad took me down to the bank, we remortgaged the house—which you already know because of the divorce decree. While we were there, he had your name removed from the deed, which legally you'd have to sign and agree to. Dad knew he was getting sicker. When I turned eighteen, he added my name to the deed. He wanted to make sure that I had a home for however long I needed."

"Well, how about his medical bills? How are you handling that?"

"His pension. Since he didn't have a spouse and I'm too old to receive the benefits, it all went towards the estate, i.e., his care. I've had to pay for some myself. Trust me.... It wasn't cheap."

Kathy sat there for a moment, quietly pondering Tess' words. *Looking for a loophole*, Tess thought as she absently rubbed Otter's soft head, her eyes never leaving her mother's face.

As the silence stretched on, to the point of becoming awkward, Sharon finally stood up and stretched, breaking the tension.

"Anyone need a refill?" she asked with forced cheerfulness, holding up her empty glass. Kathy ignored her, staring blindly at a spot on the rug.

Grateful for the diversion, Tess moved to get up, jostling Otter in the process. "Yes, please. Anyone hungry? I can make sandwiches!"

"Oh! Yes, honey! I'll help," Sharon exclaimed, overly eager as she nearly tripped over herself to get to the kitchen, Tess and Otter hot on her heels. Kathy remained quiet on the couch.

"What in the hell is going on here?" Tess whispered to her aunt when they were tucked away in the safety of the kitchen. "Why is she *really* here?"

"Grilled cheese?" Sharon ignored Tess's question as she dug around in the fridge. Tess gave her a halfhearted nod, unwilling to let the subject drop.

"Seriously, Aunt Sharon.... After almost ten years, why did it take Dad dying for her to come creeping back? And how do I make her go away?" Tess made a shooing motion with her hands that caused a grin to cross her aunt's face.

"Dear Tess," sighed the older woman, "My sister is a mystery all of her own. I honestly don't know why she's here but I did try to stop her. I knew this wasn't a good idea."

"Well, you could have at least warned me," grumped Tess as she set about making grilled cheese sandwiches and tomato soup.

"I did try, dear. Multiple times, but you wouldn't answer your phone. You were too busy solving crimes and putting bad guys in jail, huh?" Sharon fondly wrapped her arm around Tess and leaned her head against Tess's bicep. Sharon was on the shorter side and only came up to Tess's chin.

Grinning, Tess laid down her spoon and turned to embrace her aunt. "I'm glad you're here, Aunt Sharon.... Now help me get rid of her," she whispered into her aunt's mess of graying curls.

This elicited a snort from Sharon and caused the two women to giggle. It was going to be a long day, but Tess was glad to have her aunt by her side.

# Chapter Twenty-Four

---



Kathy stayed in a hotel that night, much to Tess's silent delight. Having her mother suddenly show up had thrown Tess off balance and she was only just coming to grips with the fact that her father was gone.

With a sigh, Tess continued looking out into the night from where she sat curled up in her favorite chair next to the window with Otter on her lap. Another light rain had moved in an hour or so before, the droplets pelting out a rhythm on the glass before sliding downward to pool on the windowsill outside.

Tess had tried to read some smut on her Kindle, thinking that would take her mind off of her mother and even the O'Leary case for just a little while, but to no avail. *This is bad if even smut can't get me to check out of reality for a while*, she thought to herself as she finally gave up.

Setting the Kindle on the small wooden table next to her, she picked up her phone to check the time. It was nearly eleven. Aunt Sharon had gone to bed over an hour ago, although the light glow coming from under her door had Tess suspecting that she was also up reading.

About to give up and go to bed herself, Tess shifted slightly, causing Otter to lift his big black head and gaze up at her with large brown eyes. She smiled down at her dog and booped his nose.

"I love you, boy," she cooed. She was awarded with a tail wag. "What are we going to do about Mom, though? She seems to think we have a bunch of money and wants some of it." She made a snort sound, one she knew made Otter excited, and sure enough, he stood up and crawled higher up her lab, excitedly snooting her. She giggled quietly as she rubbed his soft ears, enjoying his full-body wag.

Just then, her cell phone chimed. Glancing at it, she smiled when she saw a text from Denny.

Denny: You awake?

Tess: Yes. Can't sleep. Mom's in town.

Her phone immediately started ringing and she answered it. She petted Otter's warm body as Denny's deep voice filled her ear.

"What do you mean, in town?"

"She just showed up at my door today like the last ten years never happened. Sharon got here a few minutes before, trying to cut her off at the pass, but Mom just waltzed right in like she owned the place. Which is what she wants, by the way."

"She came to take ownership of the house?" Denny asked incredulously. "After ghosting you and your dad for this long, she actually thinks there's something here for her? Incredible."

"My thoughts exactly," Tess sighed, earning a side-eye look from Otter. "I have Aunt Sharon staying with me, but as you know, she's always welcome. I told Mom to go find a hotel. *My* house was full."

"You think she's been waiting for Tommy to die so she could swoop in, or is there something else going on?"

"I don't even know. We didn't make it that far. She thought that Dad left her the house or money of some kind even though in their divorce paperwork, she got some money, and he got the house. Why on Earth she thinks he'd leave it to her after all of this time is beyond me."

"Do you need me to do anything? I can't come over right now, though. Natalie's in bed, but if you need to talk, scream, Facetime wearing that cute little..."

"I am not about to Facetime you wearing that thing when Aunt Sharon is twenty feet away!" Tess whispered in a hoarse giggle, casting a glance at the guest room door. The pale blue scrap of lace that Denny was referring to would *not* be making an appearance tonight.

His warm laugh came across the phone, "I'd rather see it on you in person anyway."

"Sure thing. Just help me get my mom to leave, and I'm all yours," Tess snarked. "What are you and Natalie doing this weekend? I've been so out of the loop with Dad and the funeral ... and now I'm dealing with Mom. I'm not even sure what day it is. I just want to get back to work."

"We don't have any set plans for Saturday, but my sister has been begging for Nat to come spend the night and play with cousins again. You can always come over if you want. We could even stop at that farmers market you mentioned the other day. I'd love to see you again."

"Oh, that sound fun, doesn't it?" Tess smiled, already in a better mood just from talking to Denny. "Well, count me in, barring any movement with the O'Leary case or issues with the Life Giver."

"Life Giver...? Oh, your mom?" Denny laughed, "Does that make you a Womb Goblin?"

"Oh, good lord, Denny," Tess stifled a moan, "These are bad."

"You started it."

"Very true," a smile filled her voice. "Thanks, Den."

"For what?"

"For making me laugh. Getting my mind off of everything here. I really needed it."

"Anytime, sweetheart. Let me know if there is anything else I can do to help. I love you."

"I love you, too." Tess sighed as she finished the call. She might not know how to handle her mother, but she did know one thing: She was totally and irrevocably smitten with Denny Haywood.

# Chapter Twenty-Five



The house was dark except for the random flashes of lightning that lit it up at uneven intervals. *Another damn storm*, thought Kevin, as he lay in bed, wide awake listening to the rain pelt the tin roof of the old farmhouse.

He'd always loved a good thunderstorm, even as a kid. Back before his mom had died and his dad had disappeared—been murdered, he now knew—Kevin would sneak up from his bed and sit at the bedroom window to watch the storms roll in. Sometimes his brother, Brandon, would join him and they would count the seconds in between lightning flashes to see how far away the storm was.

Now, as Kevin lay in his bed alone in an empty old farmhouse, he tried thinking of better times, hoping that he could fall back asleep. The past few days had started taking their toll on him, both emotionally and physically, and he wished he could just stop time. He needed to process things. His father, who he thought had abandoned him all those years ago, had been murdered and left to rot in the cold, hard ground just yards from the farmyard where Kevin worked every day. All those years that Kevin had longed for his father to come home only to learn that he'd never left...

With a sigh, Kevin gave up after a few moments of tossing and turning amongst lightning flashes and rumbling thunder. The rain came down in sheets, pelting the windowpanes and wooden siding, causing a racket.

Deciding on a quick trip to the restroom and maybe a late-night snack, Kevin padded barefoot down the hallway, the wooden floorboards creaking as he went. Rubbing sleep from his eyes, he reached out to flip on the hall light before descending the stairs. He was rewarded with a click. Irritation coursed through him as he realized the electricity was out again due to the storm.

Grumbling to himself, he felt his way along the darkened corridor until he found the bathroom door. Lightning flashed outside, illuminating the small bathroom for a brief second as he made his way to the toilet.

After relieving himself, he skipped flushing due to the electricity being out to the well but opted for a quick hand wash before making his way back out toward the hallway. He was standing at the top of the stairs, debating if he needed a snack badly enough to feel his way around in the shadows of the old house, when a noise caught his attention.

He turned his head to listen intently for any more sounds other than the thunder and rain. After a moment, he was about to head back to bed when he heard it again. A thud.

Coming from downstairs.

Who or what was down there? Thinking he'd imagined the whole thing since he lived alone, Kevin rubbed his temples and then leaned over the banister for one more visual check in the inky darkness below, and that's when he saw it.

A whisper of light was slowly moving from the downstairs hallway into the living room. It was too bright to be a candle, too dim to be a flashlight.

Kevin stood perfectly still, the hair on the back of his neck standing on end as he tried to decide his next move. He was barefoot, standing at the top of the stairs in an old tee shirt and boxers—hardly attire for fighting an animal or intruder.

He thought about his rifle, hidden away in his closet, but knew he'd make a lot of noise if he crept back to the bedroom. As he debated his options, he heard another thud, followed by a scraping sound, and whatever it was made its way closer to the stairs.

Just then, a loud crack of lightning stabbed to the ground just outside the window, the grumble of thunder immediately answering. Kevin jumped at the sudden stimulus and, to his horror, noticed the light moving toward the base of the stairs.

Whoever was down there was coming up the stairs!

He turned, noise be damned, and swiftly made his way back to his bedroom, closing the door and cursing himself for never updating the original knobs. The skeleton keys for the old locks were gone long before he took over the farm.

With only seconds to spare before the intruder found him, alone and in his underwear, Kevin opened the closet door, extracted his rifle, and dumped the box of ammo onto his bed. He loaded the firearm with practiced fingers as the squeak of the nob heralded the intruder's approach.

Turning toward the door, he watched in horror as the knob turned, illuminated by yet another bolt of lightning.

The hair on the back of his neck and arms stood on end as he gripped the weapon with clammy palms. A bullet slipped from his shaking fingers and landed on the floor with a muted thud. Kevin let out a quick breath of relief, for once glad he'd left his dirty jeans in a heap by his bed.

The door knob slipped and Kevin fell to his knees beside the bed, blindly patting around, searching for the dropped bullet.

The room got brighter suddenly, and to Kevin's horror, he realized it wasn't from lightning outside but from the intruder's cell phone light. That was the light he'd seen from the upstairs railing. Not a candle or an actual flashlight, but the small glow of a cell phone flashlight app. But who would be prowling around his house on a night like this? And why? Surely, Kevin had nothing of value. Wracking his brain for anything he could offer the intruder in exchange for his life, he remained hunkered down between the bed and the wall. The rifle only had one bullet in it so far. He'd dropped the other one like an idiot. Cursing his own stupidity, he slowly tried to peer under the bed to locate the intruder.

At first, it was too dark to see anything, just shadows and dust bunnies. Kevin slowly turned his head, searching for signs of his unwanted guests, but saw nothing. It had gone dark again. Had they left, perhaps thinking the room or house was empty? Surely not.

He paused, listening intently for signs of breathing, creaks in the floorboards, anything. All he heard was the rain that continued to fall against the panes of glass and the thunder beyond.

Moments passed, and nothing happened. His leg was beginning to cramp from staying in such an awkward crouch for so long. He tried wiggling his toes, moving his ankle. Anything to aid in circulation, but the cramp wouldn't leave.

Finally, when he could bear it no longer, Kevin slowly stood from his hiding space. As blood began circulating in his lower limbs once again, he kept his eyes sweeping around the darkened bedroom. Where had the nighttime visitor gone? Had he imagined them?

Tentatively, he took a step forward, grabbing two more bullets off of the bed and loading them deftly into the rifle. Racking the firearm, he slowly made his way toward his now-open bedroom door, fully aware that he'd closed the door. Kevin was sure that someone had entered his home and was very likely still lurking somewhere in the shadows. He hadn't been dreaming it after all.

Taking a few calming breaths before heading out to the hallway, he tried to devise a plan. His cell phone was down on the kitchen counter where he'd stupidly left it to charge all night. He had no landline. Kicking himself for his lack of planning, he held his breath for a moment before releasing it slowly. It was now or never.

Just as he was about to step out into the hallway, a shadowy figure moved in front of him to block his path. At the same time, a bolt of lightning illuminated the figure's face, catching Kevin off guard.

"Boo!" they hissed. A sneer spread across their face as they raised something over their head. Seconds later, Kevin O'Leary lay sprawled in a puddle of his own blood, a huge gash across his head.

# Chapter Twenty-Six

*Sunday, September 16th 9:34 AM*

"Look, Sheriff, I know I'm supposed to be out on bereavement, but if I have to stay one more day in that house with my mother...." Tess sighed, dropping into an old leather chair in Malone's office. "Please, just let me back on duty now."

"Are you sure, Tess?" Malone grinned slightly, watching Tess leaning back in her seat to stare at the ceiling. "You could just ask your mother to leave if she's bothering you so much."

"Oh, trust me. I asked her *and* told her. She's not budging." Tess pulled a face at Malone. "She said she isn't leaving until Sharon leaves! But I *like* Aunt Sharon!" Tess growled in frustration. "She didn't want to mother me when I needed her, and I sure as hell don't need her now."

Malone busied himself with some papers on his desk, trying to hide his grin from Tess. He'd never seen her so fired up.

"And I swear," Tess continued her rant, "if she makes one more snide comment about Otter, his hair or his drool, I'm going to let him bite her in the ass."

A laugh finally erupted from the sheriff, "You know that dog doesn't have a mean bone in his body."

"Then maybe *I'll* bite her if it makes her go away," Tess snarked, abruptly sitting forward in her seat, hands on her knees. She sighed heavily, her chin falling to her chest.

"Now, Tess, we can't have our officers going around assaulting family members," Malone jokingly reprimanded. "Seriously though, if you want to come back early, I won't stop you. I just want to make sure you're okay."

"I am, at least as much as can be expected. Of course, I'm going to miss Dad terribly, but at the same time, I'm glad he's at rest," Tess sighed again, standing to her feet. "Besides, I have a bag of bones down at the morgue and a cold case to close."

"Those old bones have waited years for justice, Tess. Another few days or weeks aren't going to change anything."

"True, but the detective in me is always working. And you know, it's what Dad would have done: find the killer, lock them up." A broken smile crossed her face as she willed her tears not to fall.

Malone nodded solemnly, understanding all too well where Tess was coming from. Once a detective, always a detective.

"Stay safe out there, Dane," the sheriff nodded his consent to have her back from bereavement leave early.

"Thank you, sir. I'll let dispatch know I'm back on duty." And with that, Tess turned and left Sheriff Malone's office, softly closing the wooden door behind her.

***

Twenty minutes later, Tess was sitting at her desk, going through work emails that had been unanswered during the past week or so that she'd been out on personal leave. Luckily there wasn't anything overly urgent to deal with but she liked staying on top of things and having a nice clean inbox.

Suddenly, her office phone rang. Malone was on line two.

"Yes, sir?" she greeted, absently clicking 'delete' on an obsolete message.

"Dispatch just got a call. Seems like your guy, Kevin O'Leary, was attacked last night."

"What?" Tess was suddenly all business, her mind going into overdrive. "When? Is he okay?"

"His son found him this morning and called it in. They are taking him to General."

"Good, so he's not dead?"

"Not that I've heard. I was told he was unconscious but that it didn't look good."

"Has anyone talked to the son yet? Checked the scene?" Tess asked, already grabbing her keys.

"No, the call came in just moments ago. We have a patrol officer headed there now. They'll be waiting for you. I'll send Miles to stand guard over O'Leary until we find out what the hell is going on."

"Thanks, Sheriff. I'll head over to the farm now." She disconnected the call and ran out the door.

# Chapter Twenty-Seven



Tess pulled up behind Scafferty's cruiser parked in front of the old O'Leary farmhouse. Another county vehicle sat parked next to a blaze blue Dodge Charger. The morning sun set the porch aglow in a warm golden hue, but Tess knew that the house was anything but warm. Something terrible had happened there last night and she had to find out what.

Climbing the steps to the sagging front porch, just as she'd done just a few days before, she took a deep breath, held it, and then let it out slowly.

Before she'd even knocked on the screen door, she heard Scafferty call to her from the bowels of the house, "Come on in, Dane. We're in the living room."

She entered the darkened home, letting the screen door slam shut with a smack, and made her way to the living room. Breck O'Leary sat slumped over, eyes red and puffy, on the worn couch in the middle of the room. Deputy

Scafferty sat across from him, typing something into his tablet.

Tess could hear movement upstairs and threw a questioning glance at Scafferty. He answered with a shrug.

"Norton is up there with Cooper. CSI is on the way out," he informed her, casting a glance over at Breck, who hadn't moved an inch since Tess's arrival.

"Deputy Scafferty, a word, please." Tess stepped back into the foyer and waited for her coworker to approach. When he appeared, she glanced over his shoulder. Breck still hadn't moved.

"So, what do you know so far?" Tess asked in a hushed tone. "Malone said Kevin was attacked last night, and Breck found him this morning. That's it."

"That's the gist of it, yes," Scaffery concurred. "The kid hasn't said much of anything since we got here. Just kinda catatonic."

Choosing to ignore the fact that Scafferty had referred to Breck as a kid when he was roughly the same age as Tess, she sighed with worry for Kevin.

"How is Mr. O'Leary?" she asked. "Alive, I hope."

"For now, but barely." Scafferty's face was grim. "I got here about thirty seconds before EMS. They took one look at him, and all hell broke loose. I'm sure they tried to keep the scene as clean as possible, but God, what a mess." The two of them looked around at the dusty footprints all over the entryway to the home, and Tess groaned inwardly.

Scafferty muttered something about heading out to look for footprints or signs of entry anywhere around the home's perimeter, and Tess nodded.

"I'll go try to speak with Breck. Hopefully, he'll talk to me," Tess commented, casting another look over at Kevin

O'Leary's son. She nearly jumped when she found him staring right back at her, unblinking.

"Hey, Breck," she greeted him, turning to head back into the living room. "I'm Detective Dane. We all spoke about your grandfather, Garrett, remember?"

"Yes," Breck mumbled, dropping his eyes to the floor again as Tess approached. She slipped into the chair that Scafferty had just been sitting in. "Have you heard anything about my dad?"

"No, not yet," Tess's face softened. "I'm sorry you had to find him like that. Any idea who would want to hurt him?"

"No, not really. Everybody likes Dad, or so I thought," Breck sucked in a ragged breath as his eyes welled up again. "I can't think of anyone who would do... that to him. There was blood everywhere..." The tears started sliding down his face, even though he tried to brush them away with the back of his hand.

"I'm sorry this is hard to discuss, but we need to so that my coworkers and I can catch the guilty party."

Breck slumped for a moment and then, with resolve, sat up, wiped his eyes, and looked at Tess again. "I got here around 8:30 this morning. Dad and I were supposed to go fishing. Normally, he's up and at it by that time, feeding the animals and whatnot. I poked around the barn, looking for him, but he wasn't out there. Didn't answer me when I called him, so I headed inside, calling for him. The house was quiet, almost eerily so. I yelled, but he never answered, and by that point, I was starting to get concerned."

"Concerned how?"

"Well, he's not that old, what... forty-seven? Forty-eight? But still, I was thinking, what if he fell, had a heart attack? That kind of thing. I searched downstairs and then went upstairs. That's... that's when I found him. Layin' in the hallway in a puddle of blood." Breck's voice broke as he relayed the last part, and Tess sympathized with him. She couldn't even imagine finding her father lying on the ground in a puddle of blood.

"Was he breathing? Did you check for a pulse?"

"Yes, he was lying on his back with his head turned to the side, so I had to move his head to look for it. That made the blood start coming again, but yeah, he had a pulse. It was hard to find, but it was there. I think I saw his chest move, too, but that could have been a trick of my eyes. When I felt the pulse though, I called 911 and they told me what to do until y'all showed up.

"Well, I'm sure the doctors and nurses are doing all they can to help your father now. Our CSI team will be here any moment to begin their investigation. Tell me, Breck, did you touch or move anything else while you were upstairs near your father?"

"No, I don't think so. I don't remember. Everything was a blur once I found Dad."

"That's understandable," Tess offered. She sat for a moment, quietly watching as Breck searched his pockets for something. When he eventually pulled out a scrunched up tissue and blew his nose loudly, she looked away, giving him some privacy.

"When was the last time you spoke to your dad?" she asked, watching Breck again. His gray tee shirt had wet spots on it, most likely from wiping at his eyes. The black gym shorts he wore looked like they'd missed the tears… for now.

"Just yesterday."

"And did he mention anything that might be important? Mention anyone giving him grief over something? Someone showing up at the house uninvited?"

"Nah, not really. We just talked about the fishing trip today," Breck shrugged. "Oh, and he mentioned he was going to go to the grocery store. Other than that, it was business as usual, I guess." He leaned back in his seat and crossed his leg over his knee. "I just… I just don't know who coulda done this to him."

"Have you noticed anything missing?" Tess asked, making some notes to herself in her notebook. "Or anything that is here now that shouldn't be?"

When Breck said nothing for a few seconds, she looked up to find him absently picking at his leather flip-flop while looking around the room, deep in thought.

"I don't know," he said eventually, standing then to move about the room and toward the foyer. "I wasn't even looking for stuff like that when I got here. I came into the house looking for my dad. When I found him, he's all I thought about."

Tess stood and followed Breck, making sure that he didn't touch anything. "Hey, because this is a crime scene, I'd like it if you could wear some booties over your shoes. Also, for now, we'll just stand in the doorway of the downstairs rooms and you do a visual check of things, okay? CSI will be here any moment."

As if on cue, Mike Seawell pulled up outside in the black Swain County CSI van and hopped out. Stacie and another CSI, who Tess hadn't met yet, climbed out of the van and approached the house.

"Come on in, Seawell," Tess said as a way of greeting, holding the screen door open for the trio of crime techs to enter the farmhouse.

"We gotta quit meeting this way, Detective," Seawell quipped. Noticing Breck standing behind Tess, he offered a quick nod. He was awarded for his efforts with a sullen look from Breck.

"Deputy Cooper is already upstairs, where Mr. O'Leary was found. I was just about to take Breck, Mr. O'Leary's son, on a quick walk through–visual only, no touchy–to see if anything obvious was missing or left behind." Tess explained. "We are just staying in the front hallway here and peering into the rooms on the first floors. First responders and EMS have already been through the hall so any footprints left by the perp are most likely destroyed."

"Here," Stacie said, offering Breck and Tess each a pair of blue shoe covers. "Put these on."

As Tess and Breck donned the foot coverings, the CSIs began bringing in their gear to start processing the scene. Tess hoped they'd find some answers. Kevin O'Leary seemed to be a nice guy. Could the attack be connected with the murder of Garrett O'Leary? His bones had only just been discovered, and now his son had been assaulted in his own home. Or was it totally coincidental? A random attack that had absolutely nothing to do with the bones found in the mound?

Tess mulled over different scenarios, forming a myriad of questions. She had to get to the bottom of it all— did she now have two cases to solve or just one?

# Chapter
# Twenty-Eight

*Sunday, September 16th, 10:52 AM*

"Okay, Breck. Let's begin in the back of the house." Tess motioned for him to follow her. When he did, she led him down the hall, pausing in the kitchen doorway. "Take a look, please. Is there anything that stands out as unusual to you?"

The large farmhouse kitchen was open and cheery, despite the dark events from the previous night. Sunlight bled through the yellow gingham curtains, illuminating dust motes falling loosely through the air.

The wide-planked wooden floor, though worn, seemed clean and the white cabinets on the wall looked to be original. A bowl of eggs, brown and smooth, sat on the counter, next to a couple of plastic grocery bags. Tess could see the tops of canned soup and a box of cereal sticking out of them. Perhaps Kevin had made it to the grocery after all?

A few dirty dishes filled the sink, as evident from the sound of a fly buzzing around happily. From where Tess stood, it looked like just a skillet, a plate or two, and a cup half-filled with a brown liquid. Nothing exciting.

Next to the back door, tossed haphazardly on a black plastic shoe tray, sat a pair of men's leather work boots, worn and muddy. Above them, a homemade-looking white-washed coat rack with black metal hooks hung on the butter-yellow walls. From one of the hooks hung what appeared to be a man's dark blue raincoat.

The center of the room was dominated by a large oak antique table and six Shaker-style chairs. Though obviously well used, they, like the floor, seemed to be clean and well polished. The table was clear of clutter except for a small stack of mail and a dog-eared Stephen King novel.

Nothing seemed amiss to Tess, but again, she'd never been in the O'Leary's kitchen. She stood silently for a few moments, giving Breck time to survey the room.

After a few moments, Breck shrugged. "Nothing seems outta place. It always kinda looks like this."

"Okay then, let's go look at the dining room," Tess instructed, moving along the wooden-planked corridor to the next room. She could feel Breck shuffling in his shoe booties behind her.

The dining room was just off of the kitchen. Though it appeared to not be used much nowadays, the furniture was well maintained. An antique dining table dominated the room. Surrounded by six matching chairs, the table appeared covered by a white linen table runner, two brass candelabras, and a thin layer of dust. Across the room from where Tess stood, a large brick fireplace took up most of the wall. Above the mantle hung an old oil painting of an elderly couple, possibly a past generation of O'Leary's, Tess surmised.

A sideboard sat against another wall, also topped with a white linen table runner and some kind of statue Tess couldn't discern from where she stood.

She glanced toward Breck and watched as he slowly looked around the dining room for anything out of the ordinary, but from the look of dismay on his face, she wasn't hopeful.

"Anything?"

"Nothing seems out of sorts." Breck shrugged. "We don't use this room much anyway, so even if something was missing, I'm not sure if I'd even notice."

"That's fair," Tess offered. She didn't want to make him feel as though he had to find something. Maybe there wasn't anything to be found. Perhaps Kevin O'Leary had startled the intruder before they'd had a chance to finish their mission. "Let's check that room back there." She pointed to another doorway further down the hall, next to what she assumed was the basement stairway.

"That's Dad's office," Breck supplied as he took the lead. He paused by the basement door and seemed to contemplate opening it to check the stairwell. Pointing to the chain latch, he asked, "Don't suppose somebody would have come up from the basement last night to rob the place only to take the time to latch the door back before hurting Dad, huh?"

"Not likely," Tess agreed, "but we'll have people go down there to check anyway."

Breck nodded solemnly and then pivoted to enter the room that housed his father's home office.

The room was chaotic.

"Holy..." Breck let the comment die on his lips as he looked around the room in despair.

"I'm guessing it doesn't normally look like this?" Tess asked, looking around at the mess. The room was in complete disarray. Had it been ransacked? Or did Kevin prefer his workspace to be like that? She'd known officers who'd worked in worse conditions and didn't seem fazed. Tess, for one, preferred a tidy workspace.

"No, never," Breck answered, his breathing hitched. "Dad keeps it neat and tidy in here. 'Messy space, messy mind' he always says. What *happened* last night?" His voice cracked and he seemed to struggle maintaining his composure. Tess could empathize with him, especially with having lost her father so recently. Luckily, for Breck, his father was still alive. For now.

"Do you see anything missing or left behind? Something that is out of the ordinary?" Tess gently prodded the man next to her. She could feel his anxiety pouring off of him as he began to sweat. His breathing hitched as he frantically stood in the doorway and looked around at what was left of his father's office.

"Oh, god... why is it like this?" he asked, his eyes slowly roaming over the papers and books scattered on the floor. "What were they looking for?"

"Who?" Tess asked, hoping Breck might slip and give her a name amid his obvious stress. He just turned to her, his eyes puffy and red.

"Whoever hurt my dad," he sniped, "Who do you think?"

"I was just double checking that you didn't have any idea who it might be," Tess answered, holding her hands up, palms out. "Maybe something in here triggered a thought or memory..."

"No, I don't know who broke in and hurt Dad, and I don't know what they wanted," Breck snapped. "Look, I'm just really upset by all of this and—" he sighed, letting his thoughts go. Turning away from Tess, he continued to look around the room.

Tess held in a silent breath, not willing to let Breck know his outburst affected her. She understood how he must be feeling about the state of things. To give him time, she surveyed the room, looking for anything obvious.

The office was adorned with floor to ceiling built-in bookcases with yet another large fireplace that was a twin of the one in the dining room. On the wall opposite Tess, a pair of French doors appeared to open out onto a small seating area overlooking the fields and duck pond beyond. Late morning sunlight streamed through the glass doors, giving the room a warm, welcoming feeling had it not been for the ransacked room.

A large antique cherry desk dominated the space, the drawers each pulled out, their contents scattered. From her vantage point, Tess could see the top half of a matching chair laying on its side behind the desk.

On the wall behind the desk hung framed photos of Garrett and Kane as children. Garrett was hard to miss with his bright red hair and huge smile. Another photo showed Kevin laughing while holding a young Breck on his shoulders. A Cincinnati Reds baseball cap was crammed down on Breck's head and his grin revealed he was missing his two front teeth.

"Cute picture," Tess commented, nodding toward the photo. Breck looked in the direction she indicated, smiling when he saw which one she was talking about.

"Yeah, that was my first Reds game," he sighed, losing himself momentarily to the memory. After a beat, he tore his gaze away from the image to continue his search for anything out of the ordinary.

Tess paused when Breck sucked in a breath as he stared over at the bookshelves. She followed his gaze and, not having ever been in the office before, Tess didn't notice anything at first.

"There," Breck indicated, pointing a shaking finger at a glass display case on one of the shelves. The inside of the case was empty except for some dark blue velvet. "They're gone."

"What's gone?" Tess asked, looking back and forth between Breck and the bookshelf. "What was in the case?"

"Artifacts. Dad's collection of Hopewell artifacts," Breck explained shakily as he ran his fingers through his dark hair. "Every last one is gone."

# Chapter Twenty-Nine



"Apparently, there were two stone pipes, some kind of bowl, and a knife with a bone handle," Tess explained to Malone over the Bluetooth in her county vehicle as she headed back to the station. "Oh, and a handful of flint arrowheads. Seawell and his team are processing the scene now."

It had been a long day, processing the upstairs of the old farmhouse where Kevin had been attacked. And then, just about every single member of the O'Leary family either called or stopped by to get more information– or demand justice–once they learned about the intrusion.

Tess stifled a yawn as she took a curve in the road before hitting her blinker to make a turn onto Rt 72 toward Crawley.

"That's it?" Malone's voice floated out of the car's speaker. "Someone killed Kevin O'Leary over some old artifacts?"

"Yes. Wait— what?" Tess jolted out of her stupor. "Kevin didn't make it?" The news hit her harder than she'd expected, like a punch in the gut when she was already down. Familiar tears threatened the back of her eyelids, and she thought, briefly, that she risked conflating her grief for her father with the O'Leary family's devastation. She usually didn't get involved enough with the families she worked with, but for some reason, Kevin O'Leary's attack bothered her. Perhaps it was because she'd only recently lost her father.

"Yeah. About an hour ago," Malone let out a heavy sigh. "I had just gotten off the phone with the hospital when you called. Sorry, I didn't mean to blurt it out; I was just surprised about the 'why' of it all."

"Shit," Tess mumbled, trying not to let her voice give away her feelings. How had this happened? Who would break in and attack Kevin over a few prehistoric relics? "There has to be something that we are missing. A few artifacts like that can't be worth that much... right?"

"I have no idea. But there is also the question of why he was attacked upstairs, but the artifacts were downstairs, right? Didn't you say they were in the office?"

"Yes," Tess agreed, her mind racing. "And the point of entry seemed to be the french doors which were off of the office. They overlook a small deck."

"Was the glass broken? Knob removed? Tool marks?" Malone asked curiously.

"Lock was jimmied," Tess answered, double-checking that her headlights were on as the sun dipped lower in the horizon. The shadows cast by trees flanking the rural road stretched like gnarled fingers from the earth and would soon join the darkening sky.

"Jimmied..." Malone echoed. "And do you think that the attack and the theft are connected or separate?"

"Well, that's the strange part... No," Tess sighed, her beams catching a rabbit scurrying across the roadway into the weeds beyond. "My gut says no, they aren't connected. But, Sheriff, what were the chances that two crimes would occur the same night at the same house during a thunderstorm? It almost sounds... absurd. Right?"

"It does sound a little abnormal, but Tess, your gut has never led you astray yet, has it? Trust it. If something seems off, then something's probably off."

"You're right, Malone," Tess agreed, taking another turn in the road. "I'll try to look at it objectively, like always, but this whole O'Leary case is..." Her voice trailed off.

"I get it, Tess," Malone replied, empathy filling his voice. "You've had a long day. Just go home and get some rest. Looking at it with fresh eyes in the morning may trigger something you missed today."

"Thanks, Sheriff," Tess sighed. "And I'm sorry to hear about Kevin. He seemed like a nice guy."

"I know, Tess. Try to have a nice night," Malone said before disconnecting the call.

Tess pulled into the shoulder of the road, gravel crunching under the tires of the SUV as she fought to control her churning emotions. She put the vehicle into 'park' and sat for a moment, watching insects bounce around in the beams of her headlights. Her vision blurred as tears pooled in her eyes, and she sucked in a breath. It wasn't fair!

She smacked the steering wheel with an angry palm, tears streaking down her face, reveling in the cathartic nature of the repeated motion.

Seconds later, the crackle of her police radio broke the relative silence, jarring Tess from her turmoil. It was a call about a motor vehicle accident, and a deputy responded as en route; it was nothing that concerned her at the moment, but she was grateful for the distraction.

Tess composed herself, taking a deep breath. She leaned over and extracted a napkin from her stash of take-out restaurants leftovers she kept in her glove box. The texture was rough on her nose but made a decent tissue in a pinch.

"Okay, Tess, time to get it together," she consoled herself as she eyed herself in the rear-view mirror. With a glance over her shoulder to check for oncoming traffic, she pulled out onto the roadway and headed home.

# Chapter Thirty



Tess's living room light was on when she pulled up at her house. She still didn't know how she felt about coming home and having a house guest. Aunt Sharon was one thing, but her mother was another. Even with her mother staying in a hotel close by, showing up at Tess's house out of the blue was enough to drive Tess batty.

So far, Tess had been mostly able to avoid speaking with Kathy and when she was forced to interact, Sharon had been there to be a buffer. Tess found herself perpetually surprised at how much anger and resentment she'd built up toward her mother through the years. If she'd been asked how much her mom had hurt her, she'd have said not much, but now that she was forced to confront her feelings, the old wounds she'd thought were long scarred over were erupting, festering things that went much deeper than she'd realized. Grabbing her things, Tess parked the county SUV in the driveway and headed up the front walk to unlock her front door. Through the glass, she could see Otter losing his mind with excitement, a stuffed duck hanging from his mouth.

"Hey, buddy!" Tess exclaimed as she opened the door, and Otter bounded up to her, letting out an excited whine. She knelt and rubbed the dog's ears, peppering his wiggling face with kisses. "I know. I missed you too, bud."

Locking the door behind her, she led Otter into the kitchen.

"I bet you're hungry, huh? I know I am!" she said, pulling the fridge open to survey the contents. Grabbing some lunch meat, mayo, and cheese, she stepped back to shut the door and let out a startled squeal.

"Mom! What the heck are you doing? You can't go sneaking around like that in other people's houses. It's a good way to get shot!" Tess glared at Kathy while pointing to her service weapon still holstered on her hip for emphasis.

"Calm down, Contessa, you're being dramatic," Kathy brushed her off as she slid past her to put an empty cup in the sink. "And I already fed the dog. He really needs to eat less, he's going to get fat."

"He's not fat, thank you. Not that it is any of your business," Tess seethed, slamming the fridge door with so much force a magnet holding a takeout menu fell to the ground. She bent to pick it up so Otter wouldn't swallow it. "However, thank you for feeding him. I'm sure he appreciates it."

"I'm sure he did, sitting here all alone while you're running around for hours at a time. I never know when you're coming home, when to expect you. You're just like your father in that regard, I suppose."

Tess saw red. Flames of anger scalded her cheeks, and she wanted to reach out and throttle the woman who stood before her. She now understood how some women get pushed too far, and then one day, they just snap.

"Let's get a couple of things straight once and for all. First, I do not fucking answer to you, do you understand me? I am twenty-six years old and have pretty much raised myself since you walked out on me– your *child*. Two, yes, I am a cop just like my father, and yes, I work long, unpredictable hours. I will absolutely not apologize for that. I take Otter on a walk or two every day, and he goes to doggy daycare multiple days a week. I also take him to the dog park. He has a doggie door and a large fenced-in yard with water bowls inside and out that I fill multiple times a day. If I'm going to be especially long, I have my neighbor on speed dial, and she comes over and feeds him. Stop. Fucking. Judging. Me!" Tess yelled, her skin hot and her blood pressure rising. "Thirdly, I swear if you call me Contessa one more time I'll arrest your ass for... *something*... just to get rid of you for a while. I hate that name! My name is Tess Dane, for now and always. Either call me that or don't speak to me. Got it?" Her eyes were wild with anger as she glared down at her mother.

Kathy stood frozen at the kitchen entryway, her bottom lip quivering as if she were about to cry but couldn't decide if doing so would be to her advantage.

Tess blew out a long breath, leaning her shoulder against the cool stainless steel of the fridge.

"Why are you here, Mom?" she asked, the fight in her voice gone. "It can't *really* be because you didn't think I couldn't handle the paperwork after Dad passed. And despite the fact that I've made it abundantly clear that I don't *need* you, you're still lurking around Crawley. Just tell me why you're here already."

Kathy remained silent and for a moment Tess thought she wouldn't answer. Then finally, her mother raised her eyes up and looked at her daughter fully.

"I have cancer. And I know that I've screwed up and I deserve all your anger and contempt. I deserve to be kicked out, but I want you to know that I'm sorry. I'm sorry for leaving you when you both needed me the most. I'm sorry for staying away. I'm sorry for not calling you back and making an effort. I need you to see how sorry I am. I can't take back the past, my bad decisions, the lost time; All I have left is the here and now and I'd like to make amends with you. Before it's too late" Two large tears broke free and slid down Kathy's cheeks as she covered her mouth, pivoted, and ran from the room.

Tess stood there alone in her kitchen, her emotions playing havoc on her. She wanted to scream, cry, hit something, and be held all at once.

She wanted her dad.

A sob tore at Tess's throat, but she forced it back, clawing with her restraint to school her emotions. A part of her knew internalizing them would catch up with her eventually in the form of another panic attack. She was completely ignoring her father's death. She knew the situation with the O'Leary case was spiraling. And now, just when she thought she'd had enough to deal with, her absentee mother had pushed into the fray. It was too much at once. She knew Denny would be encouraging her to speak with a professional, someone who could help, instead of keeping everything bottled up, but Tess couldn't see how that would help. She'd never tried therapy except when forced to after the death of Sheriff Burrows. Laying on a stranger's couch and talking about feelings had seemed so foreign to her. It wasn't that she didn't see its value; she'd just never tried it herself.

As she remained standing in front of her fridge, her mouth open in a silent cry as her shoulders shook with emotion. Perhaps she should call someone tomorrow? But for now, she had to remain strong.

If she let herself melt down now, she feared she'd never put herself back together again. Absently, she heard Sharon whisper something to her mom, the front door open and close quietly and the house was silent around her again.

Lost in her thoughts, she leaned back against the cool firmness of the stainless steel fridge and slid down to the floor. She felt lost. Broken. Alone.

Sitting in the quiet for a while, thinking about her life, missing her dad, contemplating what she'd say to her mom, Tess didn't hear the front door open again.

Suddenly, two male hands appeared in her line of sight, jarring her from her dark thoughts. She jumped, the dismal spell she'd been under broken, and she found herself staring up into a pair of familiar dark blue eyes. Waves of concern filled them as they traveled over her face.

The emotional dam broke as she reached out, sobbing, and Denny pulled her up.

His strong arms enveloped her as she cried, anguish wracking her body. Denny ran one hand up and down her spine while the other hand held her head close to his heart. She tried focusing on the steady rhythm as she took solace in his embrace.

They stood like that in the kitchen for a while; she was crying, and he was soothing her, each finding strength in the other's presence.

Tess sniffled, pulling back to wipe her eyes with the cuff of her sleeve when she noticed something different about his appearance.

"Wait, why are you wearing a hoodie? You're always warm. And how did you get in? How did you even know I needed you?" she asked, looking up at Denny's handsome face.

He grinned. "Well, a few reasons. First, I was playing basketball with a couple of guys, and my tee shirt was sweaty, so I took it off. I didn't have anything else with me but this," he pointed to the navy blue hooded sweatshirt he was currently wearing. "Do I know it's September in Ohio and still pretty warm out? Yes. Was I sweaty? Sure, from playing basketball. But it's because I'm *hot* that I had to wear the sweatshirt. I don't think old Mrs. McCrae from next door could handle me walking around here without my shirt." He waggled his eyebrows at Tess, causing her to snort with laughter.

"Thanks," she smiled, her face still red from crying. "I needed that mental picture. I can barely handle you without your shirt, and I'm less than a third her age." She grabbed handfuls of the fleece and pulled him down for a kiss. "I like seeing you in street clothes. You're typically dressed for work. Basketball shorts look nice on you. And so does this hoodie."

Tess stood on her tiptoes to look over his shoulders to the living room beyond.

"She's not here," he said simply. When Tess pulled her confused gaze back to his, he continued, "Your mom. She's not here. Sharon called me about thirty minutes ago and said you needed me and that she and your mom are going to go stay at Kathy's hotel tonight to give you some space. I told Claybourne and the guys I needed to go and just... left. I came here, and luckily, your mom left the door unlocked when she took off."

Something warm and wet bumped into Tess's hand, causing her to startle again as she processed what he'd said. She looked down to find Otter booping her with his nose as though he were checking on her.

She leaned down to scratch his head while she looked up at Denny. "Thanks for coming. I mean it. You didn't have to drop everything, but you did." Her voice cracked again as her words grew thick in her throat.

"Hey, don't ever think like that. I will always drop everything for you. And Natalie, of course. I love you two; you're my family." He reached and tucked a piece of loose dark hair behind her ear. "You don't have to tell me what happened, but if or when you do, I'll be here to listen." He leaned forward and kissed her forehead.

Tess's heart swelled at his endearment, and a warm feeling filled her. *His family*. Denny saw her as part of his family. She felt more tears prickle the backs of her eyelids, but this time, they were happy tears. For so long, it had just been her and her dad against the world, so much like Denny and Natalie.

Now that her father was dead, Tess only had distant relatives, except for Aunt Sharon, and even she was distant in the fact that she lived in Anchorage. To be counted as part of Denny's family meant more to Tess than she thought it would. Being a part of the family meant she'd have the one man she loved for years but was only recently able to admit out loud. She'd get to be an important part of Natalie's life.

"First things first... Where is Natalie?" Tess asked, reaching up to wrap her arms around Denny's neck, savoring the closeness.

"She's spending the night with cousins because there is no school tomorrow. It's so nice having my sister available to help babysit sometimes. Single parenting isn't for the faint of heart," Denny replied, holding Tess close. "Natalie can't spend the night on school nights, and it's not up for debate. During the summers, though, I try to let her stay as much as she wants. She just has so much fun..."

"But you miss her." Tess waited for him to deny it. He didn't. Instead, he just grinned.

"So, you're staying the night, right?" she asked, pulling back to look at him closely.

"If you'll have me," he answered, a wicked grin splitting his face in two.

"I'll have you multiple times tonight if you want but you need to take a shower first, Mr. Hoodie," Tess smirked, even as she watched his expression change from playful to one full of desire.

"Yes, ma'am," Denny nodded, pulling the navy sweatshirt off his muscular frame and flexing a little more than was necessary. "I might need your help, though. You know... washing my back or... other parts." He flexed his bicep and kissed it before pivoting toward the hallway.

Tess barked a laugh, "Well, hurry up then! Get in there. I'm not waiting forever." And she took off down the hall after him, Otter close behind.

As Denny headed for the shower, Tess pondered over her mother's revelation. She didn't quite know how she felt about everything yet: her sudden reappearance in Tess's life, the cancer diagnosis, the plea for reconciliation.

It wasn't something that Tess could take lightly, like deciding where to eat out after a long day at work or what shoes to wear for a date. The choices she made now regarding her mother could either help heal her or break her even further. She needed to decide how much she was willing to risk.

# Chapter Thirty-One



"Hi, Remi," Tess greeted as she walked into the cool, darkened interior of the tiny house that Remi Nightsong called home.

"Hey, Detective, come on in and have a seat." Remi grinned, hanging over the edge of the hand-hewn bannister of the small loft above Tess. "I'll be down in a sec."

"You know you can call me Tess, right?"

"Yeah, yeah. You told me on the phone," Remi acknowledged as she climbed down the ladder from the loft, her long, lean legs making quick work of the rungs. "Old habit, I guess." Hopping off the last rung, she shrugged. "Want a tour of this mansion on wheels first? Most people do."

"I *am* a little curious," Tess admitted, looking around the small house built on a trailer. "How many square feet is this?"

"About 400 square feet, 500 if you count the deck," Remi smiled proudly. "It has all the amenities I need: heat, air conditioning, electricity, water, and best of all: a composting toilet."

"What kind of toilet?" Tess asked, scrunching up her nose in confusion.

"Composting toilet. It separates the… solids from the liquids and turns it into compost. I just empty it as needed, and I don't need to be attached to a sewer system or septic tank."

"Huh," Tess nodded, still mulling the idea over, uncertain if she'd be up to living like that. "What about washing your clothes?"

"I wash them over at Dad's house once a week when I visit. If the weather is nice, I dry them on the line out back," Remi supplied, pointing a thumb over her shoulder.

Tess glanced into the small yet functional kitchen, and Remi continued to show her all the bells and whistles of 'tiny living' before continuing to the loft and then back down the ladder to the small bathroom, home of the infamous composting toilet. Much to Tess's surprise, the toilet looked pretty normal, just more boxy on the bottom and didn't smell like she thought it might.

"See? It's not weird." Remi's smile brightened her sun-kissed face as the duo made their way back to the living area.

"Okay, you're right." Walking over to a cushion on the floor, Tess sat down, folding her long legs in front of her. Remi opted to sit on the short blue love seat opposite the front door. "Now, as I said on the phone, I had some questions about the Adena and Hopewell cultures and about some artifacts that were involved in a case I'm working on."

"The stolen ones?" Remi rolled her eyes with a sigh. Muttering something under her breath, she nodded at

Tess. "I'll tell you what I know, but I'm not so sure it'll help with your case. Didn't you say the dead guy next to the mound was some missing white man? Did you figure out who he was yet?"

"Yes. Garrett O'Leary, a past owner of the farm."

"O'Leary? As in related to the current family?" Remi asked, her eyes round with surprise.

Tess nodded. "He went missing nearly thirty years ago, only for his remains to be found now. I've been digging into the past, trying to figure out who might have wanted him dead. The O'Leary family, for the most part, have been well-loved members of the community. Their dramas have at least managed to stay off the official radar."

"It just seems fishy to me that everything is quiet on the old farm until the bones are found, and now, suddenly, the house is broken into, and the place is robbed. In the days leading to his passing, Kevin reported strange phone calls in the middle of the night. The caller doesn't say anything, just breathes."

"Perv." Remi made a face.

"Yeah." Tess nodded. "And the calls all lead back to a burner phone."

"The same one?"

"Yep."

"The skeleton turned out to be who then? Kevin's father? ...and now Kevin is dead, too?" Remi asked, not bothering to mask her horror.

Tess nodded, "Yeah, and now I'm trying to figure out if the murders are connected or just two random attacks on the same family. Do you know the O'Leary's?"

"A little. I went to school with their kids. Luke was in my freshman biology class." Remi shrugged.

"Breck, Kevin's son, seems pretty torn up about his father's death. The whole family, really." Tess sighed, taking a sip of tea. Remi nodded somberly.

"So, back to the robbery part," Remi changed the subject, her expression thoughtful. "You said nothing was missing except the Adena and Hopewell artifacts that the O'Leary family had?"

"Yes," Tess confirmed. "I'd like to pick your brain, see what you know about the cultures and where someone might try to sell something like that to make a quick buck."

Remi sighed, stretching out her legs on the couch. "The Adena culture was here way before they became known as the Hopewell. It took like 500 years for the Adena culture to slowly transform into what you'd call Hopewell culture. And it wasn't just one tribe of people—it was a large group of people from different cultures, mostly part-time farmers living in villages throughout what is now Ohio, Indiana, Illinois, and Kentucky. Even Tennessee."

"So, where are they today?"

"Back around 500 CE, the Hopewell mound building just... stopped. No more art, no more artifacts. Some historians think that cultural decline is to blame. Maybe war with other tribes? Maybe sickness? Some even speculate that a cosmic airburst did it."

"A what?"

"Comet. The Ohio Valley has an increased concentration and diversity of meteor space dust— you know, fragments of space rocks," Remi paused, holding her hands up and wiggling her fingers around cryptically. "Archaeologists have found it in jewelry, instruments, and even burial gifts in the mounds.

"So you're saying the Hopewell people just... disappeared because they got hit by a comet?" Tess asked incredulously. "Are Mulder and Scully coming to this meeting, too?"

"No," Remi half-heartedly glared at Tess. "The ancestors of the Hopewell are federally recognized tribes that include the Wyandotte like me, Delaware, Kickapoo, Miami, Ottawa, Peoria, Potawatomi, Seneca, Shawnee, and....." She counted off on her fingers. "Oh! And Chippewa!" She grinned at Tess.

"Dang, you sure know your history." Tess was impressed. She couldn't recite her lineage beyond Great Grandpa Dane and his older brother Henry, who'd fought in the trenches together in WWII.

"Someone has to," Remi stated, serious once again. "I pride myself in learning all I can about my people and our past so that we can have a better future and not repeat the mistakes of our ancestors." As she said the last part, she waved her hand between herself and Tess, including her in the decree.

"So... where would someone go to sell artifacts that they'd *found*?" Tess asked, hoping to get some new leads.

"Well, unfortunately there is always going to be someone interested in something like that, huh? A private collector, a museum, maybe? Since they were stolen, I'd check with a private collector first. My dad knows some shady people from his casino days. Want me to ask around? He might even know of somewhere on the dark web where antiquities of that kind could bring in the highest profit. How did the O'Leary's even come across them in the first place?"

"Apparently, the past generations of O'Leary's weren't as respectful of the dead as the current generation is. Kevin claimed that his grandfather, Shamus O'Leary, dug them out of the mound as a teen on a dare. When the farmers market was all the rage back in the day, Shamus would bring the artifacts out and charge people to see them, claiming they had healing powers." Tess rolled her eyes. "At least that's what some of the family mentioned to me."

"Anything for money, eh?" Remi grumped. Mumbling something under her breath, she stood and walked a few feet into her tiny kitchen. "Sweet tea?" she offered, pulling a turquoise pitcher out of the short refrigerator. When Tess nodded, Remi retrieved two glasses and filled them with tea.

"Thank you." Tess accepted the proffered glass as Remi reclaimed her perch on the couch. After swallowing a cool mouthful of the sweet liquid, Tess continued her questioning. "How much do you think the artifacts would even go for? And where would anyone even sell them?"

She got a snort from Remi. The black haired woman looked at Tess for a moment before replying. "It depends really on what you have to sell. I've seen listings on online selling sites for random knife blades, arrowheads... Prices seem to be anywhere from a few dollars on up." She sighed and took another drink. "I heard of one auction, down in Cincinnati, that went for over $160,000! Now, there were like 380 different pieces of artifacts, but still! If you can find a buyer, there is money to be had."

"Who has that many pieces to sell?" Tess asked, eyes wide.

"A collector of antiquities, most likely. Many people are interested—obsessed—with preserving the past for future generations. I'm guessing the items came from a situation like that."

"Well, according to the O'Leary's, they are missing more like ten or twelve artifacts, namely a very distinct knife. Hopefully, that helps with tracking it down," Tess sighed.

"What's so special about it?" Remi asked curiously. She leaned forward in her seat.

"This one has a handle made of bone, painted red with some kind of blue design on it." She pulled up an old photo of the knife on her phone that Jamie O'Leary had emailed her. Remi leaned in to take a look, zooming in with her fingers.

"Hmmm," Remi thought for a moment, "Typically, the artifacts I've seen seem to be plain or are just a blade. I'll keep my eye out for anything like that."

"Thank you, Remi," Tess smiled her appreciation.

# Chapter Thirty-Two



After leaving Remi's tiny house, Tess called Denny to tell him all about the composting toilet and what she'd learned about the missing artifacts and Hopewell and Adena cultures. Although he laughed at her excitement over the composting toilet, he was interested in the Native American history and mentioned taking her and Natalie on a date to the Ohio Historical Society Museum in Columbus. According to Denny they had a large selection of ancient artifacts and displays full of early American history and Tess was interested in learning more.

Tess had just ended the Bluetooth call when another call came through her car's speakers. As she took a turn in the road headed back to the office, she answered the call.

"Detective Dane," she greeted as she glanced in the rearview mirror.

"Con– I mean, Tess…" Kathy's voice filled the SUV. Tess felt her mood instantly sour.

"Yes, Mom? What do you need? I'm on duty and can't stay on the phone," Tess sighed inwardly. It was a total lie, of course. She was driving, and as long as a work call didn't come through…

"I'm sorry about last night," Kathy sighed. "I shouldn't have blurted out what I did, and I shouldn't have left you like that."

"No, you shouldn't have, but I'm used to it," Tess said, a slight bite in her voice. "Denny came over and took care of me." She didn't add how he took care of her; she and her mom didn't have that kind of relationship. But as Tess thought back to the multiple times that Denny had 'taken care' of her last night, it was enough to bring a smile to her face even though she was speaking on the phone to the woman who caused all the grief in the first place...

"Good. That's good, Tess. I'm glad he was there," Kathy rambled. "Look, I... I just wanted to let you know that after the way things went last night with you and I... Well, maybe I should just move on. Maybe I should just rent a place somewhere warm for the next few months and be done. You have your life and, if I'm being honest, you seem like you're happy and doing well for yourself."

"Mom, do you even have anywhere to go? What about your house in Florida?" Tess sighed, her shoulders and neck tensing. If she continued at this rate, she'd have a migraine by lunchtime.

There was silence on the other end of the phone.

"You lost it, didn't you?" Tess asked, smacking the steering wheel.

"Tess..."

"Look, where are you now?

"I just got to your house. Sharon and I are meeting up to go thrifting."

"Fine. Listen, we'll talk about this more tonight when I get home, okay? I'm following up on some leads to a case I'm working on, or I'd come home now."

"Okay, Tess, I'll wait for you," Kathy answered before disconnecting the call.

Tess stared out the windshield as she entered Crawley, her mind going a million miles a minute. She couldn't– wouldn't– let her mom move in with her... would she? No.

She gripped the steering wheel harder than she needed to, her knuckles blanching, as she turned into the Swain County Sheriff's Department parking lot, a pit forming in her already knotted stomach as dread consumed her.

One way or another, she was going to have to deal with her mother, once and for all.

# Chapter Thirty-Three

*Monday, September 17th, 5:38 PM*

"So this is the way I see it, Mom," Tess said, wanting to storm off to her bedroom like an angsty teenager. "You've admitted that you have nowhere to go, you've lost your house, and now you're drowning in medical bills. Is that the gist of it?"

The three women, and Otter, once again found themselves camped out in Tess's living room having a tense conversation about Kathy's future. It had taken Tess some finagling but she'd finally been able to pry enough of the truth from her mother to get an idea of what was going on.

Kathy Dane-Humpheries, who'd claimed her third husband was an oil tycoon who own a beachside mansion and yacht in Florida had been full of shit. All of it had been embellished. In truth, Greg Humpheries operated a Texaco franchise in Florida and owned a late model bass boat he liked to take out in the Gulf on weekends. That was where he met his latest girlfriend, Tiffani, who was four years younger than Tess.

Needless to say, he'd kicked Kathy out of their two-bedroom, single-bath home bordering a swamp and filed for divorce. He'd never let Kathy put her name on anything important, like the bank accounts or deed, so she was pretty much up Shit Creek. He didn't seem to care that she'd been diagnosed with liver cancer either.

Greg sounded like a real winner.

"Yeah, that pretty much sums it up, Tess," Kathy said glumly. "Thanks for painting my life so beautifully."

"You picked the paints. Don't get upset how they land on the canvas."

Kathy stared at her sullenly and then grabbed another tissue and began dabbing at her eyes.

"Well, my plane leaves in a few days, guys," Sharon piped up from her quiet corner of the room. "I'd like to help as much as I can before I fly back to Anchorage. We can sit here and throw barbs at each other all day, or we can actually be productive." She gave Tess a reproachful look. "My offer still stands for you to come up to Alaska, Kathy, you know... if things don't work out down here for you."

"Thanks, sister, but I really would rather not get eaten by a bear. Besides, it's much too cold there," Kathy said with a sniff. Sharon rolled her eyes and muttered something about bears running from Kathy.

Tess stifled a grin at Sharon's snarky comment but caught her mother's dour gaze.

Tess sighed, "Okay, fine. Mom, where do you want to be? Florida? Zimbabwe? Oklahoma? London? Like... tell me what you want and then we can work on figuring out... I don't know... Life."

"Here."

"Here?" Tess asked. "Like Ohio? Crawley?"

"Here in Swain County," Kathy sighed. "I'm not asking to live with you, mostly because we'd just fight all the time and because you'd say no. But I would like to find somewhere of my own. Maybe a small house to rent, or an apartment. Sure, I'm sick, but I can still work." She looked down at her hands, folded in her lap. "Like I've told you before, Tess, I've made some mistakes in my life. Bad ones. But I'm trying to change that now, before it's too late. I... I want to be a part of your life if you'll let me. Sharon told me about Denny. Even showed me his picture. Darn, Tess.... He's a looker! I can't wait to meet him."

Tess felt herself grin despite the tears sliding down her face. Even Aunt Sharon let out a wet-sounding giggle.

"Anyway, I want to know you. Be a part of your life," Kathy nearly whispered, her voice full of emotion. "Do you think that's something we could do?"

"And you're sure this isn't just because you don't have anywhere else to go except Alaska?" Tess asked, wanting to accept her mother's apology but still extremely apprehensive.

"She's been talking about this for a while, Tess," Sharon piped up again. "Even before Tiffani bounced into the picture."

Tess turned and looked at her mom for confirmation. Kathy looked her directly in the eye and nodded. "It's true. Every word."

Tess wondered if she could trust her mother after all these years. There had been so much betrayal. Tess had been hurt, shattered beyond what any child should ever go through. But she was an adult now, who could think logically and empathize somewhat with the woman Kathy once was and who she'd turned into.

Maybe this was the new beginning Tess had hoped for all those years ago after nights of longing for her mother, crying into her pillow in the shadows of her bedroom, feeling lost and alone. Tess's teenage years had been tumultuous. She'd longed for a day when her mother would come home to be with her, to *choose* her, once and for all.

After a moment of hesitation, Tess sighed. "Okay, but here are the rules: You can stay in the guest room after Sharon leaves until we find you a rental. You do not boss me around or call me Contessa. You do not call my dog fat. You clean up after yourself. Also, I can amend this list at any time as needed. Agreed?"

"Thank you, Tess," Kathy gushed, jumping up to throw her arms around Tess for the first time in over a decade. The sudden show of affection caught Tess off guard, but the feeling of her mother's embrace seemed to shift something deep inside her. It felt like healing.

# Chapter Thirty-Four

*Tuesday, September 18th, 1:30 PM*

The sun beat down on Remi Nightsong's head as she pulled her basket of dirty laundry from the backseat of her beat-up Chevy and shut the car door with her hip. Before making it even two feet from her vehicle, she was assaulted by her father's trio of mixed-breed dogs.

"Hi, boys," she greeted them as she walked across the yard to her father's log cabin. Between the dog's snorting, barking, and prancing, she barely heard her father's voice as she approached the front porch.

"How is my beautiful daughter today?" he asked, stepping off the porch to take the clothes basket from Remi. Setting it on the patio table near the sliding glass door of his house, he watched as Remi reached into the fray of dog flesh to greet them. This only caused the level of canine sounds to amplify.

"I'm well, Dad," Remi offered over the barking and panting of the dogs. "How are you doing?" She stood then and headed toward her father, leaving the dogs to get over their excitement in favor of the shady area under a large live oak near the house.

"I'm great. Balanced and well, and now you are here!" Gordon Nightsong smiled, his arms enveloping his only child. After a moment, he pulled back and looked in her face. "Come. I have a surprise for you. Go do your laundry, and I'll get it."

Intrigued, Remi grabbed her dirty clothes from the table and followed her father into the cabin. While he moved about the kitchen, Remi ducked into the laundry room to start a load before returning.

"Ta-da!" he grinned mischievously, holding a plate of chocolate No-Bake cookies, Remi's favorite. "Eat as many as you want, I have a whole container for you to take home."

Remi let out an excited squeal before selecting a cookie and taking a large bite. She closed her eyes as the chocolatey peanut butter taste coated her mouth. It was pure ecstasy. Gordon laughed at her exaggerated reaction.

Once a casino mogul out West, Gordon Nightsong was now a self-proclaimed self-help guru who loved cooking and baking. He spent his days trying new recipes and using Remi as his test tester. He claimed he was writing a cookbook and, based on Remi's responses to his recipes, his own recipes would fill the pages. Chocolate No-Bakes, however, were Remi's favorite, and he made them for her from time to time.

"Have you heard any updates about that skeleton they found out on the O'Leary farm?" Gordon asked as he poured Remi a glass of milk. He slid the glass across the granite countertop toward Remi as she swallowed the last bite of her cookie.

"Nothing that hasn't been on the news." Remi tipped the glass to her lips and took a long drink.

"I thought you said you were going to meet with the detective?" Gordon asked, shoving the gallon of milk back into the fridge.

"Oh, I did. She just had some questions about the Hopewell and Adena people."

"Ah, so you showed her how smart you are?" Gordon grinned. Remi rolled her eyes.

"Sure, Dad, that was it," she smirked. "I talked her ear off about history, artifacts, myths, and legends. Oh, and she liked my composting toilet."

Gordon barked out a laugh. "I bet you're the talk of the sheriff's department now!"

"Oh, great," Remi replied deadpan.

*** 

The clothes were still warm from the dryer as Remi dumped them into her basket to fold on the couch before they wrinkled. Gordon was outside, still talking to one of the dogs. His soft voice made Remi smile. Ever since her mother had died, her father had been alone, except for his dogs, which he treated like family.

Remi thought of her mother now, as she folded a purple tee shirt from last summer's pow-wow. As she thought about all the fun they had that day, her dark-eyed gaze roamed over her father's living room. Family portraits of the three of them hung on the walls and various shelves throughout the cozy space.

She pulled a pair of denim shorts out of the basket to fold when one photo in particular caught her eye. She walked over to the frame and leaned in to get a better look at her mother's smiling face.

The picture showed a rare summer vacation to Myrtle Beach when Remi was around nine or ten years old. The three Nightsongs all stood on the beach, seafoam swirling around their ankles, as the waning sun streaked the sky in pinks and oranges. The photo had captured Remi and her mother mid-laugh, and as Gordon looked on, a wide smile spread across his face. Looking at the memory, Remi was thankful for the random beachgoer who had stopped to ask if they'd like their photo taken.

Turning back to the pile of laundry on the couch, something caught her eye that she hadn't noticed before, and she paused, her heart racing in her chest.

There, up on a shelf over her father's recliner, where he kept some of his artifacts and family heirlooms, sat a new acquisition. A knife with a bone handle, painted red, with some kind of blue design on it. She'd only heard of a knife like that one other time.

It was the perfect fit for Detective Dane's description of the missing artifact from the break-in at the O'Leary Farm.

# Chapter Thirty-Five

*Tuesday, September 18th, 4:03 PM*

"I can't take it, Denny," Tess whined, dramatically flopping down next to him on the wooden bench. Natalie played a few yards away on a new play structure that the local metro park had recently opened. Being the newest attraction to the area, the play structure was currently crawling with children.

Despite the bright sunlight, the cloudless cerulean sky, and the squeals of laughter coming from the playground, Tess was still in a sour mood. When Denny had found out about her dismal outlook for the day, he'd invited her to join him and Natalie at the park that was conveniently located halfway between their houses.

"Hello to you too, Sunshine," he flashed her a bright smile. She knew his eyes were sparkling with mischief even though they were hidden behind his sunglasses. "What can't you take, my love?" He held out a bottle of water as a peace offering when she glared at him.

"Trying to figure out my life with Mom. I have a case that is so cold it's frozen. And now I have a new murder case involving the same family and a bunch of stolen Hopewell artifacts. I don't know if you're going to lose your job, and I just want my Dad back," Tess cried, pulling her legs up and burying her head between her knees. As quiet tears slid down her cheeks, she felt Denny reach over and pull her into his embrace.

"Shhh... I'm here for you, babe," he murmured against her temple. "How can I help? Want to talk through the case? We can work through it tonight if you want. I'll drop Natalie at Steph's house, and you can come over to my place if you feel like it, and we can work the cases out. Bounce ideas around. Bring Otter, he'll love it."

Tess sat up, wiping at her eyes and sniffling. Embarrassed that she had just lost her shit, especially in front of Denny, she tried to get a hold of her emotions but struggled.

"I'm sorry."

"For what?" Concern filled his voice as he reached over to smooth out her long ponytail.

"For being... so emotional. I'm not normally like that, and it's... weird." Tess let out a small wet laugh and a sniffle. "Hell... stress, life... the job... I even had a panic attack. That was new." She scrubbed a hand down her face in frustration. She was quiet for a moment before finally admitting aloud, "I'm thinking about going to talk to someone, like you suggested."

"I think that'll be good for you if you find the right person. When I was struggling and finally decided to talk about things, I tried two or three therapists before finding 'my person.' It's okay to seek help and try different people. It's worth it in the end."

Tess nodded slowly, absorbing his words. She knew he was right; she did need to talk to a professional. A lot was going on in her life, and if left unchecked, she'd only be hurting herself and those she loved.

"Hey, Tess?"

"Yeah?" She finally looked over at Denny's concerned face, his dark blue eyes watching her intently.

"You're human," he stated simply. "It's okay to feel things. To get upset, angry, horny, happy…"

"Did you say horny?" she grinned at him, her cheeks still pink from crying.

"Yep," Denny nodded seriously. "It's okay to see a man sitting on a park bench, watching his kid play, and just want to ravish him. Those feelings are totally normal."

Tess let out a snort. She nudged him with her elbow and grinned.

"You're ridiculous," she smiled, leaning in to give him a gentle kiss.

"You're my life," he grinned before pressing his lips to hers.

"Ewww!" came a young voice, causing Tess and Denny to pull back. Natalie stood in front of them with an amused look on her face, arms crossed over her chest, foot tapping the asphalt path encircling the mulched playground.

"Ewww?" Tess asked, feigning disbelief. "Come 'ere, twerp!" Natalie squealed as Tess let out a laugh and lunged at her. Scooping up the nine-year-old, Tess gave her a big hug. "How ya been, kiddo?"

"Good. Putting up with him," Natalie thumbed over her shoulder at her dad, an ornery grin spreading across her face. "I don't know what you see in him. I mean, he snores and sometimes…." she leaned up to whisper into Tess's ear, "he farts. Super gross."

Tess burst out laughing and squeezed the girl again before putting her back on the ground.

"What did you tell her?" Denny asked, eyeing Natalie's widening grin with suspicion.

"Ain't telling," she called over her shoulder as she ran back to the playground.

"Wait... what did she just tell you?" Denny asked, sounding mildly concerned. Tess shrugged, feigning innocence. She was having too much fun watching him squirm, wondering what Natalie had said.

# Chapter Thirty-Six

*Tuesday, September 18th, 6:30 PM*

Tess pulled up to Denny's ranch-style house, which was nestled in an older neighborhood on the Swain County line, with Otter in tow.

He'd lived in the same house since he'd married his now-deceased wife, Cassidy, who passed away from lymphoma. At the time, Natalie was only around two so Denny had thought moving right after losing her mom would have been too much for the toddler. Now, as a young girl, Natalie was thriving, seeming to be content living wherever her dad was.

Tess parked her Jeep and began making her way up the front walk to the porch. The dark blue door opened before her and Otter dashed forward to greet Denny first. The black Labrador was wagging his tail so aggressively his whole lythe body seemed to join in, his four paws prancing on the porch in excitement.

"Hey, babe, perfect timing," Denny greeted Tess, wrapping his arms around her as she approached. She nestled into his embrace, finally feeling the stress of the past few days slip away.

"Hey yourself. Sure smells good in there," Tess sighed, breathing in the aromatic scent of Denny's cooking wafting from the open doorway. Otter also caught the scent and followed his nose inside as though he lived there.

"Sorry, my dog is feral," Tess apologized, pulling out of Denny's embrace to go find him before he got into trouble. "Come here, Otter!"

She could hear Denny's laughter behind her as she slipped into the house to track Otter down before he cleared the counters. She found the dog sitting on a rug in front of the kitchen sink, snout in the air, sniffing the scent of something Italian baking in the oven.

"Otter, get over here," Tess laughed, mouth watering at the wonderful smell emanating from the oven. She looked over at Denny as he entered the kitchen behind her. "Please tell me that is the baked Ziti stuff you made a while ago that I couldn't get enough of..."

"Yep, and garlic bread, too." Denny smiled, walking over to crack the oven open. A deep throated murmur escaped his lips as he checked the contents. "I hope you're hungry. Looks like there are about five more minutes left."

"I'm hungry, and now that I know you made your ziti recipe!" Tess did a happy dance, causing Denny to shake his head, a smile spreading across his handsome face. Otter popped up at the excitement, his tail wagging side to side like a metronome.

A few moments later, plates heaped high with twice-baked ziti and garlic bread, Denny and Tess sat at the kitchen table, chatting as their food cooled. Denny had also made a small side salad, complete with homemade croutons. Otter lay at their feet, chewing on a Nylabone that Denny had bought him.

"This is exactly what I needed," Tess commented in between bites. "Thank you for cooking for me. It's so much better than take-out." She sighed, closing her eyes and enjoying her meal.

"I figured it's been a while since I made it, and I knew you could use a pick-me-up." Denny smiled before taking a bite of salad. "How are you doing, Tess? For real? I know that earlier, you were upset about a lot of different things, and I totally get that. If you want to talk about it, I'll listen."

"I'm doing okay with things, I guess. It's just... I really miss my dad." Tess did her best to hold the tears at bay. The legs of Denny's chair screeched as he dragged himself across the slate tile to come to her side.

He pulled her into a wordless embrace. Tess went willingly, clinging to him as though her life depended on it. As quiet tears slid down her cheeks, Denny patiently waited, gently rubbing small circles across her spine, even as his home cooking cooled.

Eventually, her tears subsided and turned to hiccups, causing Tess to let out a small, broken laugh.

"I don't know what's more embarrassing. Snotting on you for a second time or having these hiccups," she mumbled, looking around for a tissue or napkin to wipe her nose.

"Tess, never be embarrassed in front of me. I love you no matter what." Denny bent down and kissed the crown of her head. "Go clean yourself up, and I'll warm the food back up."

She looked up at him, her blue eyes red and swollen from crying. "Thank you. For listening and giving me a safe place to land," she sniffled.

He lifted her chin until she met his gaze. "Anytime," he assured her softly.

***

One trip to the bathroom and a freakout later, Tess managed to get herself back together. As she'd feared, her face was red and splotchy, and her makeup, though minimal, had run, causing her to look like she'd done a round or two with an MMA fighter.

Giving up all pretense of being cute for Denny, Tess washed her tragic face off, ran her fingers through her long dark hair before pulling it back into a ponytail, and gave herself one more glance in the mirror before she left the bathroom.

She found Denny setting their reheated plates back on the kitchen table.

"Ah, perfect timing." Denny smiled as she slunk back to her seat. She gave him a grateful look and sat down. Picking up her fork, she sampled a bite of the ziti, not bothering to stifle her moan.

"God, this is good!" Communication ceased as they dove into their meal, Tess reveling in the savory pasta and buttery bread as Otter happily chewed on his bone at their feet.

They eventually chatted about their week, carefully avoiding discussing work and the elephant in the room. Tess was avoiding talking about her recent outward displays of emotions. She was usually one to keep a stoic face out in public and let her emotions out behind closed doors. Perhaps it was from years in law enforcement? Or maybe from trying to remain strong for her father for so long? Tess wasn't entirely sure, but what she did know was that the trifecta of her father's death, her mother's reappearance, and the O'Leary case were wrecking her emotionally. Maybe she should have taken the time off that Malone had offered after all. She pushed the thought away instantly; there wasn't time for that. The O'Leary family needed her, and at the moment, she needed them because dealing with the emotional baggage of her parents right now was too much. She welcomed the distraction of solving the case, even if it was bad for her mental health.

Tess finished her dinner and leaned back in her chair, a look of contentment crossing her face.

"So... about earlier, at the park," she began, watching as Denny continued to eat his ziti. He nodded at her to continue. "Like I said, I... I have been feeling overwhelmed. With losing Dad. With my mom showing up out of nowhere uninvited..." She paused, absently playing with her empty fork. "And this case... I've got a cold case with skeletal remains, and now a new murder, all involving the same family. Coincidence? I don't think so."

They sat in silence for a few moments, her thinking about the case, him silently chewing. When he was done, he shoved his plate away a few inches and leaned forward.

"I have something I want to show you. It might help you see things differently, catch something you didn't notice before," Denny said. He stood to collect their dirty dishes, depositing them in the sink before motioning for Tess to follow him.

"Where are we going? Your top-secret crime-solving lair?" Tess joked as they walked down the hallway, Otter tagging along behind.

"Shhh. Don't tell anyone," Denny threw her a grin as he paused at the doorway to his home office. "I do have some crime-solving... *tools*... in here." He paused in front of the closet, suddenly seeming to be a little unsure of himself. Then he winked at Tess and grasped the door knob to pull it open.

"Please tell me you don't *actually* have a murder board in your closet," Tess smirked.

"You don't?" Denny asked innocently, although Tess caught a glimmer of amusement in his eye.

"How very... serial killer-esque of you," she squinted at him. "And no, I do not have a murder board hidden at my house somewhere. Let me guess, you also have the red–"

She paused as Denny pulled out a ball of red string and smiled like a cat that had just caught a canary.

"Wow... Now I can say I've seen it all," she laughed, reaching out to snatch the ball of cotton string. "Is this how the great Denny Haywood works his cases and solves the crimes?"

"Hey, don't knock it until you've tried it," Denny mocked playfully. "Sometimes, when I'm struggling with a case and can't seem to think things through, I'll make copies of the file for myself so I can make my 'murder board', as you call it. Then I can focus on it here at home in the quiet after Natalie's gone to bed. It really seems to help." He watched Tess quietly for a moment as she considered his words. "Wanna try it?"

"Sure, bring it out here," Tess said after a moment of indecision.

Delighted, Denny pulled the corkboard from the closet and set it up on an easel in the middle of the office. Tess gathered up her case file from the living room and followed

Otter back to the office. The dog took no time to find a comfortable spot to curl up and take a nap while Tess began flipping through her file.

"Okay, let's see...where to start...," she mumbled to herself as she sat on the floor with her legs crossed, the file opened on the carpet in front of her.

"I'd start at the beginning," Denny shrugged, puffing out his chest and strutting around the small office like a know-it-all.

"Noted." A slow smile crept across her face. Denny let out a puff of air he'd been holding and stifled a laugh. "You're ornery tonight, Den. Okay, let's start with the facts that we know for sure."

"Ornery and horney." Denny leaned in to whisper to Otter loud enough for Tess to hear. Otter thumped his tail, grateful for the attention.

"Denny!" Tess laughed, swatting at him with part of the case file. "Help me with this and then you can do whatever you want to me."

A wicked grin slid across his face, igniting a hungry glint in his eyes. Leaning in close, their noses almost touching, he whispered, "Deal. The butler did it, in the pantry, with the rolling pen. Now you're mine."

"Not so fast, Casanova." Tess pushed him back with a gentle hand, even though everything in her wanted to drag him closer. "If we take the road you're suggesting, I'll never get this case solved."

Denny let out a frustrated sigh. "Okay, okay... Let's do this, then. Whatcha got?"

"We have skeletal remains found buried next to the Hopewell burial mound on the O'Leary farm," Tess announced, holding up a photo of the mound in question.

"And you're sure it's not an indigenous person from back in the day?" Denny asked, looking at the photo. When Tess said nothing, he turned and looked at her, only to find her glaring at him.

"Oh, gee! By gosh, why didn't I think to have that checked out?" Sarcasm dripped from her every word. "Of course, Denny, don't be a dick. That was the first thing I did." She shook her head, irritated at him suddenly even though she knew he probably didn't mean it the way it came out.

"Sorry, I didn't mean it like that–"

"I know, and I'm sorry for snapping." Tess sighed. "I sent the bones with Dr. Summers, and she contacted the anthropologist at OSU."

"Ohh! Brezdika?" Denny grinned, seeming to have already forgiven her harsh reaction. Tess nodded.

"She did her exam, gave me a general idea of age, height, that type of thing. With that information, I ran a missing person search and came across a cold case from nearly three decades ago, and that guy just happens to have the same last name as the family that currently owns the land the bones were found on. Coincidence? I think not."

"Hmmm... interesting," Denny confirmed, rubbing his chin in thought.

"And yes, before you ask, I did send out a DNA sample for testing, but the results won't be back for a while, of course. There is also the issue of the dental work done on the mandible. There were dental implants on the left side of the dental arcade. We couldn't find a serial number on it, and unfortunately it's been so long that old Doc Beeson has been retired and sitting on the beach for the past fifteen years. A lot of his old patient's dental records were destroyed in a flood long ago."

"Don't doctors and dentists have to keep medical records indefinitely?"

"Nope. Depending on the state or the type of records, it can range anywhere from six to ten years. Besides, Doc Beeson never had digital records, and I found a report about a flood in the office. Most of his records were destroyed. I looked through the remaining medical records in the basement at the dental clinic, and with the current Dr. Beeson, old Doc Beeson's son, we determined that the victim was not among the files. *However*, Kevin O'Leary was able to give me old medical and dental records of his fathers, and I was able to match the dental radiographs with those of the Burial Mound John Doe." Tess shrugged. "At this point, until I hear back about the DNA results, I'm working under the assumption that the skeleton in the mound is Garrett O'Leary. He was found on family land; he hasn't been seen in nearly thirty years, he matches the profile of the skeletal remains, and his dental X-rays match those of the victim." She held her hand up and counted off her fingers.

"Sounds logical," Denny shrugged. "Okay, so we have Garrett O'Leary, AKA Mr. Bones, or as you called him, Burial Mound John Doe." He picked up a pad of Post-it notes, drew a crude skull on it that made Tess roll her eyes, and wrote 'Garrett O'Leary?' on it before thumb tacking it to the Murder Board.

"Nice art," Tess mused. She watched as Denny pulled out another Post-it and made a crude drawing of a man in a straw hat.

"And that is?" Tess asked, watching him intently.

"The guy that found the body. What was his name again?"

"Kevin O'Leary, Garrett's son," Tess answered. She waited as Denny filled in the name and then hung it under the drawing of Garrett.

"Who else are the players?" Denny asked, pen poised over another Post-it. Tess shook her head and smirked.

"You're ridiculous. Kane O'Leary, Garrett's brother," Tess offered.

"Distinguishing features?" Denny asked. "You know, like the farmer hat."

"Kane looks like Santa and lives in a wheelchair...?" Tess offered, unsure of where this little exercise was going. She found out moments later when Denny slid another crude drawing of a Santa in a wheelchair onto the Murder Board next to Garrett.

"You're enjoying this, aren't you?"

"Very much. Who's next?" Denny grinned, watching Tess.

"There is Jamie O'Leary, Kane's son. Then there's Jamie's kids, Courtney and Luke... Oh, Jamie's wife's name is Lori. And then there is Kevin, Marissa, and Brandon who are all Garrett's children, but Brandon is deceased. Kevin has a son, Breck. Marissa doesn't have any children." Tess stopped to take a breath and caught Denny staring at her. "What?"

"What do you mean, what? You just rattled off these people's whole family trees like it was nothing. How did you even keep that straight?" Denny asked in awe. Tess just shrugged.

"I don't know. Kane and Garrett's parents were Shamus and Lenore O'Leary but I don't think that is important, but maybe."

"The brain on you, Tess. It never ceases to amaze me," he shook his head as he quickly made more Post-it note people and wrote down names with Tess's help. Soon, the Murder Board started looking more like a genealogy research project than that of a murder case.

"Phew... Okay. So now we have a list of possible players because, as we know from research, most people are murdered by people close to them." Denny commented, stepping back to look at his work, inspecting each drawing as though his creation held the key to the case.

He turned to Tess. "Anyone else?" he asked, a pad of sticky notes at the ready.

"There were a few people interviewed at the time, although I don't know if I'd call them suspects..." her voice trailed off as she thought through the list of potential threats.

"Names?" Denny wiggled his pen in anticipation. Tess rolled her eyes at his eagerness.

"Kenny Novak, Fred Krinsel, and Sid Miliron. All were interviewed the night Garrett was last seen. Novak and Krinsel were close friends of O'Leary. Miliron was the bartender. I haven't been able to track him down yet, though."

"You've re-interviewed Krinsel and Novak?" Denny asked, glancing down at the file spread out around Tess. She nodded, her dark ponytail sliding forward over her shoulder as she leaned to reach a printout.

"Here is a copy of the original interview from both men, along with the notes and transcript from my interview with them," Tess offered, handing the files to Denny to peruse. "They basically say the same thing. Even after nearly thirty years, both men's stories are the same: They went out to a new strip club in town, had some drinks, hung out, and Garrett left alone in his truck. He seemed fine. No one has seen him since." She shrugged.

"Someone's lying," Denny said. "Or, at least, not being completely honest. Someone knows something from that night that they either aren't telling you or don't even know that they know. Something important that they saw, heard, whatever, but they didn't think it was worth mentioning." He paused to skim the interviews.

Tess rubbed Otter's belly while Denny read the documents, her mind thinking through everything she knew, or thought she knew, about the case, which wasn't much.

"It sounds like the brother sure had mommy issues, huh?" Denny asked, holding up Kane's interview. Tess quirked her eyebrow and nodded.

"He isn't the only one," she snarked. "I understand his pain." She leaned forward and flipped through various pages of Kevin O'Leary's file. "And now, if that's not enough, I've got Garrett's son, Kevin, to worry about. The poor guy was attacked and murdered in his home. The only motive I have so far is the theft of some Hopewell artifacts. It just seems strange that Garrett and Kevin were both murdered over some artifacts, right?" She held up a photograph of the empty display cases strewn about Kevin's bookshelf.

"People kill others for all kinds of reasons. I've read about cases where people got their throats slit just for giving someone the side-eye," Denny replied. "I mean, it could all be about some old artifacts, but why now? Why wait until Garrett's body is found before attacking Kevin? And if the artifacts were that sought after, why weren't they locked up better? That display case looks nice and all, but there doesn't appear to be a lock or anything on it."

"Good point." Tess chewed her lip as she searched over the file and crime scene photos once more, looking for anything she might have missed. She couldn't rule out the possibility Kevin had been murdered for the same reason as Garrett. It was even possible, despite the passage of time, that they were murdered by the same person. There were still so many questions to find answers to, but at least now, she had Denny to bounce ideas off of. For the first time in days, she was finally starting to feel like her old self, like she was strong enough to handle the task at hand with him by her side.

# Chapter Thirty-Seven

*Wednesday, September 19th, 3:35 PM*

Sid Miliron wiped down the bar with a damp rag as he glanced at the clock near the door. It was only half past three and the club didn't open for a couple of hours. He was grateful for the time, though, as he had a long to-do list and Connie, one of his girls, had just called off for the night.

He turned and looked at the schedule he'd posted behind the bar and felt a breath of relief escape his lungs when he saw that Jimmy and Sloane would be working the floor tonight. He had Becky and Heather on stage first, Jill and Simone on second.

If he hurried, he might be able to get the inventory done before the dinner crowd began pouring in after five.

He was just about to head down the hall to the storeroom when the front door of the club opened, flooding the darkened interior of the building with bright sunlight.

"Bar's closed," Sid called out, watching a tall, dark haired woman approach. Her hair was pulled back into a neat ponytail, and aviator sunglasses obscured her eyes. From her white button-down dress shirt, the badge clipped to her hip, and gun holstered to the other, he instantly knew she was a cop.

*Shit.*

"Can I help you, Officer?" he asked wearily, hoping this visit had nothing to do with the half dozen city code violations he could think of off the top of his head, things he kept meaning to get to but never seemed to have the time for.

"I'm looking for Sid Miliron. Is that you?" the woman asked, pulling the aviators from her face. Sid sucked in a breath when he saw how blue her eyes were.

"I'm Sid," he answered slowly, trying to pull his eyes from hers.

"I'm Detective Tess Dane with the Swain County Sheriff's Department. I have a few questions to ask you about an old case I'm working on. Would you happen to have a few moments to speak with me?"

"I... I... uh, sure," stammered Sid. He chastised himself internally as he stepped around the bar. To hell with the inventory, he'd have Sloane do it when she came in.

He led Tess over to one of the tables close to the stage and gestured for Tess to have a seat. She nodded and politely accepted his invitation.

"So, this place used to be called The Booby Trap?" Tess smirked as she looked around the darkened interior. Music was playing softly over the speakers, but nothing like it would be in just a few hours. For now, the stage was empty, the strobe lights off.

"Yep, back when it first opened. I had to change it when some goody-two-shoes complained to the city council and caused a raucous few years back. I tried to change it to The Doll House, but that was taken, so we're stuck with Sid's Place. I figure that shouldn't piss anyone off, right?" He rolled his eyes. "Hey, you want a drink or something? Coke?"

"Nah, I'm good, but thanks," Tess answered. "So, I'm sure you've heard about the skeletal remains found out at the O'Leary place..."

"Yeah, poor Garrett. He was such a nice guy, too!" Sid lamented with a shake of his head. "Always seemed friendly when I worked at the Falcon's Nest."

"So you met him at the Falcon's Nest Bar before buying the strip club?" Tess asked for clarity. Sid gave her a look of disdain.

"I prefer 'gentlemen's club,' but yes, I used to bartend in town at Falcon's until I bought this place. Once I did that, though, I didn't see Garrett and his friends as much. Well, I saw Fred Krinsel all the time," Sid rolled his eyes. "That guy is hornier than a middle-school locker room, but I digress. No, once Garrett left... disappeared, I guess...his brother Kane and the other guy, Novak, didn't come round as much." He shrugged, leaning back in his chair.

"What do you remember from that night? The night that Garrett was last seen?"

"Well, I remember the club had only been open for a couple of months at that point. That particular night, I don't remember anything strange or out of the ordinary. Just that the O'Leary brothers came in to meet up with the other two guys, like normal."

"Did Kane and Garrett always come together and leave together?"

"Yeah, except that night, I remember Kane got there a lot later than Garrett. He seemed pissed about something, but then again, Kane always looked like that back then. I hear he's mellowed out with age," Sid laughed. "Krinsel and Novak were already here, sitting back there in the corner with Garrett." He pointed to a booth in the back of the bar, away from the door, but still in sight of the stage.

"And did the other three men seem to be in good spirits? Any bickering or fighting that you noticed?" Tess asked, jotting some notes down for herself.

"Nah, nothing that I saw, but then again, we were super busy with it being the weekend and still being so new."

"Do you remember anyone else coming up to them, speaking with them, Garrett specifically?"

Sid scratched his stubbled chin as he thought. "No one that stands out in particular." He paused for a moment, and then his eyes suddenly lit up. "You know, I did see a woman approach their table. She greeted them, but within moments, she was yelling something and picked up Kane's glass and threw his beer in his face."

"Did you recognize her? Hear what she said?" Tess asked, pen poised to write down a possible lead.

"No, I didn't recognize her, and all I could hear was yelling. The music was too loud, and people were talking... I'm sorry, Detective," Sid apologized, a look of defeat on his face.

"It's okay, it was thirty years ago," she shrugged, although she was disappointed. This was, however, the first time she'd heard about a mystery woman coming in and causing a scene that night. She'd have to go back and re-interview the others to see if it triggered any memories.

"When the men left that night, who left with who and how?" Tess asked, referring to her notes.

"Oh, geesh, Detective... I don't remember all that," Sid scratched his head, forehead wrinkling with worry.

She pulled out a copy of his original statement. "That night, you said you saw Garrett leave by himself and that he seemed fine. Do you remember saying that?"

"Oh yeah, he left in his pick-up, that old blue farm truck," Sid exclaimed, a memory dawning on him. "I remember because he'd recently rebuilt the bed of it with two by fours 'cause the metal had rusted outta the other one. I saw him heading out to the lot when I was dumping some trash and told him it looked nice."

This was new information, Tess thought excitedly. Was it a fact though? Or just fabricated memories because Sid wanted to appear helpful? She would ask Kane about the truck bed.

"What time was that?" She asked instead, watching Sid as he seemed lost in his thoughts.

"Oh, I don't remember. It wasn't crazy late... Maybe midnight?"

"And for the record, you don't remember when the other men left?" Tess asked, hoping to glean more information.

"No, not enough to say with certainty. To this day, Krinsel usually stays till last call. Novak and Kane were always hit and miss." Sid shrugged.

"And do any of these men still come here regularly?" Tess asked out of curiosity.

Sid snorted. "Krinsel, again, is hornier than a middle-schooler, so yeah, he's here at least three, four nights a week. One of my best clients." He grinned with a shrug. "Novak? Haven't seen him in years. It's the same for Kane. He's in a care home, isn't he? Last I heard, he was in a wheelchair."

Tess nodded. "Yes, he's had some health issues that have affected his mobility."

"Well, that's unfortunate... poor guy," Sid sighed. He was quiet for a moment. "I don't know if I helped any more than I might have years ago, Detective, but I hope you catch the bastard that hurt ol' Garrett. He sure was a good one."

# Chapter Thirty-Eight



Remi leaned back in the wooden Adirondack chair that sat on her front porch, listening to the night sounds around her. She was thinking about the artifacts she'd seen at her father's house, knowing she needed to tell Detective Dane but feeling fiercely loyal to her father. Being at war with herself, questioning her own morality was harder than pointing fingers at another. She felt a deep sense of shame for knowing something important and remaining quiet because she didn't want to hurt her father. But surely her father didn't have anything nefarious to do with the attack on Kevin O'Leary. He couldn't, could he? Deep in her heart, Remi didn't think her father could ever do something as horrible as attack someone, even if it was to return artifacts to their rightful heirs. Kevin was an old friend, maybe not a super close one, but still their neighbor, one who had helped protect the sacred mound of their ancestors through the years.

It was after 10 pm, she was sure, but the citronella candles seemed to be keeping the mosquitoes away, so she was content to sit in the shadows, enjoying the evening. In the distance, she could hear spring peepers and bullfrogs singing their songs in unison with various insects.

It was when the crickets and frogs suddenly fell silent that she knew she was not alone. Alarmed, but forcing herself to remain calm, Remi's dark eyes sought out the intruder among the darkened woodline. She found it eerie trying to determine if it were man or beast that was watching her.

"I know you're there," she called, her strong voice belying her sudden weariness. "Come on out."

In response, her visitor stepped from the shadows of the treeline near the driveway and walked towards her.

"Hey Remi," he greeted, a small smile crossing his face. Without waiting for an invitation, he mounted the porch steps and took the seat opposite her.

"It's been a while," she commented to her guest, not sure if she was pleased that he was there. Deciding to give him the benefit of the doubt, she played nice. "How have you been?"

"Oh, you know, same old same old," he commented, pulling a pack of cigarettes from his pocket and extracting one. Slipping it between his lips, he lit the end and took a puff.

"You know those things will kill you, right?" Remi chastised with a shake of her head. Some things never change.

"So you've told me a thousand times, Rem," he playfully rolled his eyes.

"I've told you a lot of things over the years, none of which you ever listened to," she huffed, leaning her head back to look up at the night sky. "Why are you here?"

"Ahh, Rem, don't be like that," he sighed, leaning toward her chair as he continued to smoke. "I missed you. Can't a man miss the one woman he loved the most? I fucked up is all. You're never going to forgive me, are you?"

"It's debatable," Remi murmured, rolling her head to look at him. "What you did was inexcusable."

"I said I was sorry like fifty times!" he moaned exasperatedly. "I don't know what else I can do to tell you I'm sorry."

"How about stop fucking every woman in town? That would have been a good start."

"So I slept with Emily—"

"And Jenna and Rosie. Did you think I wouldn't find out?" Remi glared at him. "That's at least three different women you were with while you were *supposed* to be with me. So yeah, I don't think I'm overreacting."

"But that was just once with Jenna and Rosie togeth—"

"Shut up." Remi snapped. "I absolutely do *not* want to know any of it. All that crap is old news. I'm over you. I've healed and, frankly... I think you should leave."

"But I..." he let out a discontented huff and then took a frustrated drag on his cigarette.

"What? What do you want? More money?" Remi asked incredulously. "Is that seriously why you're here again?" By the look on his face, she could tell her assumption was spot on. "Look, I didn't give you money two years ago when you came asking for it, and I'm not giving you any now. You have a gambling problem! If you need food, fine, I'll help. Do you need clothes? I'll take you shopping. But I am not going to give you money to waste at the casino."

"Remi, I'm in between jobs right now, and the bookies are—"

"Not my problem," she finished for him. "You made this mess, you can clean it up. I'm done helping you. Now, please leave.""

But Remi—"

"Leave!" She jabbed a finger in the direction of the driveway. When he didn't budge for a moment, she stood up and headed inside the house to grab her cell phone. Taking it back outside where he remained, she held it up. "Don't make me call the cops." Her voice broke slightly, her resolve shifting.

Once upon a time, she'd loved this man. Had planned a future with him, picked out baby names with him. But then she'd discovered the ultimate betrayal. Infidelity with a side of using her for her money and connections to the casino. She couldn't do that anymore. It was just too hard.

"Fine, fine, I'll leave," he said, standing with a sigh. Knowing he was her weakness, he stepped closer to Remi, and, before she could react, he pulled her in for a kiss. Taken aback by the sudden intimacy, Remi stiffened yet felt her body betray itself as it reacted to his kiss.

*Damn him.* The taste of his kiss alone—stale cigarettes and a hint of peppermint was enough to flood her mind with memories. Through the pounding of her heart, she longed to pull him closer despite the anxiety twisting in her stomach. She knew he was toxic to her. He was like a rose with thorns tipped in poison; beautiful to look at, but painful to touch.

"Leave," she breathed huskily, gently pushing him away, "Now."

He pulled back to look at her, his eyes full of something she couldn't quite decipher. Need? Hurt?

He raised a finger to her cheek and carefully brushed a few dark strands of hair behind her ear. At first she thought he was going to say something, try to get her to change her mind, but he remained quiet. Just when she was about to cave and throw caution to the wind, he dropped his hand and stepped back.

With a mischievous grin, her nighttime visitor stepped off the porch and back into the shadows.

# Chapter Thirty-Nine

*Saturday, September 22nd, 9:36 AM*

"Hey, Dad," Remi greeted her father as he parked his old truck and climbed out.

"Hey, sweetheart," Gordon Nightsong smiled as he enveloped her in a warm hug. "How have you been? Missed you this week for laundry day."

"Yeah, yeah..." Remi shrugged, gesturing for him to follow her into her tiny house. He started to climb the porch steps and then snapped his fingers.

"Wait! I almost forgot!" he exclaimed as he quickly retreated to his truck, the door hinges protesting as he opened the cab to get something. Remi leaned against the door jam and grinned, watching her father digging around in the floor well of his truck.

A moment later, he stood up and gave her a triumphant smile, his long black hair flowing in the gentle morning breeze. His exuberance caused Remi to laugh while inside a dark blanket of unease filled her heart.

She'd invited her dad over to discuss the knife she'd found, although he didn't know that... yet. After taking a few days to wrestle with herself over the morality of knowing the truth and not going to the police, Remi had finally made a decision.

She had to know where her father had gotten the knife. But was she ready for the answer? That was the real question that had kept her awake the past few nights. She couldn't see her father doing something so horrible as attacking Kevin O'Leary over some artifacts, and yet somehow, he had them in his living room. How was her father involved? And if he was somehow guilty of breaking into the O'Leary's farmhouse and hurting his neighbor, would Remi have the courage to call Detective Dane and tell her the truth?

The thought of turning her father in to the law made her stomach roil. And yet, a man was dead, and Remi's conscience wouldn't rest until she knew the truth, no matter how harsh it may be.

"I brought you something special. For your house," Gordon called to Remi as he closed his truck door with his jean-clad hip. In his hands, he held something flat and thin, covered by an old bath towel.

"Is it alive?" Remi asked, her interest piqued. She stepped forward to help him up the stairs as his arms were full with the awkwardly shaped gift.

"At one time," Gordon shrugged indifferently, an ornery twinkle in his eye.

"Dad, it better not be another one of those Jack-o-lope things you brought me last time," Remi pulled a face. "That thing looked cursed."

"Nah, nah, nothing like that," Gordon laughed as the duo wiped their feet on the sisal doormat before stepping into the living room. Remi kicked off her shoes and set them back out on the porch before padding over to the couch and sitting down in anticipation.

"So, you know how I've been taking that woodworking class down at the vocational school?" Gordon asked, taking a seat next to his daughter. When she nodded, he continued, "Well, I've been working on something for you for a while. I was going to wait until your birthday to give it to you, but I'm not patient enough for that."

"Well, now I'm very intrigued," Remi said, trying to catch a glimpse of the mystery item under the faded gray bath towel. "You used your class time to make something for me?"

"Yep," Gordon nodded proudly. "Now, don't get too excited. I'm not that good yet." After a moment of hesitation, he slowly pulled the towel off his gift, and Remi let out a gasp.

Her father held up a wooden sign roughly two feet long and one foot wide that read "Nightsong" and around the name were perfectly engraved wildflowers. The edges of the sign were expertly beveled, accentuating the warm oak stain.

"Dad... It's beautiful!" she praised, reaching for the object. Gordon grinned and handed it to her to inspect.

"I was going to add your house address so you could hang it on your mailbox or your house, but then figured, you move this little house around the country so much, the numbers wouldn't mean much. But Nightsong is who you are."

"This is amazing..." Remi breathed, tears welling up in her eyes. It was a beautiful gesture, and the craftsmanship was superb. Her father had really outdone himself. "Thanks, Dad." She leaned out and wrapped her arms around his neck, her heart warming when he reciprocated the gesture.

"So, how have you been?" Gordon asked, leaning back in his seat once again as he watched Remi trace the letters he'd etched into the wooden plank. "You kinda sounded cryptic on the phone. What did you need to talk to me about?"

Remi paused for a moment, her stomach churning with anxiety. This was it. The moment she found out the truth about her father and the stolen artifacts. The truth about Kevin O'Leary's murder.

"Can I get you a drink?" she blurted, swiftly standing to alleviate the creeping nausea. Could she do this? If he told her he was involved somehow, how could she shield him from the law? The guilt would eat at her. Could she report him to the police? Would she do it, even if there were an explanation?

Gordon raised his dark eyebrows at his daughter's sudden change of activity. "Uh... sure. You got any of that sweet tea?"

"Sure do," Remi sang as she slid past him into her kitchen. Trying to sound normal and will her hands to stop shaking, she decided to broach the subject while her back was to him. "So, Dad, did you hear about Kevin O'Leary?"

"Yeah, it's such a tragedy. Mable Walker at the post office was telling me about it." Her father's voice filtered into the kitchen as she put the pitcher of tea back into the refrigerator.

"Do the cops know who did it?" Remi asked, trying to keep her voice light but concerned as she carried their cups into the living room and set them on the end table.

"Not that I've heard, no." Gordon reached for his glass and took a sip. Releasing a contented sigh, he smiled over at Remi. "You really should bottle this stuff, you know."

"Sure, Dad...," Remi mumbled absently, still thinking about the attack at the O'Leary farm. She needed to ask the tough questions. The ones she didn't know if she wanted the answers to.

"Dad?"

"Yeah?"

"Where did you get that knife on the shelf in your living room?" Remi exhaled, pushing the question out into the universe. Her hands began shaking, and she felt suddenly light-headed.

"What knife? I have quite a few of them that I've collected over the years." Gordon looked at her, eyebrows bunched in confusion. He took another sip as he waited for his daughter to continue.

"The new one, with the bone handle. You know, the red handle with the blue emblem on it?" Remi asked, carefully watching her father for any tells.

"Oh, that one," he smiled. "I got it from an old friend who was looking to re-home it."

"That doesn't sound sus." Remi squinted at her dad, her anxiety spiking. "And does this friend have a name?"

"Does it matter?"

"Yes. Who gave it to you? And where did they get it from?"

"Why do you care so much, Rem?" Gordon leaned away from her, seeming to get a better look at her. "You don't usually care what I do and who I deal with. Why are you suddenly asking about some old knife?"

"Dad... Just tell me, who gave it to you?"

"You know who did."

"What the hell does that mean?" Remi scoffed. She stood and stretched her back in frustration at her father's obvious avoidance of the question.

"Think about it, Remi. Who do we know that is always trying to grift people? Or gamble away every dime they make?" Gordon looked down his nose at her. "This time, he got a job working for an antiquities dealer, or so he says. He knew I'm into that stuff, so I decided to help him out."

Remi's blood ran cold. She knew exactly who her father was talking about.

"But Dad... That knife... That knife looks exactly like the one stolen from Kevin O'Leary the night he was murdered."

Gordon sat there momentarily, mouth gaping open as he processed his daughter's words. As he processed the fact that his almost-son-in-law had become a cold-hearted killer.

"Remi, this is bad. What has that man gotten himself into?"

# Chapter Forty

*Saturday, September 22nd, 11:12 AM*

Tess sat at her desk, filling out some forms and answering emails. She'd been at the station for nearly two hours already. She'd like to think it was because she was just that dedicated to her job, but in reality, it was because she was avoiding her mother, even though it was Saturday.

Kathy had been acting like everything was just peachy, as though the past ten years never happened. Tess had been trying to make amends with her but so far, it wasn't working as well as she'd hoped. Yes, Tess knew she should try to be the bigger person and not stoop to Kathy's level. Tess could try to give her mother yet another chance, but where would it stop? Tess worried Kathy was still the same narcissistic liar who'd proven she'd do anything to make herself comfortable, even if it involved walking away from her daughter again. Kathy claimed that she'd changed, and on the surface, it seemed to Tess that she had or at least was trying. But would it be enough? And more importantly, was it even real?

Tess let out a frustrated sigh as she thought about the whole situation. With a huff, she tossed her pen down and grabbed her empty coffee mug, intent on refilling it.

Just as she was about to fill her Keurig, her desk phone rang. Slumping her shoulders, Tess quickly did a 180 and turned to grab the receiver.

"This is Dane."

"Detective, there is a Remi Nightsong here to see you. She says it's urgent," the receptionist's voice came through the speaker.

"Thanks, Bertie, send her back, please," Tess said, all thoughts of coffee forgotten.

A moment later, Remi rounded the corner in the hallway, clearly distressed. Tess watched her with concern and ushered her inside her office.

"Hey Remi, here have a seat," Tess gestured toward one of the worn leather office chairs opposite her desk. As Remi took a seat, Tess stepped behind her desk and sat down.

"What's going on? You look... stressed?" Tess gently pressed, watching the woman across from her. The last two times she'd seen Remi she had been bright and alert, passionate about life. But the woman sitting across from her now looked stricken and pale. What had happened?

"I... I think I know who killed Kevin O'Leary, and I think I know why," Remi blurted before bursting into tears. She buried her face in her hands and sobbed.

Taken aback by the news and the sudden outpouring of emotion, Tess sat stunned for a beat before grabbing a handful of tissues and walking around the desk to Remi.

Tess squatted down to Remi's level, holding the tissue out between them. The crying woman accepted the offering and as she began blowing her nose and dabbing her eyes, Tess discretely stood and closed the office door to give Remi some privacy.

"Take your time. I know this can be hard," she murmured, laying a comforting hand on Remi's shoulder as she passed by on her way back to her seat.

With a ragged sigh, Remi wiped at her nose a final time before sitting up straighter in her chair. With red, swollen eyes, she finally looked up at Tess, and her bottom lip quivered.

"I'm sorry," she began. "I didn't mean to come in here and cry all over the place. I'm just overwhelmed, and I'm still trying to wrap my head around it all."

"Why don't you start at the beginning then? Work your way up to where you discovered the truth?" Tess encouraged, reaching for her coffee cup, only remembering belatedly that it was still empty. Disappointed, she set it back down and waited for Remi to begin. "Do you mind if I record this? Just in case I have questions later?"

"Sure, I don't want to tell it twice." Remi slumped in her chair as though the weight of the world were on her shoulders. Tess nodded and found her digital recorder. After a quick recitation of the date and their names, Tess nodded for Remi to begin.

"Well, um.... After you came to my home, asking about the Hopewell artifacts going missing from the O'Leary farm," Remi began, "I happened to go to my father's house to do laundry. I usually do that because the laundromat in town is expensive, and it gives me an excuse to visit him. I was folding laundry in the living room when I found this on the shelf." She reached into her jacket pocket and pulled out a bone-handled knife. The blue emblem painted on the red handle was very distinct.

Tess gasped as she looked at the stolen knife, her mind immediately racing to the unsavory conclusion that Gordon Nightsong had stolen the knife and attacked Kevin O'Leary. But why? Nightsong had plenty of money from his casino days. Why attack an old friend over an ancient artifact?

"It's not what you think!" Remi cried, holding her hands in response to Tess's expression. "I thought the same thing you must be thinking. I saw it on my dad's shelf and immediately couldn't believe it. I have been sick about this for days."

"Days?" Tess asked, raising her eyebrows. "You've known about this for *days,* and you're just now bringing it to my attention?"

"I... I... Yes." Remi hung her head as her eyes filled with tears again. "I was afraid of what my dad would say if I asked him about it. I knew deep in my heart that he wouldn't–couldn't– have done something so hideous, but was worried if I asked, I wouldn't like what he said."

"So what happened when you asked him about the knife?"

"He said he got it from an old friend who was having money trouble. They claimed they'd gotten a new job with an antiquities dealer," Remi scoffed as she looked back at Tess. She shook her head in dismay, seemingly deep in thought.

"And do you know who the old friend was?" Tess gently prodded, excited for a possible break in the case.

"Sure. I almost married the guy," Remi shrugged. "It was Breck O'Leary."

# Chapter Forty-One

*Saturday, September 22nd, 11:49 AM*

"You're saying Breck O'Leary attacked and killed his father over some old artifacts?" Tess asked, horrified. "But he seemed totally distraught the entire time we were searching the house together." How had she been duped?

"Yes, unfortunately," Remi said, leaning back in her chair as she looked at Tess across the desk. "See, Breck and I used to be a thing. A hot thing. Back in high school and all during college. The problem was, he couldn't save a dime or, as I found out later, keep his dick in his pants."

"So you're saying he cheated on you *and* had money problems?" Tess asked for clarification.

"Yup. He was constantly borrowing money, saying he'd pay it back. That type of thing."

"Didn't he have a job or something?"

"Not one that lasted longer than a week or so." Remi shook her head in disdain. "He'd get fired for not showing up, or he'd quit for some dumb reason or another. He was always looking for the 'next big thing' and I was too young and naive to see past all his bullshit."

Remi paused, looking out the small window toward the parking lot beyond. Turning back to Tess, she continued.

"It wasn't until my senior year of college, after we'd been engaged for a few months, that I found out the truth about Breck and his money issues. And the other women."

"I had started planning the wedding. I wanted to go to Cabo to this all-exclusive resort that I'd been saving for. My dad had given me a huge chunk of the money to help cover it. Everything was going great. I picked out my dress and shoes. Even had the cake narrowed down to three different designs." Remi paused again, running a hand over her face as she sighed.

"One night, right before finals, I was up all night studying. I was exhausted and overwhelmed with school and wedding planning. Breck offered to take care of booking the resort and plane tickets; he just needed the money to do it. So, ever the trusting fiancee, I gave him the money so he could deal with it all." Remi let out a bitter laugh.

"Then what happened?" Tess asked, already guessing where the story was going.

"Well, everything was fine for the next few months. Or so I thought." A look of anger clouded Remi's dark eyes. "I needed to call the resort to confirm something, I don't even remember what at this point, but it doesn't matter now. You know what they told me? They had no record of our reservation! The wedding was in one month and they had no record of us! Let's just say that the conversation didn't end nicely. I was so upset and stressed. I called Breck to ask him but he didn't answer his phone, so then I decided to look up our flights. Guess what I found?"

"No flights under your names?" Tess offered with a shake of her head.

"Exactly. The fucker had taken all the money and gambled it away. It was gone, every last cent. I only found that out because I happened to go to my dad's house in a rage and one of his casino friends was there visiting. I was seeing red and just ranting about the whole thing–lots of tears and snot for sure–and Dad's friend was like, 'Wait, I know that guy. He's at my casino all the time. He's in the hole big time and has a real problem. With the ladies, too. *That's* your fiance? Breck O'Leary?'" Remi started crying again, her smile broken but appreciative when Tess handed her the box of tissues.

"Apparently, he'd been going to different casinos, racetracks, wherever he could, and gambling away his money. And mine!" Remi blew her nose. "I found out that he'd also been cheating on me with multiple different women, too. Needless to say, I broke things off immediately. Never saw a dime of my money again, either." She angrily threw the wad of used tissues into the wastebasket next to the desk.

"When was the last time you saw Breck?" Tess asked curiously.

"A few days ago. About the time the artifacts were stolen, actually. He'd been out of town, living in Columbus somewhere for a while, but he showed up at my place late one night."

"And what did he want?"

"What he always wants–sex and money." Remi rolled her eyes and scoffed.

"Did you give him any? Money, that is?" Tess asked, not caring who Remi slept with.

"I told him no on both counts. Told him to leave me the hell alone. After a few moments of begging, he finally gave up and left."

"Do you think he's capable of breaking into the farmhouse, attacking his father, and stealing ancient artifacts to pay for his gambling addiction?" Tess asked.

"I think that when someone has a problem like gambling or pornography or whatever... if it goes unchecked, it can get out of hand, and then anything can happen," Remi answered firmly. "I'd like to honestly say he wouldn't hurt a fly, but I've seen him angry. I've seen him desperate. And if the bookies are after him..." Her voice trailed off, and silence stretched between them, both women deep in thought.

"And your dad bought the artifacts off of him, knowing that they were stolen?" Tess asked, watching Remi closely.

"That I don't know for sure," Remi sighed. "He knows Breck has had gambling issues in the past. He knows Kevin O'Leary was attacked. I didn't know if he had put two and two together until I asked him about it. He honestly looked shocked when I told him."

"I'm going to have to speak to your father, Remi," Tess said. "And I'm going to have to bring Breck in, too."

"I know," Remi sighed. "I just want this mess to be over with. What is wrong with that family? First, Garrett is murdered, now Kevin."

"Well, we can't blame Breck for Garrett's murder because he wasn't even alive for that one." Tess shrugged, trying to lighten the mood.

"Very true." Remi gave her a small smile.

"Thanks for coming in, Remi. I know it was hard, but you did the right thing."

"It doesn't feel like the right thing, somehow," Remi admitted. "I feel like even though he's treated me like crap over and over again, I'm still somehow betraying Breck. But, at the end of the day, I know he needs help. I'm surprised he hasn't gotten himself killed yet because of his gambling problem. Maybe this is a good thing?" She stood slowly, her shoulders slightly drooped.

"If it wasn't for the gambling and the women, he's actually a nice guy," she sniffled. "Thanks for listening to me ramble, Tess. Maybe when this mess is over, we can... I don't know, hang out or something?"

"That sounds like fun," Tess smiled kindly. "You have my number."

Remi gave her a small smile and then slipped out the door and disappeared down the hall. Tess sighed, a slight smile playing on her lips, despite the tragic tale Remi spun. She had her first real lead on the O'Leary case.

# Chapter Forty-Two



"Thank you for coming down to speak with me, Mr. Nightsong," Tess greeted Gordon as he followed her into her office. "I thought we could chat in here, if you don't mind. It's a little more comfortable than the conference room. Besides, I bought a new coffee maker recently and I'm eager to show it off. The one in the break room is questionable at best. Would you care for some?"

"Sure, that sounds great actually," Gordon's bright smile lit up his face. "I will never pass up a cup of coffee." He ran his fingers through his long black hair, pushing it behind his ear.

"Perfect. It's a Keurig, so just pick out what flavor you want and have at it. I bought a selection since the K-cups make it easy," Tess grinned, pointing to the small coffee station she'd set up in her office. She was rather pleased with her bright red Keurig, two clean guest mugs, and assortment of flavored coffees. A small bowl filled with creamers sat next to it, along with a few sugar packets. She'd decided to only keep a few out at once to keep her coworkers from raiding her stash when she wasn't around.

She'd seen how the guys drank their coffee (and made messes while doing so!), and she wanted to avoid it.

While Gordon Nightsong set about brewing a cup of breakfast blend, Tess took a seat behind her desk, trying to center herself. She'd asked Remi not to say anything to Breck until Tess had talked with Gordon. She was hoping for some concrete evidence that Breck was indeed the source of the stolen artifacts. She couldn't get an arrest warrant just on Remi's word.

"So..." Gordon started as he finished preparing his coffee and came to take a seat across from Tess. "Remi said you needed to see me. About the O'Leary knife."

"Yes, that's correct," Tess answered. "I'm going to record our conversation for later reference, okay?" She held up her recorder.

"Am I under arrest?" he suddenly looked alarmed, as though he'd been trapped into coming in.

"No, no, nothing like that, Mr. Nightsong," Tess placated, holding her palms up. "I have Remi's side of things, now I need yours. As I move through the investigation, I'll be talking to others as well. It's easier if I can refer back to these recordings; that's all. You are not under arrest and can leave at any time. You're here under your own free will. If at any time you change your mind, you are free to go as you haven't been charged with anything."

Tess watched as Gordon let out a sigh of relief and seemed to relax. He took a slow sip of his coffee, his dark eyes watching Tess over the brim. When he slowly swallowed, she gave him a nod and proceeded to record their names, the date, and the purpose of the interview.

"So, Mr. Nightsong–"

"Please, call me Gordon."

"Okay... Gordon. Your daughter, Remi, came to me earlier and told me about a knife that she saw at your house. Do you know which one I'm talking about?"

"Yes. The ancient one with the bone handle."

"Yes, that one. What can you tell me about it?"

"It's from the Hopewell culture, possibly Adena. To be honest, I've never seen one like it before."

"So this knife is unique, would you say, Gordon?"

"Yes."

"And do you think it is worth a lot of money?"

"I'm not sure of that yet. Just for the fact that it is so old and is in excellent condition, it is worth quite a bit to the right buyer. Add the sheer uniqueness... who really knows?" Gordon shrugged.

"And how is it you came into possession of this knife?" Tess asked, watching the older man closely for any signs of untruthfulness. She hoped that his story matched Remi's, but at the same time, she knew she must keep an open mind if she were to find the truth.

"I was down at the casino, visiting with my old coworkers, when I noticed Breck O'Leary at the Blackjack table. He was in trouble. A lot of trouble," Gordon sighed and shook his head. "This isn't anything new. The boy has a problem. Always has for as long as I've known him. Can you believe I almost let him marry my girl?" The look he gave Tess was one of dismay. "Anyway, I saw Lyle and Elliot standing directly behind Breck, just waiting for him to get up off his stool so they could make their move."

"Wait, who's Lyle and Elliot?" Tess interrupted for clarity.

"Bookies. They work for The Shaman. No one knows The Shaman's real name, not even me, but if he sends his bookies after you..." Gordon's voice trailed off. "Let's just say, I've heard of more than one person leaving with Lyle and Elliot, never to be seen again."

"That's concerning," Tess commented, making notes to look into the Shaman and casino. She wrote down the names Lyle and Elliot even though they were most likely fake, but it was worth passing on to the appropriate investigators.

"Yes, very," Gordon agreed. "Anyway, I saw Breck struggling. He knew he was surrounded, knew he was a dead man the minute he stood up. So, I caused a distraction."

"Which was?"

"Pulled the fire alarm." Gordon grinned and then let out a laugh when he saw Tess's surprised expression.

"I was not expecting that, but okay... please continue," Tess grinned and shook her head.

"Everyone scattered like roaches when you turn the light on in the middle of the night. Running, screaming.... When everything calmed down, Breck was gone, and Lyle and Elliot were standing outside on the sidewalk empty-handed."

"So when was this?" Tess asked, trying to make a timeline in her head, a sequence of events leading up to the attack on Kevin O'Leary.

"The night of the storm," Gordon offered, his eyes dark and worried, "The night Kevin O'Leary was attacked."

# Chapter Forty-Three



"So the casino incident happened around what time?" Tess asked, trying to keep her breathing under control. Tess's stomach churned at the very idea that Breck might have actually beaten his father to death. And for what? Some gambling debt? But the reality was that she would have to consider it a very real possibility if the timeline of events lined up with the attack. She held her breath and waited for Gordon to continue.

"Ummm... around 8:45? 9:00?" he paused then, appearing deep in thought. "Wait, I remember getting a text from my sister right as I was walking into the casino. Hang on..." Tess watched as Gordon dug around in the pocket of his jeans for a moment before pulling out an old iPhone. He unlocked the screen and began tapping it until he found what he was looking for. After a moment, he let out a sound of triumph.

"Ah, here we go. I got to the casino around 8:53 to be exact," Gordon said, sliding his phone across the desk for Tess to see. "Meaning the fire alarm was pulled around... 9:15 if I were to guess. I responded to the text as you can see, then went inside and started chatting with some of my old coworkers. It didn't take long for me to spot Breck at the BlackJack table... or his shadows."

"And do you know if Breck saw you there?" Tess asked as she leaned in to look at the phone's timestamp. The screen was cracked and smudged with fingerprints. She made a note of the timestamp and would contact the fire department and casino to verify the time of the alarm going off.

"Not that I know of," Gordon shrugged. "The place wasn't too busy for the evening crowd, but with the amount of pressure that Lyle and Elliot must have been breathing down on Breck... He didn't seem to be looking anywhere except the table."

"Okay... So, we've established that you saw Breck at the casino around nine on the night of the attack. When did you see him again?" Tess asked, waiting for Gordon to take another swig of his coffee.

"He showed up early the next morning. I was feedin' my dogs when he pulled up. Other than seeing him across the casino, I hadn't seen him in a long time, much less spoken to him, so I was surprised when he showed up. We got to chatting and before long, he said he had gotten a new job working with an antiquities dealer. He told me that the dealer had recently come across a new collection of Hopewell and Adena artifacts and, because Breck knew I was a collector, he'd offered me first dibs."

"And you believed him?"

"The boy's never lied to me before. Didn't figure he'd start now." Gordon shrugged. His face saddened as he continued, "I knew he'd had money issues in the past, but I never thought he'd try to sell me stolen goods. Especially ones he'd taken from his own father." His shoulders slumped then, and he hung his head. Tess gave him a moment to collect himself, trying to look busy with her notebook when he sniffed.

Eventually, he looked back up and, avoiding her eyes, took another swallow from his mug with a shaky hand.

"I think... I think I didn't *fully* believe him, but I didn't want to admit he was lying to me either. I never thought for a moment that he'd stolen them from his father, much less attacked him. Even when I heard that Kevin was attacked, I didn't put two and two together. I didn't hear about the missing artifacts until Remi told me." He paused. The tears glistening in his dark eyes did nothing to diminish his firm conviction. "I don't even know what to think, what to say. I... I gave Breck money for the artifacts, choosing to believe it was for his new 'boss'... even though, in my heart, I knew somewhere that he was just trying to get money to either pay off the shaman or skip town. But to kill his father to save his own hide? I never saw that coming."

"So Breck sold you the knife and other artifacts the morning after Kevin was attacked, correct?" "Yes."

"And you paid him cash at that time?"

"Yes."

"And, for the record, you never saw the artifacts over at the O'Leary's?" Tess asked, knowing that the Nightsongs and O'Learys had been friends for years. Surely they'd been in each other's houses, right?

"No, not that I remember. I've only been to the farm a handful of times, mostly for summer barbecues and once for a Christmas party. And that was only because Remi insisted on it."

"Aren't you close friends with the family?" Tess asked, her brows scrunching together in confusion. Gordon shook his head.

"Not really, no. I mean, we are friendly, yes, but not friends, if that makes sense."

"Yes, that makes sense," Tess smiled, making a note to herself. "So, where inside the O'Leary house have you been?"

"The entryway, living room... bathroom. Oh, and the kitchen and dining room." Gordon answered, holding up his hand and ticking off fingers one by one as he thought through the rooms he'd seen at the O'Leary farm.

"Never upstairs?"

"No. Why would I go up there?" He looked very confused.

"Just asking," Tess asked with a calming smile. "How about the office downstairs?" She watched Gordon for his reaction, knowing that was the room that once housed the artifacts in custom display cases for all to see.

"Is that the doorway just past the living room or the one by the kitchen?" Gordon asked, scratching his head. "Those doors were always shut, and I never was curious enough to find out why." He shrugged.

"That's fair," Tess nodded. She'd been to a friend's home where certain doors had been shut. She'd never pried either. Unless Gordon had a reason to go into the basement or office at the O'Leary farm, she supposed there wouldn't be a reason for him to go poking around during a party. She made some notes to herself to refer to later but decided to continue with her line of questioning.

"So, Gordon, how did you first hear about Kevin getting attacked?" she asked, absently picking at a cuticle.

"Mable Walker down at the post office," he answered with a shrug. "She always seems to hear about everything that goes on around here before anyone else."

"Did Mable mention anything about the missing artifacts?" Tess asked, wondering just how much information was circling through the small town of Crawley. She knew of Mable Walker and her ability to spread a good story when she heard one.

"No, she just asked me if I'd heard about Kevin getting attacked in his own home."

Tess made a humming sound in her throat as she thought about his response. Had Mable just not mentioned it because it wasn't common knowledge yet? Or had she heard about it and knew Gordon liked to collect artifacts? Perhaps Mable thought Gordon might have had something to do with the attack and was doing some nosing around on her own. Tess shook herself. Her mind was wandering down a rabbit hole of ridiculous what-ifs, and it wouldn't be helpful. Facts. She needed to determine facts and find out exactly what happened that night.

# Chapter Forty-Four

*Monday, September 24th, 5:45 PM*

Tracking down Breck O'Leary had been almost more irritating than her mother calling her Contessa, but tracking him down is exactly what Tess did. With the help of Miles, Scafferty, and a few kind officers from the Columbus Police Department, that was.

Breck had been holed up in a coffee house in Columbus's Short North when he'd logged onto his social media account. Within moments, they knew where he was and had him apprehended. Originally, Tess had just wanted to talk with him, interview him and get his side of things. But when he'd seen the cops, he'd thrown his coffee at them and run. A chase ensued and when he'd been tackled to the ground, he'd yelled out, "He made me do it!"

Now, Breck sat in Interview 1, slumped in a metal chair, his hands cuffed in front of him to the table, waiting. Tess stood watching him on the other side of the two-way glass, letting him stew, watching his behavior.

According to his driver's license, Breck Garrett O'Leary was twenty-four years old and lived at the farm. Tess didn't believe he lived at the farm; Kevin had never mentioned it, and they hadn't seen any signs of another person living there besides Kevin.

Tess had also run Breck's credit. The Nightsongs were not joking when they said Breck had money problems. His credit score was abysmal, and he had numerous accounts currently in collections.

With a sigh, she steeled herself and opened the door to the interview room. Holding Breck's file in one hand, she slammed the door with the other to get his attention.

He jumped and eyed her wearily as she walked over toward the metal table that served as his tether. His eyes never left hers, and she noticed that his left leg started nervously bobbing up and down the second she walked in.

"Hello, Breck. So we meet again, huh?" Her smile held no humor. "I'm sure you know why you've been brought here, but for shits and giggles, let me remind you. You are here under suspicion of the theft of ancient Hopewell artifacts, and most importantly, you are here under suspicion for the murder of your father, Kevin O'Leary. As always, you have the right to remain silent. Anything you say can and will be used against you in a court of law. You have the right to a lawyer. If you can't afford one, a lawyer will be assigned to you. Do you understand these rights as I have laid them out?"

"Yes," Breck mumbled, his voice quiet and withdrawn. He dropped his gaze to the worn surface of the table, his fingers mindlessly following grooves made by so many that had come before him.

Tess picked up her voice recorder and stated, "This is the official interview of Breck O'Leary. Present are myself, Detective Tess Dane of the Swain County Sheriff's Department, and the suspect, Breck O'Leary." She added the date and time as she flipped through the file in front of her.

"Do you have anything you'd like to tell me? Anything to get off of your chest?"

Breck sat there unmoving, staring aimlessly at something on the table. Tess had hoped that he'd readily give her something, but apparently, she was wrong.

"Is your name Breck O'Leary?"

"Yes."

"Do you live at the farm on Quaker Hollow Road in Swain County?"

"No, I used to, but now I have a place in Columbus," Breck answered, confirming Tess's suspicions about the driver's license.

"Where do you work?" Tess continued asking her baseline questions, letting him relax a little before getting to the meat of the interview.

"I'm in between jobs at the moment," Breck mumbled, not meeting her eye. A muscle in his jaw twitched.

"Have you ever stolen anything?"

"Hasn't everyone at some point in their lives?" Breck deflected, but Tess heard it: the slight hint of fear mixed with righteous indignation.

"I suppose you're right. Kids do impulsive things all the time." Tess commented, making a mental note to circle back to the topic.

"Did you kill your father, Breck?" Her eyes never wavered as she watched his reaction for any tells or tics.

"No," he whispered hoarsely. He sniffed and snapped his eyes straight at Tess. "I would never hurt him." His eyes flashed with anger, and his jaw clenched as he matched her steely expression.

"But you stole the artifacts." She said it bluntly, as a statement rather than a question, gauging his response.

"No," he said again, a little louder this time.

"That's interesting, because I have a witness that says you sold them the artifacts directly. So if you didn't steal them, who did?"

"It's not what you think."

"Then enlighten me."

A minute passed, then another. Neither one said a word. Tess waited him out, willing him to fold under distress.

"I took the artifacts, but not for the reason you think. Besides, Dad was going to give them to me... eventually," Breck finally said.

"Okay... so you admit to taking the artifacts but say your dad was giving them to you? Please clarify this, Breck, because it seems awfully suspicious that he gets murdered the same night you decide to pop over to pick up your inheritance," Tess bit out.

"I..." Breck paused, his cheeks reddening, his eyes filling with unshed tears. "I was always told that I'd inherit the artifacts when he died. The problem was that I needed money now. Not thirty, forty years down the road when Dad eventually died. So... I decided to sneak in and just take them. They were already mine, technically. I figured if I took them when Dad was sleeping, then I could get in, get out, and he wouldn't notice."

"Why didn't you just ask your dad for them early? Or ask him to loan you the money you need? Why break in during a thunderstorm and steal them like a common cat burglar? Was it some kind of sick game to you?"

"No! It wasn't like that. First, Dad would never have given them to me early because I'd already asked for them.

Twice. He said I didn't respect them enough and until I 'grew up' and thought about more than just myself for once then he'd think about it. As for giving me a loan? Ha! You're hilarious."

"Why am I so amusing to you, Breck?" Tess asked, flipping through her file until she found his credit report. She held it up for him to see. "Could it be because of this?"

She watched as Breck's face reddened, with rage or embarrassment she didn't know.

"If I was your mother, I wouldn't give you a loan either," Tess shrugged. "You need help, Breck, not a loan. Your gambling problem isn't helping anyone, and I think your dad knew that. I think that's why he wouldn't give you the artifacts or even a loan. I'm betting that if I dug far enough back in his financials, I'd find that he's given you plenty of money throughout the years, all of which you've immediately taken to the casino and lost. Am I right? He knew that if he gave you even so much as a dime, you'd be down at the Blackjack table losing it.

"How much do you currently owe the Shaman?" Tess paused when she saw Breck suck in a large gulp of air. She'd hit a nerve. "Rumor has it that Lyle and Elliot have been on your ass for days now wanting their money. How long do you think the Shaman's bookies are going to give you before you end up in a ditch with your throat slit? Or worse... ?"

"What could be worse than that?" Breck swallowed audibly, his eyes large and round.

"You could be deposited into several ditches at once all across the county..." Tess replied holding her hands up, palms out as though warding off such a nasty thought.

"Alright... alright," Breck said, tugging at the handcuffs around his wrists. "I stole the artifacts. I went to the farm that night with the express intent of taking them and selling them to make money to pay off the Shaman. His men had been getting more and more... aggressive in their threats, and I was getting desperate. Can you really blame me?"

Tess just looked at him, her face devoid of emotion. Of course, she blamed him. He'd broken into the farmhouse, stolen artifacts, and killed his own father! *Allegedly.* He needed help with his gambling addiction. He needed to be held accountable for his crimes.

The two of them sat there looking at each other for a beat before Tess broke the silence.

"Okay, so you admit to entering the house that night and stealing the artifacts. Why didn't you just snatch them and run? Why did you tear the office up? Why did you go upstairs and attack your father?"

"I... I didn't. I used my key for the back door like always and slipped inside but...."

"But what?" Tess asked, remembering that there had been tool marks found on the exterior French doors to the office.

"Someone else was already there." Breck leaned forward in his seat and let out a wail. His shoulders shook as his cries wracked his body.

"Who was there, Breck?" Tess tensed, her body poised for a breakthrough in the case.

"He asked me why I was there and I told him I needed money, needed the artifacts," Breck gasped out in between sobs. "He told me to grab them and leave, now."

"Who?" Tess pleaded. She needed a name! She could feel her coworkers' eyes on her, watching from the other side of the two-way glass.

The only sound penetrating the quiet was the ticking of the clock over the door to the hallway, accompanied by Breck's harsh breathing. Tess sat silently, giving Breck a chance to speak, even when everything in her wanted to grab him by the shoulders and shout at him to answer her. She forced her face to remain neutral.

Breck was obviously dealing with an internal emotional battle, and if Tess was to make any sort of breakthrough, yelling and screaming at him during his fragile state wasn't going to work.

"He told me not to tell anyone he'd been there. He offered to pay me to keep quiet." Breck's gaze lingered at some distant point over Tess' shoulder, his eyes seeming to glaze over. He sat like that for a few moments, quietly staring at nothing, lightly chewing on his lower lip.

"Who was in the house, Breck?" whispered Tess gently, but she got no response.

"Who?" Tess slapped the table, jarring Breck out of his fugue. "Who, Breck? Who was there that night? Who killed your father?"

"I can't say it. He'll kill me too." Snot bubbled out of his nose as he let out a sob.

"Then write it down," Tess ordered, sliding over a piece of paper and a pen.

Breck stared at her for a moment, eyes red and puffy, lips trembling. For a moment, she thought he might lunge at her right then. She'd essentially given him a weapon, so she'd only have herself to blame. But then, expelling a large sigh, he reached out shaky fingers and grasped the pen awkwardly with his cuffed hands.

Tess watched as Breck wrote a name on the paper that made her blood run cold.

# Chapter Forty-Five



After Breck had written the name on the paper, he'd immediately requested a lawyer and protection. Since he was being held for the theft of the Hopewell artifacts, he was being protected enough but she'd made sure he was to receive no visitors under any circumstances, except for his lawyer. She'd also requested that the public defender's photo ID and name be sent to her before they were allowed to go speak with Breck.

Tess's mind whirled with the suggestions of Breck's admission, which had implications in Kevin O'Leary's murder as well as of his father's death nearly thirty years ago.

But the question was how? And why? Tess knew she couldn't blindly trust the accusation. Breck O'Leary was a desperate man, and desperate men were dangerous. She needed some kind of evidence to get an arrest warrant on Breck's lead. Some tangible proof of motive.

She'd run background checks and financials on all the key players. As she stood in the office, case files spread out around her, she tried to search each profile for something she might have missed. With Breck's accusation pushed to the back of her mind, but not discredited, for the moment, she wanted to take one more look at the key players involved in the case.

Pausing at James O'Leary, she looked at his finances. He was in a lot of debt, mostly medical, due to his wife's MS. Would he have killed his uncle for monetary gain to pay the bills? Possibly. According to the county auditor's site, James and Lori O'Leary owned a two bedroom, one bath house on 0.42 acres located at 462 Horse Path Rd.

Tess set Lori O'Leary's profile to the side. Breck had referred to the second intruder as 'him,' and Tess had seen how weak Lori was. She wore arm braces just to walk. There was little to no chance that she'd be able to climb a steep flight of stairs and attack a work-hardened farmer in his prime. It might not have been plausible, but it wasn't impossible.

Breck's profile remained in the pile for now, as Tess still didn't know if she thoroughly believed his story. In his defense, his emotional response was either genuine or extremely well-rehearsed. Either way, what were the chances that two separate individuals with evil intent would stalk the same farmhouse on the same night, each with their own plan?

Next in the pile was Kane O'Leary. Tess sighed, looking down at the profile. The man looked like Santa in a wheelchair! According to his financials, Kane had $148,382.00 in his retirement account and close to $75,000 in his savings. He didn't own a car, and his only debt or revolving accounts were a monthly cell phone bill, his care home, and medical costs. Nothing seemed to stand out to Tess as alarming.

She flipped through the auditor's paperwork for Kane's profile and frowned. The printout said, "No records found."

"Well, that has to be a mistake..." Tess muttered to herself. "He has shares in the farm." She slid behind her desk and pulled up the county auditor's site.

Typing in Kane's name and hitting 'search' she was soon met with the same result: No records found.

Tess typed in Kevin O'Leary's name and immediately the results appeared on her screen. The entirety of the farm belonged to Kevin. But why? Wasn't it a *family* farm? What about James? Or Kane?

Sweat began beading up on Tess's lip as she did a record search for the properties on the county clerk's website. She typed in the property address, feeling unnerved as though she were onto something big.

After a few more clicks, the most recent sale and ownership entries for the O'Leary farm were listed. According to the site, Kevin took complete ownership of the farm in 2003, which made sense to Tess if she did the math correctly. That would have been seven years after Garrett was last seen. Long enough for him to be declared legally dead.

Tess clicked an entry dated further back in time to when Garrett O'Leary took ownership of the property. May 1996, just two months before he disappeared. The previous owners were listed as Shamus and Lenore O'Leary.

Tess snapped her eyes up to the profile of Kane resting on the top of her pile. Why hadn't Kane inherited half the farm from his parents like his brother Garrett had?

Had there been something in the will prohibiting Kane from inheriting a share of the farm? Tess turned back to her computer and pulled up the country probate court website. A will filed that far back was public record and should be easy enough to find.

She typed in Lenore and Shamus O'Leary's names and waited for the search results to come through. And there it was, the last will and testament of Kane and Garrett's parents.

She clicked on the document dated from June 7, 1980, and scanned through it but paused. According to the will, the farm was to be split evenly between Kane and Garrett. So, why didn't Kane take his inheritance? And why was Garrett dead?

It was then that Tess noticed another document link. Curious, she clicked it to reveal an updated final will for Lenore O'Leary dated April 7th, 1996.

Tess sucked in her breath at the date. Lenore had updated her will just a month before she died and a couple of months before her youngest son disappeared.

**I, Lenore O'Leary, being of sound mind and body, wish to amend all previous wills in my name. With the recent death of my beloved Shamus, I must keep our family farm intact.**

**With that said, I wish to remove my son, Kane O'Leary, from any and all inheritance, both real or otherwise. He would just want to sell it for his own gain and he's never shown an interest in the farm.**

**Instead, I shall leave the farm, house, and all of the property (Parcel number 2005689032-0987) in Swain County, Ohio, to my youngest son, Garrett. He has worked the land along with his father his whole**

**life and has proven that his heart is committed to keeping our legacy alive.**

Had Garrett been murdered over an inheritance? Was it really that simple? But why Kevin? And how? Kane was in a wheelchair and almost eighty years old now.

There was only one way to find out. She printed off her findings, stuffed them in her file, and grabbed her keys. She had to get to Glade Springs Senior Living.

# Chapter Forty-Six

*Tuesday, September 25th, 12:00 PM*

"I'm sorry, Detective, but Mr. O'Leary isn't here right now," the mousy-hair receptionist explained as she looked up his name on the computer.

"What do you mean he's not here?" Tess asked. "He can't just walk out of here, so someone must know where he is."

The receptionist gave Tess a confused look. "Ma'am, it's not like he's a prisoner here. We don't check their every move; that's ridiculous."

"If it's so ridiculous, then why did you look him up? How do you know he's not home?"

"Well, for one, when a tenant calls for an Uber or taxi, we log it into our computer so we can let them know their ride is here. Comes in handy when the person needs special transport vehicles like Mr. O'Leary's wheelchair." The receptionist did very little to hide her annoyance at Tess. "Otherwise, we don't know if people are in their apartments unless we call them, and they don't answer, or if they specifically leave a message with us here at the desk. Again, our tenants are allowed to move around however their mobility and health allow. We aren't a nursing home.

We are an assisted living facility, meaning we help make their lives easier, keep an eye out for them, but we don't coddle."

Tess sighed, frustration seeping into her and threatening a headache. She rubbed her forehead to soothe it away.

"Okay, fine. Do you know when he should be back or where he might have gone? This is very important," Tess said, struggling to keep her voice even. *Important as in he might have killed two people*, Tess thought as she watched the receptionist roll her eyes at her and proceed to act as though she were looking it up on her computer.

"The computer says his son, James, came to pick him up around nine this morning. We had to have an orderly help Mr. O'Leary into the car," the receptionist shrugged. "Other than that, I don't know anything."

"Thanks..." Tess replied, already pulling out her cell phone. "That was helpful."

She exited the building and made her way back to her SUV. Unlocking the door, she climbed in and began searching for a phone number. Finding the correct one, she dialed it and waited while it rang.

"Hello?" a male voice answered.

"Hi, is this Jamie?"

"Yeah... Who is this?"

"Jamie, this is Detective Dane from the sheriff's department. Please don't say anything but yes or no. Do you understand?"

"Yes...?"

"Is your father with you?"

"No."

"Do you know where he is?"

"Yes."

"Are you alone right now?"

"Yes."

"Okay, you can answer in full sentences. Tell me, where is your father?"

"I dropped him off at his apartment twenty minutes ago," Jamie answered, confusion filling his voice. "Detective, what is this about? Is Dad okay?"

"He's fine. I just need to find him. I tried calling his cell phone earlier, but it kept going to voicemail. I can try it again," Tess said, sitting up straighter in her seat and looking around the parking lot for any signs of Kane.

"Jamie... Which apartment did you drop your dad off at?" Tess asked, wondering how on Earth she'd missed seeing Kane being dropped off.

"The senior living place, Glade Springs," Jamie answered, indicating the same place Tess was at. "Look, Detective, I don't know what's going on here, but you are making me nervous. What happened? Is my dad in some kind of trouble?"

"I just need to speak with him and haven't been able to get ahold of him. I'm here at Glade Springs and they said he wasn't back yet."

"What? Really?" The confusion in Jamie's voice sounded genuine. "Maybe I should head back over there..."

"It's okay. I'll just double-check his apartment. Maybe the receptionist was misinformed," Tess soothed, even though she was now concerned about Kane's whereabouts.

"Like I said, I dropped him off out front around... twenty-five, maybe thirty minutes ago? He should be there," Jamie reiterated. He sounded distressed. "You'll call me when you find him, right?"

"Sure. And Jamie? If somehow he shows up where you are, please let me know. It's important."

"Will do, Detective," Jamie promised before ending the call.

Tess locked her phone screen and sat there for a moment, pondering the conversation she'd just had. If Jamie had indeed dropped his father off at the senior living place just moments ago as he'd claimed, then Tess or the receptionist should have seen him. Where had he gone?

Climbing out of the Swain County SUV and locking the door, Tess kept her eye out for any signs of Kane O'Leary or his wheelchair. Perhaps something bigger was at play. Something that she'd overlooked? Had someone snatched the old man to keep him quiet about a larger crime?

The afternoon sun beat down on Tess as she walked around the front of the tan brick building, under the shadowed shelter of the portico, and on around to the far side of the Glade Springs complex.

Through a fence enclosing the back gardens of the facility, Tess could see older men and women enjoying the sun, reading books, playing chess, or chatting in small groups. From somewhere deep within, the mournful sounds of a perfectly performed cello ensemble wafted through the early autumn air.

Had Tess not been pursuing a possible murder suspect, she would have stopped to listen.

"Excuse me!" a voice called, bringing her to a halt. She turned and saw an orderly approaching the fence, his deep brown skin in stark contrast to his white scrubs.

"Yes?" Tess asked, approaching the fence from the outside perimeter.

"Not to be difficult, ma'am, but we are not allowed to let anyone loiter on the outside of the fence. Company policy. We had a... situation a few years ago so...," he shrugged. "I just don't want to lose my job." His name tag indicated his name was Shawn.

"I'm sorry, Shawn. I'm Detective Tess Dane with the Swain County Sheriff's Department, and I was actually looking for one of the residents who lives here," Tess explained, gesturing toward her badge clipped on her belt. Shawn's eyes widened in understanding.

"Oh? Who is it? Maybe I can help you." Shawn glanced over his shoulder, surveying the current tenants milling around the gardens. "We have people of varying abilities that live here. I'm out here with a small group of B Tenants."

"B Tenants?"

"Yeah, A's don't need any help at all, and B's need some help with walkers or wheelchairs. That type of thing," Shawn explained. He leaned toward the fence that separated them and whispered, "Don't tell the tenants that, though. It's the staff's way of differentiating who needs attention and who can do fine on their own. Nobody wants to be a B."

"What happens when they get to a C?" Tess asked, looking over Shawn's shoulder at the elderly people enjoying their day.

"Nursing home," he said sadly. "They require full-time nursing care at that point, and we don't offer that here."

"So, the tenant I'm looking for is Kane O'Leary. I guess he'd be your charge today. Is he out here?"

Shawn looked at her skeptically. "No, ma'am, he isn't. I saw him leave earlier today with someone, and I don't know if he's back yet. I've been out here for the past hour."

Tess sighed, "Okay then. Thanks, Shawn. Is it okay if I continue to walk the perimeter of the property?"

"Sure, I don't suppose it would hurt anything," Shawn smiled, "And I was just doin' my job earlier... You know, when I tried to run you off."

"It's fine, I get it," Tess grinned. "You see some crazy lady prowling around in dress pants and a white button-down shirt in this weather, and you gotta check it out. God, this humidity is awful, isn't it?"

Shawn hooted, "That's Ohio in mid-September for you, Detective! You never know what you're gonna get! Have a good day."

As he turned to walk back to his post, Tess stopped him. "Hey, Shawn?"

"Yeah?"

"If you see him, will you call me?" She rolled one of her cards to fit through the chain length fence.

"Sure will, Detective." Shawn accepted it, and with a grin, he stuck it in the breast pocket of his scrubs and strode back to the garden area.

# Chapter Forty-Seven

*Tuesday, September 25th, 7:45 PM*

After a fruitless search of the outside of Glade Springs and a quick apartment check to verify that Kane O'Leary was indeed not at home, Tess put an APB out for him. He couldn't have gotten far. He was wheelchair bound! Since he was a vulnerable person due to the wheelchair, it was easy to get an alert out to all law enforcement and emergency personnel in the tri-county area. Hopefully, someone would see him and report his location.

Jamie and Lori had met her at the sheriff's department, asking what could be done. Tess had little to tell them at this point. She hadn't wanted to tip them off to her suspicion that he had murdered his brother and possibly his nephew (if Breck was to be believed!). The less they knew, the better. But at the same time, Tess was worried that they may be in danger somehow, too. She didn't think so, though. If the motive truly was all about land and inheritance, then killing Jamie or Lori wouldn't make sense.

But if she was wrong...

"Tess, go home," Malone ordered. "It's almost eight. You've done all you can do for tonight. Law enforcement in three different counties are looking for him. They'll call you if anything happens, okay?"

"But—"

"No 'but's,' Tess. You're better to us rested than you are here, exhausted and wearing out the carpet with your pacing." he cast a pointed look at the floor. Tess glanced down and could see a tract she'd made already from walking a circuit around his office and down the hallway.

She let out an exasperated sigh, rolling her eyes enough to impress a teenager, causing Malone to laugh.

"Okay, Dad," Tess grinned at him, knowing he was right, even though she didn't want to admit it or do what he said.

"Leave now, young lady, or you'll be grounded until... tomorrow morning at 8:00," Malone said, trying to sound stern, which only amused Tess further. They'd been friends and coworkers long before he'd been elevated to sheriff.

Tess snorted. "See you then, Boss. Just make sure they call me if anything–"

"We will. Go!"

***

Twenty minutes later, Tess pulled up outside her house. The lights were out except for a small one in the living room she left on for Otter. *Aunt Sharon and Mom must have gone out*, Tess mused as she gathered her things and headed inside.

Otter greeted her by the door, his tail metronoming him into a full-body wag. He let out happy woofs and yips around the stuffie clenched tightly in his teeth.

"Hey, bud!" Tess greeted him with a head rub and nose boop. "Where is everyone?"

She walked into the kitchen and flipped on the light, and that's when she saw the note. A single sheet of paper was lying on the countertop next to the fruit bowl. It looked like Aunt Sharon's handwriting.

**Tess,**

**Your mom and I are taking Natalie to dinner and a movie tonight. Don't wait up for us! Denny said it was fine.**

**Natalie fed Otter and gave him treats. Lots of them. Sorry.**

**Have fun!**

**-Sharon**

Tess smiled at the note. She loved how readily Aunt Sharon, and even her mom, seemed to accept Natalie into Tess's life. Tess planned on having Denny and Natalie a part of it for as long as they were willing, and having her aunt accept them without question or prejudice meant the world to Tess.

She typed out a quick text to Denny: What this I hear about you letting Natalie go on a girls night and I wasn't invited?

Denny: Well, we stopped by to surprise you and you weren't home.

Denny: Besides, I have better plans for you...

Tess: Oh? What kind of plans?

Denny: I can't tell you, or they won't be a surprise.

Tess: :(

Denny: You home now?
Tess: Maybe.... Why, do you wanna come over?
Denny: See you in 20
Tess: :)

Now that she was in a time crunch, she decided to get a shower and forget the stresses of the day. Forget about Kane O'Leary for a few hours; wonder where he was and what he was up to.

She headed to her bedroom, gathered some clean clothes, and then made her way to the master bathroom.

Slipping off her dress pants and dropping them on the cool, tiled floor of the bathroom, Tess leaned into the shower and turned the water on. After a long day of work and tracking down a potential killer, she couldn't wait for the feel of the hot water to caress her tired muscles.

As she unbuttoned her shirt and added it to the pair of pants at her feet, her cell phone chimed. Glancing at it, she smiled.

Denny: I'm almost there. I kept hitting all the red lights.

"You have a key now. Come find me," Tess texted back. Hitting 'send,' she finished undressing and then stepped into the shower.

Enjoying the water coursing over her, Tess shampooed her hair and was rinsing it when she heard Otter barking in the living room. Denny must be there. A smile crept across her face, and she wondered if he'd come to find her or if he'd hear the shower running and wait for her on the couch.

Her question was answered a few minutes later when the bathroom door cracked open, and Denny stuck his head in the room.

Feeling emboldened, Tess made a show of rinsing her long dark hair and letting the suds slide down her body. She could feel his eyes on her and felt her temperature rise.

She glanced at him and gave him a come-hither look, which he gratefully seemed to accept.

His blue eyes dark with need, Denny stepped fully into the bathroom and shut the door behind him, the shower steam swirling around his tall frame.

Tess continued to rinse herself, never pulling her eyes from his. His breath quickened, and he stepped closer to the shower door, his gaze finally leaving Tess's face and sliding across her wet body.

"Need any help?" he asked, his voice thick as his gaze lingered on her breasts before sliding back up to her face.

"Maybe..." she informed him with a smirk. "Sometimes I can't reach certain... places...very well."

That was all she needed to say. Without another word, Denny reached up and started undoing his neck tie, his heated gaze remaining on Tess the whole time. He made quick work of his buttoned-down shirt and dress pants. Only when he laid his phone down gently did he take his eyes off of Tess's naked form.

Once his clothes were lying in a pile next to hers, he opened the shower door and stepped inside, instantly taking Tess into his arms. The steamy water slid over their entwined body as Denny molded his lips to hers in a passionate kiss. It had been a few days since they'd had a quiet moment to fully enjoy each other's company, and they both seemed to want to enjoy their time.

"God, you're beautiful," Denny whispered in her ear as he left a trail of kisses down her neck. His hands slid down to cup her wet ass. She looked up at him and grinned before sliding her hands from his shoulders to his chest.

"You make me feel beautiful," she said, staring up into his eyes, suddenly feeling more emotional than normal. "Otherwise, I'm just Tess." She shrugged, a small smile playing on her lips.

"You're never 'just Tess' to me," Denny murmured as his hands continued exploring her. "You are my present, my future. You're my everything, and I can't imagine my life without you." His hand slid lower in between her legs, and she let out a soft moan.

As the warm water coursed down their bodies, Tess and Denny lost themselves in each other. Their eyes remained locked on each other through the shower steam as their hands explored.

"Turn around," Denny whispered hoarsely in her ear, his hands gently yet firmly urging her to face the shower wall. Tess moaned lightly as he trailed kisses down her neck and across her shoulder as he took her from behind.

Between the passion and the echo of water against glass, they didn't hear their phones ring. First Tess's, then, seconds later, Denny's. It wasn't until both phones began ringing again, in tandem, that the couple were finally jarred back to reality.

"Something's happened," Tess said, a worried look overtaking her once-blissful face. Denny pulled away from her, turning the water off before following her out of the shower.

Wrapping a towel around herself, Tess picked up her still-ringing phone. It was Malone. And he'd called four times already. Casting a glance at Denny, she watched as he, too, picked up his ringing phone.

"Dane," she answered, even as she heard Denny do the same. The bathroom door squeaked open as he stepped into the hallway to answer his phone.

"Dane, there's been a kidnapping," Malone barked, cutting to the point. "It's Natalie. She's gone."

# Chapter Forty-Eight

*Tuesday, September 25th, 8:25 PM*

Glad for once that she'd driven her department car home, Tess slid into the front seat, turned the ignition, and backed out of the driveway at record speed. By the time she approached the first intersection, she already had her lights and sirens going and was on the radio with dispatch.

Denny sat immobile next to her as she raced toward the mall a few miles down the road. Tess had tried to get him to agree for her to drop him off at the station, but he'd declined with a shake of his head. He was an emotional mess, and Tess didn't know what they'd find at the mall or where their investigation would take them. Having Denny there to worry about was an added stressor.

She risked a glance at Denny and sucked in a breath at what she saw. Silent tears slid down his tormented face, and she could tell he was barely keeping it together. His child had been kidnapped, and his world was shattered.

Tess reached over and gently laid a consoling hand on his thigh, letting him know she was there without saying a word. She was about to move her hand back to the steering wheel when Denny suddenly grasped her fingers tightly in his grip, as though he were afraid to lose her, too.

As Tess pulled into the large parking lot nearest the main entrance of the mall, she was relieved to see Miles and Scafferty's cruiser pulling in behind her.

"Wait here a sec," she told Denny, "I need to see if this is the correct entrance." She knew her excuse was lame, but she needed to speak to Miles and Scafferty in private, and Denny didn't seem to notice. Her stomach churned with anxiety, and her hands were clammy. *Deep breath in, deep breath out.* She tried to relax as best as she could, considering the severity of the moment. She wanted—no, needed— to avoid another panic attack. What good was she to Natalie and Denny if she let her anxiety win?

She parked her SUV before getting out to speak to her coworkers. Their empathetic expressions did little to improve the situation but comforted Tess nonetheless. The trio talked in low tones, sharing what they knew so far from the initial 911 call, which wasn't much.

"Okay, guys, I'm going in to speak to my mother and aunt. I need you two to wrangle Denny. Take him to the station or keep him out here, anywhere but in there," Tess instructed, jabbing a finger toward the glass door of the mall. "He's not taking this well, and I don't blame him. But you know how it is... We don't know what we'll find, and we can't have the distraction. Or having him go rogue because emotions are involved."

Miles and Scafferty nodded in understanding. They'd seen parents get tangled up in investigations and it always ended up in chaos.

"We have this, Dane." Miles nodded. "Go ahead and do what you need to do. Find that little girl." He and Scafferty turned and headed toward Tess's SUV to care for Denny while Tess slipped away to begin investigating.

Within moments, she found herself racing into the nearly deserted Buckeye Valley Mall, where her mother, Aunt Sharon, and two members of mall security stood huddled in front of a Bath and Body Works. Both women were sobbing uncontrollably while one of the mall security officers stood there staring at them, hands shoved in his pockets. The other officer paced nearby, speaking to someone on his cell phone.

Giving the young officer little mind as he stood there doing absolutely nothing helpful, Tess brushed past him and went directly to her Aunt Sharon.

"What happened? Tell me everything." She tried to reign in the panic in her voice to not worsen the anxiety of the situation, but knew she was failing. Usually, she was even-minded and cool-tempered, even while under duress, but it was Natalie! Poor, sweet little Natalie!

"We... We were just coming out of the theater, and Natalie asked to use the restroom. She went in by herself, but your mom and I were standing right outside in the hallway! We were watching everyone who went in or came out," Sharon sobbed, dabbing at her eyes with a wadded-up ball of soggy tissues.

"She'd just come out to us when a large family went into the restroom. There was chaos, and someone bumped into me," Kathy inserted, rubbing a reddened area on her forehead. "I hit my head on the wall. When I turned around, Natalie was gone." She started crying again in earnest.

"Did you see who took her? Where they went?" Tess urged gently, trying to keep the two women on task.

"I heard her squeal—that's what made me look up—and I saw a man carrying her away through the crowd. He had his hand over her mouth by then, and she was fighting him. Kicking and hitting him," Sharon recalled. "They were headed towards the exit by the Old Navy."

"Did you see his face? What did he look like?"

"No, not his face, just his sweatshirt. He had the hood pulled up over his head. He was about your height, average weight. Jeans, dark green hoodie with some kind if white logo on the back." Sharon paused for a moment, as though trying to recall what exactly she'd seen.

"Do you remember what the logo looked like?" Tess asked, getting frustrated but trying not to let it show.

"Like maybe a leaf or a tree?" Kathy offered.

"Yeah, it was like a leaf and maybe a word?" Sharon agreed excitedly. "It was a simple design, but it all happened so fast that I don't even know if I really paid much attention, to be honest."

"Great, guys. This is helpful. We'll get the information to the media and issue an Amber Alert. We've already got extra patrol out looking," Tess comforted the two women as she saw movement out of the corner of her eye. Miles, Scafferty, and Denny came barreling toward them.

"What do you have?" Miles asked, panic in his voice. Tess avoided Denny's gaze.

This was bad. Very bad.

"Miles, a word, please," Tess gestured with her head. Miles nodded and stepped away from Denny and Scafferty, who were already asking Sharon and Kathy the same questions she'd just asked them. The women were sobbing and apologizing to Denny, and Tess feared they'd need an ambulance for them if they didn't calm down. This couldn't be good for their health.

Already a crowd was forming, whispering voices rising in the echoing halls of the enclosed mall. People were sticking their heads out of stores trying to spy at what was going on, getting a front row view at the latest drama unfolding before their eyes.

"Why is Denny still here? He needs to be at the office. He's a mess," Tess asked Miles, her voice low and even as she relayed her concern. "You know what happens when emotions get involved. Hell, Malone might even yank *me* off of this case. I need you to help get Denny out of here so he's not a liability or a distraction."

"I understand. Trust me, Tess. We tried. He wouldn't stay put. He's already called his special agent friends at BCI to help us, which can't be a bad thing, can it?" Miles asked, his voice full of empathy.

"No. No, I guess not. But either way, you have to help me keep an eye on him, okay? Now, let's break up, work the crowd, show Natalie's picture to everyone, see if anyone else saw anything, okay? No one leaves until they are asked, got it?"

"Yes, got it," Miles nodded, turning to give orders to mall security.

Stepping out toward the forming crowd, Tess held up her hand for silence. After a moment or so the crowd finally calmed down enough that her voice could be heard.

"My name is Detective Tess Dane with the Swain County Sheriff's Department. There was a kidnapping here tonight of a nine-year-old girl. Her name is Natalie Haywood." Tess's voice cracked when she said the name. "She was last seen near the restrooms by the movie theater. We have officers at the two main mall exits with photos of Natalie. All the other exits have been closed for the evening. We ask that you exit through one of the two main exits and view the photos. If you recognize the young girl, if you saw anything, heard anything.... Anything that you think may be helpful, please let a member of law enforcement or mall security know immediately. Thank you."

As soon as she stepped back, the volume of murmuring voices escalated as people began making their way toward the exits.

Tess risked a glance at Denny and instantly regretted it. She'd never seen someone look so shattered, so desperate. His eyes were bloodshot, and his face was pale. He looked as if a piece of himself had been sucked out by Natalie's disappearance, like he'd become the gaunt duplicate of his normal, vibrant self.

Tears welled up behind her eyelids, and Tess willed them away. If she broke down now, what good would she be to her little buddy? She tried not to think of what horrors were playing out on the innocent young girl. As a cop, she knew the kidnapping most likely wasn't a random act of violence and that there was some kind of explanation. But as a woman who had feelings and a relationship with Natalie, it was easy to think of the worst case scenario: that the kidnapping was to appease someone's sick perversion.

As these thoughts wrestled in Tess's mind, she tried rationalizing what she knew to be fact. Denny had good relationships with everyone in his family, so it was highly unlikely they'd be involved. But what about her family? Tess's mother seemed to thrive on drama and had proven herself to be a volatile wild card. Tess shuddered to think about the implications.

But what if it wasn't about family at all, but about their jobs? As far as Tess knew, Denny wasn't working any especially high-profile cases at the moment. At least, none that he'd told her about.

Or what about the O'Leary case? It had already proven to be full of violence and mystery. Tess had been tracking Kane O'Leary down because of Garrett and Kevin's deaths. But what about Breck? He was currently sitting in county lock-up for stealing ancient artifacts from his father to repay bookies. Could Natalie's abduction somehow be connected to the Shaman and Breck's unpaid debts? If Breck was locked up, the Shaman wouldn't get paid, and that could be a motive.

If the kidnapping was because of any of the open O'Leary cases, Tess couldn't help but blame herself. She was getting too close to the truth of what had happened to Garrett and Kevin O'Leary. And whether the guilt fell on Kane or an unnamed person that had yet to make themselves known, Tess feared the worst. Someone wanted to threaten her by taking Natalie.

The mere thought of it made Tess's stomach roil. Dear god, what if this was all her fault? What if Natalie was killed because of—

"Detective?" a voice behind Tess pulled her from her dark thoughts. She turned to find a young wisp of a teenage girl standing behind her, long strawberry blonde hair pulled back in an elaborate braid that trailed over her shoulder.

"Yes? How can I help you?" Tess forced a smile as she watched the girl fiddle with the strap of her Hello Kitty purse.

"Can I see the picture? Of Natalie? I... I might have seen something."

"Yes, of course," Tess said, showing the girl two different pictures of Natalie. Tess almost shouted out when she saw the girl's eyes widen in recognition.

"I saw her! I saw her with a man!"

"Where? What did he look like? Tell me everything," Tess asked, reigning in her excitement. She didn't want to scare the girl, but this was possibly a huge lead.

"I saw them when I was standing near the theater exit, waiting for my friend, and I saw that girl being led out by some guy wearing a hoodie."

"Was she okay? Did she look hurt?"

"She looked really scared, but really pissed off too–am I allowed to say that?" the girl replied, her eyes going wide again. "Like a feral cat that wants you to leave it alone but will eat your face if you touch it."

*That sounds exactly like Natalie*, Tess thought, glad that Natalie was full of spunk and sass.

"What did the man look like? Was he White? Black? Old? Young?"

"He was an old white guy," the girl made a face.

"Old like... Santa Claus?" Tess asked, even though it sounded ridiculous to her, "Or old like.... That security officer over there with the glasses?" Tess pointed to the mall cop who appeared to be in his mid-fifties.

"In between? More like the cop? He was older than my dad and had black hair, blue eyes, and a mustache. He was holding her arm tight and kinda dragging her with him, like she didn't really want to go. To be honest, I thought she was his kid, and she was just mad at her dad, and they were fighting. My dad used to drag me out of stores when I caused trouble so..." The girl shrugged.

"Do you remember what color the sweatshirt was? What else was he wearing?"

"Dark green with some kind of white logo. A tree, maybe? Jeans, work boots. Typical guy stuff."

"Did you happen to see where they went? What kind of car they had? License plate number?"

"No, sorry. They walked out the door and down the aisle of cars directly outside the door. My friend came back then, so I lost track of where they went."

"Thanks, you've been a huge help. If you don't mind, I'll need you to write all of this down for your official statement. You can do that now or go down to the station. If you're under eighteen, you'll need a parent or guardian to accompany you. Are they here now?"

The girl shook her head. "I'm only sixteen, and my sister dropped me off. Can I call my Dad and have him take me to the station?"

"Sure thing," Tess smiled. She got the girl's name and phone number to follow up with and then went over to Miles and Scafferty. Denny looked up when she approached, desperately searching her face for any new information.

"We might have a lead. A young girl saw a man leading Natalie out of the front door of the theater and down the main aisle in the parking lot. If we can pull those tapes, we can hopefully catch this bastard on video and get the make, model, and color of the vehicle. She was also able to provide more of a description of the kidnapper."

"Then let's watch those tapes," Scafferty said, as he headed to track down the security guard.

# Chapter Forty-Nine



Across town, a cell phone emitted a hideous loud beep that broke the silence as an Amber Alert came through. A child was missing.

"About damn time," the kidnapper muttered to himself as he sat watching the news bulletin on his phone. **Breaking news! Local girl kidnapped!**

He scoffed. They'd never find her, at least not any time soon. They were already looking for the wrong guy. According to the news, the suspect had black hair, a mustache, blue eyes, and was in his mid-fifties. Hadn't they thought he might have worn a disguise?

*Idiots.*

He'd learned early on that if you were going to do something illegal, you had to cover your tracks. That's why so many criminals get caught. Just doing dumb shit.

During his daily jogs, he liked to listen to true crime podcasts and it was always the idiots who Googled shit on their phones or personal computers that got caught.

He shook his head at the thought. Amateurs.

Nah, he had planned this out well. He'd been watching, waiting, looking for any kind of weakness in that bitch detective's armor. And he'd found it.

When she'd started sniffing around, asking questions about the night Garrett disappeared, he knew she'd have to be stopped. That's when she just kept buzzing around like an annoying gnat at a picnic, constantly getting involved with everything. Then Kevin ended up dead.

He let out a sigh. He hadn't meant to kill Kevin, at least not initially. He'd wanted to hurt him, yes. Get him to listen, yes. But kill him? Maybe, if he was being honest with himself.

He stood up and turned his phone off. The room was suddenly silent except for the sound of the crickets and frogs outside. He let out a yawn and stretched his back before moving to his backpack to look for something to eat.

Glancing at the small lump lying on the corner of the confined space, he listened for the girl's breathing. At first, he heard nothing and started to panic, but then it came, short ragged breaths as though she'd been crying.

"You awake?" he asked, toeing her with his boot. She didn't move. He thought about kicking her, but he wasn't cruel. He wasn't a monster.

"Suit yourself then," he said to the immobile form at his feet. "You just have to stay here long enough for me to get rid of the cop, got it?"

That got a reaction. The girl started flailing against her restraints, her voice muffled against the gag in her mouth.

He let out a laugh. "Relax, little one. I won't kill her. Immediately." Then he stepped over the child and opened the door leading outside before locking it behind him and walking away.

# Chapter Fifty



*Wednesday, September 26th, 12:42 AM*

"Can you zoom in a little more? The girl said she saw the guy dragging Natalie down the main aisle, there," Tess pointed to the small surveillance screen in front of her.

Denny, Tess, Deputy Miles, and the older mall security officer were crammed into a tiny office roughly the size of a powder room. The temperature was stifling but the urgency of the situation was more pressing at the moment. The media had already shown up and been given a description of the kidnapper, and for now, Tess had been given permission to view the video footage of the parking lot. She was relieved that they hadn't made her get a warrant given what they were up against.

"There!" Denny gasped, aggressively tapping the monitor. On the video feed, two people could be seen walking down the aisle; a taller adult-sized individual wearing a green hooded sweatshirt and a young girl. Natalie.

Tess felt her heart shatter as she watched, the horror of it all too big to process as the man half dragged the girl down the line of vehicle, stopping at an older model red extended cab pick-up. Beside her, Tess heard Denny let out a sob as they watched the man on screen grab the girl around the waist and force her into the vehicle at knife point. Tess could only assume the knife had been under the truck seat or in his pocket. The video was too grainy, and there were too many obstructions to get a perfect play-by-play of events.

Regardless, it was enough to at least give them an idea of the type of make and model of the escape vehicle to further assist in their search.

"Let's get this video over to forensics STAT," Tess commanded. "I want every IT, computer engineer, high school hacker, I don't care.... Everyone is to work on this video! We need it enhanced; make, model, license plate. Check traffic cameras, business security cameras... We need all the information we can get. And send the vehicle description over to update the Amber Alert now!"

"I'm on it," came a voice from the doorway. Tess turned and saw Special Agent Aaron Claybourne from BCI. He was a coworker and close friend of Denny's and had worked with Tess during the Torture Killer case. Tess trusted his abilities and was grateful to have him there.

"Thanks, Claybourne," she gave him a broken smile. He nodded at her before leaning in to say something to Denny. Denny listened carefully and nodded solemnly.

The mall security officer finished making a copy of the video and handed it to Tess who immediately handed it to Claybourne. She knew BCI had access to better state of the art computers and enhancement software than she did and they'd make it a priority.

After signing the appropriate chain of custody forms, Claybourne checked on Denny one last time and then left for the BCI lab in London, Ohio to get started on digitally enhancing the video.

Deputy Miles and the security guard headed out to inform the other officers that had shown up to help about what they had found on the video. Until more details came through, they would be looking for an older model red extended cab pick up. Tess hoped that soon they'd be able to add a make, model, license plate, and even an owner to it.

***

Hours that felt like years passed as they waited for a call from BCI. Tess had been pacing a hole in her hardwood floor, trying to calm her aunt and mother and offer solace to Denny, all while also doing her job.

Officer Kennedy, the Liaison Officer, had arrived just after midnight and was currently sitting with Kathy and Sharon in Tess's living room, offering hot tea and a comforting shoulder. An occasional sniffle could be heard, and the last time Tess checked, Kathy had Otter wrapped in a bear hug. The dog didn't seem to care, though, and let the woman cry all she needed to into his ebony fur. Oh, how her opinion of him had changed!

Denny retreated to the bedroom. Tess had found him there, sitting in the dark, on the edge of her bed, with his head in his hands.

She silently glided into the room and sat down next to him, wrapping her arm around his broad shoulders. She didn't say anything. What could she say? *Everything will be okay? We'll find her?* She wouldn't make promises she didn't know she could keep.

The first twenty four hours after a kidnapping were the most crucial. After that, the chances of survival...

She couldn't think that way. Not yet.

"I can't believe she's gone," Denny finally broke the silence, his voice strained. "Who would do this? I keep thinking about the cases I'm currently working on. If this could be some kind of sick... retribution for one of them. I...I worked a sexual assault case a year ago and... oh my God..." He jumped up and ran to the bathroom. Tess felt tears burn the back of her eyes as she heard him vomit.

How had they been so happy, so carefree just hours ago? Where did this nightmare begin? Would it ever end? Tess pulled her legs up to her chest and wrapped her arms around them, dropped her face in her knees and sobbed.

A few moments later, she heard the bathroom door squeak on its hinges and felt Denny sit back down beside her.

"Den?"

"Yeah?"

"What if this isn't about you? What if it's about me?"

"You? What do you mean?"

"Well, I'm working on a cold case, right? And now there's been another murder and stolen artifacts. I've arrested the suspect for the stolen artifacts, but I can't find the person of interest for the murders. And it's a stretch, anyway."

"Why is that?" Denny asked, turning to Tess.

"Well, I'm pretty sure Kane O'Leary is the one responsible for the murder of Garrett nearly thirty years ago. I need more proof, though. The problem is, I went to speak with him today and no one can find him. He's an old man who's wheelchair bound and has health problems. How can he just disappear? He couldn't have killed Kevin. It's impossible for someone who can't even walk to climb a steep flight of stairs, attack and kill a healthy man, and then escape all without leaving a trace.... Right? What if there is someone else involved? A second murderer that I haven't figured out yet? What if they took Natalie to use as a pawn somehow?"

Denny sat silently, seeming to mull the new theory over. Running his fingers through his short, cropped hair, he sighed.

"I don't know, Tess. It's possible. I mean–"

Tess's phone rang, startling both of them. She grabbed it and answered in record time.

"This is Dane," she all but shouted, excited for some positive news.

"Hey, Tess, this is Claybourne. Forensics was able to get some information on the truck."

"Wait, I'm putting you on speaker. I have Denny here with me," Tess said as she pressed the speaker button.

"Hey, man," Claybourne greeted Denny. "We were able to find out some info about the truck. It's a Chevy Silverado, Ohio plates RP7263. It's registered to a Steven Sweeney over in Hillvale. The problem is he reported it stolen three days ago."

"Shit," Tess muttered. "And does this Sweeney guy match the description of the perp?"

"Negative. He's a Black man with silver hair, balding on top. Your witness said the guy she saw was tall, White, blue eyes, black hair?"

"Yeah, and a mustache," Tess confirmed.

"Definitely not the same guy then. Besides, Steve Sweeney has another distinguishing feature," Claybourne offered.

"Which is...?"

"He only has one arm. Lost the other serving in the military. I'm sure if Sweeney was the same guy that took Natalie, your witness would have noticed his missing appendage."

Tess let out a growl of frustration. Claybourne was right. Steve Sweeney wasn't their guy, however, his truck had been used in the commission of a crime. She wanted to pull the incident report and see what details she could glean from it. Better yet, she wanted to speak to Mr. Sweeney. Maybe he'd seen something when his truck was taken? Maybe it wouldn't be a dead end after all?

"Thanks, Claybourne. You've been a huge help. I'll keep you updated, okay?" Tess said.

"You're welcome, and I'll do the same. And Denny, we'll do the best we can. Try to get some rest. We have a lot of our guys working on this, okay?"

"Thanks, Aaron," Denny's voice sounded ragged. Tess said goodbye to Claybourne with his promise of sending over all of the information he'd obtained so far.

With some resistance, she was able to get Denny to agree to lie down and attempt to get some rest, even though they both knew no one would be sleeping tonight.

Once he was tucked in her bed, she quietly crept back out into the living room. It appeared that Sharon had retreated to the guest room, and Kathy was curled up on the couch under an Afghan. Otter lay snoozing in his dog bed next to Tess's favorite chair.

The living room was dark except for a small lamp in the corner, which provided just enough light to move around without tripping over something.

When Otter heard Tess pad down the hallway, he lifted his head, and his tail began thumping out a rhythm. She smiled and motioned for him to follow her as she quietly slipped into the kitchen.

"Any word?" Officer Kennedy asked in a hushed tone from where she worked quietly on her laptop at the kitchen table.

Tess nodded. "BCI just called. They got some information about the truck used in the getaway."

Trying to be quiet so she didn't wake the sleeping woman in the living room, she crept over to fill a mug of fresh brewed coffee. "Thanks for making this." She indicated the carafe of coffee.

"Not a problem. I figured we'd need it on a night like tonight." Kennedy attempted a smile. "God, I hate when kids are involved."

"I know. Especially one of our own." Tess slid into a chair across from Kennedy with a sigh. Taking a sip from her mug, she willed herself not to start crying again. "They say the truck was reported stolen a few days ago."

"Crap. So this was probably planned?"

"Possibly," Tess shrugged. "Most likely. I'd guess one of two things. Either the owner of the truck knows who took the truck and reported it missing to cover his own butt or the perp saw an opportunity and struck. How convenient that his getaway vehicle just happened to be stolen and untraceable back to him?"

"How about your other suspect? The one you were looking for earlier? Does he have any vehicles?" Kennedy asked, looking up from her computer screen. "I heard Denny ask something earlier about some guy you were looking for."

"Oh, that guy is elderly and immobile. He's confined to a wheelchair and lives in an assisted living facility for seniors. No one can seem to find him either. I have an APB out on him."

"What's his name?"

"Kane O'Leary," Tess said, taking another sip of coffee. She felt a dog snoot bump her thigh and reached down to caress Otter's soft fur. "Why do you ask?"

"Just curious. We have some time right now while forensics are checking the CCTV cameras and stuff. Figured we could try to be useful here. It's not like I'm going to be able to sleep anyway," Kennedy answered warmly.

"Good point," Tess agreed. "I feel like we are just sitting here wasting precious time. She's out there somewhere, in the dark, all alone..."

Officer Kennedy reached over and laid a comforting hand on Tess's and gave it a light squeeze.

"What was the name of the truck owner?" Kennedy asked, changing the subject.

"Steven Sweeney," Tess answered, moving over to sit next to Kennedy so she could see the computer screen as the liaison officer typed the name into the police database.

"There are two Steven Sweeneys in Swain County," Kennedy informed Tess, leaning out of the way so Tess could look closer.

"That one, in Hillvale," Tess answered confidently, pointing at the first option.

"Perfect," Kennedy mumbled to herself as she clicked on it and pulled up the man's file. The two women quickly read the short entry and let out a collective sigh.

Steven Sweeney was a Boy Scout; not so much as a speeding ticket.

"Ugh... I don't know what I was hoping for, but I guess we should be glad he's not some criminal mastermind, right?" Tess mused, chewing her bottom lip.

"Yeah. I guess I was just kind of hoping it would have something that would stand out to you and also match up with Kane O'Leary. You know, some weird, abstract connection we haven't noticed until now." Kennedy admitted.

"There may not be a connection; that's the problem," Tess sighed. "I feel like they're connected, but I don't want to force an idea if it's not there."

"Wait, this guy only has one arm?" Kennedy asked, her nose wrinkling as she read the rest of the file.

"Yeah, why do you ask?"

"Well, for two reasons. One, it says here he lost it in combat during his time in the service. Did O'Leary ever serve? And if he only had one arm, did he attend any kind of...I don't know... handicap support group or physical therapy where he might have met O'Leary?" Kennedy thought aloud.

"We have to see if and when their paths crossed," Tess said, snapping her fingers, the light finally switching on in her head. "God, why didn't I think of that? Am I losing my touch?"

"No, you're just very close to this victim, and you're not thinking things through clearly. You're also exhausted, Tess," Kennedy empathized. "Tell you what, why don't I work on this, and you go try to get an hour or two of sleep? You'll need it for tomorrow."

Tess thought about it for a second, torn between exhaustion and the need to find Natalie.

"You sure?" she finally asked, looking over at Kennedy.

"Yes. Besides, I took a nap this afternoon and feel pretty good. I'll work on finding any connections between the two men. There may be none, but we have to do something, right? If any news comes in, I'll come get you, I promise."

"Okay then... If you're sure," Tess sighed, feeling guilty.

"Go," Kennedy waved her off as she went back to her laptop.

"Thanks," Tess said, sliding her cell phone across the kitchen table before motioning for Otter to follow her down the hall.

# Chapter Fifty-One

*Wednesday, September 26th, 5:22 AM*

It was still dark when Officer Kennedy gently nudged Tess's shoulder, rousing her from sleep.

Tess sat up in bed, immediately alert, still fully dressed from the night before. She'd wanted to be ready to go in case there was any word on Natalie's whereabouts.

Denny stirred next to her, instantly awakened as well. He rubbed his eyes and looked between Tess and Kennedy for any news.

"I think I might have found something," Kennedy said, "A connection."

"Really?" Tess hopped out of bed like a bolt of lightning had hit her, Denny and Otter hot on her heels. They followed Kennedy to the kitchen and sat at the table, waiting impatiently for Kennedy to gather her thoughts.

"Okay, so I looked through your case file for Kane O'Leary and double checked just for peace of mind that he did *not* serve in the military. You were correct, there was no connection there," Kennedy began, looking back down at her computer screen while  she spoke.

"And…?" Tess ground out with an impatient gesture. "Get to the good stuff."

Kennedy gave her a look of reproach. "I'm getting there."

"Sorry."

"So, I looked into Mr. Sweeney a little more. Where he works, who lives with him, who he hangs out with, that type of thing. That's when I found something that might be important. According to Sweeny's social media account, his daughter, Jasmine, and grandson, Shawn, live with him. I took that information and looked up each of them. Jasmine rarely posts on social media and when she does, it's mostly cute pictures of kittens or animals."

"Okay, but what does this have to do with Natalie?" Denny finally entered the conversation, his voice strained.

"I'm getting to that part. That's when I clicked on the grandson's Facebook page and found this." Kennedy turned her computer around so that Denny and Tess could see the screen.

On the screen was a picture of a handsome Black man with a bright smile spread across his face. On his white scrubs was a logo that Tess had seen multiple times before. The caption under the photo read, *"I love my job! I get to meet some of the coolest people and hear some crazy stories. I oughta write a book! Whata y'all think?"*

"I just talked to that guy yesterday! Along the fence at Glade Springs when I was looking for O'Leary..." Tess breathed, suddenly feeling faint. "Dear God... this *is* about me after all. Someone took Natalie, and possibly Kane, because of me."

She shoved away from the table and barely made it to the bathroom in time to lose the contents of her stomach.

# Chapter Fifty-Two



*Wednesday, September 26th, 7:50 AM*

"Swain County Sheriff's Department, open up!" Tess pounded on the door of Steven Sweeney's red brick home on the eastern side of Hillvale near the county line. It was barely eight in the morning, but she'd secured a search warrant to look for Natalie before driving all the way out there.

Officers Scafferty, Miles, and Cooper, as well as Denny and Agent Claybourne, had pulled up behind her.

She raised her hand again to pound on the wooden door and announce herself when it finally opened and an older one-armed Black man stood there glaring at Tess.

"Why are you pounding on my door like that so early in the morning? Did you find my truck?" He asked. His deep voice was smooth and held a hint of the South. "You about gave me a heart attack with all that carrying on."

"I'm sorry I scared you, sir, but this is a rather urgent matter. I'm Detective Tess Dane, and we are with–"

"The Swain County Sheriff's Department," the old man tutted. "I know, I heard you the first time. Don't let the gray hair fool you none. I'm old, but I ain't deaf."

"Is your grandson, Shawn, here?" Tess asked. "We need to speak with him immediately."

"What's he done? He's a good boy, Detective," the man bristled.

"Mr. Sweeney, a young girl has been kidnapped, and we believe your truck was used in that crime. I'm also working on a murder case that involves someone that your grandson comes in contact with. We are starting to think that perhaps both the murders and the kidnapping are connected somehow and that your grandson, Shawn, may know something. May have seen something that he doesn't even know is important."

"Oh, Lord..." Sweeney took a step backward, his face stricken. He turned suddenly and yelled, "Shawn!! Get yo ass out here! The police wanna talk to you!" He looked back to the officers.

"C'mon in," he gestured, opening the door wider for Tess, Denny, and Miles to enter the home. "I'll go get him."

Miles followed Sweeney a few steps so he could see down the hallway, making sure that Shawn wasn't going to make a run for it. The other officers outside would watch the windows.

Tess looked around the small living room for any signs that Natalie had been there but came up empty handed.

A blue velvet couch with white throw pillows sat under a large oil painting of Bourbon Street during Mardi Gras. In the corner, next to a window, stood a narrow bookshelf filled with the works of Tananarive Due, S.A. Cosby, Tiffany D. Jackson, and Victor LaValle.

An electric blue Beta swam around its watery kingdom atop an upright piano against the front wall. Tess leaned in to watch it for a moment when she heard a sound from the hallway.

Glancing over, she saw Shawn standing there, wearing sleep pants and a groggy expression. He caught her eye as he slid a tee shirt over his head.

"Hey, Detective, what's this about? Did I do something wrong? I thought we were cool." He almost looked hurt.

"I'm sorry, Shawn. No, I don't think you did anything, but... but something happened yesterday after I left you at Glade Springs, and we need to talk."

"Is everything okay? Did you find Mr. O'Leary? I kept an eye out for him, like you asked but I never saw him."

"At all? Your entire shift?" Tess asked, and an alarm bell went off in her head. This did not bode well.

"No, ma'am," Shawn answered, looking concerned. He glanced between Tess and Denny, then back again.

"Shawn, why don't you have a seat?" Tess gestured for the couch. She waited for him to take a seat before taking one herself. "Last night, a young girl was kidnapped from a theater in Crawley. Forensics was able to determine through surveillance video that the vehicle used in the getaway was your grandfather's truck."

Shawn's eyes rounded as he processed the information. He cast a worried look at his grandfather and then back at Tess.

"Have you found the little girl?"

"Not yet. That's why we are here. Her name is Natalie, and that's her dad," Tess gestured toward Denny, who solemnly nodded to Shawn, his lips in a grim line.

"According to our records, you reported the truck stolen three days ago now, correct, Mr. Sweeney?" Tess asked, looking up at the older man standing in the corner.

"Yes, that's correct."

"Were you the last one to drive it?" she asked him pointedly. He shook his head.

"I drove it. It was the vehicle I used to get to and from work," Shawn offered, his shoulders slumping in dismay.

"Okay, so you were driving it then. Why didn't you report it stolen?" Tess asked, "Why did your grandfather do it?"

"I don't know. Because the truck and insurance were in his name? Because I had to work the next day so I had to borrow his other car," Shawn shrugged. "You see, I was making payments to Granddad for the truck. It was getting too bulky for him to maneuver, especially with his disability, so I offered to buy it off of him. I had to work the night it was stolen, but I met up with a friend beforehand. We decided to grab a late lunch but overstayed at the restaurant, and I was almost late for work. My friend dropped me off at work to save time. The truck was parked on the street near her house a block away, so I figured I'd just walk to get it after my shift. I came out of work, ready to get home and sleep, but when I got to her place, it was gone. I was pissed, but I think it was kinda my fault it was stolen in the first place."

"And why is that?" Tess asked.

"Because I usually just throw the keys under the visor and call it a day. Nobody's going to steal an old truck, right? I guess I was wrong. That day, though, I'd been distracted because I was running late. I don't remember putting the keys under the visor. I'm worried I left them on the seat."

"You might have been being watched even then. Or someone could have just walked by and seen their keys randomly lying on the seat..." Tess thought through the information. She'd like to see the security tapes from the night of the theft. She made a note to herself to contact the responding officer from that night to get a look at any footage they had found.

"How'd you get home that night?"

"Granddad drove all the way to get me in his old Toyota Corolla. I drove him home. That's what I've been using to get to work the past couple of days. If you don't believe me, check the security cameras at work," Shawn said, panic starting to fill his voice.

"Shawn, take a deep breath," Tess soothed. She reached out and grasped his hand calmly. "Just breathe. You aren't in trouble. We are just trying to figure out how and when someone had access to your vehicle."

Shawn took a few deep breaths, but his leg was still nervously bouncing.

"When was the last time you saw Kane O'Leary?" Tess asked, letting go of Shawn's hand and folding her hands in her lap.

"The day before yesterday, like I told you already. What's he got to do with this?"

"I'm working on two other cases currently, a cold case and a new one. I believe Mr. O'Leary could be involved in one or both of them. And now he's missing. Is he on the run? Or was he taken just like Natalie? That is what we are trying to find out."

"How is this little girl involved, though?" Shawn asked, wrinkling his nose in confusion.

"Because she's like a daughter to me, and the closer I get to closing these cases, the harder someone is trying to get to me."

"Well, shit," Shawn muttered. "How can I help? What can I do to help?"

"Don't discuss this with anyone, especially at work. I don't want the news getting out. If Mr. O'Leary *does* have something to do with all of this, I don't want to spook him into hiding. I just need you to keep an eye and ear open for any signs of him, any chatter about his whereabouts, any strange sounds coming from his apartment..."

"Got it. I won't say a word," Shawn swore in earnest.

# Chapter Fifty-Three

*Wednesday, September 26th, 11:15 AM*

Shawn strode down the hallway leading toward Kane O'Leary's apartment. Since the police had awoken him that morning, he couldn't stop thinking about that little girl. Was she still alive? Could Mr. O'Leary really have hurt her, or was he a victim too?

The older man had always been kind to Shawn. It was just hard for him to imagine the nice old man hurting a fly. The fact that no one had seen Mr. O'Leary since yesterday morning was also concerning. Had anyone checked his apartment? What if he'd fallen and was hurt?

Nina, one of the other orderlies, was walking down the hallway toward Shawn as he approached Mr.O'Leary's door. She cast him a shy smile as she passed, lowering her eyes.

"Hey, did you hear that?" Shawn asked, even though he'd heard nothing.

Nina skidded to a halt and looked at Shawn wide-eyed. "No, I didn't hear anything."

"I swear... I heard something coming from that apartment." He pointed toward O'Leary's unit.

"Like something falling?" Nina asked, her voice small. Shawn went with it and nodded.

"That's Mr. O'Leary's. He's in a wheelchair. Maybe we should check on him?" he asked.

"Yeah, let's knock." Nina stepped up to the door and tentatively knocked, her petite knuckles barely emanating a sound. Shawn stood by and watched the abysmal attempt for a few moments before reaching out above her and knocking for himself.

Regardless, he was pretty sure that O'Leary wasn't in the apartment, just like Detective Dane had suggested. After a moment of waiting for the old man to answer the door, Shawn pulled out his pass key.

"He could have fallen out of his chair," he suggested, hoping that Nina took the bait.

She looked skeptical for a moment as though she were warring with her conscience. He held a breath, waiting.

Finally, Nina shrugged, seeming to come to some internal decision within herself.

"You're right. He could be hurt," Nina agreed, stepping aside for Shawn to open the door.

Sliding the card into the slot over the handle, they waited for the beeping sound. Shawn knew he could lose his job over this. If he got caught going into a tenants apartment without a legit reason, there would be immediate termination.

With sweaty hands, he gently turned the knob and pushed the door open. The apartment was dark, and the air was stagnant.

"Mr. O'Leary?" he called into the dark recesses of the small apartment. Inhaling deeply, he was relieved not to smell the sweet, tangy scent of death. He'd smelled it before, once a year ago when old lady McGarvey had passed in her sleep and hadn't been found for two days.

"Mr. O'Leary? Are you here?" he called again. He was met with silence.

"I don't think he's here," Nina whispered, tentatively following Shawn into the apartment.

Shawn flipped the light switch on, casting a dim light across the entryway and into the living room.

"I just want to make sure, in case he's unconscious," Shawn threw over his shoulder as he made his way deeper into the apartment. "You can stay here if you want. It's up to you."

Glancing through the living room revealed nothing obvious: no young girl duct taped to a chair, no old man sprawled dead in a puddle of his own juices.

Shawn headed toward the kitchen but found it empty as well. A glance over his shoulder revealed a nervous-looking Nina watching his every move. Making sure to play the part of worried orderly and not amateur sleuth, he shrugged.

"I'm going to check the bedroom and bathroom real quick just in case. Hang on," he said before slipping into the darkened room to his right.

Flipping on the light, he found himself standing in Kane O'Leary's bedroom. The room was deserted, and the bed appeared undisturbed. The room appeared very organized and neat.

A queen bed with a navy blue comforter dominated the room while matching bedside tables flanked it, each donning a clear glass lamp. Across the room sat a matching chest of drawers on top of which sat a framed photo that caught Shawn's eye.

Walking closer and picking up the frame for a better look, he realized he was looking at a picture of Mr. O'Leary from back in his younger days. In the picture, O'Leary appeared to be fishing with a teenage boy. Maybe his son?

"Did you find anything?" a voice said from behind him, causing Shawn to jump. He whirled around, setting the frame back down on the chest of drawers but missing the mark. It fell to the floor with a crash.

"Damn it, Nina! Why'd you sneak up on me like that?" he snapped, suddenly irritated with himself for even involving her in this scheme in the first place.

"Sorry," she mumbled, holding her hands up placatingly. "You were just taking so long and now..." She gestured to the broken glass from the photo frame.

"I'll clean this mess up. How about you go find a broom or something?" Shawn suggested with an irritated tone as he bent down to begin gathering up the larger pieces of glass, wondering how he was going to explain it to his boss if he was asked.

Nina shoved off the door frame with a slightly irritated look and disappeared into the kitchen. Shawn rolled his eyes and picked up the remnants of the frame.

It was then that he noticed something strange about the backing of the frame. Lifting the corner revealed a second picture hidden beneath. When Shawn realized what he was looking at and what it meant, he gasped. He pulled the photo from its hiding spot and slid it into the pocket of his scrubs.

He had to hurry and call Detective Dane. The photo changed everything.

# Chapter Fifty-Four

*Wednesday, September 26th, 1:24 PM*

The old bastard could walk! Better yet, he could run! He wasn't the feeble, frail grandpa he'd made everyone believe he was.

Tess felt like an idiot for not figuring it out sooner. Thankfully, Shawn Sweeney had called her, talking so fast she could hardly keep up. Something about finding a photograph in Kane's apartment.

Once she'd calmed him down enough to get him to make sense, she couldn't believe what he was telling her. She was already en route to Glade Spring Senior Living and when she pulled in, Shawn was waiting outside.

She'd barely pulled her SUV to a stop when Shawn ran up to her window and held the photo up. Slamming the vehicle into park, Tess climbed out and grabbed the photo.

"Holy crap..." she said, completely dumbfounded. "And you had no idea?"

"None," Shawn answered, his face pale despite his dark skin. "Never once would I have guessed this."

In the photo, a very buff and tanned Kane O'Leary stood topless and sweaty, holding up a trophy somewhere in the desert. His arms and torso were well muscled considering his age, evidence of a life of physical activity. His hair was snowy white, and his eyes matched the cerulean sky above him. The smile on his face was contagious, as evident from the two people that flanked him on either side. Behind the trio hung a red banner that read "58th Annual Zuma Race for Multiple Sclerosis".

"Dude looks healthier than I do, and I'm only twenty-five!" Shawn said excitedly. "And that was taken this year! I know because I already Googled it. It's from 2 months ago! Now you tell me, Detective Dane, how does an old man that looks like a slightly plump little Santa Claus in a wheelchair go running marathons like he's freaking Schwarzenegger? It doesn't make any sense!"

"It doesn't. This has been a huge grift this whole time," Tess bit out as she looked at the photo. How had he played them all, even his own family? Did they know he was able-bodied this whole time? Or were they in the dark just as she had been?

She was going to find out. Natalie's life was at stake, and she was done playing games with the O'Learys.

Tess thanked Shawn for his help and made him swear to be quiet yet vigilant, which he promised to do. The poor guy seemed rather shaken up by everything but he told her he wasn't going to ask to go home early just in case O'Leary showed back up. He laughingly called himself The Mole Man.

"Just watch yourself, Shawn. You know what they say: Snitches get stitches or wind up in ditches," she quipped as she put her SUV in gear.

"Damn, Detective! You don't play," Shawn called as she pulled away from the curb.

"No, I do not," she grinned with a wave. As soon as she was out of sight of Shawn, she called Malone to give him an update, and then Denny.

"I'm going over to Jamie and Lori's house to speak to them directly," Tess told Denny as she drove down the highway. "I want to see their reactions in person when I show them this picture and ask them about Kane."

"Awesome, Tess. Thank you," Denny sighed, relief in his voice. "I've been following up with Claybourne on the forensic eval of the CCTV footage around town. So far, they've been able to track the truck leaving the mall, headed down past the feed store and post office, left at Bernie's Pizza, and then we lost sight of it until that Ford dealership out on Route 72."

"Like the truck went to the Ford dealership or just drove by?" Tess asked, excited by all the new information.

"Drove by, headed westbound toward Camden Town and Milbren area."

"Well at least we have a direction of travel now! This is great work. You don't think he'd take her to the farm, do you? That would be the first place we'd look. Do you think he has another apartment or house he's keeping her at?"

"I don't know, but now that we know it's Kane and that he's living a double life, anything is possible," Denny answered. "I mean, he doesn't live there or own it. He'd probably be expecting us to check there. If I were him, I wouldn't go there. There's too much police activity with Kevin's death and everything. Unless he's hoping to use reverse psychology on us, you know, hoping we don't search there because of those reasons."

"All good points. We need to check. There's over 1,500 acres and since we don't have any other areas to search right now, that might be a place to start," Tess countered.

"Agreed," came Denny's reply over the Bluetooth. "While you speak with Jamie and Lori, Claybourne and I will start pooling resources together to start searching the O'Leary property."

"Perfect. I'm almost to Jamie's now," Tess said. "I'll call you in an hour with an update." Then, she disconnected the call.

***

Moments later, she pulled up in front of Jamie and Lori's moss green two-storied Cape Cod a few miles outside of Camden Town. The curtains were drawn, and there were no cars in the driveway.

Tess tried not to feel disappointed at catching the couple out. She'd wanted to speak to them in person. She pulled into the driveway anyway to turn around as the rural road was narrow and had deep ditches on either side.

When she pulled in the driveway, however, Tess noticed an old red pickup truck parked toward the back of the property, almost completely obscured by a ramshackle barn.

She sucked in a breath. It matched the description enough that it warranted follow-up, but she tried to control her hope, just in case it was nothing. Was Kane O'Leary here somewhere watching her even now? And where was Natalie?

Her heart quickened in excitement as Tess slid her phone from her pocket and silently confirmed that her backup pistol was holstered at her ankle. With it hidden under her pant leg, she felt as though her dad was with her, even if things went sideways. After grabbing her duty belt from the passenger seat and securing it around her waist like in her patrol days, she tapped out a quick text to Denny.

Tess: Not home? Haven't knocked. Red truck noted behind barn. Going to investigate.

Denny: Wait for backup. Could be dangerous. Sending someone now.

Tess: I'll knock first. Want to talk to J and L. Plz send backup.

Denny: Sounds good. I love you!

Tess: Love you, too!

Sliding out of the SUV, Tess shut the door and locked it behind her before walking up the flagstone steps to the front door. The doorbell appeared to be broken so she used the brass knocker on the burgundy wood door.

The home was quiet. Save for the birdsong coming from the large maple shading the front yard and a barking dog somewhere off in the distance, the property was silent.

After a few seconds, she knocked again but was met with the same result. It appeared no one was home. That wouldn't stop her from strolling around back to check out the truck's license plate. With it being parked where it was, it was in clear view from the driveway, thus giving her an exception to getting a search warrant. *A small victory,* Tess mused as she cautiously strode across the uneven terrain.

She kept her hand on the gun holstered at her hip, ready to draw at a second's notice. She cast her gaze cautiously around her, determined to miss nothing from the rusted swing set surrounded by weeds, the small chicken coop with its beady-eyed occupants watching her every move, to the small white wooden cross with 'Buddy' painted in black jabbed into the ground near the woodline.

The early autumn sun beat down, warming her skin as she cautiously approached the old barn. Tall weeds surrounded its listing walls, and the door was slightly ajar. The large equipment door appeared to have long ago rotted off its track.

A feeling of unease coursed down her spine as she unsnapped her holster and withdrew her firearm. She kept the barrel aimed at the ground as she crept to the entrance of the old barn and listened. She was greeted with silence.

As she let her eyes adjust to the dim interior of the outbuilding, she silently slipped into the barn, checking her surroundings for signs of danger. For signs of Natalie. Except for the comforting coo of mourning doves in the rafters and the scurrying sound of something small in the old hay strewn at her feet, Tess was alone.

Breathing a sigh of relief, but still keeping her guard up, she checked the old tack room and horse stalls, equipment area, and antique tractor abandoned in the middle of the breezeway. She found nothing. Frustrated yet determined, Tess continued toward the other side of the barn, where she could see the pickup truck parked. Like the front of the barn, the back door had also rotted away long ago and made what remained of the structure open to the outside.

As Tess approached the vehicle, she sucked in a breath. It was an extended cab Chevy Silverado, just like Steven Sweeney's stolen vehicle. She glanced at the license plates and felt a sob building in her chest. It *was* Steven Sweeney's truck.

Natalie had been in that vehicle at some point. Was she still around here now? Did Kane have her held somewhere inside the home?

Tess lowered her gun as she ran around to the driver's side to peer in the window, looking for anything that may help her find Natalie. Any signs that would prove in court that this was the truck that was used in the kidnapping.

The interior of the cab appeared decently clean, except for a small bottle of hand sanitizer and an ink pen in the console. The hoodie on the seat bothered Tess. It was dark green with some kind of white logo on it that looked like a leaf of some kind. She couldn't see the whole thing because it was hidden under a plastic bag that had something black and furry in it.

Tess dug around in her duty belt for a rubber glove and then tried opening the truck door. Whatever was in that bag was in plain view, but she was apprehensive to touch something furry and potentially dead.

The door was unlocked. It opened with a creak of hinges and a gust of heat from inside the closed-up cab. Tess reached in and grasped the bag, pulling it to herself to look inside. Confused, she pulled the item out to inspect it.

It was a black wig! And in the bottom of the bag was a matching moustache. It was Kane O'Leary, acting alone the whole time. He'd stolen the truck from the senior living facility and then waited for his time to strike. It was easy for him to do while wearing a costume.

Tess began to shake with anger at being duped. She needed to find Natalie!

Reaching into her pocket she pulled out her phone to call Denny when all of a sudden there was a rustling sound behind her. She whirled around to find Kane O'Leary standing behind her, a gun trained on her every move.

"Drop the gun, Detective," he commanded. "And the phone."

Tess glared at him but obliged. She knew backup was en route but didn't know when they'd show up.

"Kick them under the truck. Now!" he barked. Not taking her eyes off of him, she toed her firearm and phone under the vehicle. Tess was looking at a man who killed his brother and likely his nephew, too. Even if there were more to the story, he certainly kidnapped Natalie, and there was a good chance he intended to kill her, too. After piecing together the parts of the puzzle, it was all becoming clearer to Tess.

"You're not getting away with this, Kane. Backup will be here in minutes," she continued to glare at him.

"That's a load of bull hockey. You didn't even make a call." he rolled his eyes at her and gestured to the phone lying in the grass under the truck.

She shrugged, "Believe what you want to believe then. Where is Natalie?"

"Why should I tell you anything?" Kane growled, jabbing the gun at her.

"Because I have enough circumstantial evidence against you," she paused to look over her shoulder at the hoodie and wig, "And physical, to put you away for the rest of your miserable life."

He just sneered at her and said nothing. Tess sighed and rolled her eyes in frustration.

"Are we seriously going to do this? She's just a kid, Kane! What happened to the Santa Claus jokester? I like that version of you way better."

He snorted, "Please. It was all an act."

"Obviously," she muttered, trying to buy time for backup to arrive. "Look, just take me to Natalie and—"

The sound of a car on gravel traveled to them, and in the blink of an eye, Tess turned to see Jamie and Lori pulling up in the driveway behind her SUV just as something hit her in the side of the head. Pain erupted in a starburst of confusion, and everything went black.

# Chapter Fifty-Five



*Wednesday. September 26th, 2:22 PM*

Tess woke with a start, her head throbbing and the side of her face crusted in dried blood. Her cheek was pressed up against the window of the red pickup as it jostled down a narrow, rutted tract in the woods.

"Where are we?" she muttered, turning her head to find Kane O'Leary behind the wheel of the stolen vehicle.

"About time you woke up," he commented. "Light weight." He grinned at her, although she found no humor in his joke.

"Seriously?" Tess glared, rattling her handcuffed hands at him. "You do realize you just added a whole laundry list of new crimes to your list of dirty deeds, right?"

Pulling at the handcuffs again, her anger surged. They were her own handcuffs, she was sure. She'd been hit on the head and then subdued with her own freaking handcuffs. Though she couldn't bend and check, she was sure that her service weapon and the backup pistol her father had given her were also missing. *Mother fucker.* If she got out of this situation alive...

"Whatever. Don't even act like you weren't about to use them on me," Kane snarked, casting her a dark look.

"Where are you taking me?" she asked as the truck hit another tree root, jostling her to and fro. "Where are Jamie and Lori?"

"Who cares?" he asked. "They don't know about the truck, they didn't know I was there. All they found was your SUV, abandoned in their driveway. It means nothing."

"But they know you've supposedly been missing," Tess commented, trying to gauge how much the couple knew about Kane's double life.

"I called them last night after I dumped the girl. Told Jamie I had met someone and we were going out to dinner. He told me to call you," Kane shrugged. "I told him I would. That, in truth, was a lie."

"Nearly everything you say is a lie," Tess snapped. "Tell me, does your precious Jamie know you run marathons in the desert?"

"So I see you've been snooping around in my apartment, Detective. Tsk, tsk. Don't you need a warrant for that?"

"I've never even stepped foot in your stupid apartment," Tess growled. Her head throbbed.

Kane shot her a look that said he didn't believe that for a moment before returning his gaze to the narrow overgrown tract. The truck continued to jostle along, branches scraping it from all sides.

"So tell me, Kane, since we are going on this adventurous road trip into the unknown... Why did you kill your brother? Was it really because Mommy and Daddy didn't give you an inheritance?"

"Shut up," he snapped, pressing the gas pedal and causing the truck to lurch forward, narrowly missing a tree.

"I can see I've hit a nerve," Tess goaded. She decided to pick at the wound further to see what he'd reveal. "Is that why you attacked Kevin, too? I liked Kevin. I find you lacking."

"That's funny. You seemed to find me amusing when I looked like Grandpa Kane," he snapped. "Now, shut up!"

They'd entered a small clearing in the middle of the woods. Tess had no way of knowing how long she'd been knocked out or if they were even on Jamie and Lori's land anymore.

Kane slammed on the brakes, causing Tess to fall forward, nearly hitting her forehead on the dash. She heard him snicker and wanted to throat punch him. Instead, she chose to remain calm and not allow him to see her anger.

Turning off the ignition, Kane climbed out and came around to the passenger side. Tess pulled away as he yanked open the door and reached for her.

"C'mon. Let's get this over with," he growled. As he tugged her out of the vehicle, she realized just how strong he really was.

He had forty years on her, though, and even with his muscular physique, youth and agility were on her side. She had to plan an escape.

As he led her towards the middle of the clearing, she looked around for any signs of humanity. There was nothing. They were surrounded by woods on all sides. Where were they? Yardley Game Reserve? Had he taken her back to the farm? Were they still on Jamie's land?

"Stop your lollygagging. Get a move on," Kane snapped, getting behind her to shove her forward. She noticed then that he'd pulled a gun– her gun, by the looks of it– from the back of his jeans.

They'd almost made it across the clearing when Kane stopped her by pressing the barrel of the gun between her sweaty shoulder blades.

"Sit down on that stump," he commanded, pointing with his chin.

"If you're going to kill me, just do it and get it over with," Tess said, looking him straight in the eye. She was shaking on the inside, but she would not show fear.

"I'm not going to kill you... yet." His face cracked into a hideous grin. "We're playing a little game now."

"What kind of game?" Tess asked, confused and thirsty. Her head was pounding. She squinted up at the sun and watched as Kane pulled her cell phone out of his pocket. He held it up.

"Smile pretty," he cooed cheerfully as he snapped a picture, then used her face to unlock the screen before pressing some buttons.

"What the fuck is wrong with you? Where is Natalie? Why are you doing this?"

"Just wait," he said with a grin. Within seconds, Tess's phone started ringing.

"Oh, it's for me," Kane announced. He pressed the green button to answer the call, "Ahh, Agent Haywood, I thought I'd be hearing from you soon.

"Denny! Help! He's got a gun! We're in the woods!" Tess screamed. Kane jutted the gun out in her direction.

"Hold it down. I'm on the phone," Kane snapped at Tess. "Sorry about that, Agent Haywood. Yes, I'm here." A slight pause. "No, I will not go fuck myself and no, I will not tell you where your daughter is. Well, I might." Kane glanced at Tess. She could hear Denny yelling something over the phone.

"My, my, but your temper is just about as bad as Detective Dane's! No wonder you guys seem to get along so well together. Now listen, enough of your ranting. If you want to see Dane or the little brat again, you're going to do something for me, got it? You're going to destroy all the records of this investigation that Dane has on me. All the stuff about Garrett, about Kevin... all of it. It disappears, poof! Once you send me proof that it's been destroyed and give me your word that I walk away a free man, then I'll tell you the location to pick her up."

More yelling from Denny and more glaring from Kane. Tess wanted to scream in frustration. If he wasn't standing two feet from her with a gun trained on her sternum, she'd run. She'd kick him and run.

"What do I mean by 'pick her up'? Well, you don't think I'm giving *both* of them back to you, do you? You have to pick your favorite. You have one hour." With a sinister leer, Kane disconnected the call.

"Well, that was a nice chat, wouldn't you say?" Kane asked Tess casually, as though they'd just chatted about golf or the latest State of the Union Address. "Tell you what, since we all know he's going to pick to save his spawn and I'll get to kill you, why don't we just have a little story time until we hear back from lover boy, eh? I know you're dying to ask your stupid questions again." He rolled his eyes and waved the gun around wildly. "Yes, I killed my brother. Yes, I killed my nephew. And yes, I'm going to kill you."

# Then

# Chapter Fifty-Six



*September 1995*

One evening in late September, Kane O'Leary found himself walking up the long gravel driveway toward his family's farmhouse. It had been a little over sixteen years since he'd last traversed the rutted tract, and from the looks of it, nothing had changed. The mailbox down at the road needed painting, and as he got closer to the house, he realized it, too, could use an update.

Maybe if he offered to paint the place or mend some fences, his dad wouldn't mind if he hung out for a few weeks. Whatever happened, there was no way in hell that he was staying on at the farm long-term. He was only stopping by now because he needed the money and a place to lick his figurative wounds.

He hadn't seen his family in so long that he was almost nervous to climb the wooden steps to the porch. As he approached the front door, he found the screen door latched, but the main door open, allowing the low hum of voices and laughter to escape. With it came the scent of something delicious– turkey? Chicken? Kane's mouth watered at the scent as he raised his hand to knock on the door's wooden frame.

The house fell silent as Kane's knock echoed through the front hall. He felt the sudden urge to leave. He hadn't told them he was coming, hadn't announced his reappearance into society after years of absence. He'd basically made himself disappear years ago.

"Son, run see who it is," a deep male voice said from within the house. Kane heard the scrape of chair legs on the wooden floor and footsteps coming closer. It was too late to chicken out now.

A teenage boy came to the door, his tall, lanky form filling the frame as he spoke through the screen. "Can I help you?"

"Hi...uh, is Garrett here?" Kane asked, not entirely sure where to begin. He didn't know if he was speaking to little Kevin or Brandon. The last time he'd been at the farm, the two boys had been kids.

"Yes, sir. Who should I tell him is here?" the teenager asked, his eyes roaming over Kane. If the boy recognized him, he didn't let on.

"His brother."

"Uncle Kane?" he exclaimed, his eyebrows rising in surprise. "We thought you were dead. Dad is going to be so excited!" He turned his head and called for Garrett over his shoulder.

*Dead? My family thought I was dead? Damn, maybe I should have come home sooner,* Kane's mind raced.

"Yep! I'm back in town, kiddo! Kevin, right?" Kane plastered on a smile, despite the anxiety churning in his gut. The teen nodded, a wide smile splitting his face. "Wow, you're all grown up! Practically a man!" Kane exclaimed, the words scalding his tongue. He'd missed so much, lost so much time, but he only had himself to blame. He'd chosen to stay away for so long, to live life on his terms. And now, after another business deal had turned to dust, he was broke with nowhere left to go.

At the commotion, Garrett approached the entryway and gasped.

"Kane! I can't believe it's you! You're really here?" he exclaimed as he unlocked the screen door and rushed to wrap his arms around his older brother's torso.

"Yeah, baby brother, I'm back," Kane laughed, returning the embrace. "I'm really here."

"Where have you been?" Garrett asked at the same time that Kane called out for his mother.

"Mama! Mama!" he paused and looked at Garrett, trying to push past him, "Where's mom?"

"She's gone, Kane." Garrett sighed, his arms falling to his sides.

"Gone where? She'll be back soon, right?"

"She's gone to Heaven, Uncle Kane," Kevin announced glumly. "Two months ago now. It was her heart."

"What's the boy talking about, Garrett?" Kane whirled around to his brother for answers, an anguished look on his face. "Where's Mom?"

"She passed away two months ago, like Kevin said," Garrett relayed, his shoulders sagging.

Kane struggled to process that his mother was dead. He'd never been close to her by any means, but he didn't want things to end like this. He would have liked to at least say goodbye. Kane wanted to lash out, punch something, when a little voice bubbled up inside him, *"Your selfish decisions are why you didn't get to say goodbye. This is all your fault."* Emotions he hadn't felt in a while tore at him: sorrow, loss, and anger. Pain.

"Where's Dad?" he asked, afraid to ask but needing to know the answer. When Garrett and Kevin didn't immediately answer, he took off into the bowels of the house, calling for his dead parents.

***

Once the shock of learning that both his parents were dead had worn off, Kane still struggled with being home in Ohio. Garrett acted as though he thought life would return to normal on the farm, to the way it had been before Kane had even left. His constant comments about the 'good old days' and his overly happy demeanor annoyed the piss out of Kane daily and he quickly remembered why he left in the first place. He and Garrett were as different as day and night.

Kane had been home for a few weeks, working the farm alongside Garrett and Kevin as they prepared for the harvest season. It was one of the busiest times of the year for the family, and Kane knew that Garrett could use the extra hands. Since Kane needed the money, and only because Garrett had agreed to pay him, Kane had signed on to help at least with the harvest. If things went well, he may stay on for the spring planting, too.

"You seen Jess Holloway around these days?" Kane asked casually, grabbing a wrench before shimmying back under the old reaper he and his brother were repairing. The old rig needed to be up and running by next week's harvest or they were going to be in a world of hurt.

Garrett smirked down at his brother before removing his ball cap and wiping the sweat from his brow. "I ain't seen her 'round much, no. But then again, I ain't been looking. I'm surprised you haven't looked her up yet, if I'm being honest."

"Well, I've been gone for nearly fifteen years. Surely she's moved on," Kane commented, his voice muffled from under the farm machine. He slid back out to grin up at his brother, "But I'm sure she hasn't forgotten me. I'm hard to forget if you know what I mean."

"God, Kane, I ain't never met somebody so full of themselves," Garrett snorted, replacing his hat on his head before getting back to work.

"You're just jealous, little brother," Kane scoffed, sliding back under the reaper. "You shoulda came with me, traveled the world. I've traveled to places most people only dream about. Loved women on every continent. But I'm ready to settle down now. Once I sell my share of the farm, I'm taking my inheritance and heading somewhere warm, living out my days by the sea."

"Selling what share of the farm?" Garrett asked, confused for a moment. "Mom left it all to me." As soon as the words escaped his lips, Garrett sucked in a breath of air. Even though Kane was under the reaper, he heard it. He could feel his brother tense next to him, waiting to see what Kane would do. Garrett had always done that, even as a kid. He'd spout off at the mouth and then freeze like a deer, waiting for Kane's wrath.

There was a beat or two of silence as Kane processed Garrett's words. Suddenly, he slid out from under the reaper, a full scowl covering his face.

"What the hell do you mean, they left everything to you?" he spat, sitting up abruptly and hitting his head on the metal frame of the broken-down farm machinery.

Cursing, he rubbed his forehead where a red welt was already forming. "We were supposed to get half and half, split right down the middle." He needed that land. He'd been relying on it. Had his parents truly hated him so much that they took away his inheritance? A rage began thrumming deep within Kane's gut, growing in intensity as his thoughts ran rampant.

Garrett just stood there, saying nothing, which angered Kane further. His scowl turned to a glare as he climbed to his feet and stalked towards his brother, stopping when they were nose to nose.

"Well...?" Kane growled, impatience dripping from his tone. Garrett took a step backwards, avoiding eye contact. He'd always hated confrontation, even as a kid. It was one of the things that Kane liked using against him. Kane had been exploiting his brother's soft, pliable nature for years to get what he wanted. He should have known that Kane would be pissed when he found out about the farm.

"Well, after you disappeared and then Dad died, Mom thought you were dead, too, I guess." Garrett shrugged, casting a leery glance at his brother. "Don't blame me. It wasn't my fault Mom had her will changed. It wasn't up to me, Kane. You weren't around. Nobody knew where you were, if you were alive or dead. Hell, just two more months or so, and we coulda had you declared legally dead. Poof." He made an explosive motion with his hands before dropping them back to his sides.

"Well, I ain't," Kane growled, waving the wrench in his hand around for emphasis before throwing it to the ground with enough force it made a thudding sound on the grass at his feet. "And I want what's mine. I'm entitled to my half, same as you." Kane mulled over the information. Maybe if he played his cards just right, Garrett would change his mind, especially now that he knew Kane wasn't dead. Surely he could deed his brother some of the land, right?

"You're welcome to live here, work the farm with me," Garrett said quietly. "We can build another house, down by the pond, if you'd like. The kids–"

"To hell with the farm. It's just work, work, work, with little to show for it. That's why I left in the first place," Kane huffed, turning his back on Garrett for a moment. His hands shoved in his pockets, he took a deep breath and then turned back around to glare at Garrett.

"Look, how about we just take a break from this conversation. I'll think about it. Maybe we can find a resolution to all of this that will make both of us happy, don't you think? I want to look into this mess."

"Sure, Kane. We can talk about it all later." Garrett sounded relieved to drop the subject. "I'm sure all of this has come as a shock. I honestly didn't know about it until after Mom died."

"I bet you didn't," muttered Kane under his breath. In an angry huff, he grabbed his water bottle and stomped back toward the farmhouse, leaving Garret in the middle of the field.

# Chapter Fifty-Seven

*July 20th, 1996, 8:20 PM*

The sun dipped low in the western sky, leaving streaks of pinks and purples in its wake. Kane cast a glance up at the porch, already darkening with evening shadows, and a look of annoyance crossed over his face. *Where was Garrett?* Grumbling to himself, he kicked the tire of the old Ford pick-up out of frustration and stalked back towards the house.

"Hey, Garrett! You comin'?" he called, trying to keep the anger out of his voice. It was getting harder and harder to do these days, however, and he'd been thinking of just moving on again. Hell, he didn't need the farm, the land, or his stupid family's money. He'd lived all over the globe before, he could do it again, right?

Except he didn't want to. Not really. It was lonely, hopping from town to town, country to county. Sure, he always had "friends" and people around him, but they weren't... family. They were fair-weather friends at best: there to party and hang with... until the money ran out.

Where had his friends been the night he'd been mugged in Singapore and left, broken and battered, on the roadside? They'd left him, scattering like dry leaves in a brisk autumn breeze. Or what about the time he had been mistaken by the police in Paris, accused of robbery? He'd spent a night in jail for that, but had his friends come to bail him out? No. Had they verified his alibi? That he'd been with them the whole evening, partying down on the beach? No. In the end, a young wisp of a woman he didn't even know had come forward and vouched for him; she'd seen him at the beach during the time of the robbery. Saved by a complete stranger!

No, Kane didn't want to go back to that life. Yes, he'd had fun. He'd sowed his wild oats, but he was ready to stay in one place, settle down. And he wouldn't stop working toward that goal until he got it.

He'd been talking with lawyers, trying to verify or even contest his parent's will, trying to find some loophole. But so far, he'd hit brick wall after brick wall. According to three different lawyers, his mother's last will was legit and overrode the one that she and Shamus O'Leary, Kane and Garrett's father, had made when the boys were young.

His mother had truly written him out of the will.

Every time he thought about it, he just wanted to choke her. Anger would fill him until he began seeing red. She'd always preferred Garrett over him anyway. If the bitch was still alive he'd wrap his hands around her neck and...

"Yeah, yeah, I'm coming," Garrett hollered through the screen door, jarring Kane from his angry thoughts.

Suddenly Garrett appeared, wallet and keys in hand, as he shoved past the door and let it slap the frame behind him.

"You said nine o'clock. It's not even eight-thirty," he pointed out as he clumped out onto the porch and down the stairs over to the pickup. Sliding his wallet into the pocket of his Levi's, he opened the creaking door of the old Ford and slid behind the driver's seat.

Kane scowled in annoyance as he climbed into the passenger seat as his brother turned the engine over and they drove down the rutted driveway. Still angry, more at their mother than his brother, Kane sat staring out the window as Garrett drove them to town for a guys' night out.

"What flew up your ass?" Garrett asked after a few moments of awkward silence. Kane said nothing.

"Okay, fine. Don't talk to me then," Garrett sighed, turning on the radio instead. A Garth Brooks song soon filled the truck cab.

"Nothing," muttered Kane, turning to glance at his brother. Garrett cast a look back at him, holding his gaze for a moment before turning back to the road.

"Doesn't seem like nothin', Kane," Garrett sighed. "You don't seem happy. You're only in your forties and not tied down to anything or anyone. How can you *not* be happy?"

"Are you happy?" Kane countered, turning the conversation away from himself. He didn't feel like getting into this with Garrett, talking about his feelings and shit. "You have a wife, kids, a house..."

"I'm happy enough, I guess," Garrett shrugged. "We fight sometimes, but then we make up. And sure, the kids can get under my skin occasionally and irritate the hell outta me, but I wouldn't change that." The truck hit a pothole as they made their way to the edge of town, jostling the brothers.

"I see they still haven't fixed that hole," Kane grumped, glancing in the side mirror at the large pothole that had been there for years yet had gone unrepaired.

"I heard it swallowed Frank Lennon's bicycle a few years ago," Garrett commented deadpan. Kane snorted.

"Gary Fletcher said he saw a mermaid swimming around in there once. He nearly fell in while trying to get a glance of her tits," he grinned.

"Gary Fletcher is a damn drunk," Garrett smirked, rolling his eyes at his brother. Kane let out a bark of a laugh as Garret pulled up into the parking lot of The Falcon's Nest.

"And we should be, too, tonight," Kane laughed, his anger simmering low for the moment. He just wanted to relax, have some fun, maybe even find a woman to warm his bed for the night.

"Go have fun, brother. Just as long as you promise not to puke in my truck on the way home," Garrett grinned, pocketing his keys and wallet as he followed his brother's long-legged stride through the busy parking lot.

By the time they got there, the Falcon's Nest was already hopping. Live music filled the air as a country band played on a wooden stage along the back wall. The dance floor was crowded as people in various levels of intoxication danced along to the music. The scent of alcohol, tobacco smoke, and stale food hung in the air. Through the darkened interior, Kane could make out people playing pool at the tables in the corner.

He followed his brother to an empty table and slid into the booth, positioning himself so that he could see most of the bar from his position. He'd been jumped too many times to turn his back to a room.

"Hi, boys, what'll it be?" a young blonde woman cooed as she approached their table, menus in hand. There was a lot wrong with Kane's life at the moment, but he could find no fault in the way the waitress's ass-cheeks hung out the back of her cutoffs as she leaned over to lay the menus on the worn wooden table in front of them. He'd like to bend her over the table himself if given the chance.

"I'll take a Corona, sweetheart," he gazed up at her with hooded eyes and a grin on his face. The woman looked him over for a moment and then, seeming to like what she saw, smiled down at him with a wink.

"It's Charity," she said loudly, trying to be heard over the music. "My name. It's Charity." She giggled then, watching Kane's look of confusion change as he processed what she'd said.

"Well, Charity, that's a beautiful name," Kane grinned, already thinking about taking her home tonight.

"I'll take a Corona, too, please," Garrett inserted, "and some onion rings. You want onion rings, Kane?" He was oblivious to everything around him, and Kane tried not to roll his eyes.

"No, I don't want your damn onion rings," Kane hissed low enough for only Garrett to hear him.

"Okay, if that's it, I'll go put your order in," Charity slipped away from the table and headed back toward the bar, Kane's eyes never leaving her ass the entire time.

"Well, well, if it isn't Kane O'Leary, back from the dead," came a woman's voice from behind him. He begrudgingly tore his eyes away from Charity's ample backside and looked to see the owner of the voice.

Jess Holloway, Kane's ex-girlfriend, came to a halt at the edge of the O'Leary's table. She folded her arms over her chest and looked down at him through slitted eyes.

"When did you get back in town, Kane?" she demanded with a rough tone that didn't quite meet the fire in her eyes. She'd always been a feisty one, sassy and short-tempered, but that's what he'd loved about her all those years ago. She had all the attitude of a feral cat in attack mode but none of the bite.

"It's been a bit," Kane mused, giving her a lazy smile. It seemed to do the trick, just like it always did. He watched as she dropped her arms to her sides and let out a sigh.

"You coulda called, Kane. And I'm not talking about last week or even a month ago. I'm talking about years ago," Jess stated, her eyes never leaving Kane's face.

"I know...." Kane started, then trailed off with a noncommittal shrug. Garrett, seeming to want to avoid the conversation at all costs, began studying the menu as though it were the final exam for AP Biology.

"Kane, just stop," Jess threw her hand up, palm out. "I've been waiting for you to come home for fifteen years, but truly? I don't even know why. You're just as self-centered as you were then."

Her statement caused Garrett to finally look up, a look of sudden enlightenment on his face. Kane chose to ignore him. His brother always was one for theatrics.

"Now, Jess... You know it ain't like that," Kane sighed, scooting over. "Sit, baby. I missed you," Kane cooed. Jess looked at him skeptically but slid into the booth.

"Why didn't you call? After you left me?" Jess asked, picking at the bent edge of the laminated menu on the table in front of her. She didn't look at him, but he was pretty sure he'd see tears in her eyes if she had. *Shit.*

"You know why. I had to get away for a while. Think about things," Kane sighed, feeling like an asshole. "Time just got away from me, babe." It was a lame excuse, he knew, but as more and more time had passed from when he'd left her standing on her front porch, tears running down her face, it had just been easier to stay away.

"You're despicable, Kane O'Leary," Jess hissed, finally turning to look at him in the dark interior of the bar. She held his gaze for a moment, the noise and activity around them falling away as though they didn't exist.

"Here you go, two Coronas and some onion rings," Charity's sing-song voice broke the awkward tension at the table. Jess pulled her gaze from Kane and used the distraction to leave.

Garrett grabbed his beer and downed half of it while still avoiding eye contact with his brother. Charity, seeming to realize she'd walked into something, shoved the plate of onion rings towards Garrett and left the table.

"Don't leave, Jess," Kane growled, his face darkening with frustration. He knew he'd messed up with her, but he wanted to make things right. He wanted to talk to her, but The Falcon's Nest wasn't the right place.

"I have nothing to say to you," Jess snapped, turning to move away from the table. Kane reached out and grabbed her wrist, gently pulling her back to the table. She started to resist him, but the sudden change in his expression seemed to have caught her off guard.

"Please," he practically begged. "I want to talk to you, just not here. Can we go somewhere else?"

Jess Holloway paused for a moment, a look of skepticism on her face. At first, Kane was sure that she was going to turn on her heel and walk off, leaving him as he'd left her all those years ago. He knew he deserved it. She didn't owe him anything.

With a long, suffering sigh, she finally shrugged. "Fine. Got a pen?" When Garrett silently slid one across the table toward her, she gave him an appreciative smile before grabbing it and scrawling her phone number down on a napkin. Laying the pen down in front of Garrett, she slid the napkin toward Kane.

"This is your last chance. Don't fuck it up." She turned on her heel and left. Kane wrestled with the desire to follow her but watched her go instead.

"You're an idiot," Garrett commented as he poured copious amounts of ketchup onto his plate. "You need to talk to her."

"Fuck off, Gar. You don't know shit," Kane growled, tipping his beer to his lips and taking a long swig.

"I know more than you do." Garrett stuck an onion ring in his mouth and began chewing.

"About what?" Kane rolled his eyes as he absently started picking at the label on his bottle. "You don't know anything about Jess and me."

"I know you messed her up when you left."

"So. It ain't any of your business."

"I know she's been working two jobs just to make ends meet."

"So she can't handle her money? Not my fault." Kane took another swallow of his beer and shook his head at his younger brother.

"It kinda is," Garrett said so quietly that Kane almost didn't hear him.

"And why do you think that?" Kane asked although he didn't really want to know.

"Maybe you should just get over yourself and just talk to Jess," Garrett muttered.

Suddenly, anger overtook him. Casting a glare at his brother, Kane clenched his fists under the table. He wanted to beat the crap out of Garrett, wipe that smug look off of his face. But no, not here. Not at the bar where people would talk. They already thought he was the black sheep anyway.

"Fuck you, Garrett," Kane growled as he grabbed Garrett's keys, slid out of the booth, and stalked out the door to find Jess.

# Chapter Fifty-Eight



It didn't take Kane long to find Jess Holloway's run-down trailer on the outskirts of town. She'd lived there with her mom, stepdad, and two sisters back when she and Kane used to be an item. The trailer was in poor condition back then and he wasn't expecting what he'd found when he pulled up outside it tonight.

Nestled in the back of the Buckeye Trails Trailer Park, Jess's 1972 single wide had long ago seen its glory days. Once a pretty blue color, its paint was now faded to an uneven hue that resembled watercolors blended together by a four-year old. Rust had taken hold of the trim, eating away at it as it spread across the skirting and window frames. Missing siding left areas of exposed wood, and the sagging roof appeared as though it was one thunderstorm away from collapse.

The yard was small but neat, as opposed to the neighbors' yards, which were crowded with junk and old cars. Kane could make out some tomato plants lining the front garden beds, their green vines heavy with red fruit. In addition to the tomatoes, there were what appeared to be onions, carrots, and string beans planted around the house.

Kane smiled to himself, even as he looked at the dismal structure. Jess had never come from money, but she was resourceful.

Sliding the truck into 'park' and turning off the ignition, he paused for a moment, wondering if he was making a good decision. Talking to Jess after so many years of avoiding her. What if she hated him now? What if she was married and had kids?

A thought hit him.

He hadn't spoken to Jess in… what, almost sixteen years, now? And Garrett said she'd been working two jobs to make ends meet which meant she probably didn't have a man supporting her but what if…?

Did Jess Holloway have a kid? *His* kid?

The thought of it was enough to make Kane's hands sweaty and his breath hitch. Had he really fathered a kid all those years ago? Why hadn't Jess told him?

His mind instantly flew back to all the voicemails she'd left, begging him to call her. The emails that he'd never opened. Had he somehow known? Had he suspected and was he too weak to face the repercussions? To take claim of his actions and do right by her and the kid?

He rubbed his eyes, feeling a headache coming on. He needed to do this. It had been long enough, and if there *was* a kid, it wasn't the kid's fault.

Opening the truck door, he climbed out slowly, looking over the trailer again for any signs of Jess or evidence of a kid. Seeing nothing, he closed the truck door and quietly walked up the crooked pavers that served as a walkway, across the sagging front porch, to knock on the door.

Someone stirred inside. Kane didn't know if he was excited or nervous about it. Maybe a little of both. A second before he lost his nerve and fled, the door flung open.

Jess stood on the other side of the screen door, her dark blond hair pulled up in a messy bun atop her head. She'd changed into cutoffs and a spaghetti-strap tank top since leaving the bar, and Kane found himself struggling to keep his eyes on her face.

"I wondered when you'd come by," Jess greeted, her voice quiet and weary. "Might as well come in." She stepped to the side and shoved the door open for him, taking care not to shove her hand through the large hole in the screen.

Kane stepped into the trailer, his tall frame instantly making the small room feel even smaller. He didn't know what to do with himself so he just stood there awkwardly looking around, kicking himself for not thinking this through better.

"You want a drink?" Jess asked, opening a magnet-covered fridge and extracting two bottles of beer before he could answer. With practiced ease, she popped the tops and handed one to Kane.

"Thanks," he mumbled, taking a swig for something to do.

An awkward silence yawned between them, each one sipping from their bottles but avoiding the other's eyes. Kane noticed that the kitchen cabinets had been painted white since the last time he'd been there. And the creepy cat clock with the bulging eyes that Jess's mom liked so much wasn't hanging on the wall anymore. Even the kitchen flooring looked to be recently redone; the old country blue and pink linoleum had been replaced with a vinyl that looked like real wood.

"Nice floor," he commented, instantly chastising himself for saying something so lame.

"Thanks, I did it myself," she beamed. "I went to the library and got some of those home repair books out. I like the ones that have lots of pictures."

"Too bad there isn't somewhere on the internet you could watch how-to videos. Wouldn't that be awesome?" Kane mused.

"If that ever existed, I'd be able to do even more stuff without a man around..." Jess answered, her voice trailing off.

"I'm sorry, Jess," Kane swallowed audibly. His stomach suddenly felt uneasy. This was it. This was the talk.

"For what, exactly?" Jess asked, staring him directly in the eye. Apparently, she wasn't going to make this easy.

"For all of it. For leaving, for not calling. For not being here for..." Kane's voice trailed off as he took in a ragged breath.

"Is it true, you gotta kid?" he finally asked, tired of beating around the bush. He watched her closely, wondering if she would deny anything.

"He's in his room studying for a science test," she said after a moment of hesitation. "He's obsessed with science and is in a special internship program for junior scientists through the local community college. It's not really a test, more of a project, but he's wanting it to be perfect." Seeming to realize she was rambling, she shut her mouth and looked away from his piercing gaze.

"Is he... mine?" he asked, his brows knitted together. He had to hear her say the words; he had to have her make this real for him.

"Yes, without a doubt, Kane," Jess said, his name coming out as a sob. Her eyes watered, but she didn't cry.

Kane felt like all the air had suddenly been sucked out of the room, felt like someone had punched him in the gut. Like he was drowning in a turbulent sea.

Finally, he inhaled, and his breathing hitched. Had Garrett known about this? Had anyone else known? Why hadn't they told him?

"What's his...what's his.." Kane suddenly couldn't form words as emotions wormed their way through his mind.

"Jamie. Well, James Kane Holloway, but I call him Jamie," Jess smiled, a tear breaking free and sliding down a freckled cheek.

Kane stood there in her kitchen, staring at the floor as a million thoughts played through his mind.

"Hey, Mom?"

Kane whirled around to see a teenage boy standing behind him in the kitchen doorway leading to the living room. The boy had the same dark hair as Kane. The same blue eyes. He even had the same lanky frame.

"Yeah, baby, what's up?" Jess asked the boy as she wiped her eyes.

"I just wanted to remind you about the field trip money for tomorrow," he said as he cast a shy glance in Kane's direction.

Kane was at a loss for words. He had so many things he wanted to say, to ask, but at the same time he was speechless. This was his son! Though this whole reality was new to him, Kane was surprised at the calm feeling deep inside of him. Maybe, after all the years of selfish decisions and hard living, he could find redemption. Maybe he could find the love he'd always felt he'd been denied. Even when he was a young man, he'd vowed that if he ever had children of his own, he'd never let them feel unloved or second-best like he'd felt as a kid. This was his chance.

Jess blew out a breath. "Oh, yeah, I forgot. How much was it?" She reached for her purse.

"Ten dollars."

"Shit..." Kane heard Jess whisper under her breath as she dug around in her wallet. "Jamie, I only have seven on me. We'll have to stop by the bank in the morning."

"Here, I have cash," Kane said, pulling out his wallet and withdrawing all the bills. He wadded it up and thrust out his hand toward Jamie.

"Kane, you don't need to do that," Jess sighed, looking up at him and then at her son as he reached out to accept the cash.

Jamie paused when she mentioned Kane's name and he yanked his eyes away from the money back up to Kane's face. Glancing at his mom, his eyes widened when he saw her splotchy, tear-streaked face.

"You're...?" he sputtered, turning back to Kane, his outstretched hand shaking slightly.

Jess blew out a breath and hung her head. "Umm, maybe we should go into the living room for a while." She glanced at her watch. "It's late, and you have your field trip tomorrow, but..."

"I don't need your money," Jamie snapped, throwing the bills back at Kane. They fell to the floor like faded green leaves in the fall.

Kane made no effort to pick them up. He stood there, silently watching the array of emotions play over his son's face at his sudden appearance in Jess's kitchen.

Jamie took a step forward into the kitchen, standing tall in front of Kane. "I don't need you at all. Mom and I have done just fine without you." His face reddened, and his shoulders shook with bottled-up emotion. Angry tears threatened to fall as he glared at Kane. "You need to leave. You aren't welcome here."

He turned and fled down the hall, but not before Kane saw angry tears coursing down Jamie's cheeks. Shit. He'd really fucked up.

Seconds later, a door slammed from down the hallway, causing Jess to wince, disrupting her quiet crying.

This isn't how he'd wanted things to go. He didn't think it'd be all hugs and kisses and greetings of love, but he didn't think it would be open hostility straight out of the gate.

Kane had messed up so much in his life and made so many selfish decisions. If he'd known he'd had a kid, he would have come home sooner. He could argue that no one told him he had a son, but he knew that was a lie. Jess had tried to contact him multiple times when he first left and he'd chosen to ignore her.

This was on him. All of it. And although his brain was still processing the fact that he had fathered a child sixteen years ago, he vowed to himself, right then and there, that he would do whatever he could to be there for his son.

"Jess..." Kane started.

"Please, just go. You've done enough for one night," she turned to him, her eyes full of sorrow. "I'll talk to him. I just got home myself and hadn't had time to warn him you were back in town."

Kane let out a ragged sigh, his heart aching for the things he'd missed and the things he couldn't change.

Without another word, he hung his head and left Jess Holloway standing in her kitchen, alone and crying, just like he had sixteen years ago.

# Chapter Fifty-Nine

*July 21, 1996 12:34 AM*

Kane pulled onto Route 72 and headed back toward Crawley. It was well after midnight at this point, but he was tired of driving. He'd left Jess's place an hour or so ago and had been driving around the county, trying to clear his thoughts. He'd sat at Lake Amelia for a while, listening to the water lap at the dock and the frogs singing from their hidden places in the reeds along the shore.

He'd even laid back onto the newly built dock to gaze up at the stars in the heavens, wondering how he'd fucked his life up to much. He'd missed out on knowing his kid, he'd been cut out of his inheritance... hell, even his own parents didn't care about what happened to him. Well, not that they could now anyway. They were dead.

Maybe that was the answer. Maybe he should be, too. No one would miss him anyway.

All these years, he'd traveled the globe, lived how he wanted to live, done what he'd wanted to do... or what he'd *thought* he'd wanted to do. But as it turned out, maybe he'd been wrong. Maybe he should have stayed here in Crawley and worked the farm alongside his brother, married Jess, and raised Jamie together with her. If he'd done that, maybe he wouldn't feel so goddamn lonely now.

As he drove back toward Crawley, he decided that, in the short term, he needed to get drunk and possibly laid. Maybe that would get his mind off of the dark thoughts churning in his mind.

He pulled into the parking lot of the new strip club, The Booby Trap, hoping to try his luck somewhere new for once. Groaning inwardly when he saw Kenny Novak's new Ford parked next to Fred Krinsel's piece of crap rusted-out pick-up, Kane could only guess that his brother was inside as well. He supposed it worked out for him since he'd technically stolen Garrett's truck to go find Jess to begin with.

After finding a spot, Kane parked and strode toward the front door of the club. He could already hear the pulsating music before he even went inside.

Stepping inside, he was immediately enveloped in a throng of moving bodies, neon strobe lights, loud music, and the scent of beer, stale food, and straight-up primal lust.

On stage, he could see two women twisting and gyrating around black metal poles wearing nothing but string thongs that were so skimpy they could have been made out of dental floss. Another woman was giving a lap dance to a large man in the corner. By the look on his face and the sweat on his brow, he wasn't going to last much longer. *Gross.*

Kane shook his head in pity for the man's lack of stamina and went to find his brother.

He found him and his friends sitting at the bar, ogling a big titted blonde serving drinks while wearing a white tee-shirt that barely covered her chest and a pair of cut-offs that would have made Daisy Duke blush.

"Here's your keys," Kane said, slapping them down on the bar. Garrett cast him an annoyed look and shoved them into his jeans pocket.

"Where'd you go, anyway?" Garrett asked, raising his voice over the din of the music. "I had to ride over here with Kenny. Next time, just ask for the keys, Kane. I spent twenty minutes looking for them at Falcon's Nest."

Kane didn't apologize, just ignored his brother and flagged down the waitress for a beer.

"Why don't you go get a lap dance or something?" Kane muttered when he could feel Garrett's eyes still boring into him.

The blonde slid the beer across the bar, and Kane grabbed it, taking a swig for something to do. He was agitated and angry, and if he didn't watch it, he'd punch someone before the night was through.

"You still pissed at me from earlier?" Garrett asked, leaning closer to be heard over the pounding bass.

Kane turned to glower at him. "What do you think? Has anything changed in the past two hours?" He rolled his eyes and shoved away from the bar, intent on finding a booth to sit and drown his sorrows in. Finding an empty one on the corner, he claimed it for himself, sliding into the booth to continue his sulking.

He'd been sitting there with his head resting on the table for only a few moments when he felt someone standing next to him. With a start, he glanced up to find a slightly younger version of Jess Holloway standing in front of him.

"You son of a bitch!" she snapped, leaning into his space. "I just got off the phone with my sister. You know what Jess told me? I'll tell you what! That you made her cry *again*, that you dropped the ball *again*, that you are a piece of shit dad just like our daddy was and she wished she'd met Garrett first because he's been more of a dad to Jamie than you ever have." She picked up Kane's glass of beer and threw the contents in his face. "Stay away from my sister and *her* son!" she yelled before stomping off and disappearing into the fray.

Kane sat there for a moment, beer dripping from his face. He knew he deserved every bit of that, but at the same time, he seethed with anger. How could he have known he'd had a kid if no one had told him? His brother had obviously suspected all these years but hadn't bothered to mention it.

He grabbed a napkin and wiped his face off before unfolding himself and stalking to the bar for another beer. Throwing some bills on the bar, he grabbed the beer with a grunt of appreciation to the bartender.

Taking a few steps away toward the stage, he paused to watch a hot redhead writhe suggestively around a pole, her large breasts lightly dusted with freckles.

After a few minutes of watching the redhead and nursing his beer, Kane was about to find some barfly to chat with for a hookup when he turned around and found Garrett standing directly behind him.

"For fuck's sake, Gar," Kane grouched, bunching his eyebrows. "What? Why are you following me? Leave me alone."

"I just wanted to make sure you're okay," Garrett said, taking a step back from Kane's angry pose. "Did you talk with Jess?"

"That's none of your business, brother. Now leave me alone," Kane snapped, anger flashing in his eyes.

"Well... I just worry about you and–"

"You do not, Garrett. You don't give a shit about me or what I have going on," Kane growled. "I'm outta here." He turned to leave, the writhing redhead all but forgotten.

"Here, I'll drive you home," Garrett offered, taking a step to follow him.

"Nah, stay here with your friends," Kane brushed him off, "I'll walk, I have a lot of steam to blow off anyhow."

"Kane, it's like ten miles to the farm," Garrett inserted, taking another step toward the door with Kane.

"Then I better get started, huh?" Kane turned and walked out, fueled by anger. He didn't look back once, even when he heard his little brother calling for him across the gravel parking lot of the strip club.

# Chapter Sixty

*July 21st, 1:21 AM*

It was a little after one in the morning, and Kane had been walking for a while, fueled by anger and resentment. He was so hot around the collar he could probably walk the ten miles to the farm and back and still want to punch someone.

He'd toyed with cutting through the woods and fields as a shortcut but didn't have a flashlight, and he sure as hell wasn't going to end up in a ravine overnight with a twisted ankle. No matter. Kane had always been incredibly fit, and even sticking to the road, his long-legged strides carried him through Crawley in a matter of minutes. He strode past the Crawley Theater, Hanlon's Drug, the Swain County Public Library, and three different churches. Luckily for him, the streets were empty this time of night, giving him a chance to think.

Time to think about his past, his present, and most importantly, his future. Now that he knew he had a kid, he had to be better. Had to be present. He'd get a good paying job somewhere and save up. Maybe he could rekindle things with Jess, and they could be a family. They could even buy a—

*Damnit.*

If it wasn't for his parents, his *mother*, he'd have had land to build a house on. He'd probably even have enough money to start a life, a nice life, with Jess and Jamie if it hadn't been for his stupid family messing everything up.

A new flood of anger coursed through him as he thought about it. With each step he took on the lonely rural road in the dead of night, Kane O'Leary's body pulsated with an anger that quickly turned to rage.

He was the Prodigal Son. The one that had gone away but now came home to make things right. *Where was all the fanfare? Where were all the welcome parties, the well wishes?* Instead, all he seemed to get were the looks of disdain and the whispers of the local gossips.

He was Kane O'Leary, the black sheep of the family. The Fuck-up, The Worthless One, and now, based on tonight's big-reveal, The Deadbeat Dad.

Meanwhile, Garrett was the favorite; the Golden Child, the Perfect Son, the one that could do no wrong.

He knew, deep down, that he only had himself to blame when it came to leaving all those years ago. It was his fault that he never answered his phone when Jess had reached out to him. It was his fault that he'd never supplied his family with a forwarding address. But why hadn't they mentioned Jamie when he'd called home a handful of times during the early years? Why had Garrett waited *months* to tell him about Jamie now? He'd been back in town since September! Now it was July!

Kane clenched his hands into fists as he thought about it. He could make excuses for some of the other things, but Garrett? He knew and could have told Kane months ago! *Damn him!* Kane seethed.

He'd gone nearly four miles when he crested a hill and heard a vehicle coming up behind him as he walked along the guardrail. He stuck his thumb up toward the heavens.

The vehicle pulled over onto the gravel shoulder. When Kane turned to greet the driver, he stiffened. It was Garrett.

"Kane, just get in the truck. Stop being like this," Garrett called through the open passenger window.

"Leave me alone," Kane muttered, waving off his brother without slowing his pace.

"I'm not leaving you here. Please, get in the truck."

The truck tires crunch along the gravel on the side of the road, the sound competing with Kane's heavy breathing and the insects hiding in the weeds along the roadway.

Neither brother said anything for a few moments, each lost in their own thoughts.

Garrett glanced back over at Kane once more through the open truck window. "You seriously are a stubborn sonofabitch."

Kane turned then and sneered at his brother, "You'd know. She always liked you better, anyhow."

"Not true. Now get in the truck. This is stupid," Garrett hissed, annoyance finally getting the best of him. His hands began to shake in anger at the situation. "Why won't you just get in the damn truck? Just get over your anger for once? You're always mad, always going off about this or that."

Garrett jumped when the truck door opened suddenly. Kane folded himself into the passenger seat and slammed the door. Staring straight ahead, Kane remained quiet as anger radiated off of him.

Shuddering as though an uneasy feeling were coursing down his spine, Garrett checked his side mirror for oncoming traffic. As he pulled back out onto the deserted roadway, he remained quiet all the way back to the farm.

***

The farmhouse was shrouded in shadow when Garrett pulled the old Ford up the driveway, past the house and into the yard near the barn. Moonlight did little to illuminate the fields beyond, but Kane could make out the dark silhouettes of deer grazing near the woodline.

Climbing out of the truck, Kane watched as Garrett turned back around to gather his wallet and a travel mug of cold coffee. Kane did very little to hide his contempt for Garrett, his glare boring into the top of his brother's skull.

Garrett slowly lifted his gaze and found Kane staring at him. At seeing his brother's eyes dark and rage-filled, Garrett stepped back from the truck, his eyes round with surprise. Garrett had never seen that look on his brother's face because Kane had never been this angry. He was so overcome with it that he could feel his hands shaking.

"Uh…You comin', Kane?" Garrett asked, his voice light. Even Kane could hear the tremble in it.

Kane ignored him and slammed the passenger door. As he walked around the truck bed, the dusk-to-dawn light finally clicked on, casting a yellow-tinted glow across the farmyard. The buzzing sound it made irritated Kane, and he tried to ignore it as he watched Garrett standing there, mouth agape, staring up at the mosquitoes and moths ramming themselves into the light. *Idiots.*

With a shake of his head, Kane started walking toward the farmhouse, jarring Garrett from his reverie. He started to follow Kane inside the house when suddenly Kane halted without warning. When Garrett nearly ran into him, Kane whirled around and grabbed him by the shoulders.

"You know what, Gar, we need to talk. Enough is enough," Kane growled, bending slightly to stare Garrett in the eyes.

Garrett swallowed audibly.

Kane wanted him to be afraid. He'd never been this angry at his brother. They'd had their differences in the past, and they'd beat each other up a time or two, but never had he shown such malice and hatred toward Garrett.

Catching his off guard, Kane pushed Garrett toward the barn instead of the comfort of the house. With each step, a dark and foreboding feeling filled the air and Kane welcomed it. He was so angry, so hurt,that he needed to get it out. He needed to yell and rant, to tell Garrett how he truly felt after all these years. Enough was enough. He was through internalizing his feelings. Garrett needed to know how much pain he'd caused with his silence.

Kane knew that whatever happened in the barn, a screaming match or a full-on brawl, would change their relationship forever.

"What is this all about, Kane?" Garrett asked, dirt and gravel crunching under his shoes. "Did you talk to Jess? Is this about Jamie?"

Kane sucked in a breath as anger surged through him. *How dare he act so casual about it all!* Garrett had kept Jamie from him for years. Even when Kane had randomly called home when he'd first left town, Garrett hadn't said a word about it.

As they approached the red door of the old barn, Kane stopped walking and tugged the door open.

"Get inside." Kane shoved Garrett forward through the doorway. Garrett stumbled into the dark interior of the barn. The sounds of small critters scurrying and large beasts moving around matched the sound of the men's footfalls as they stumbled into the darkness. From somewhere deep in the darkness, a Holstein mooed, and then another.

"The office," Kane indicated, flipping a switch on one of the overhead lights. The single bulb only illuminated the central walkway enough to see a third of the way down the length of the barn. Past that was nothing but shadow.

The murky shadows seemed to move on their own in the most eerie way but Kane soon realized it was just the black and white hides of the Holsteins playing tricks on his overactive imagination.

Garrett paused too long to catch his bearings so Kane gave him a shove. "I said the office."

'The Office' was a nickname they'd made up as teenagers for the room in the barn where they stored some smaller equipment and animal feed. Garrett had thought it was funny at the time because he and Kane would take their Playboy out there and tell each other "I'm headed to the office. I have some work to do." It was the perfect cover for each other and they thought it was amusing.

Now, Kane thought it was anything but funny. He walked down the main aisle behind his brother, avoiding looking the cows in the eye. Could they feel his anger? See his clenched hands balled at his sides?

They approached the office door, and Kane reached through the darkness to find the light switch. Soon, the small room was aglow with warm overhead light, enshrouded by years of cobwebs and dust.

The space was small, perhaps ten feet by ten feet, and had old gray metal shelving on three walls. Musty-smelling boxes, crates, machinery, and animal supplies filled the shelves. In the middle of the room sat a stack of feed bags, a small table, and two folding chairs.

"Sit," Kane indicated the chair closest to the door as he half shoved Garrett into it.

"Why are you doing this?" Garrett asked, his voice edged with worry. "You don't have to be so aggressive, Kane."

"Don't I?" Kane snapped as he slid into the opposite chair. He glared over at Garrett. "I'm tired of the bullshit around here, Garrett. I'm tired of playing second fiddle. I'm tired of all of it. And it stops tonight."

"What are you even talking about?" Garrett asked, his eyebrows raised. Kane wasn't buying the innocent look anymore. Garrett had proven that he couldn't be trusted.

"I did talk to Jess Holloway tonight," Kane stated, his voice barely above a whisper. He was staring somewhere over Garrett's shoulder, seemingly lost in thought.

"And what did she say?" Garrett asked, sweat beading up on his brow. Kane couldn't tell if it was from fear or the stifling heat of the small windowless room.

"She told me I had a son. Jamie," Kane said. He turned then, staring directly into Garrett's eyes. "But then again, you've known about that since the beginning, haven't you?"

# Chapter Sixty-One

---



"If you suspected I had a kid all these years, how come you never thought to tell me?" Kane hissed, leaning over the table toward Garrett. "You figured you'd just keep that little tidbit to yourself so you'd look better to Mom and Dad? Poor Garrett has a wife and kids. Of course he needs the whole fucking farm. But Kane? Nah. He's just a fuck up who ran away from his responsibilities."

"That isn't true, and you know it, Kane!" Garrett spouted, even though they both knew better.

Garrett was quiet for a moment before admitting, "Maybe I was a little jealous of you. Maybe I did like to see you fail at something. Our entire lives you were always the stronger one, the quicker one, the one Dad listened to first. If I'm being honest with myself, I was glad when you left. It finally gave me a chance to prove to Dad that I was worthy, that I was capable."

"Wow..." Kane scoffed. "So you *do* admit it? Did you purposely keep Jamie a secret from me?"

"I admitted to being jealous growing up. Now, I just find you pathetic." Garrett spat. "Your relationship with everyone else is on you. I couldn't care less."

"Don't lie to me, Gar! I saw how smug you looked when you told me about Mom changing the will. You enjoyed every moment of it," Kane snapped, his face reddening as rage poured from him.

Kane watched Garrett work through something, his chest heaving.

"So what? Maybe I did enjoy it a little bit?" Garrett finally admitted, his lips curling into a smirk. "Probably as much as I liked fucking Jess every time I went over there to give her money or groceries to help raise *your* son."

At Garrett's admission, something snapped in Kane. In a rage, he lunged at Garrett.

Garrett barely had time to brace himself for impact as Kane's shoulder rammed into his gut, causing Garrett to stumble backward and double over with a grunt. Sucking in a ragged breath, Garrett whirled in time to dodge Kane's fist as it came flying towards his face. He wasn't fast enough for the second punch, and Kane relished the sound of his brother's nose crushing under the impact and the sight of blood dripping onto his shirt.

Garrett pivoted and threw some punches of his own into his brother's solar plexus and was rewarded with a swift kick to the knee. On impact, Garrett fell to the ground, holding his injured leg.

"Get up you piece of shit," Kane taunted as he stood over Garrett's prone form. When Garrett didn't move fast enough, Kane's booted foot made contact with Garrett's ribs, causing him to cry out.

"Enough!" Garrett pleaded, holding up his palm in surrender as blood poured from his nose. He wiped at it absently but just made the mess worse.

"Enough?" Kane sneered. "Enough? Don't you get it? It'll never be enough until I get my share of the farm. Until I get what's mine. Until I get the life I should have had! The one you kept secret from me!"

"I don't–" Garrett began but stopped in horror as Kane suddenly pulled a knife from a hidden ankle holster. He pointed the blade at Garrett's throat, its edge long and wicked. He felt a small thrill of satisfaction at seeing the way Garrett's eyes rounded in fear.

"Yes, you do," Kane spat. "You've been a thorn in my side since we were kids. Always the good one, the perfect one. I'm sick of it. And I'm sick of getting overlooked in this family. My own parents wrote me out of their will! Fuck them! And fuck you!" He moved to stand over Garrett, the knife still trained on Garrett's jugular. "They may have written me out, but if you aren't around to have it, well... then I guess it goes to me, right?"

"But... don't do this, Kane..." Garrett pleaded. "You don't have to be like this. It doesn't have to end like this. It's just a piece of land, a stupid old farm. Besides, the will says–"

"I don't care what the will says, Garrett. You kept my kid a secret, you cheated on your wife with the only woman I've ever loved, and you turned my parents against me." Kane glowered. "I have a family of my own now to look out for. If you aren't going to give me my half of the farm... I'll just have to take it." And then, without hesitation, Kane O'Leary thrust the knife into his younger brother's chest again, and again, and again.

With each thrust of the knife, Kane felt a part of his anger break away, like an ice pick chips away at a block of ice to form something beautiful and new. With Garrett out of the picture, Kane felt he could finally be the man he was meant to be: a man worthy of love, worthy of a family, and most importantly, worthy of his inheritance.

# Now

# Chapter Sixty-Two



*Wednesday, September 26th, 3:38 PM*

"So it was all originally about the farm? The land?" Tess asked, trying to keep Kane talking while she devised a plan to escape. "From what I've been told, you didn't even want the farm. At least, you didn't want to work it. You were going to sell it, weren't you?"

"My part, at least. That was the initial plan, but then my parents nixed that for me." Kane glared down at Tess as he stood over her sitting on the stump.

"How'd it work out for you after killing your brother?" Tess goaded him, trying to get him to admit more. "Last time I checked, Kevin held the deed to the farm. You still have nothing."

Kane's hand flew out and backhanded Tess before she could move out of the way. She instantly tasted blood as she felt her split lip with her tongue.

"You can shut up now," Kane glowered. He raised his closed fist in front of her face and shook it threateningly. "And besides, Kevin is dead."

"Is that why you killed him? To get his share of the farm? Good grief, Kane. Is your niece Marissa next? Please tell me you aren't going to play Whack-a-Mole with your entire family just to get a farm," Tess spat out angrily.

"Kevin was an obstacle, yes. He was just like Garrett; always happy to work that stupid farm, never complained about getting up at the crack of dawn, never complained about being broke. He was just... happy. And damnit, he was taking my inheritance! At least, it was my share that my son should have gotten. Now Jamie gets nothing because I got nothing and how fair is that? Poor Lori is sick and I see how hard Jamie works to pay her medical bills, and I can't help them. But if things had gone as they were supposed to, then I'd have the land. I'd have the money to help my son." Kane's face had turned a disturbing shade of purplish red, and Tess was worried he'd have a medical issue and no one would find them for days. She found the thought even more disturbing than the color of his face.

"I didn't even know about Jamie until he was fifteen. I'd missed so much of his life by that point, I'd vowed to try to make up for it. At first, he wouldn't have anything to do with me. He'd only talk to Garrett, only wanted to spend time with Garrett. It pissed me off, even though I knew I deserved his anger. It wasn't until about a year or two after Garrett "disappeared" that Jamie finally came around. He'd been working on a car, an old Mustang he'd bought off of Craigslist, and couldn't get it running. Prom was a week away, and he'd asked Lori to go with him, so it was a pretty big deal. I'd offered to help get the car running multiple times before, but he'd always declined. One day, he finally changed his mind." Kane's face had relaxed to its normal color once again as he relayed his story. "We ended up talking finally and found that we had stuff in common. It took us a few hours, but we got the Mustang running, too. Something changed that day. Jamie and I bonded somehow. I'd kinda given up by that point, but then things turned around for us. And now, we are like any other father and son."

"Except he thinks you can't walk," Tess chimed in deadpan. Kane glared at her.

"Judge me all you want, Dane, but know this," he spat as his anger rekindled. "I might not have started out being 'Father of the Year,' but I sure as hell didn't give up. When I found out I had a kid, I stayed around, even when there wasn't anything here for me. Even when I had nothing."

"So have you been seething and planning how to get the land this whole time? That sounds exhausting," Tess said.

"The farm was a touchy subject for years. But then Lori got sick and the medical bills started coming in. Life started getting harder for Jamie. I wanted to help him. I don't have much myself, nothing to give my son. I *should* have had half that farm."

"I tried reasoning with Kevin," Kane raged on. "But he wouldn't give me my share. Said he just couldn't do it. Offered to let Jamie and Lori build a home on the land but he refused to deed any of it to me. None of it! Every time I tried to speak to him about it, the answer was always the same. Eventually, I'd had enough and decided that *my* son deserved his fair share. That *I* deserved a fair share." he jabbed a finger angrily at Tess for emphasis. "The only thing standing in my way at that point was Kevin."

"But you have the problem of Kevin's last will and testament," she commented casually as if it weren't that important, even though that was the furthest thing from the truth.

"The last time I checked, he didn't even have a will." With a haughty huff, Kane sneered as he began pacing while keeping the gun barrel trained on Tess.

"Again, you're wrong, Kane. Kevin did have a will. The farm and all of Kevin's assets are to go to his sister, Marissa."

"Marissa?" Kane whipped around to gape at Tess once more. "Whatever for? Why not give his half of the farm's holdings to his own son? Or even me?"

"Marissa and Kevin were Garrett's last remaining children, so of course he would have left the farm to them. There was a clause that stated that in the event of the death of one of Garrett's children, their portion was to be divided among the living children, which is what happened to Brandon's share when he was killed in the car accident. The date on Garrett's will was just a couple of weeks after everything from your parents' will was finalized. It appears that Garrett knew that Kevin would be the one to stay and work the farm, so he willed it to Kevin and Marissa with the clause that the property could never be divided and sold into smaller sections. In essence, they would remain co-owners of O'Leary Farms and Holdings. So, according to Garrett's will, with Kevin dead, Kevin's portion of the farm would get deeded to his sister. According to Kevin's will, he agreed with his parents. All land and holdings are to go to Marissa."

"So now Marissa owns *all* of it?" Kane growled. "What about *my* kid? *My* family?" He paused his rant, apparently deep in thought. "Why not Breck? I assumed he'd give it to Breck."

"I don't know why he didn't leave his share to his son. I'm only telling you what the will said. You'd have to ask

Breck, but I'm guessing it had to do with his extensive gambling problem. I'd speculate that Kevin knew exactly what his son would try to do if he ever inherited such a vast chunk of prime farmland. It'd be wagered away faster than you could say 'ante up!'" Tess shrugged, her arms pulling at the restraints around her wrists.

"Pansy-assed little..." Kane mumbled as he stomped around the clearing, visibly rattled. "I assumed the land would go to Breck, which would be like taking candy from a baby. That little shit can't keep a dime longer than a minute. I could dangle ten, twenty grand in front of his face, and he'd be drooling like one of Pavlov's hounds. He'd sign that deed over to me so fast it'd make your head spin."

"I'm guessing he didn't leave it to you because you are– were– in a wheelchair and had made your mind known about not wanting to work the farm. According to multiple witnesses, you've been wanting to get your hands on the land for years now to sell it for a quick buck. Garrett and his son Kevin poured their blood, sweat, and tears into that soil, just like your parents, Shamus and... Lenore, was it? Except Lenore knew what kind of son you were; the kind that would destroy the family legacy with the swipe of a pen on a bill of sale." Tess watched as her jab hit its mark. "Tell me, Kane. Who else knows that you can walk? That you are, in fact, highly capable and have been playing on their emotions for years?"

"My granddaughter, Courtney, knows I can walk... a little." Kane grinned wickedly at Tess. "She caught me one day. I was in the kitchen at my apartment, cooking breakfast, and she used her key to come in unannounced. The look on her face..." he sighed at the memory. Glancing back at Tess, he continued, "I had enough time to 'shuffle' to the couch and slowly sit down. Act like my back was giving me grief."

"But why go to all that trouble?" Tess wondered aloud. "Seems like a pain in the butt."

"Oh, it was," Kane assured her. "But it was necessary for me to get into that apartment."

Tess gave him a quizzical look as she continued attempting to untie her restraints.

"Look... Judge me all you want, but seriously. I was in my sixties, unmarried, and alone. I didn't have a house or inheritance, thanks to my parents, and I didn't have a wife to take care of me. So, I acted all feeble and worked the system to get into an assisted living home. They keep the common areas clean, there's a pool and gym, neighbors around my age, social events, plenty of women to warm my bed if you get me..." he paused to wink at Tess. When she wrinkled her nose in repulsion, he barked out a laugh. "All I have to do is live normally inside my apartment and then act all frail when I go out. I tell a few jokes here and there. The ladies love me!" He shrugged. "Hell, even my groceries get delivered! Between that and Amazon, you don't ever have to leave your house if you don't want to."

"I just can't see you being the water aerobics type," Tess said. She squinted at him for a moment. "Maybe a Silver Sneakers guy."

Kane snorted a laugh and pointed at her. "That's a good one. And no, I don't do either. I have my own routine. Now, enough of the chit-chat."

He stalked over to her and abruptly grabbed her around the arm, yanking her to her feet. His fingers bit into her flesh, and Tess knew without looking that she'd have bruises.

"Do you think that I don't know what you've been up to? Talking and wasting time, hoping that your big bad cop boyfriend will come save you," Kane whispered hoarsely in her ear as he half-dragged her through the woods toward a four-wheeler hidden under a camouflage tarp. "Right where I left it. Perfection." He muttered to himself as he pulled the tarp off and threw it to the side. Turning back to Tess, "Agent Haywood? He's too busy looking for his brat kid. Why would he give two shits about you. They'll be too busy chasing their tails back at Jamie's, wondering where you went since your SUV is still parked in the driveway. I bet they are combing the woods right now. They'll give up soon enough, though. It's only an acre or so, and you're not worth the resources. Trust me, the girl's going to get more attention, not some meddling cop."

With a firm shove, he pushed her in front of him. "Saddle up, and no funny business."

The four-wheeler was built for two but Tess had no desire to go for a ride. The phrase, "If you ride, you die" kept going through her mind. If she got on and left with Kane, she may never be seen again. She may never find Natalie.

She may never see Denny again.

"No," she said as she pivoted and made a run for it, her long legs carrying her deep into the woods.

She could hear Kane behind her, keeping pace, as she stumbled and fell against trees, running in a zig-zag formation. With her hands still tied behind her back, her equilibrium was off but still she pressed forward. If he caught her again, he'd kill her. She already knew what he'd done to his brother. What would stop him from doing it to her, too?

Her breath came in hitches, and her lungs burned, but she kept running, expecting bullets to start flying at any second. As her feet pounded across the uneven terrain, she thought about looking behind her but didn't want to risk falling. The minutes passed with her jumping over fallen logs, dodging branches, and getting smacked in the face with leaves.

In the distance, she suddenly saw a familiar site. He'd taken her to the farm! She could barely make out the silhouette of the burial mound that had once held Garrett O'Leary.

Just as she was about to jump over another fallen log, her breathing painful and ragged, Kane pounced, knocking the wind from her lungs. Tess landed over the log awkwardly, gasping for air as her chest hurt with each attempt. Pain shot up through her ankle, and she gingerly attempted to move her foot to assess the damage. Could she still run? Regardless if it was broken or not, she still couldn't breathe properly, her lungs struggling to accept fresh air.

Tess cautiously looked over her shoulder. Standing over her, Kane sneered and pulled out something from his back pocket.

Opening her mouth to scream for help, she instantly knew her efforts were futile because as soon as she inhaled, something came from behind her, and everything went black again.

# Chapter Sixty-Three

*Wednesday, September 26th, 5:20 PM*

Tess landed on the hard-packed floor of the old woodshed with a thud, her shoulder taking a bulk of the impact. With a grunt, she bit her lip to keep from crying out at the pain coursing through her arm.

Once the pain subsided and her eyes adjusted to the dark interior of the shed, Tess tried to see around the blindfold. When she'd fallen, it had shifted just a small amount, allowing her to see a just sliver of her surroundings.

The small space was sparsely filled. An old rake leaned against the wall in the corner, its green painted handle faded and chipping with age. A small stack of terracotta pots, cracked and dirty, sat on a rickety shelf next to Tess, directly under a small, grimy window.

Shifting around as best she could, her hands handcuffed behind her, Tess tried to get another look of her surroundings. The building smelled musty, like rotten leaves and decay. A strong ammonia smell dominated the area however. Had some animal taken up residence here? Would they come back soon?

Tess felt her panic rising again as she thought of Natalie alone somewhere out there, having God only knows what done to her. And it was all Tess's fault.

Feeling warm tears sliding down her cheeks and soaking into the blindfold, Tess tried to calm herself. Duct tape covered her mouth, and if she cried too much and became congested, then she'd have difficulty breathing.

Turning her head to the side, she tried to rub her face on her shoulder to pull off the duct tape but realized, much to her dismay, that it was wrapped completely around her head. Giving up on rubbing the tape off, she tried using her spit to loosen the tape, but again, that seemed futile.

Suddenly, she heard something. A soft scraping sound somewhere to her left. Trying to control her breathing, Tess strained her ears to listen.

Nothing.

And then, just when she was about to shift her position and begin working on getting the blindfold off, she heard the sound again, this time closer.

Straining to hear, Tess didn't move a muscle. She could hear birds singing outside, but inside the quiet woodshed, all she could hear was breathing.

And then she realized it wasn't her own.

The realization hit her at the same time as she felt a hand reach out and touch her arm. The hair on the back of her neck stood on end as she knew, without a doubt, she was not alone. Pulling away from the touch, Tess maneuvered toward the person to kick out at them when suddenly everything changed.

"Tess?" a small voice whispered from the shadows of the small shed.

"Natalie?" Tess exclaimed, her words muffled by duct tape, her tears suddenly changing to those of joy. "Where are you?" Turning her head blindly, left to right, she tried to ascertain where the young girl was.

"I'm here, Tess," Natalie cried, throwing herself into Tess's lap as relief washed over them both. "I knew you'd find me!" Tess could feel the child's small arms wrap around her waist tightly, and Tess's heart broke for the girl. She must be so scared!

"Nat, blindfold," Tess mumbled against the tape across her mouth. It must have sounded close enough to Natalie because the small girl reached up and pulled the blindfold off of Tess's eyes.

Staring into Natalie's dark blue eyes, so much like her father's, caused Tess to tear up. The girl leaned into Tess and wiped the tears away.

"It's okay, Tess. You came for me. I knew you would; that's what family does." Natalie then proceeded to pick at the duct tape until she found a loose end and tried to pull it off of Tess.

Growing frustrated with the sticky tape, Natalie looked around for a pair of scissors or a knife but found nothing. Finally, with some muffled instructions from Tess, Natalie was able to pull the tape downward, away from Tess's face.

"Oh, sweet girl, come here," Tess commanded gently once her mouth was freed of the sticky bonds. She sucked in a fresh lungful of air as Natalie came closer and snuggled into her.

"We were so scared for you. Your dad and I have been looking for you everywhere."

The young girl shook her head. "I was so scared. It happened so fast. The bad man grabbed me and brought me here. Where is Daddy? I want to go home."

Tess's heart broke for the young girl. The trauma of the day would not be easy to recover from. She'd probably have trust issues for some time.

"Your dad is out looking for you right now, just like I was. He will be here soon... I hope. We need to get out of here, though, before the old man comes back."

"How do we get those off of you?" Natalie asked, gesturing towards the handcuffs around Tess's wrist.

"You'll just have to help me. I can walk just fine, but I'll need you to open the door and stuff."

"It's locked. I already tried that," Natalie rolled her eyes. Tess coughed out a laugh.

"Yep, that's my Nat, Always thinking, always sassy," she grinned at the young girl. Natalie smiled, her dirty, bruised face full of affection for Tess.

"I love you, too, Tess, but stop being mushy. We gotta get moving," Natalie assured, hopping to her feet, seeming suddenly invigorated now that Tess was with her.

Tess chortled as she awkwardly climbed to her feet. Her legs were sore, and her ankle felt sprained. And she was so thirsty!

"Okay, Smarty Pants, have you tried breaking out through the window over there?" Tess asked, pointing her chin in the direction of the grimy window over the shelves. "I'm a woman on a mission to get some water. I'm thirsty."

"I tried, but I'm too short," Natalie said, bending to pick something up. Holding it out, she offered it to Tess. It was a bottle of water, but to thirsty Tess, it was like winning the lottery.

"Thank you," Tess said gratefully, as she bent lower to accept the bottle that Natalie held to Tess's lips. Within seconds, she'd chugged half the contents. She wanted all of it but knew she should save some for Natalie.

"Ahh, refreshing!" she licked her lips with a smile as the young girl pulled the water bottle away. "Now, we need to break the window. I nominate using the pottery there on the shelf." She walked over to the shelf and attempted to look out the window. The glass was so dirty she could barely make out the edge of woods and what appeared to be a fenced-in field beyond.

"Here goes nothing," Tess said, nudging a medium-sized terracotta pot to the edge of the shelf with her shoulder for Natalie to reach. "Go ahead and give this a big heave-ho, lady. I want out of here."

Natalie was able to reach the pot now, and Tess watched as the young girl sized the window up, the tip of her tongue sticking out as she focused, and threw the planter at the window with all her might.

The glass shattered, shards of it raining down on the floor like prisms. Tess stepped back, blocking Natalie from the spray. The sudden burst of sound from the exploding window would surely bring Kane running if he were in the vicinity still.

Tess made a shushing sound to Natalie so they could listen for signs of Kane's return, but they heard nothing. Relief, though fleeting, coursed through Tess.

"C'mon. Let's get out of here before he decides to come back. Watch the glass," Tess glanced around, "Is that a blanket? Grab that and throw it on top of the shelf."

She watched as Natalie grabbed a small blue blanket that was lying on the floor where Natalie had been sitting. The young girl tossed it up on the shelf as best she could but was too short to make the blanket stay.

"Here, try again, I'll help you. Just watch the glass," Tess instructed. Together, they got the blanket on the shelf and Tess was able to spread it over the window sill. She turned to Natalie.

"So we don't cut ourselves," she explained. "Now, can you please toss the water out the window so we have something to drink?" She watched the girl fling the half-filled water bottle through the window, where it landed with a plasticy splat sound. "Perfect. Okay, now come over here, Nat. I'm going to give you a boost. I need you to climb up and over. Got it?"

"Got it," Natalie nodded solemnly, her dark blue eyes full of apprehension. She looked exhausted and pale, and Tess wanted to take her in her arms and tell her everything was going to be okay. But she didn't know they would be. She couldn't look her in the eye and lie to her, especially after everything she'd already been through.

Getting down on one knee, Tess instructed Natalie to use her leg as a step-stool and gave a boost as the young girl carefully attempted to climb the rickety wooden shelf. At first, Tess was afraid the shelving unit wouldn't hold the girl but Natalie was able to reach the window frame and cautiously peek out.

"Do you see anyone?" Tess asked. Natalie shook her head and continued to shimmy out the window. With some light grunts, a whispered curse word that made Tess grin, and a triumphant giggle, Natalie finally made it through the window and onto the ground outside.

She gave Tess two thumbs-up and a huge grin when Tess spied at her through the broken window.

"My turn!" Tess smiled, trying to make a scary situation more of a game for the nine-year-old. "This should be fun with these on my wrists." She shrugged.

"You can do it!" Natalie whispered loudly before looking around her suddenly.

"What's wrong?" Tess asked, panic suddenly filling her.

"I thought I heard something. Just hurry up. I want to get out of here."

"Me too," Tess agreed with a nod. She didn't trust the shelving unit, but just in case it was stronger than it looked, she stepped up on the middle shelf and instantly heard it moan and creak. Moving quickly, she shimmied herself up by the window sill using her elbows and shoulders. With a grunt and a heave, she pulled her knee up onto the window sill just as the shelving unit collapsed below her. With her wrists still bound together, she pushed through the window frame headfirst and landed in a pile of weeds on the other side. Her already injured shoulder howled with pain, and her head throbbed. She let out a gasp as she lay there for a moment, staring up at the canopy of trees overhead.

Natalie moved into her line of vision. "That looked... embarrassing. Are you okay?"

"Yes, Twerp," grunted Tess with a smile. "Now help me up, and let's get out of here."

Natalie reached out and grabbed Tess's arm and helped pull her to her feet. As the girl bent to pick up the water bottle, Tess looked around to get a better idea of where they were.

"I don't know for sure where we are, but I think we are still on the farm. Let's follow the fenceline. Stay alert, be quiet," Tess whispered. "I wanted to check the other side of this shed first, see what we can see."

Motioning for Natalie to follow, Tess surveyed the field on the other side of the fence to look for any signs of life. Two fields over, she could see a barn, but it didn't look like the O'Leary barn. It was difficult to tell where in the state she was in. She was so turned around!

Walking around the woodshed, the twosome stayed alert for any signs of humanity. All they could see were trees and dense undergrowth. With a sigh of frustration, Tess led Natalie over the uneven terrain back toward the fence.

Overhead, birds sang, oblivious to the peril Tess and Natalie found themselves in. *Maybe ignorance really* was *bliss*, Tess mused as she stumbled yet again on a hidden tree root. Gnats buzzed around her face annoyingly, but she'd long since given up swatting at them with her bruised, bound hands. Instead, she'd resorted to swishing her hair around like a horse's tail, even though she knew it must look like a matted mess by this point.

"How are you doing, Nat?" Tess asked softly over her shoulder. She could hear Natalie stumbling around behind her, but the young girl said nothing. Tess halted her steps and turned to find Natalie silently sobbing as she trailed after Tess, trying to keep up.

"Sweet girl, what? What happened? Am I walking too fast?" Tess asked, bending down to look Natalie in the eye. The girl stopped and looked up at Tess, her blue eyes pooling with tears.

"I'm so scared," Natalie sobbed. "I just want to go home to Daddy. Where is Daddy?" Her tears fell in earnest now. She sucked in a breath before letting it out again in another sob. "Please take me home, Tess." She hiccuped another sob, breaking Tess's heart.

"Natalie, your dad and I love you more than you know. He is trying his hardest to find you. To find us," Tess leaned out, pressing her forehead to the young girl's, looking her straight in the eyes. "I will do whatever I need to do to get you back to your dad safely, no matter how long it takes. And I know your dad is working as hard as he can to find us. All of his work buddies are looking, too. That is how much you are loved." It was the one thing that Tess could promise Natalie. Everything else was out of her hands.

Natalie looked at her in wonder for a few moments and then suddenly threw herself at Tess, wrapping her arms around her middle.

"I love you too, Tess! Now, let's find my dad."

# Chapter Sixty-Four

*Wednesday, September 26th, 5:30 PM*

"Slow down, Haywood! Good grief!" Claybourne complained, his knuckles blanched from where he grasped the dashboard. "I told you I should have driven." He pursed his lips as Denny took a curve way too fast.

"You drive like an old man, Claybourne," Denny snapped as he accelerated into the curve before Quaker Hollow Road. "Jamie O'Leary admitted to seeing an old red pick-up truck pull away from their house this morning minutes after they pulled up. The fact that Tess's county owned vehicle was parked, abandoned, in their driveway and she hasn't been seen since says a lot."

"Okay, then why are we headed to the farm at like... 300 miles an hour?" Claybourne snapped as Denny slowed the Tahoe enough to barely take the turn in the road safely. Behind him, three deputy sheriff cruisers followed.

"I told you. The woods surrounding Jamie and Lori's place are about two acres at most. They've got deputies searching it now to be thorough. I was already gathering men and preparing to head to the farm to search for Nat when I got this." He handed his phone to Claybourne.

"Shit," Claybourne murmured, looking at a photo of a battered and bloodied Tess sitting on a stump. "That's when you called me to trace Tess's phone?"

Denny nodded. "Kane sent that and then called me from Tess's phone. Told me I had an hour to decide which one I wanted to save." His grip on the steering wheel tightened. He pressed the accelerator, urging the vehicle faster down the bumpy rural road.

"The phone just pinged around here, Haywood. It doesn't say exactly where–"

"The farm is huge, and Kane grew up there. He knows all the nooks and crannies. He took them there," Denny assured. He didn't know for a fact. It was more of a feeling in his bones. He wanted both of them back. Just the thought of going through life without one of them...

He felt his throat tighten with emotion at the thought of losing them. Pushing the darkness from his mind, he flipped on his turn signal as he finally slowed his Tahoe to take the turn up the O'Leary's long and bumpy driveway. A glance in the rearview mirror revealed the trio of deputy vehicles doing the same.

Up ahead, Denny could still make out the remnants of yellow and black crime scene tape around the old white farmhouse. It appeared that someone had cut the seal across the door meant to secure the door.

"I thought the scene hadn't been released yet?" Claybourne asked curiously as he, too, noticed the crime tape.

"I'm pretty sure Tess told me they've officially released it but the victim's sister wants everyone to stay out until the crime scene clean up crew comes through," Denny answered as he parked the vehicle and the two men got out, cautiously looking around for signs of Kane, Tess or Natalie.

Denny heard the other law enforcement vehicles roll to a stop, their ignitions turning off as the officers began piling out, pulling their firearms. Holding them at the ready, they signaled to one another and slowly surrounded the house. They'd brought extra officers in each vehicle, including BCI agents that worked with Denny. It was the BCI agents that swiftly made their way toward the barn to clear the structure, while some of the county deputies surrounded the house or checked the other outbuildings.

"Kane O'Leary, this is the Swain County Sheriff's Department! Come out with your hands up!" Sheriff Malone called into a bullhorn from his position near his cruiser parked behind Denny.

It was silent except for a light breeze wrestling the leaves of the live oak over their heads. A crow cawed in the distance, and cicadas hummed. The autumn air was surprisingly warm and humid as Denny and the officers waited for signs of life in the old farmhouse.

"Kane O'Leary! This is your last chance! Come out now, or we are coming in," Malone announced into the bullhorn.

The minutes ticked on, the cicada seemed to get louder, and Denny's anger climbed. As he was about to order his men to advance, an upstairs window slid open. All eyes on that side of the house went to the window.

The muzzle of a rifle could be seen pointing out from behind a curtain.

"You make one step to come in here, Agent Haywood, and I'll slit this little brat's throat," came a deep, gravely voice.

Denny swallowed audibly yet kept his face blank. His daughter was up there with that mad man! His mind was racing with different scenarios and rescue plans.

"Why don't you just come down here so we can talk face to face?" Denny called up loudly. He was hoping the sound of his voice would give Natalie hope. God, he wanted to hold her now; he wanted to know she was safe.

"Yeah, right, I ain't stupid. The minute I walk out there, you're either going to kill me or arrest me," Kane hollered back. The curtain moved slightly, giving Denny an idea as to where Kane was standing. If he could get a clear shot...

But no, he didn't know where Natalie was. He couldn't risk accidentally hitting her.

"Let me talk to Natalie then," he called up.

"Why should I allow that?" Kane asked. "Is she the one you choose to save? Or do you want to save the detective?"

"Show me my daughter you sonofabitch!" Denny seethed.

"Daddy, help me!" Natalie's voice came from the window.

"Natalie!" Denny called, making a move towards the house.

A voice crackled in Denny's ear, "Agent Haywood, this is Officer Cooper. I can see two people walking along the fenceline. One looks like a kid. The other looks like Dane. Repeat, I have them in my sights. Over."

"Daddy, help me!" Natalie's voice came from the window again. The same volume, the same inflections. A recording.

"Copy," Denny said as he pressed his radio button. He turned to Claybourne, relief coursing through him. "They've been seen. This is a trap. Kane doesn't have them in there. We need to flush him out, arrest him." He wanted to go get his family.

Claybourne nodded, and as he turned to tell the others, a shot rang out. Claybourne flew backwards, gasping as the bullet ripped through his shoulder with a spray of crimson. Denny lifted his gun and began firing at the window where he'd suspected Kane had been standing.

"Officer down! Officer down! Send a medic!" someone barked into a radio.

More shots rang out from above, this time from a handgun, peppering the farmyard with bullets. As the officers ran for cover, firing shots at the gunman in the upstairs window, some of them slipped up the front steps and kicked in the front door.

In what sounded like a Wild West brawl, the officers held their ground as Kane kept firing shots. With his lack of lag time to reload, Denny surmised that he had barricaded himself inside with a small arsenal. Who knew how long this could go on?

Denny glanced over at Claybourne's prone form on the packed dirt driveway, his blood soaking into the ground. He had to get his friend out of harm's way. After a moment's hesitation, he lowered his head and slunk out from behind the chicken coop where he'd taken cover and grasped his friend under the arms. With a grunt of pain, Claybourne offered no resistance as Denny pulled him to safety.

"Thanks, Haywood," Claybourne gasped through the pain.

Inside the house, a struggle ensued. Something shattered, and someone shouted. It was then that Denny noticed that the shooting had stopped, and an eerie silence had fallen over the farmyard.

Denny checked Claybourne's wound and looked for something to place over it. It had missed Claybourne's bulletproof vest by mere centimeters. Cautiously, He ran back to his Tahoe, now covered in bullet holes, and dug around inside. Finding a clean pair of Natalie's socks, he took them back to Claybourne and pressed them to the hemorrhaging wound. While applying pressure, he waited for an ambulance, hoping they brought two. He had no idea what shape his family would be in when he finally got to see them.

# Chapter Sixty-Five

*Wednesday, September 26th, 5:38 PM*

"I feel like we've been walking for hours," Natalie whined as she smacked at another mosquito. Tess didn't blame her.

"Same, child, same," Tess offered a smile. "We should be getting close to the farmho–"

Gunshots suddenly filled the air, causing Tess and Natalie to dive for cover. Natalie was screaming, covering her ears, as they hid in the waist-high grass. The torrent of shots continued, and at one point, Tess thought she could hear men shouting. It had to be at the farmhouse! Denny had arrived with backup!

"C'mon, Natalie," she encouraged gently. "I know it's scary, but we're close. It sounds like your dad has arrived, and he brought friends."

Natalie looked skeptical but finally stood on shaking legs and dusted her dirty knees off. Her shorts and tee shirt were filthy at that point, and her hair was a matted mess, but Tess was just glad to see her alive and well. They were almost out of this mess!

"Here, hold my hand if you want," she offered. Natalie finally reached out and wrapped her small hand around Tess's.

Together, the duo cautiously climbed the fence and made their way across the field toward the sound of the shootout. Stepping around random piles of cow manure, vaulting over groundhog holes, and swatting away pesky insects, Tess and Natalie crossed the vast field.

As they crept closer to the farmyard, Tess bent lower, using the tall grasses in the field as camouflage from danger. The sound of bullets flying had slowed dramatically, and for the past few moments, all seemed quiet at the house. But where was Denny? Though she was confident in Denny's ability to handle the situation, she couldn't dismiss the fear that Kane might have gotten away. He could be on the run or looking for them even now.

The barn was the closest place to hide to get their bearings. Getting Natalie's attention, Tess pointed with her chin, and the girl nodded. They altered their course and slunk through the grasses toward the large red barn.

"Psst, over here!" came a whisper from somewhere close by. A smile broke through Tess's focus when she saw Deputy Miles peek around from behind the barn. A sob built in her chest as she stumbled toward her colleague.

Seeing her struggling at the fence separating her from the barn, Miles crept over and helped her and Natalie through the slats. Shielding them from behind, he guided them behind the barn.

"God, Tess, you're a sight for sore eyes!" he said quietly as he reached for his handcuff keys and released her wrists. Once freed, she rubbed her red wrists, the skin already bruised and raw.

"You too, Miles!" she flung her arms around his neck, catching him off guard. After a second, he let out a soft chuckle and returned her hug.

"I missed you too, Dane, but you need a bath," he grinned as she pulled away. She gave him a scowl that caused Natalie to giggle.

"I know, I can smell myself," Tess made a face. She glanced from Natalie back to Miles. "So what's going on? We heard gunshots."

"O'Leary was holed up in the house. We had the place surrounded, thought one or both of you were in there with him. Then Cooper saw you two walking on the other side of the field and called it into Haywood. That's when they realized O'Leary was alone in there. I was back here, but I heard the 10-00, so I knew things went south."

*Shit*... 10-00: Officer Down.

"Who?" Tess breathed, afraid to hear the answer, tears pressing on the back of her eyelids. Her breath hitched as Miles glanced down at Natalie before quickly finding Tess's face again.

"Claybourne. He's okay; he took one in the shoulder, I think. The ambulance should be arriving any minute."

"Claybourne?" Tess asked, letting out a relieved breath. She liked Claybourne, of course, and wished him no ill will. But the thought of losing Denny tore at her heart in a way that she was unable to process.

Suddenly, the wail of sirens filled the air, and the trio turned and watched as, in the distance, two ambulances sped down Quaker Hollow Road, lights and sirens blaring.

"Suspect is in custody. Repeat, suspect is in custody," Sheriff Malone's voice came across the radio.

"Copy," Miles replied, pressing the button on his shoulder. "I have Dane and Natalie with me. Both are fine."

"This is Haywood," the radio crackled. "Miles, where are you? I have to see them for myself." Denny's familiar voice calmed Tess and made her smile. Natalie must have felt it, too, because Tess found herself nestled in Natalie's embrace, the young child's arms wrapped around Tess in a tight grip.

"We are near the barn, coming to you now. Over," Miles said with a grin.

They made their way around the barn. The setting sun alighted the red paint in a golden glow. If it wasn't for the traumatic events of the day, Tess could have paused to enjoy the scene of the sun on the fields and pastures in the distance. She was so exhausted, both mentally and physically, and she just wanted to see Denny and Otter.

"Daddy!" squealed Natalie, tearing away from Tess's side and bounding across the farmyard to Denny. The look of pure love and delight that filled his face when he saw his daughter pulled at Tess's heart.

Denny bent and scooped Natalie up, tears in his eyes as he held her. She clung to him, sobbing, her little legs and arms wrapped around him like a spider monkey. Tess could see her whispering to him as he held her close. They stood like that, holding each other, both crying for a long time.

Tess wanted to rush to him, too, but she knew that Natalie needed her time with her dad. The girl had been through a lot in the past twenty-four hours or so and would need time to process everything. Tess vowed in her heart that she and Denny would make sure Natalie got the help she needed to get through this successfully.

It was then that Denny caught sight of Tess standing off to the side, quietly waiting. She watched as he sucked in a breath when he saw her and something changed in his demeanor. He was exhausted from the events of the last few hours. His eyes were red and swollen with emotion, yet they held something else.

He held out a hand to Tess, beckoning her to him, which she immediately accepted. Stepping into his embrace, he pulled her close and nestled his nose in her hair. It was then that she noticed his shoulders were shaking.

He was silently sobbing.

Tess wrapped her arms around him and Natalie as tight as she could, feeling at peace for the first time since her father died. This was her family now. That realization hit her with such force that she felt her knees weaken.

"Sir, can we check the little girl?" one of the paramedics asked Denny. Tess hadn't even heard them approach. She reluctantly let go of Natalie and Denny, even as Natalie informed the paramedic she was fine, with sass that only a nine-year-old could muster.

"C'mon, kiddo, let's get you checked out." Denny gently took his daughter's hand and followed the paramedic to the back of a waiting ambulance.

"Ma'am?" another paramedic beckoned to Tess. She felt fine, if not exhausted and thirsty, but went to get checked out. At this point, she was willing to do anything to avoid going to the hospital and just wanted to get home and into the shower, followed closely by bed.

# Chapter Sixty-Six

*Wednesday, September 26th, 6: 15 PM*

Tess had one last thing she wanted to do before she headed to the hospital to have her head looked at.

She made her way to the back of the waiting ambulance that held a spitting mad Kane O'Leary. She could hear him shouting and carrying on before she even saw him. Rounding the open back of the vehicle, he yelled expletives when he saw her.

"Calm down, O'Leary," Tess scolded, holding her hands up placatingly. "Crazy is very unbecoming on you."

"Get off my land, bitch," he raged, pulling at the restraints on his gurney. Spittle sprayed from his mouth with each word, and his eyes were devoid of reason. His hair, once nicely maintained, now stood up in disheveled tufts all over his head.

"Now, now, O'Leary. We've discussed this, remember? The land belongs to your niece, Marissa, now."

"I'm going to make her give me my share so I can get my money. I've already written to her about it."

"And has she written you back?" Tess asked, knowing that Marissa was indeed not going to be writing him back any time soon. Her lawyer had advised her to cut off all contact with Kane O'Leary immediately.

"Not yet, but she will," Kane answered smugly.

"Doubt it. Besides, even if she did decide to go along with your hair-brained idea, she can't," Tess rebutted his smugness with some of her own.

"And what makes you think that?"

"Well, your dear mother.... You know, the one you loved oh so much? She made sure you couldn't have it. Ever." Tess pulled out the copy of Lenore O'Leary's Last Will and Testament. "Pay special attention to the last part," she said as she cleared her throat and began to read it aloud for Kane.

**"I, Lenore O'Leary, being of sound mind and body, wish to amend all previous wills in my name. With the recent death of my beloved Shamus, I must keep our family farm intact.**

**With that said, I wish to remove my son, Kane O'Leary, from any and all inheritance, both real or otherwise. He would just want to sell it for his own gain and he's never shown an interest in the farm.**

**Instead, I shall leave the farm, house, and all of the property (Parcel number 2005689032-0987) in Swain County, Ohio, to my youngest son, Garrett. He has worked the land along with his father his whole life and has proven that his heart is committed to keeping our legacy alive."**

"You've already told me this part. What's the big deal? Kevin's dead. I'll just get Marissa to give it to me and Jamie. I was always her favorite uncle, anyway," Kane snapped, spittle flying from his mouth. His eyes were wild with rage.

"Like I said, pay attention to the last part," Tess sighed with annoyance at being interrupted. She held up the will and continued to read:

**"There is one condition with this arrangement, however, and that is this: The land is never to be divided to sell under any circumstance. If there is no heir to inherit the property, it is to be donated, in its entirety, to the county as a working farm and Native American Historical site. It is meant to be a place for people from all walks of life to come to visit, learn about animals and farming, learn the histories of the people who have come before us, and enjoy all that rural Ohio has to offer."**

When Tess was done reading, she folded the paper up to stick in her pocket and glanced up at Kane. His face had gone from a bright beet red to a pale vampiric white within seconds. His eyes snapped with anger as he clenched and unclenched his jaw.

"There was an addendum like this signed by Garrett and Kevin both on the part about not dividing or selling the land," Tess explained. "I'm not sure why your lawyers didn't find it as it's public record." She shrugged. "Since Marissa owns the farm now and has no children, it will go to the state upon her death. You will never get the O'Leary land. Your mother made sure of it, and your family has honored her wishes. They know that if given the chance, you'd have sold them out the first chance you got. Now, they've ensured that something good will come of their work and provide a positive legacy for the O'Leary name here in Swain County. I spoke to Marissa on the phone a couple of days ago and let her know about the will and the addendum. She told me she wasn't surprised. Apparently, it was common knowledge that your father made up the story about you joining the military so that people would think you were some great war hero, but your mom never played along with it. She was realistic about who you were from the beginning. She just let people think what they wanted to think. She saw through your bullshit just like Kevin and Marissa. Just like I'm sure Garrett did."

A vein snaked across Kane's forehead as his face contorted into an even deeper rage. Tess had seen a lot in her line of work, but never had she seen someone so angry over not getting their way.

"You bitch! You're just like my mother!" he roared, lunging at her but getting yanked back by the restraints on his gurney.

"You can't blame everything on your mom, Kane. I don't know what all you did to piss her off but just remember, if you break the rules like a bad little boy," Tess scolded, "in the end, Mommy wins." With a smirk and a head shake, she slammed the back of the ambulance and gave it two taps with her open palm. From the other side, she could still hear Kane O'Leary raging.

# Chapter Sixty-Seven

*Thursday, September 27th, 2:12 A.M.*

Both Natalie and Tess were diagnosed with mild dehydration and exhaustion, and other than a few scrapes and bruises, Natalie appeared fine. Tess was taken to the hospital for closer examination due to being knocked out not once, but twice. Luckily, her scans came back clear, and radiographs showed that her ankle was sprained and her ribs bruised but not broken.

Denny and Natalie had refused to leave Tess at the hospital, so after a few grueling hours, when Tess was finally discharged, the trio rode home in silence.

Once home, Denny tucked Natalie into her bed and then helped Tess get a quick shower as she was so tired she could barely stand. After ridding her of the dried blood, dirt, and sweat crusted on her skin, he dressed her in his old BCI tee-shirt and tucked her into bed. She was vaguely aware of him climbing into bed behind her, but she passed out asleep almost as soon as her head hit the pillow.

***

It was almost ten the next morning when Tess finally woke up. Late morning light streamed through the window next to the bed, warming her skin. She climbed out of bed, stretched, and went in search of Natalie and Denny.

She found Denny standing quietly in Natalie's doorway, watching her sleep. He looked over at her when she stepped out into the hallway and smiled. Quietly closing Natalie's door, he walked toward Tess and wrapped his arms around her.

"How'd you sleep?" he asked, his voice muffled in her hair.

"Like the dead," Tess smiled against his chest. "You?"

"Never better, especially now that I know both of you are okay." He pulled away, his gaze falling over her face. "I can't believe she's still asleep. I keep checking on her...." his voice hitched. "She's been so quiet, I just have to make sure she's still in there."

"It's going to take a while to not think like that. I'm on edge, too," Tess admitted, chewing her bottom lip.

"Tess... I... Thank you. I don't know what I would have done if I'd lost her," he said, smoothing a stray piece of hair back from Tess's face. "Or you. I can't imagine my life without you in it, Tess. This whole ordeal has shown me how fragile our lives truly are, how little control we actually have. We have no promise of tomorrow, do we? Everything can change in an instant." He paused, leaning his forehead down to touch hers.

"I wouldn't get too close to me. I haven't brushed my teeth yet, and I have bed-head," Tess whispered a warning, as she gazed into his deep blue eyes.

"You're a little crazy-haired, but who cares?" Denny grinned before becoming serious again. "What I'm trying to say is... I'm trying to say that I don't want to miss any more time with you, Tess. I don't want to miss any more days or nights separated from you. I told you before, you are my present and my future. I want to grow old with you. I want to make babies with you if you want them. I want to haunt Natalie when we die just to pester her because it sounds like fun." An ornery grin crossed his face. Tess laughed, relishing in his carefree, happy spirit despite the seriousness of the moment. "Marry me, Tess. Today, tomorrow, five years from now, I don't care. I just want to be with you. And if you don't like the idea of marriage, I won't tie you down. We can live together, not live together, we can buy a house or not. It's up to you. You and Natalie are what matter the most to me."

"And what does Natalie say to all of this?" Tess breathed, tears of joy leaking from her eyes. Her breath hitched as she waited for his response.

"I've been thinking about it for a while now, but Natalie is the one that told me I'm an idiot if I let you slip through the cracks. She said, and I quote, 'she's a keeper, 10/10 recommend.'"

Tess snorted a laugh. "That does sound like Natalie." She stood up straighter to look at Denny head-on. "As for your questions... I need you in my life more than I need air. This whole ordeal... has taught me that. I also can't imagine being separated from you for any length of time again. I want you and Natalie in my life on a forever basis. Whether living together or married, I want to be with you. You two are my family now. Am I ready to be a stepmom? I have no idea, but I'm willing to try." She smiled. "You know I'm leery of marriage considering my parent's history, and I'm not saying no to that, but maybe can we start small? Maybe we move in together and adjust to that. If we still feel the need to legalize it, then we do. Either way, I don't want to change my last name."

Denny grinned. "I didn't expect you to. And yes, we can live in your house if you want, and I can rent this one out to your mom, or we can buy a new house together. Whatever you want. My house holds memories of my old life before Cass died. I think it's time Natalie and I move on. Whether that's in with you or into a new place we all get together, it is up to you. That's her idea, by the way."

"Really?" Tess grinned, wrinkling her nose.

"Yep. And she told me she's already been looking for houses with big yards because Otter needs a sister." Denny raised his eyebrows. Tess threw her head back and laughed quietly, blissfully happy.

"Yes, Denny Haywood, I will marry you. Someday," she smiled up at him, "But for now, you better move your murder board into my house while we search for a new place with a big backyard for Natalie's new puppy."

"What puppy?" Natalie asked as she stepped out of her bedroom, rubbing her eyes and yawning. Natalie looked at Tess and then shot a glance at her dad. "Wait... Did she say yes?!"

Denny nodded, and Natalie squealed, running at the two of them and flinging her small arms around their middles. The adults enclosed her with their arms, and Natalie beamed while the newly formed family held each other.

# Author's Note

This book briefly mentions a real world issue that I would like to shed some light on. Even if I only raise awareness to one person, it is worth it to me.

When Remi Nightsong's character first approaches Tess at the mound, she mentions the alarming rate at which Native American women and girls go missing or end up murdered. I was not writing that to be dramatic; it is a disturbing truth.

According to research, Native women and girls are at a 10% higher risk of being victims of murder. This is due to under reporting, lack of media attention, minimal investigative tools, and inaction by law enforcement. A 2016 report by The National Crime Information Center revealed "that there were 5,712 reports of missing American Indian and Alaskan Native women and girls though the US Department of Justice Federal missing person database, NamUs, only logged 116 cases" (www.nativehope.org/missing-and-murdered-indigenous -women-mmiw).

According to the Urban Indian Health Institute, Native people make up only 2% of the US population, and yet the third cause of death in Native women is murder. The

National Congress of American Indians (NCAI) reports that 84.3% of all Native women will be victims of violence at some point in their lives; 56.1% will fall victim to sexual assault, and 55.5% will be victimized at the hand of a domestic partner.

Please join me in spreading awareness for these women and girls. They deserve to live happy, full lives free from violence. For more information, please visit the websites listed below or search the hashtags #NoMoreStolenSisters and #MMIW

www.ncai.org          www.nativehope.org

# Thank You!

I would like to take the time to say "Thank you" to some of the behind-the-scenes people who helped make this book possible. It was with their knowledge and kindness that I was able to bring *Hill of Bones* to life.

First, I would like to thank the Wyandotte Nation, especially Beci Wright and Ciara Cotter, for their assistance in answering my questions and providing their sensitivity reader expertise. Without this, I was worried about saying something offensive about or toward the Wyandotte Nation or Native Americans as a whole, and that is the last thing I would ever want to do.

I would also like to thank the friendly staff at The Great Circle Earthworks at Moundbuilders Park in Newark, Ohio, for their compassion and knowledge of the early Native American tribes that once called Ohio their home. I went to them to verify some facts I had found and to ask their opinion on a few key details of the storyline for *Hill of Bones*. They assured me that I was on the right track and were very excited to help me in any way they could.

The Native American Indian Center of Central Ohio (NAICCO) was also very helpful and timely in helping answer my questions. If I needed answers they couldn't provide, they put me in contact with those who could. This was a huge help, and I am very grateful.

I would like to thank my friend and fellow author, Jill N. Davies, for her help editing the manuscript, listening to me rant and whine (trust me, there was plenty! haha!), and giving me ideas for things to research further to provide the best version of *Hill of Bones* possible. Thanks Jill!

And finally, I would like to thank my readers. Without you, my books would be sitting on a shelf somewhere, collecting dust, or perhaps I would have given up writing them by now. All of your emails, DM's, videos, and smiling faces at book signings truly mean the world to me! I love hearing back from you, whether you're sharing your thoughts about who you think is guilty or how the ending caught you off guard. It all makes me smile! Please don't stop staying in touch!

# About the Author

A.L. Hatcher holds bachelor's degrees in both forensic investigation and forensic pathology as well as an associate's degree in veterinary technology. Because of her love of animals, she was a registered veterinary technician for over twenty-three years but her true passion has always been writing.

Today, she spends her time caring for her child, reading, listening to true crime podcasts, and writing fiction about crime, suspense, and all things dark. She lives in the Midwest with her family, some chickens, and a pair of rambunctious dogs.

# We'd love to hear from you!

If you enjoyed this book, please consider leaving a review on Amazon, Goodreads, or wherever you review books. Reviews help other readers find books that may interest them and also help provide author feedback.

Please feel free to follow the author on Facebook, Instagram, Threads, BlueSky, Lemon8, and TikTok
@alhatcherauthor
or sign up for her newsletter at
http://www.alhatcherauthor.com
Email: alhatcherauthor@gmail.com

9 798988 943860